"YOU MUST BE OUT OF YOUR MIND! I'D SOONER MARRY A RATTLESNAKE!"

He steadied her with a smile that was possessively intimate. "I don't ordinarily kiss little girls, Talitha. But you're at a dreamy age. Now you have a starting point for your reveries."

"If I dreamed of you, it would be a nightmare!" Backing toward the door, she rubbed her mouth vigorously with her hand.

"You'll dream. And after a while you'll start to try to imagine what comes after the kiss."

"I won't!"

"You will." His long fingers touched her cheek, caressed the side of her throat. "You'll be ripening for me, Talitha, and I can be patient, for I've many worlds to conquer. But in four years, when you're eighteen, you'll marry me. If I still want you. I think I will."

Books by Jeanne Williams

Bride of Thunder
Daughter of the Sword
A Lady Bought with Rifles
The Valiant Women
A Woman Clothed in Sun

Published by POCKET BOOKS

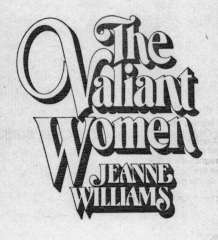

The Valiant Women

JEANNE WILLIAMS

PUBLISHED BY POCKET BOOKS NEW YORK

Another *Original* publication of POCKET BOOKS

POCKET BOOKS, a Simon & Schuster division of
GULF & WESTERN CORPORATION
1230 Avenue of the Americas, New York, N.Y. 10020

ISBN: 0-671-82536-4

First Pocket Books printing August, 1980

10 9 8 7 6 5 4 3 2 1

POCKET and colophon are trademarks of Simon & Schuster.

Interior design by Catherine Carucci

Printed in the U.S.A.

For Alice Papcun,
a most lovely and valiant lady
whose shining spirit inspires
those fortunate enough to know her

SOURCES AND PEOPLE
THAT HELPED MAKE THIS BOOK

A lot of background reading is necessary for a book of this kind so I am listing only sources that were especially helpful. The Rio Grande Press's new editions of Carl Lumholtz's *New Trails in Mexico* (1971) and *Unknown Mexico*, Vol. I (1973) Glorieta, New Mexico, are fascinating. Carolyn Niethammer's *American Indian Food and Lore* (Macmillan, 1974) is a wonderfully interesting book for anyone wanting to know about Western plant foods. I was lucky enough to take Carrie's field course on gathering and preparing wild foods and learned much from her.

Good general books are: *Early Arizona, Prehistory to Civil War* by Jay J. Wagoner, University of Arizona Press, 1975; *The Far Southwest 1846–1912, A Territorial History* by Howard Roberts Lamar, Norton, 1970; and *Pioneer Days in Arizona* by Frank C. Lockwood, Macmillan, 1932. There is a wealth of material in Thomas J. Farish's *History of Arizona*, San Francisco, eight volumes, 1915–1918. *Friars, Soldiers and Reformers* by John L. Kessell, University of Arizona Press, 1976, brilliantly depicts Hispanic Arizona.

Philip St. George Cooke tells of the Mormon Battalion in his *The Conquest of New Mexico and California*, Biobooks, Oakland, California, 1952. *My Confession* by Samuel Chamberlain, Harper, 1956, tells about the execution of the San Patricios and the author's later association with Arizona scalp hunters. Chamberlain must be taken with a salt cellar, but his illustrations are beguiling and he captures the spirit of the era. *The Warrior Apaches* by Gordon Baldwin, Tucson, 1966; *Cycles of Conquest: The Impact of Spain, Mexico and the United States on the Indians of the Southwest, 1533–1960,* by Edward Spicer, University of

Arizona Press, 1962; *History of the Cattle Industry in Southern Arizona* by Jay J. Wagoner, University of Arizona Press, 1952; *The Mining Frontier* edited by Marvin Lewis, University of Oklahoma Press, 1967, were valuable.

Also helpful were *Vanguards of the Frontier* by Everett Dick, University of Nebraska Press, 1965; *Sonoran Strongman, Ignacio Pesqueira and His Times* by Rodolfo F. Acuna, University of Arizona Press, 1974; *Destiny Road, the Gila Trail and the Opening of the Southwest* by Odie B. Faulk, Oxford University Press, 1973; *The Tarahumar of Mexico* by Campbell W. Pennington, University of Utah Press, 1963; *Mexico's Ancient and Native Remedies* by Evelyne Winter, Editorial Fournier, S.A., Mexico, D.F. 1968; *Adventures in the Apache Country* by J. Ross Browne, University of Arizona Press, 1974; *Arizona and Sonora* by Sylvester Mowry, Harper & Brothers, 1864; *Building a State in Apache Land* by Charles D. Poston, Aztec Press, Tempe, Arizona, 1963; *Latest from Arizona, the Hesperian Letters, 1859–1861,* edited by Constance Altshuler, Arizona Pioneers' Historical Society, Tucson, Arizona, 1969; *The Mexican War* by the Editors of Time/Life Books, text by David Niven, Time/Life, 1978; and *Year of Decision, 1846* by Bernard DeVoto, Little, Brown & Co., 1943.

Several *Smoke Signals,* a publication of the Tucson Corral of the Westerners, were extremely useful: *The Military Posts on Sonoita Creek* by James E. Serven, Fall, 1965; *Calabazas of the Rio Rico* by Bernard Fontana, Fall, 1971; *Journalism in Pre-Territorial Arizona* by Kenneth Hufford, Fall, 1966; *Charles Debrille Poston: Prince of Arizona Pioneers* by Dr. B. Sacks, Spring, 1963; and *Wagon-Freighting in Arizona* by Henry P. "Pick" Walker, Fall, 1973.

Also helpful were *The Apaches, Eagles of the Southwest* by Donald E. Worcester, University of Oklahoma Press, 1979, and *Camera, Spade and Pen* by Marc and Marnie Gaede, the essay on "Sierra Pinacate" by Julian Hayden, University of Arizona, 1980.

The Journal of Arizona History published by the Arizona Historical Society, Tucson, Arizona, gave me much aid and

SOURCES

comfort, especially in these articles: "Brother Burro" by George W. Harvey and Charles Fletcher Lummis, Winter, 1976; "Pozole, Atole and Tamales" by Alberto Francisco Pradeau, Spring, 1974; "Poston and the Birth of Yuma" by Frank Love, Winter, 1978; and an engrossing account of ranching and stock raising, "Echoes of the Conquistadores" by Yjinio F. Aguirre, Autumn, 1975.

"Bring Cats! A Feline History of the West" by Reginald Bretnar, in *The American West*, the Magazine of Western History, Buffalo Bill Historical Center, Cody, Wyoming, Nov./Dec. 1978, makes one wish for a whole book on the cat as pioneer. Doris W. Bent's *The History of Tubac, 1752–1948*, M.A. thesis, University of Arizona, 1949, was among the most useful of the unpublished materials I found in the files of the Arizona Pioneers' Historical Society in Tucson. A reprint of Arizona's first newspaper, *The Weekly Arizonian, 1859*, really took me back to those days. The reprint was done by Donald B. Sayner and Robert P. Hale, Compilers, Printers and Publishers. Both are in the Department of General Biology at the University of Arizona and were advised by Margaret S. Bret Harte, Head Librarian, Arizona Historical Society.

Those wishing to learn more about the desert will enjoy A Sierra Club Naturalist's Guide, *The Deserts of the Southwest* by Peggy Larson, Sierra Club, 1977, and *Desert: The American Southwest* by Ruth Kirk, Houghton Mifflin, 1973.

I wish to thank the staff of The Arizona Historical Society for their help. Tracy Row, Editor of the *Journal of Arizona History*, gave me out-of-print material, and Don Bufkin, Assistant to the Director, also Art Editor of the *Journal*, and the leading cartographer for the area, has kindly made the map.

Dr. C. L. Sonnichsen, now Senior Editor for the *Journal*, has been an inspiration, adviser and gadfly. In a small way, I am acknowledging his graciousness by spelling Mangus that way instead of Mangas though it meant changing the word throughout the first half of the book.

Virginia Roberts of Tucson, overhearing my laments to the librarian in the Arizona Pioneers' Historical Society

Library, generously told me of a letter found in her research which established that Dr. Bernard J. D. Irwin, a suitor of my fictional Talitha, was indeed a bachelor at that time.

Julian Hayden generously supplied me with a copy of Dr. W. J. McGee's treatise, *Desert Thirst as a Disease,* and kindly read the part of the book taking place in the Pinacates which he knows better than any living man, perhaps better than the vanished *Areneños.*

I would also thank Alessandro Jacques of Sonora for telling me of his family's ranching experiences and giving me a glimpse of old cow camps scattered across the Altar Valley. Without Bill Broyles, I wouldn't know the Pinacates or the *Camino del Diablo.* I cannot thank him enough for taking me to wild places of Arizona and Mexico and sharing his knowledge of them. Al McGinnis has been a good companion on some explorations and Betty and Dana Smith first showed me the Sea of Cortez where once Poston and others dreamed of a port for Arizona. My debt to all these friends is more than I can express, for through them I have come to love this region, from the sea and dead volcanoes through deserts and river valley to the mountains.

Martin Asher, my editor at Pocket Books, opened the way for me to do this book by saying "What do you want to do?" and being supportive and encouraging ever since. Thanks also to my other conscientious and sensitive editors, Janet Kronstadt and Meg Blackstone. My friend and agent, Claire Smith, is a constant support and refuge. Kristin, my daughter, read the manuscript and made excellent suggestions. My son, Michael, read with an expert eye for weapons and military background. Leila Madeheim once again wrestled clean copy out of chaos and caught my blinded-eye spelling of Gadsen for Gadsden.

Thanking is a happy task. I've had lots of help. My mistakes are my own.

JEANNE WILLIAMS
Tucson, Arizona
March, 1979

WHO'S REAL?

Though my principal characters are imaginary, they move in real country and real events, among real people.

Mangus Coloradas and Cochise are true. So are Charles Poston, Fred Hulsemann, the Penningtons and Pages, Gray, Schuchard, Pete Kitchen and Doña Rosa, Colonel Douglass, Captain Ewell and Dr. Irwin. The names of the commanders of the forts and presidios are real, and of course the background figures in government, commerce and military affairs are actual. Except for the Rancho del Socorro, Don Narcisco's mine and the enterprises of Judah Frost and Marc Revier, the mines and companies mentioned did exist, and the raids and expeditions are as detailed, though I omitted some Apache raids. There were simply too many of them to record.

This is a work of fiction trying to reflect a reality. I have allowed my characters to communicate rather more easily than they probably could have in view of their different languages—that is, I accelerated the speed with which they'd have acquired each other's tongues. Also, Apaches did not use real names in address or in referring to someone, but this is awkward to duplicate.

Shea's ordeal by thirst and conviction that he had died is taken from the true experience of Pablo Valencia who endured six days without water in the scorching desert August of 1905. Valencia's story was written by W. F. McGee, who found and saved him, and published in the *Interstate Medical Journal*, 1906. In effect, all four of my principal starting characters have died—by extreme disasters, they have lost the lives they expected to lead, but in that end was their beginning.

"Among the above-mentioned favors which our lord has granted us in these expeditions . . . one is the great, good and abundant fruit which, in the service of the two Majesties, can be secured, not only in the discovered parts, but also in this very extensive northern district of all this North America, which is the greatest and best remaining portion of the world. . . .

"We could make exact maps of this entire unknown North America which are usually drawn with so many mistakes, malevolent exaggerations and imaginary wealth of a crowned king that is carried in chairs of gold, of towers and walled cities, of lakes of gold and quicksilver. . . .

". . . that the principal and true riches that do exist are the innumerable souls . . ."

—Father Eusebio Kino, S.J., 1699,
Letter to Philip V, 1704

"For most of these lands are very rich and fertile, most of the Indians industrious, many of the lands mineral bearing, and most of them of a climate so good that it is very similar to the best of Europe or that of Castilla. . . ."

—Father Eusebio Kino, S.J., 1699,
Historical Memoir of Pimería Alta

"All that will be said is . . . over there once stood a mission called Tumacácori; at the foot of the Santa Catalinas was another called San Xavier, and so on with all the rest—but all were destroyed by Apaches."

—Father Bartolome Ximeno, Letter, March 5, 1773,
written from Tumacácori

". . . so desolated, desert and God-forsaken that a wolf could not make a living on it."

—Kit Carson quoted during hearings
on Gadsden Purchase, 1854

"Now we should pay Mexico ten million to take it back."
—Senatorial wit after Gadsden Purchase

"From 1848 to 1860, then, Arizona was a no man's land, into which the golden hopes, the expansionist dreams and the sectional fears of the United States were projected with extraordinary vigor."
—Howard Roberts Lamar,
The Far Southwest: A Territorial History, 1846–1912

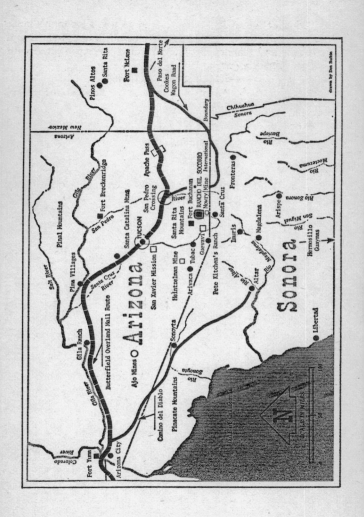

drawn by Don Bufkin

Pinos Altos • Santa Rita • Fort McLane
Paso del Norte
Cookes Wagon Road

Chihuahua
Sonora

Boundary

New Mexico
Arizona

Gila River

Pinal Mountains

Fort Breckenridge

San Pedro

Santa Catalina Mtns.

Apache Pass

San Pedro River Crossing

SOCORRO
RANCH DEL Mowry Mine
Fort Buchanan
INTERNATIONAL

Fronteras

Rio Bavispe

Rio Moctezuma

Rio Sonora

Arispe

Salt River

Pima Villages

Santa Cruz River

TUCSON

Santa Rita Mountains

Santa Cruz

Magdalena

San Miguel

Rio

San Xavier Mission

Heintzelman Mine

Arivaca Tubac

Sonoyta

Guevavi

Imuris

Pete Kitchen's Ranch

Sonora

Hermosillo
Guaymas

Gila Ranch

Butterfield Overland Mail Route

Ajo Mines

Rio Altar

Altar

Magdalena

Rio

Colorado River

Gila River

Camino del Diablo

Pinacate Mountains

Rio Sonoyta

Libertad

Gulf of California

Fort Yuma

Arizona City

SCALE IN MILES

N

PART I

THE
SAN PATRICIO

1

She followed the gray-yellow shadow because it was alive, stumbling on after the coyote had vanished. The empty leather water jug slapped mockingly against her thigh. She had drained the last tepid drops yesterday, chewed the last parched corn and dried meat.

How many days had she wandered since the Indians killed her father and the others? Four? Five? The *Areneños* had lanced the water skins, looted the wagon, stripped the four escorting soldiers of clothing and weapons. Consuelo, her maid, had been used by all the *Indios* before they cut her throat because, perhaps, she kept screaming.

Socorro hadn't screamed; had fought silently till her mind retreated into merciful numbness. They may have thought her dead. Whyever, they hadn't killed her.

She forced the nightmare away as she came upon a trail, narrow and at times lost among rocks and barren earth. It must be used by the coyote and other creatures. Perhaps it led to water. All living things must drink.

Doves flew up from what seemed merely a pile of more blackish rocks. Another trail joined the one she followed, running toward the flight of doves.

Doves, two trails joining. Socorro had seldom been outside Alamos, the ancient silver city, and knew little about the wilderness, but the doves seemed a sign of hope to her, and the worn tracks *must* mean something. She pressed on.

Abruptly she was looking down into a deep broad cañon, almost choked in spots with the large iron-woods, paloverdes, and piles of gray-black rock worn smooth by floods. Directly below glinted water, reflecting the sky, a hollow in the stone perhaps eight feet across. Beyond that was another natural cistern or *tinaja*. From it, a deer streaked away.

Socorro's ragged skirt caught often on thorns and branches as she hurried down the trail, sliding on loose volcanic rubble, checking a fall by gripping an acacia which pronged her hand with its whitish thorns. She scarcely felt it, moaning with eagerness, seeing only the water, that wonderful blessing for her cracked lips and dry throat.

Falling on her knees, she lowered her face and drank gratefully though it was scummed with green in which were tufted bits of feather, bird droppings, small insects. Nothing had ever tasted so good. She knew, though, that too much water at once could make her sick. When her most violent thirst was calmed, she splashed her face and arms, washed off her father's blood and the blood of the Indian he'd killed in his last moments.

Only Enrique, an arrow in his chest, had still been alive when she'd recovered enough to drag herself painfully to see what had happened to the others. She'd seen with a shuddering sob that her father was dead, crossed herself and crept to Enrique. Blood frothed from his mouth and he groaned. The arrow jerked up and down with his gasping breaths. Socorro, gritting her teeth, took hold of the cane arrow and started to tug.

"Leave it!" he cried, flinching. "I'm dying, my lady. Listen! Take water and food. Go north. There's a ranch beyond that highest mountain, Pinacate. If you stay here, those *Indios* will be back." His voice choked off in pinkish foam.

She found a wineskin, tipped it to his lips. He swallowed. "It will just leak out of me." He grinned, sweat standing on his leathery face. "Go! You can't help me."

But she stayed with him till he died, holding him in her arms, bathing his face. Outside the wagon, her father was skewered on a lance. He had an arrow in his shoulder, another in his thigh. His eyes stared at the sun. Beyond him sprawled the soldiers, naked and mutilated, brought down in the first seconds of the ambush, muskets unfired.

Socorro had retched when she found Consuelo. They had grown up together and the girl was more friend than servant, her mother the housekeeper for widowed Don Esteban Quintana, assuming even more control after the recent death of Socorro's aunt and dueña, Doña Catalina.

Socorro covered the ruined body. Then she pressed her foot against her father to tear out the lance.

She dragged him to an arroyo. At the brink, she kissed him, closed his eyes, whispered a prayer, asked him to forgive her that she couldn't dig a grave in the rocky soil. Next she dragged Enrique over, then Consuelo, and shoved rocks down till the bodies were covered and no hand or knee protruded.

Sickening to send boulders down on top of those she loved, but better that than letting them be torn by birds and beasts.

She was exhausted now. The poor men of the escort would simply have to lie as they were, but she knelt by them and prayed for their souls, crossed each of them and promised to burn candles for them if she lived to reach a shrine.

The chests had been ransacked. They had held her wedding finery and heirlooms, including a dozen silver goblets given to a Quintana by the King of Spain, intended for the home she was to have established with her second cousin who waited for her in Los Angeles.

Such things couldn't help her now. She was grateful for the few things the *Areneños* had left. In a blue cotton rebozo she tied as much dried corn and meat as she thought she could carry without losing speed, fastened a knife around her waist, and the precious water jug.

Kneeling once more by the burial arroyo, she turned her face north, toward the distant purple mountain.

How far? And the ranch beyond? When?

Dread had frozen the girl. For a moment she hesitated. Perhaps she should follow the wagon ruts and hope to meet some merchant from Caborca or the south. She hated to lose the track of human beings, the sign of where they had at least been and might come again. It was also where the *Areneños,* or Sand Papagos, waited for travelers. And the travelers . . . Socorro shivered.

Luck to meet a merchant in this region below the Gran Desierto. Bandits, more likely, or scalp hunters, many of them gringos who often didn't care whether they collected bounty for Mexican or Papago scalps instead of Apache. Even Socorro's sheltered upbringing hadn't shielded her from the grim realities of life in Sonora in 1847. The government had long been powerless against the Apaches and the war with the United States had left the frontier even more exposed. Battling the terror that rose in her, she left the crude road and moved northward.

The farming Indians with settled villages had usually accepted the padres and baptism, though the Yaqui of her own region had adopted the faith of the Spaniards without their government, ferociously resisting Mexico City's occasional attempts to colonize the rich delta.

In this northern area, even though they'd rebelled in 1751, Pima and Papago had generally been glad of any protection Spanish, and now Mexican, troops could give them. They were frequently raided by various Apache bands who roamed the vast mountain ranges of northern Sonora and Chihuahua and spilled over into the plains of Texas, which had successfully revolted against Mexico in 1836 and been annexed to the United States in 1845.

There was no end to the problems caused by Texas. Instead of its proper boundary of the Nueces River, it had claimed all the land to the Rio Grande, which would have included that far northern outpost of the Spanish, Santa Fe, as well as southeast to the Gulf.

Father had said the Yanquis only wanted any excuse to seize California and as much land as possible. The United States had, in the spring of 1846, occupied the disputed miles of brush and desert between the Nueces and Rio Grande; Mexican troops crossed the river, and since then battles had raged through central Mexico as the Yanquis fought their way south. Buena Vista, Saltillo, Monterrey . . . At the latest news they were advancing on Mexico City itself. That was when her father had decided to take her without delay to California.

"If the Yanquis take California, it may be impossible to have the wedding for years," he'd worried. "Your cousin is twenty-seven. He can't be expected to wait forever."

"He could come to Alamos, Papa, and marry me in our cathedral."

"He can't leave his ranch," returned her father. "And it was agreed that you should travel to him. No, we shall leave as soon as I can get an escort."

Her poor harassed father. He'd gone to death, not a wedding.

Socorro drank again, from the higher water hole, wiped a wispy feather from her lip. The cañon wound like a great serpent, curving out of sight. She filled her water jug, hesitated before she climbed slowly up the steep rocky wall. Once there, where the trails met, she stared at the mountain, her goal for days. It seemed no nearer than when she'd started. Certainly it was farther than this jug could take her. And she had no food.

She shrank from the idea of killing any of the birds or animals coming for water, but she might learn from them what could be eaten. She'd have a better chance of reaching that ranch behind the mountain if she rested a few days near this water, collected such food as she could.

The sun was sinking beyond the scattered peaks and

worn-away rims of what had been volcanoes. Light turned the distant sand dunes a luminous rose and the mountains half-buried by them glowed blue as the madonna's robe. Socorro knew the softness was a cruel deceit, a trick of sun and desert air. The dunes were said to run all the way to the muddy salt flats of the bay and those enchanted mountains were really barren gray stone like those west and north.

As she had done the other nights of her ordeal, she found a stretch of fine sand amid a spill of rocks and left her jug there while she searched for food before darkness fell.

It was early October, not the time for bird eggs, and such cactus fruits as hadn't been devoured were starting to dry up, but she picked these into a fold of her rebozo, as well as any small tender prickly pear pads she found.

Some animal with either sharp hoofs or horns had broken open and eaten part of a great mass of hundred-headed cactus. With her knife, she cut out a chunk of the greenish-white pulp, chewed it cautiously.

Almost tasteless, but at least it was filling and contained considerable moisture. She ate several more pieces, then, with her knife, rearranged the broken part to shelter the cavity. Tomorrow she'd eat from it again. Now it was twilight, time to retreat to her chosen place of rest.

With great care, she peeled some of the cactus fruits, being sure to get off the tiny tufts of spines. They had a tangy taste like wild berries.

Tomorrow she must look for something with more strength in it. She had no flint and steel for making fire so she couldn't cook anything, but perhaps she could find seeds. And it might be that the pods of acacia, ironwood and paloverde could be eaten like mesquite beans. She wrapped the extra rebozo closer against the cooling desert night, sighed and curled up next to the sun-warmed rocks.

There were paddings and sounds but these didn't

frighten her as much as before. Apart from snakes and man she had little to fear. This wasn't bear territory. Coyotes didn't attack people and mountain lions seldom did.

Several times in the night she woke shivering, turned on her other side and burrowed deeper in the sand. An impossible country! One burned by day and froze by night! But the knowledge that she was near water, didn't have to press on tomorrow in a desperate search for it, let her drift back to sleep till her final waking with the sun dazzling in her eyes as it climbed above reddish craters and black cones.

After a breakfast of cactus fruit and water, she started on another food hunt, first leaning several dead yucca stalks together to mark the descent to the water hole and orienting herself, the long crater east, that elusive purple mountain north, shimmering dunes south and west.

Within a few hours she filled her rebozo with acacia and ironwood pods and more cactus fruit, or *tunas*. The beans in the pods were much too hard for chewing, but by the water hole she'd seen several hollows in the rocks that would serve for *metates*.

Returning, she selected a depression shaded by a large ironwood and soon found a smooth black elongated stone that fitted the inside of the hollow.

As she husked beans into the grinding hole, Socorro's spine chilled. Wasn't it likely that these natural *metates* were used by *Areneño* women? Certainly the Indians living in this arid wasteland knew every water hole. Sooner or later they were bound to turn up here.

Holding her breath, she looked slowly up and down both rims of the cañon, relaxed a trifle when she saw no one, but her sense of refuge was shattered. She would risk spending tomorrow near the water but the next morning she'd move on.

She ground beans till her arms ached. Since there was no way to bake or cook gruel, she mixed enough water with the meal to make small flat cakes which she spread to sun-dry on the rocks.

That afternoon when she was gathering more pods and cactus fruit, she saw an eagle swoop, the gold of his plumage shining. His talons closed on a large rabbit, which after one frantic convulsion was limp.

Socorro didn't pause to argue the rights of robbing the eagle of meat she wouldn't have killed herself. Snatching up a dead branch, she shouted, running forward. For a moment it seemed that the giant bird, whose wingspan was more than her height, might battle, but when she struck at it the eagle gave an angry shriek and winged upward, abandoning its prey.

Socorro couldn't eat the raw flesh and she felt sick by the time she'd unskillfully cut and peeled off the hide. She cut the meat in thin strips and thrust them on an all-thorn bush to dry. She simply couldn't do anything with the intestines and heart, so she left these far from camp to make some other creature's dinner. She did save the bigger bits of furry skin. Her soft leather shoes were wearing out and she could pad the soles with the luckless rabbit's coat.

Late that afternoon she bathed in the lower water hole, and then luxuriated in what, even without salt, seemed a magnificent feast of meal cakes, partially dried meat, *tunas* and wedges cut from the hundred-headed cactus.

It was strange. During the day, heartened by the acquisition of meat and growing stack of cakes, she'd begun to have a real hope of getting out of the desert alive. But when darkness fell, she huddled in her rebozo and felt as if she were the only human in all the world. Her father seemed to watch from the shadows. She tried to talk to him but he couldn't answer. At last she slept.

It was gray dawn when she woke to an unearthly cry. Terrified, she waited for a moment. The agony of that call echoed in her mind. She couldn't ignore it. Springing up, she hurried up the bank in the direction of the sound.

A dark heap lay sprawled among the rocks. Whatever it was couldn't hurt her; but could she help it?

Approaching, she bent over a shriveled leathery skeleton. It was still breathing.

He was dying and his friends were dead. Not only the Patricios hanged as deserters because they'd thrown in with their fellow Catholics, the Mexicans, to fight the damned blue-bellies, but Michael, his twin brother, who'd escaped with him the night they were branded and flogged. The guard had been lax, jubilating over the fall of Mexico City and not expecting prisoners who'd been bloodily whipped to feel like moving.

But the O'Sheas had, before they could be fitted with those fine iron collars ornamented with six-inch spikes. No lady would be hugging a man decked out in one of those!

In spite of being overrun by Yanquis, the common Mexicans had been kind to the fugitives, feeding them, helping them evade the victorious United States troops. The brothers might have hidden till Old Rough-and-Ready Taylor and "Fuss and Feathers" Scott were back across the Rio, but Michael had a wish to go to California and so they'd struck out on the dim tracks that would lead through old volcanic mountains to the Gran Desierto and beyond into California.

In spite of warnings from the last peons who had given them food, the O'Sheas hadn't realized what they were getting into. Nothing they'd seen in Mexico, from the brush thickets of the Rio Grande to the high barren mountains, had prepared them for this. The *tinaja* they'd been told about was dry, and they'd been out of water for half a day when they reached it.

Michael's blue eyes had widened with shock, and the crusted, puckering brand on his cheek had twisted. "How far did that old man say it was to the next water?"

"Seventy miles."

"Shea, lad, we'll never make it." Perhaps because their father's name had been Patrick, his widow had

11

called his namesake "Shea" and so, of course, had everyone else. Michael looked despairingly back the way they'd come. "And we'll never last that!"

Shea nodded. "But the old man said there were a few tanks off the road."

"And only *Areneños* know where they are!"

They'd agreed to gamble on finding the secret *tinajas,* watching for animal trails or the flight of dove and quail. The few trails they found vanished in stretches of black lava or jumbled rocks and the only birds they saw were a pair of ravens, high-circling eagles, and a few hawks.

They lost track of time. There were only blazing suns that stupefied them till the cooling night revived them enough to crawl onward. Michael had died in the last sun, baked to leather, lips peeled back from his teeth, the inside of his nostrils blackened, his blood so thick it no longer oozed from cuts and scratches.

Shea had refused to believe his twin was dead. To escape the Famine, fight through the wildest battles of the Mexican War, survive floggings that had wrecked some men for life, and then to die for lack of water! Shea had pleaded and cursed and wept, but Michael only grimaced horribly at the sun, eyelids so dried and shriveled that most of the eyeballs showed.

Too weak to dig a proper grave, Shea scratched enough sand from the creek bed to give his brother a thin shelter, put a cross of paloverde twigs in his hands, and prayed. Michael had been a good lad, rough and liking his whiskey, but merry, generous and warmhearted. Even if his fleshly sins landed him in purgatory, their mother would soon have him out, for Rosaleen O'Shea had been a saintly woman, not even hating the English as she starved to death when the potatoes rotted in the fields the summer of '45. She'd urged her sons to go to America. Had she known—

Wouldn't it be best just to stay here with Michael, at least die close to the body of a loved one? Shea was mightily tempted. But something made him drag on, ridden with fever and delirium so that he tore off his ragged clothes except for his shoes, which were too hard to get off, and then shivered by night, drinking the trickle of urine he voided with great pain though part of his brain remembered that made thirst deadlier.

There seemed to be thundering in his ears, blinding light in his eyes. His throat felt sealed. Before him there seemed to be a shining glitter of a crystal water pitcher surrounded by goblets. He seized one, pressed it to his face. Only then did his mind clear enough to see that he gripped a segment of multi-spined cholla. Clawing it off, he crept on, his tongue and mouth so numbed that they scarcely felt the needles.

He thought he saw a pool, dug at it frantically till a nail ripped and he saw it was only the shadow of a rock. After these phantasms, it was a blessing when his mind, escaping his tortured body, played tricks. He and Michael, new troopers, joining the Army because it seemed the only way to earn their keep while getting used to this big new country, were back across the Rio Grande from Matamoros, building Fort Brown. Mexicans waved at them in friendly fashion from the adobe town.

In the evening, women came to bathe, the curving of the young ones beautiful beneath falls of long black hair that didn't hide much. While they sent a man's blood pounding with their laughter and pretty games, you could look beyond them to the church.

The Mexicans must have been grand Catholics because they had more Saint's Day processions than there were saints, at least that the O'Sheas had heard of. A fine sight to see banners proudly borne with music and people following.

A stirring sight to the O'Sheas whose earliest memory of the Mass was its being said by stealth in the fields, a watch out for safety, since the only priests who could lawfully hold services were pitiful ones who'd foresworn their loyalty to the Stuarts, the rightful Catholic rulers. The O'Sheas and most like them counted for naught the prayers of a traitor. It was a revelation that Catholicism *was* the religion of Mexico, openly revered as the true faith, a wonder almost past believing, though after Emancipation in 1829, the worst weight of the Penal Laws had been lifted.

This code, punishing the Irish for supporting James II, a Catholic Stuart, against the usurping William III of Orange back in 1690, had barred Catholics from voting, holding office, military and civil service, law and teaching. There were no Catholic schools, nor could a Catholic leave all his land to one son. He was compelled to divide it equally among all male heirs so that none could make a living and their holdings would pass into the hands of Protestants.

Patrick O'Shea, the twins' father, had died before they were weaned because he'd rebelled at a particularly spiteful part of the Laws. A Catholic couldn't own a horse worth more than five pounds. O'Shea did, a once weakling colt he'd taken as pay from a Protestant farmer.

He'd nurtured and tended the colt till it grew into a splendid beast the farmer coveted. The law was that a Protestant could take such a horse and force the owner to accept five pounds as payment. O'Shea had thrown the farmer's five pounds back in his face, followed with a brawny fist.

The farmer's help joined in and then there were soldiers. O'Shea died of his beating while the horse was led away, though the farmer, a church-goer, had left the five pounds for Rosaleen who'd been held back by three men while the others killed her proud young husband.

The twins grew up considering the farmer their father's murderer. When they were fourteen, Patrick slipped off from Michael one night and found the farmer eating alone in his kitchen. A strapping man in his prime, he was three times the size of the underfed boy, but Patrick scorned to attack him unwarned. Besides,

14

he wanted the farmer to know why he was carrying a freshly whetted scythe.

As the farmer gawped at him, jowls reddening, Patrick gasped, "I've come to do ye for Patrick O'Shea, him ye killed and stole his horse!"

"Ye young whelp!" cried the farmer, starting up.

If his huge hands had closed on Patrick, that would have been all of it, but the boy swerved and swept the scythe with all his might.

It caught the farmer under the ribs and curved up. Patrick gave it a final tug before it was wrested from his grip. He retreated. The farmer took a few ponderous steps forward, grappling with the scythe, and then collapsed, driving the blade completely through him. He gave a choking, wheezing groan, his feet and hands groped, and he was still.

Patrick fought an urge to retch while sudden bright hope dawned. He'd been resigned to being taken for a killer and hanged, the main reason he hadn't let Michael in on his plan. But the way the corpse lay now—

It took only minutes to find the whetstone and put it where it looked as if the farmer had been sharpening his scythe and met with an accident.

That was what it was called. It was the one secret Patrick never told his twin.

He kept the mortal sin on his soul, even after leaving Ireland, because he was not sorry. And he would never be.

At Ft. Brown there'd been a sergeant who hated the O'Sheas' guts, who called them "micks," "damn mackerel snappers" and more profane things. He had them at hard labor most of the time and there was no appeal from his edicts. To the young Irishmen and other Catholic volunteers, including Poles and Frenchmen, the sergeant became the army, became the voice and face of the country they'd hoped would welcome them, though indeed it was said that almost half of Zachary Taylor's men, encamped there on the Rio Grande that spring of 1846, were foreigners.

15

Of course there were things Shea liked. Major Ringgold's light artillery—now there was something to see! No monstrous long iron cannon on bulky carriages, but bronze barrels four feet long that could hurl a six-pound iron ball up to fifteen hundred yards. The two-wheeled caissons that carried them were attached to a two-wheeled limber that carried the ammunition. Six good horses pulled each gun and part of the crew hung on to the caisson while the others rode.

It was a joy to watch them drill and if Shea could have been with the guns, he might never have taken that fateful swim across the Rio. A battery of four guns would wheel at the order and the men dropped off, unlimbered the gun, and got out the things they were going to need.

While an officer arranged the gun, the men rammed in powder sewed up in oiled flannel bags, then the ball, shell or canister, a bagful of lead bullets. A slow-burning torch lit the quick match which set off the powder. The gun leaped, but the men swabbed it out and in ten seconds were ready to fire again.

But Shea couldn't even watch the drill in peace. The sergeant was after him like a great stinging horse fly.

Then one afternoon Sgt. John Riley of the Fifth Infantry, an Irishman said to have deserted the British Army in Canada and to have been a drillmaster at West Point, swam the river to Mass and never came back. That set the O'Sheas—and others—thinking.

Across the Rio were pretty girls, music and the Mass. Mexico was offering Catholics who would come over to its army special privileges and 320 acres of land, in contrast to the United States which had given the O'Sheas a cold welcome and considerable pain. One night the brothers swam across.

They weren't the only ones. Gradually, enough men, many Irish, deserted from the United States Army to form Mexico's fiercest fighting group, the Battalion of San Patricio. The nuns of San Luis Potosí made them

16

a fine brave flag, green, with Saint Patrick himself on it, a harp and shamrock. Ah, that flag had seen glorious fighting! No wonder. The San Patricios knew that if they were captured, they would surely hang.

The end came last month at Churubusco on August 20, 1847. General Scott's grape, canister and muskets had raked the church and convent. The Patricios fought on long after the Mexicans tried to surrender, in fact they shot down men trying to run up white flags, but at last it was over. The lucky San Patricios were those who died fighting.

Though you had to admire the way the others had gone to even a dog's death like hanging. Out of the eighty tried for desertion, the fifty-four who'd deserted after war was declared were hanged on three different days, the last bunch put on wagons beneath the gallows, not to be hanged till the U.S. flag could be seen flying in victory from the Castle of Chapultepec.

"Oh, Colonel darlin,'" one condemned man had called out to redheaded Colonel Harney, the hangman who took such pleasure in his work. "Would ye be givin' me pipe a light from your fine whiskers?"

Harney struck the man across the face with his saber hilt, knocking out several teeth, but the Irishman cried through his blood, "Bad luck to ye, for I'll never hold my pipe again as long as I live!"

Another of those seated on the wagon shouted to Harney that if they waited to hang till the U.S. flag flew from the castle, they'd live to eat the goose that would fatten on Harney's own grave. Several complimented Harney on his skill at hanging. "For didn't you rape Seminole girls in Florida and hang them next morning, Colonel dear?"

For sure he'd hung the Patricios, even the one who'd lost both legs at Contreras and was dying.

And then . . . Shea's mind veered from the flogging, the red-hot iron biting into his flesh.

At least he hadn't hanged. Nor had Michael, though that would have been easier than this. . . .

With his last strength, Shea commended his soul to the Blessed Mother and began to ask forgiveness for his sins, but even with death upon him he couldn't repent of the farmer's death. Not with hell before him.

The Virgin had a smile like his mother's. He watched that, not the flickering fires of brimstone.

Then suddenly he was floating above his scarred body, purple-gray, gashed, still marked with the flogging. Like Michael, he could not bleed; his lips were scorched away from his teeth in a wolf grin. Skin baked to bone, except for red-gold hair, he could have been some poor devil of an Indian or Mexican.

Nothing to admire or linger around, that corpse, yet though it was dead, his spirit couldn't quite desert it. Though several times he tried to leave, something held his consciousness all that day near the wrecked body.

It never moved. Buzzards circled but didn't light. A gaunt coyote sniffed, gave the face a tentative lick, then trotted on. *Not good enough for varmints!* he chuckled at himself. Still his essence hovered as if it feared being lost in the distance between this hell and the next.

The sun plunged down. A cooling breeze waked, stirred the bright hair. *Poor lad,* thought his spirit with detached pity. Then, to the spirit's great surprise, the corpse began to move, set one scratched hand forward, clawing the lava, raised a bit on raw knees, inched onward, collapsed, then hitched jerkily, clumsily ahead.

The spirit hovered, disbelieving.

Craziness! Can a dead man move?

This one did, falling prostrate often, sometimes for so long that the spirit began to slip away when it was called back, disgusted, disbelieving, but unable to leave while the corpse struggled. All night, Shea's body crawled through lava and thorns. The sun rose in a flood of liquid fire, striking the shriveled form so that it curled into itself like a scorched spider.

Scornfully regretful, the spirit drifted, at last knowing the foolish battle was ended. Poor bones and flesh, to cling to torment! But that ruin had one more surprise in it.

Bruised fingers dug deep, the head raised. From the inner core of what had been a man, a great cry forced through charred throat and mouth, echoed on the rocks. Then Patrick O'Shea was still. At last his spirit was done with his body.

II

Sand was being forced down his throat. Wet sand, scratching, choking. His eyes fell open. Without comprehension, he saw a tender line of cheek and throat, dark eyes full of tears.

He tried to say, "Why do you give me sand?" but his lips rasped like old snakeskin and the inside of his windpipe felt as if that last shout had burned it with a white-hot poker.

"Drink," the girl told him in Spanish.

The damp sand again.

She looked so kind! Why didn't she give him real water? Maybe if he sucked enough moisture from the grains he could wet his tongue enough to tell her what she was doing. But the stuff gagged him.

He retched weakly, spewing up what he'd swallowed.

"Perhaps it goes better if you only hold it in your mouth and let it slide down very slowly," she murmured, wiping his face, urging on him more of the watery graininess.

If she could just understand! But he obeyed, didn't try to swallow the mass but let it seep gradually down his throat. In between doses, the girl applied deliciously soothing wet cloths to his skin, carefully trickled fluid from the jug over them.

It *looked* like water, brackish, but not the mud it tasted like. For the first time in his life as a male, he lay on a firmly soft and lovely breast without lustful thoughts, as if he'd been a babe.

He floated in and out of awareness, rousing at her coaxing, at last finding the contents of the jug tasting more like water and less like sand. After what must have been a long time, she placed a finely mashed tangy sweetness in his mouth.

"A cactus fruit. Can you chew it?"

He could, weakly, savoring the taste, but when he tried to swallow, he gagged and seemed to lose all the water she'd so painstakingly got down him.

"Pardon me," he tried to say, but she soothed him, washing his face, and began once more to urge fluid into the rawhide skeleton he'd become.

The next food she tried was a very thin gruel. He kept a few cautious swallows of it down. Only when she smiled, eyes shining like stars, did he realize how fearful she had been; how beautiful she was.

After a judicious wait she fed him more gruel. This, too, stayed inside him. She kneaded water into his dry, leatherlike skin and kept giving him small sips. As it grew hotter, she kept wetting the cloths covering him.

He drowsed, still feverish, felt a hand touch his hair, glanced up to see her move shyly away. "When you can walk with my help," she said, "we'll go down to the water hole where there is shade."

For the first time he was lucid enough to wonder what such a woman was doing out here, apparently alone. He'd been in Mexico long enough to recognize that she was a *hidalga,* gently bred, and besides, this seemed no region for even the toughest wood-cutters or farmers to squeeze a living.

She was a miracle, he decided. Like his return from death. For he had died, he was sure of that, and his soul had watched all night while his body crept on.

The girl was a miracle. His miracle.

And it was a miracle, too, that a few mouthfuls of food and a jug of water could begin turning a mummy into a man, could restore his power to think.

If they were near water, their worst problem was solved, but the girl didn't seem to be eating too well. Her dress was so torn that she used her rebozo to cover what needed it, though Shea was feeling pesky enough to wish she'd forget.

Next time she gave him a drink, he tried again to speak, glad that unlike most of the San Patricios, he'd learned all the Spanish he could, and not just for courting the *señoritas*. He liked to know what was going on and what people were thinking, as much as they'd tell.

"How—" His tongue felt stuffed with sawdust and the words garbled. "How did you come here?"

Her eyes widened with such remembered horror that he tried to reach out with a calming gesture but lacked the strength. He wished he could take the question back. As the words came from her, painfully slow at first, then so rapidly that he could only catch the gist, he knew that this girl, his miracle, badly needed one herself, though he couldn't escape chagrin that she'd found water when he hadn't.

He suspected that she hadn't told him everything. Damned unlikely for a woman not to be ravished. The wonder was that she'd survived such treatment, used and left to die.

And this cousin she was going to marry—

Tears welled from those dark, beautiful eyes again. She shook her head determinedly as if she'd already thought that out. Then she seemed to think it was time *he* answered some questions.

"Do not try to talk if it hurts you. But I should like to know who you are, where you come from."

He told her the barest facts in between swallows of water, gruel and the wild strawberry-tasting cactus fruits which she softened for him with a stick.

"Now," he said at last, trying to grin, but finding his face muscles wouldn't work, "reckon—if you'll help— I can make that water hole."

If he'd been able to stand upright, she'd have fitted under his arm. As it was, she put her arm determinedly about his waist and he sort of folded over her. Good thing he was starved way down from his usual 170 pounds. Even so, they made the trip in stages and when she finally eased him down beneath what was a big tree for that country, he was so done in that he couldn't thank her in words; but he brushed her cheek.

She shrank away, terror flaring in her eyes. He cursed himself. Must remember what she'd gone through. She shouldn't have to wonder if she'd saved a wild beast who'd hurt her when its strength came back.

Then she smiled. To Shea, it was like the lighting of candles in a church.

Next day he could chew on bits of dried rabbit meat that Socorro had soaked and shredded. He hated to lie in the shade like a lummox, eating her small hoard of food, but he had to get strong in order to pull them out of here. His baked skin peeled, leaving more layers to come off, and he wondered if he'd ever have his own proper covering again.

And his beard was growing. He didn't like its itching heat and longed for a razor.

Desert creatures still came to drink at the lower *tinaja,* their thirst more powerful than wariness of the intruders. Deer, gray foxes, rabbits and coyotes were the common visitors, along with doves which flew in mornings and evenings and quail which came late in the afternoon and spent the night in sheltering bushes, watering next morning before they flew away.

Three bighorn sheep filed down one evening, majestic horns curving like the whorls of a massive shell. A solitary badger, gray and squat, dug a ground squirrel out of its burrow, dined and then slapped down to the water on its short legs with mighty curving claws. One twilight a mountain lion sprang on a deer, breaking its neck instantly.

When Shea was strong enough, he'd get them a deer. On the fourth day after his resurrection, he collected a dozen good throwing stones. When Socorro came back from harvesting acacia, paloverde and ironwood beans, his throwing had garnered a big rabbit, a medium rattlesnake and one small lizard.

She looked with sadness at the rabbit, with revulsion at the reptiles, before she recovered and smiled. "Why, you're getting food for us without leaving your bed! I think, *señor,* you must be a shrewd and lazy man!"

Though dampened by this, he laughed and said, "Shrewd, no, but lazy, loafing in the shade while you rustle around in the heat! Let me have the knife and I'll fix the meat for drying." At her expression, he grinned and said encouragingly, "Snake tastes a lot like chicken and I'll bet the lizard's not bad."

The truth was, of course, that unsalted meat tasted pretty glum, but at least the sun-drying took out some of the rawness. Taking his kills beyond the water hole, he skinned the rabbit carefully, saved the brains and offal for tanning by digging a hole in the sand, lining it with leaves, sand and a rock too large for animals to paw away. He saved the snakeskin, too.

Long before he'd cut the creatures into strips he was exhausted, but he made himself hang the meat on a thorn bush and toss the bones and refuse as far as he could along the rocky bank. The snake's head, of course, he'd cut off and buried. He'd heard too many stories about dead snakes biting.

"Shea!" Socorro stood by him with the water jug and a gourd of gruel. "Eat, drink and lie down!"

"Yes, lady," he said with teasing obedience. But he was glad enough to lie down on the grass and vines beneath the tree.

During the next few days he killed two more rabbits and five lizards. Socorro's pile of meal cakes grew. Together they worked all the flesh off the rabbit skins and then Shea spread brains and offal on them.

There wouldn't be time to tan the hides well, but he wanted them as soft as possible to make Socorro's footgear. The soles of her little leather shoes were now completely worn out. Fortunately he still had his shoes, though his garment was Socorro's extra rebozo, kilted about his waist. Almost as much as he wanted a deer for food, he wanted one's hide to cover himself in more manly fashion.

As he grew stronger, they talked more, especially at night while the stars glittered above them, owls hooted and coyotes sang in the distance.

"I don't think I ever thanked you for saving me," he said, aghast at the realization. "God's whiskers! Well, lady, I'm thanking you now and always will."

He sensed her smile in the darkness. "I saved you for myself, Shea. It is not good—it's almost impossible—to walk the Gran Desierto alone."

He knew she spoke of more than a desert journey.

When he told her about Michael, she reached across the space between them on the sand and pressed his hand. "He is with your mother," she said softly, "and the mother of us all. But to lose your twin! When you came from so far away. A green land, you say? *Big* trees? Tell me about it, Shea."

And he did, the country he loved, and the English overlordship he hated. He even made a stab at trying to explain to her and himself how the United States and Mexico had come to seem more and more to him like England and Ireland.

"Your cheek is better now," she told him. "And your back is almost healed."

But he knew he'd carry the scars to his grave; and with them a hatred of the United States as searing as the iron that had branded him forever.

She was still touching him. Sweet pain ran through his nerves, gorged his veins. He made himself keep his hands off her, breaking into sweat with the effort. She was still afraid of men; he sensed it when they happened to touch and she swiftly moved away, or when he was watching her, guard down, and she happened to glance up to meet his eyes. He was sure she liked him, was proud of him in a fiercely protective way because she'd saved his life; but he also knew fear when he saw it.

Socorro was afraid. He mustn't risk making that dread worse.

"Tell me about Alamos," he said abruptly, and breathed easier when she took her hand away though he hungered for that light, brushing touch.

She told him of the old colonial silver town nestled among the mountains, of its great cathedral still bearing the Royal Arms of Spain over the entrance, the Plaza de las Armas, her father's house with the long gallery.

"Don't you want to go back?" Shea asked.

"No," she said so quickly that he knew she'd already thought about it. "My uncle would make me marry his brother-in-law, an awful old man who smells like a goat and has already buried four wives! It was partly to stop his urging the match that my father betrothed me to my cousin in California."

Shea's heart stopped. But sure, what had he expected? A young woman of her class would naturally marry a Spaniard of good blood and family, someone picked by her folks.

"Well, I'll get you out there," Shea promised grimly. He owed her that. He owed her anything.

"I—I don't want to go."

Shea could scarcely believe the whisper. He lay transfixed for a moment. Except as a fleeting dream, he hadn't let himself think she might stay with him.

"What do you want then, lady?"

Silence. Then muffled weeping. Shea sat up, leaned awkwardly above her. "Socorro! *Chiquita!*"

Sobs wrenched her. To hell with whether or not it scared her, she needed badly to be held! Cradling her against him, he rocked her as he might a child till stiffness ebbed from her and she clung to him, weeping in a hopeless way that stirred him to the depths, made him ache to protect her, though there was that other almost overwhelming urge in him, too, to kiss that sweet mouth, know the soft breasts and thighs, lose himself utterly in possessing her.

"What is it?" he soothed, stroking her hair. "What is it, little one? Are you sure you don't want to go to your cousin?"

27

"Not *now*."

"But if he loves you—"

She laughed bitterly. "How can he? We've never seen each other. It was a thing arranged." Straightening, she said in a matter-of-fact way, "Even if I loved him, it would be impossible. To him. I am damaged, ruined."

"Don't say that!" So it was true. The *Areneños* had raped her.

"Maybe I am ruined—not the way he'd mean but in a worse one. Shea!" She struck at him with her fist, not really at him, but at her devils. "Shea, what can I do?"

"Why, sure, *chiquita,* you'll be doing whatever you want if it's possible or I can make it that way."

"It's stupid, what I want. And it—it's not fair."

"Never mind. What is it?"

She buried her face against him. "Shea, I want to stay with you but—" He could scarcely make out the despairing cry. "I have fear! I have much fear!"

Joyful relief weakened him. She cared about him, then! He was no green boy, to rush or hurt or disgust her. He knew the wounds of the spirit healed more slowly than those of the body, but with time and patience . . .

He laughed exultantly, kissed where the hair swirled back from her forehead. "Now if that's all your worry, you're God's lucky lass! I'd rather have you with me than all the hosts of heaven and may I be damned to the blackest hell before I hurt you!"

"But—you're a man!"

"To be sure." He wiped her eyes with her rebozo, brought up her face and grinned till, shyly, she smiled back. "Before we're through, it's my hope to make you mightily glad of that! But there's more to a man than desire, *chiquita.* Much more to loving."

She trusted him, that was the hell of it. Once she had his assurance, she seemed to think it was straight and easy, that he didn't have to battle himself. Instead of shrinking from his touch, she sought it, lay in his arms till he started to tremble with suppressed longing.

How could she press against him like that, only the torn dress between her body and his, if she really didn't want the passion and strength and tenderness he burned to envelop her in till they were utterly joined, completely each other's?

Take her! Take her! Why fool around with what must be? Later she'd be glad. . . .

Was that how he'd repay her for saving his life? Force her as those killers of her father had?

Shea put her from him. "It's time we slept, lass. Tomorrow I'll try for a deer, and you get all the beans you can. We need to be moving out. Those *Areneños* are bound to turn up soon or late."

"Yes, Shea." She curled up beside him, so close he felt the warmth of her, smelled the musky yucca root with which she washed herself.

She was asleep at once, trustfully, as if all her troubles were over. But Shea had a feeling his were just starting.

He didn't think he could sneak up on a deer and kill it with a knife so he decided to dig a hole in the sand at the bottom of the trail, covering it with twigs and leaves disguised by sand and small rocks.

The trap would bear the weight of small creatures. Anything heavy enough to break through should supply the meat they needed for the walk out of this place that looked like the dregs of God's wrath when He was too sick of what He'd made to finish properly.

During the day Shea worked at Socorro's footgear, double-soled, coming up around the ankles to tie with bits of rawhide. He stitched them by punching holes with the knife and then dragging through yucca fibers still attached to the sharp needlelike point.

He saved several stalks and bound them together with more fiber to make a fire drill, peeled an old leaf so it would act as punk. It might not work but, by God's whiskers, he was going to *try* to make them a fire tonight, the way he'd seen a Mexican do it.

Socorro giggled when she tried on the "boots," but she quickly sobered. "*Maravilloso,* Shea! They are very nice."

"Better than nothing, anyhow." Quail were coming to water and the sun was almost down. Shea picked up the knife, glanced toward the trap. "Wish me luck."

She didn't say anything. "We have to eat," he said roughly, and moved along the cañon, taking his place downwind from the trap. He was glad, though, that it was a buck mule deer, not a doe or fawn, which came finally down the trail. It had spikes instead of antlers, but looked big for a yearling. As it came closer Shea could tell from its corded muscles and places where the hide was loose or wrinkled that this must be an old buck, so far past his mating prime that he no longer developed the full rack of ten points.

The sticks broke under him. Going down, the buck scrambled for footing but Shea was upon him, slit the throat with one deep gashing, jumped back while blood poured and the deer sank slowly in a heap.

"Sorry, old fellow," Shea told him. "Reckon you're going to be tough and stringy, but you'll help us out of here!"

He'd poached a few deer in his time and hunted a little to get fresh meat while with the San Patricios. Dragging the buck off the trail, he filled in the trap so it would take nothing else and dressed his kill.

Hitching the carcass into the fork of a paloverde to bleed, Shea washed the blood off and set about spindling the yucca drill in the middle of the dry, pithy leaf.

Not only would cooked meat taste good, but a fire would help protect the bulk of the meat from some hungry mountain lion.

A fire *might* catch the eye of *Areneños,* but they wouldn't be roaming after dark and Shea reasoned that none would be close enough to see the glow. If they were, they'd surely come to camp at the water hole.

Twilight deepened into night. Shea swore and twirled and twirled and swore. Socorro made soft, commiserating noises, gave a cry of delight when at last a spark glowed, grew into hesitant flame.

"Fire! Oh, Shea, how beautiful!"

He added more pith, small twigs, then the larger ones he'd put in readiness beside his drill. When it was really a fire, not the hope of one, he stood up.

"Keep it going, *chiquita*. I'll be back in a minute with supper!"

He cut off several slices of meat, skewered them on peeled acacia limbs, and rigged them on rocks built up on either side of the precious, cheering flame. He watched the venison while he finished skinning the buck, dumped the head and legs up the cañon, cut up the meat and carried it to camp in the hide.

Socorro greeted him with smoking meat, still on its skewer, and several meal cakes. They used these to catch the drippings. Even without seasoning and tough as the old deer's flesh was, it tasted flavorsome and strengthening.

"As you can tell," Shea said, "this is not any tender young doe or fawn!"

"Yes." Her eyes danced though her voice was mock-solemn. "I thought perhaps you found him expired among the rocks, a victim of old age."

"He soon would have been." Shea was glad that she'd made up her mind to be sensible about their necessities. He wanted to linger with her by the fire, watch the play of warm light and soft shadow on her face and throat, but the hide had to be scraped and the meat cut for drying.

He was slicing strips for jerky when Socorro brought the rock scraper she'd used on the rabbit skins and went to work on the part of the hide not heaped with cuts of venison.

31

At last they were through. He spread brains and intestines on the hide, edged a heavy long-dead ironwood stump into the fire and lay down by Socorro, too weary for wild yearnings, just grateful she was there. Without her there would be only the haunting absence of his twin. She was not only Shea's miracle that had saved his life, but a promise of what that life could be.

"We'll take it easy today," Shea said next morning as Socorro yawned and tossed back her long shining hair. "Eat plenty of venison, tan that hide, find gourds for carrying water, add some more cakes to your pile—"

She wrinkled her nose at him. *"Ay de mí,* a day of leisure!"

"Make the most of it," he warned, building up the smoldering coals of the ironwood stump and skewering some venison above them.

It was a good day, busy without the forced pace of butchering. Socorro brought in *tunas* and bean pods. He helped grind meal, singed fine hairy needles off the *tunas* and worked on the hide, rubbing and kneading. It stayed discouragingly stiff.

"I think you must wear my rebozo a little longer," Socorro told him. "Besides," she twinkled, "it matches your eyes! Real *norteño* eyes you have, the shade of a storm sky!"

By late afternoon he had to admit she was right, though he didn't relish the idea of toting an offal-smeared hide. She'd found several gourds and he'd cut small holes in the tops, saving the pieces for stoppers, cleaning out the pith and seeds. They wouldn't hold much water but it could make the difference in survival. They'd also saved and cleaned the deer bladder for an additional canteen.

After she had bathed that night and washed her hair, he got a bit of yucca root and did the same, scrubbing himself from head to toes. He was still bony, but at least he didn't look like a skeleton wrapped in rawhide.

The water and breeze caressing his naked body made him think of the girl just a few strides away. He waded as deep as he could into the water, paddled about frantically like a frog in a teacup, and at last nature relieved his aching predicament. He was thankful for that, though he couldn't help but think it was a shocking sad waste.

III

They were up before dawn and breakfasted on the last of the fresh meat before Shea reluctantly covered over the fire that had been their companion and helper. He insisted that Socorro drink long after she protested that she was splitting.

"Sure, it's uncomfortable," he agreed. "But we can make canteens of our bellies and use that much less of what we carry."

He'd saved one of the buck's spikes for a dagger or tool and carried that in the snakeskin belt in the loose ends of which he'd secured the largest of the gourds and the deer bladder. The leather jug swung over his shoulder. With Socorro's rebozo kilted about him and the stiff deerhide across his shoulders, he looked barbaric enough without the strips of jerky fastened on the back of the hide to finish drying as they traveled.

Socorro had her knife fastened about her waist in the folded rawhide scabbard Shea had made for her, and the rabbit boots were fastened at her ankles. Meal cakes and *tunas* were tied in one end of her serape which draped over head and shoulders to hold the other gourds in the opposite side, tied in the corners to hold the stoppers in place.

She looked regretfully at the sheltering tree, the savior water hole, the sand where they'd slept these past ten nights. "I'm sad to leave, Shea. This has seemed—*pues,* almost like home."

"We'll find a better one," he promised. "One where we won't have to worry about *Areneños* dropping in."

"If we go north, we'll be in Apache lands." She shrugged. "Much farther east are the fierce Comanches

35

who raid Mexico each fall for slaves, mules and horses. They even raid the Tejanos who are said to have horns and eat babies raw." She frowned up at him, hurrying to match his steps which he shortened to fit hers. "You've been in Texas. Is it true, the horns?"

Shea laughed at her perplexity. "Never mind, *chiquita*. Texans, the ones who aren't Mexican, look like any other Yanquis; in fact most of them came from Tennessee best as I can figure." He gestured to the north. "What else is ahead of us?"

"Far northeast, hundreds on hundreds of miles through the deserts and mountains of the Apache, is Santa Fe. Beyond its province of New Mexico is the United States, though now that you say it has won the war with Mexico, I suppose it will take over all that region as well as California."

"How do you feel about that?"

Her brow furrowed and at last she sighed. "Perhaps I should be very angry, but the truth is, Shea, that the Mexican government hasn't been able to defend the frontiers. My father often talked of it. The Apache laugh at the few soldiers in the forts or presidos. Missions and ranches have been abandoned. California and New Mexico are separated from Mexico by this vast wilderness controlled by Indians. Some of them, the Pima and Papago, are friendly enough, but the Apache terrorize them, too." She shrugged again. "I think most Mexicans of the frontier want protection from the Apache and are past caring who gives it!"

"I'm not keen on winding up in country the United States may claim," Shea said. "It's true Michael and I deserted before war actually broke out, which is why we weren't hanged, but since I didn't wear their iron yoke at hard labor, some army officer who saw this brand and remembered the San Patricios might give me a fair amount of trouble."

"Sonora stretches far north," she reassured him. "There are trappers in the mountains, but otherwise the Yanquis seem to have no interest in it."

"It lies between the rest of the United States and California," Shea growled. "California has ports for the China trade. Right now American ships have to go all the way around Cape Horn. First thing you know, there'll be soldiers and railroads and settlers flocking west. If the northern part of Sonora's the best route, you can bet the Americans will grab it!"

"I say they're welcome if they control the Apaches!"

Shea sucked in a disgusted breath. "Spare me the blue-bellies and I'll take care of the Apache!"

She shook her head. "You don't understand about Apaches. They're dreaded throughout New Mexico, Sonora and Chihuahua by the Pueblo Indians and Pima and Papago as much as by white settlements. Apaches call Mexican stockmen their herders who raise sheep, cattle and mules for them. For two hundred years they've been at war with Spain or Mexico."

"Two hundred years!" Shea whistled. "Sounds like England and Ireland!"

"Spain created a Commandancy General of the Interior Provinces for the single need of fighting off Apaches. There were special *compañias volantes,* flying companies, cavalry to swiftly pursue raiders. But since Mexico won its freedom from Spain twenty-six years ago, the government has been too busy to spare much worry for the frontier. In order to get rid of the domination of the Spanish-born, Mexican Centralists, wealthy conservatives and the church allied briefly with the Federalists who stood for more equality and a loose federation of states. Once Spain withdrew, the two factions started a struggle for power. It's gone on ever since."

"And lately Mexico has had to fight the Americans."

"Yes. The Apache control the wilderness. Have no doubt about that!" She added bitterly, "The *Proyecto de Guerra* has just made things worse!"

"What's that?"

"Sonora created a special fund in 1835 to pay for

scalps of Apaches. A hundred pesos for a man, fifty for a woman, twenty-five for children."

"God above!" His stomach turned at the thought. "Women? Babies?"

"Some say they should pay more for women since without them the tribe would die out."

These words from Socorro's sensitive mouth convinced him of the implacable hatred between Mexicans and Apaches. "But you say it hasn't worked?"

"Scalp hunters have taken hair from friendly Indians, too. They've even killed Mexicans and collected for them! And, of course, it's infuriated the Apache. They raid worse than ever."

He decided not to tell her his low opinion of the fighting abilities of her countrymen. Whatever else could be said about the United States Army, it had been outnumbered tremendously all the way. Why, at Churubusco, there'd been fifteen thousand Mexicans against six thousand Americans.

But the frontier Americans were a ferocious lot, often carrying vicious Bowie knives in addition to better firearms than most Mexicans had.

Mexico had no small-arms factories and used mostly European discards like the Jaeger, a Prussian flintlock.

Flintlocks were fired by a spark and couldn't be trusted in rain when the power was damp or the spark failed. Many U.S. soldiers had percussion rifles. A watertight percussion cap held powder that could be ignited by a blow.

The Texas Rangers were equipped with Colt revolvers, fantastic guns that could fire six times without reloading.

Of course, Shea hadn't blamed the poor common Mexican soldiers for not wanting to fight. Dragged from their homes and families who often knew starvation without them, brutally drilled and treated, the peons fought a lot better than anyone could have expected. But if troops like that had been the defense of the frontier, it was no wonder the Apache ruled the roost.

"This ranch we're headed for," he said. "What do you know about it?"

"Only that it's there. Enrique told me as he was dying. He used to take trade goods to Tubac and Tucson. The ranch must have been one of his stops."

"Do you know the name of that mountain?"

"It's called Pinacate for the black beetle found hereabouts. Enrique told me when we first sighted it that the Papagos think one of their principal gods, Elder Brother, has one home in a cave there. His other dwelling is at Baboquivari, further northwest. It's also said that Padre Kino, a Jesuit who founded many Sonoran missions, climbed Pinacate and from there could see to the gulf and the Vermilion Sea, or Sea of Cortez, while beyond, westward, he saw Baja California."

"That must have been a rare sight. But right now I'd rather spy that ranch!"

The morning cool was gone. They stopped talking since that took energy and dried the mouth. At midmorning Shea called a halt beneath a big paloverde in a dry arroyo.

They drank the contents of one gourd rather than sipping just enough to wet their mouths. "I'm for drinking what we need as long as we have it," Shea said. "We can travel faster that way and feel a lot better. If you agree."

"It's all in God's hands. But," she added practically, "let's have some chunks from that hundred-headed cactus yonder and carry some with us when we go on."

Shea, with great care because of the vicious curving thorns, carved off the top of one protrusion and took out a big piece of the pulp. They ate slices of it along with a few bites of venison and walked till the sun was straight above.

They had been following the cañon from the top. Now it ended in a jumble of boulders and rocks scattered with ironwood and acacia. Resting in the shade, they ate and drank.

"Might as well sleep if we can," suggested Shea.

"Stirring around in this heat makes us need more water. If we leave midafternoon we can walk till twilight unless we're real lucky and find water."

They both slept, finding a sandy hollow between trees and rocks. As they drank from their third and last gourd before starting on, Shea had a nightmarish flash of crawling through the lava, drinking his few pitiful drops of urine. He couldn't stand that again, but, Mary Mother, it mustn't happen to Socorro!

Of course, back down the cañon was water. But they couldn't stay at that *tinaja* forever, they had to make the break. Even so, walking away from the end of the cañon gave Shea a strange feeling and he guessed Socorro felt it too. They were leaving their place of refuge and familiarity.

They made for Pinacate, luminous blue to the northwest, following animal trails as often as possible, several times detouring to see if there was water at the end of a promising track.

All they found were crusted hollows. Shea had tried to keep oriented by looking back frequently and lining the *tinaja* cañon up between a distant pyramid-shaped cone and a long reddish crater. If they didn't find water tomorrow, he'd leave Socorro with the deer bladder and gourds filled from the jug and take that back to the *tinaja*. If he got back to her with two-thirds of the jug, it'd carry them an extra day. By then, even if they found no water, surely they'd make the ranch.

They found no water, though when they camped in a dry wash Shea dug at the lowest place in the sand till Socorro made him stop.

"You could bury me in that hole, Shea, and the sand isn't the least bit damp! Let it go. We still have the jug and deer bladder." She added hopefully, "Pinacate *does* look closer, at last! All the days I walked alone it never seemed the tiniest bit nearer."

He put the deer spike aside, took the venison and cakes she proffered, noticed that she was favoring her left foot.

"Have you got a blister?" he demanded.

She looked guilty. "I—it's nothing."

"Let's see that foot."

Reluctantly, she sat down and let him draw off the boot. "Well," he said sternly, "you don't have a blister; now, you've got two broken ones! How you've managed to walk God knows and may He forgive me for not noticing! Saints above, girl, don't try to be brave about your feet! You need them to get you out of here!"

Her lip quivered. She hung her head. Ashamed of himself, Shea said gruffly, "Sorry, *chiquita*. But next time something goes wrong, tell me right away, will you?"

She nodded but added with a flash of fire, "And you, you also promise to say if you have pain!"

He smothered an earthy, masculine reply to that. She hadn't a notion of what she did to him. Now that she had to use her rebozo mostly as a food carrier, she couldn't drape the ends over the tears in her dress. It was taking unfair advantage, but God's whiskers! How could a man, however hard he tried, keep from seeing those sweet curvings, the budding tips of her breasts, the warm, graceful turn of waist and thigh?

Stop it, you ungrateful blackguard! he told himself harshly. She had been martyred in her womanhood in a way as cruel as his death by thirst. She'd saved him from that. He damned well had to keep a curb bit on himself till it was time to coax back into blooming that female deepness of her that had been invaded, torn, left plundered.

So he said gravely, "Let's agree, *chiquita*, that if we're sick or hurt, we'll tell each other." He grinned. "And I give you leave, if I get blisters, to use on me this cure I learned off a Mexican soldier!"

He'd noticed an agave on the side of the slope. Taking the knife, he went up to it and cut off part of one of the long, fleshy, barbed leaves.

"This will sting."

He knelt by Socorro, wrapped bits of the leaf which

41

he'd peeled and mashed over the blisters with a strip cut off his snakeskin. She bit her lip but didn't flinch. "Now," he said, making her a footrest of heaped-up sand, "you keep off that foot tonight. Is the other one all right?"

"Yes, I swear it!" She tucked it hastily beneath her.

"I'll cobble you out some kind of open sandal to wear till those blisters heal," he said.

Measuring deerhide to Socorro's slim, high-arched foot, he shaped a sandal with latchets of hide to tie around ankle and foot.

If only they'd find water tomorrow! That ranch couldn't be more than three or four days away. If Socorro could walk.

At their noon halt next day, she glanced up at him apologetically. "Shea. The other foot. I'm so sorry—"

"No, I'm sorry that you've got to hobble in these poor half-cured skins!" Making her sit down in the shade, he examined the shapely foot, the reddened spots forming in several places. "Let's try some agave and let the air at it. I'll make another sandal while we're resting."

They traveled more slowly because Socorro had to pick her way with care, though Shea helped by walking in front. Along one drifted former streambed where big burrs grew thick, he simply carried her. Her hair was soft on his lips and the feel of her against him was sweet torment. He was ready to put her down by the time they got through the burrs, though.

He still didn't have his strength back. He thought again of Michael, the thin line between life and death. Michael had borne the flogging, the red-hot iron; but three days without water had finished him. *Socorro's praying for you, lad. Her prayers are better than mine.*

She shaded her eyes and pointed. "Shea! See those doves? Look! They've dropped out of sight!"

"Let's hope it's to water!"

It was. Walking toward the point where the birds

had vanished, they descended into a broad sandy wash, followed it up between rock walls, climbing over boulders till they looked down at a rock hollow that must have been twelve feet across.

The grayish-brown, black-billed mourning doves were drinking. "Let them finish," Socorro urged, touching Shea's arm. "They led us here!"

"That they did," Shea agreed. "Sure, we won't grudge them their drink."

He was greatly relieved. If they'd had a dry camp, he'd intended to leave before dawn next morning, trying to find the first *tinaja,* but he'd hated the thought of leaving Socorro alone. A day-and-a-half's hard journey for a half-jug of water was a high price.

As they drew back to wait for the birds, Shea gave the nearly empty jug to Socorro. "Drink up, lady! We're going to stay here a few days while your feet heal! And maybe this dratted hide will get to where I can wear it!"

She laughed up at him and he knew she'd been just as worried as he was. "Let us pray," she said as she handed him the water, "that I don't need any more sandals!"

Shea needed the rest almost as much as Socorro's blisters needed it, but he didn't idle. Saving their dried meat, they ate what he brought down with hurled stones; two rabbits and a big chuckwalla lizard. They cooked these over a fire fanned from another yucca drill. Socorro roasted some of the plump yucca fruit and flavored some water with crushed *tunas.*

"It's a feast!" Shea told her.

When she fed him a piece of the sweet yucca, he was sure that they'd never again taste anything so good. Though the meat *could* do with some salt. He grinned and reckoned that even in paradise the angels grumbled that their halos weren't bright enough.

Two days later they started on, having added two more gourds to their water supply. These, and the other gourds, were carried in slings of the new rabbit hides, and scraps of buckskin. The jerky was dry enough to be carried in the blue rebozo along with the other food.

Shea's buckskin garment was far from handsome. He'd shaped it to cover as much as possible of his body below the waist in order to ward off thorns and brush, so it reached variously from midthigh to midcalf, depending on where he'd taken the parts for Socorro's sandals.

The sandals were also stowed in the rebozo Shea carried. He'd padded the toes of her boots with the softest strips of rabbit fur and she had firm orders to call a halt if a blister started.

Pinacate increased steadily in size, a longish mountain with its highest elevation on the south. Shea began to suspect uneasily that to know a ranch lay beyond it was like knowing there was a water hole on this side. It could mean almost anywhere.

They reached the bottom of the rocky, scrub-grown peak that evening, camped in a silted wash and began the ascent next morning before dawn.

"Moses must have felt like this when he was fixing to pass out of the desert into the Promised Land," Shea said as they paused for breath.

"I think the Promised Land was also a desert."

"What?" He gazed at her in shock. "Then what's all that about milk and honey?"

"Bees make honey in the desert, very fine honey from mesquite, acacia and cactus flowers." Her chin poked out stubbornly. "That milk must have come from goats because you don't hear much about cattle. The scriptures tell about shepherds, not vaqueros. It is *muy claro* that a country that uses mules and camels instead of horses *must* be desert!"

"But the Jordan River! The Dead Sea—"

"That tells you! It's full of salt. As for the Jordan, *pues,* don't you remember how Naaman, commander of the Syrian hosts, came to Elisha to be healed of his leprosy?"

"Can't say that I do." Getting to Mass and confession when his mother began to fear for his soul had been about the total of his religious education.

"When the prophet told Naaman to wash in the Jordan, he became furious! He said the rivers of Damascus were much cleaner and better. It took his servants a time to persuade him to bathe in the Jordan, even to cure his leprosy."

"Did it?"

"Of course!"

"Then I'd call it a pretty good old river."

She glared at him. "It wasn't the river at all, you redhead burro!"

Startled as if a hummingbird had suddenly attacked, Shea blinked, then covered a grin, delighted that she had a temper. It was a sign she was human, had passion that could be reached.

"Not the river?" he asked innocently. "What was it, then?"

"Faith!" she fairly shrieked at him. "Faith and humility!"

He could no longer control his laughter. Flushing, she stamped her foot, but after an indignant sputter, she laughed, too. They were still chuckling when they reached the top of the ridge and looked down and away.

The ranch lay just beyond them, but when they saw it, their smiles froze.

IV

Corrals, a rambling adobe house with smaller ones close by, several *ramadas,* open shelters for working in the shade where one could catch a breeze. There was a well by some watering troughs with a cluster of trees scattered along an old riverbed.

What Shea didn't want to see were the bodies.

Socorro gasped and caught his arm. He led her over to a shallow cave, made her sit down. "Stay here. I'll see if anyone's alive." He doubted it from the way buzzards, ravens and coyotes had been feeding.

Leaving everything but the jug and knife with Socorro, he went warily down the slope. As he neared a corral, made by stacking rough lengths of wood between uprights, a coyote trotted into the brush and several ravens scolded as they rose heavily.

What must have been two men sprawled there, eyes pecked out, faces with a strange melted look because the scalps were gone. Shea swallowed the hot scalding in his throat, walked on, watching for any movement. The corpses stank. Must have happened yesterday; much longer than that and the wild scavengers would've left nothing but bones.

Four more men lay between the corrals and houses, so mutilated that he couldn't tell how they'd died. No arrows sticking out of them, though. Buzzards flopped only a little way off, bald red heads grotesquely small on hulking bodies with wingspans almost as much as Shea's six foot two.

The big house was where the real carnage was. Apparently the attackers had surprised the six men outside, but eight more men, three women and a half-dozen

47

children, from a babe to ones of ten or eleven years, had taken refuge in the house.

They'd fought for their lives. A few still gripped the makeshift weapons they'd snatched up, a hunk of wood, an iron ladle, part of a broken yoke. Such real weapons as they'd had must have been looted by their murderers.

All were scalped, even a baby that had held to its mother's breast as she tried to protect it. The skirts of all the women, from a toothless aged one to a girl so young she had no breasts, were rucked up about their hips.

Shea leaned against the lintel. He'd seen battlefields, but nothing like this. Birds and beasts had feasted here, too, but he could see that several of the men had been shot. And weren't Apaches said to usually take children, often women, into captivity?

Dazed, he made the women's clothes as decent as possible and put the baby's head beneath its mother's arm so its wound didn't show.

He had to get these people buried, a huge task in itself. He didn't want Socorro to see that. As for the Promised Land—if this was any sample, they'd be better off at one of their *tinajas!* Except, sometime, the *Areneños* would turn up.

Stepping out the open back door, he found two more children, evidently caught as they tried to run in from play or chores. They were so chewed up that he couldn't tell whether they were boys or girls, they were just thin and brown and little.

Faint at the sight and stench, he circled the buildings and corrals. The remains of a butchered cow lay by the trough which was dry. Cattle were crowding up, evidently hoping for water.

Going over to the well, he lowered the big rawhide bucket by its rawhide rope which passed over a pulley. It must have held over ten gallons, weighing close to a hundred pounds, so it didn't take too long to water the stock enough to hold them till he could finish the job.

Had to get back to Socorro, tell her to wait while he took care of the bodies.

She wasn't in the shallow cave. Shea's heart plunged. Then he saw her down the slope quite a distance, not far from the most outlying corral, kneeling by something obscured by the brush which had kept him from seeing her as he climbed.

He ran toward her. She glanced about imploringly. He could see now that she was giving water to a man, supporting his head and shoulders.

The man's left thigh looked to be half-shot away. It teemed with maggots; good thing, ugly as they were. Cleaned out rotten flesh better than any surgeon.

He choked on the water, struggled feebly, moaning. "Out of his head, poor devil," said Shea, dropping on one knee to examine the wound. "Looks like a musket ball passed through, tore a big hole on its way out. Don't think it touched the joint."

"He has fever. If we could get him into some shade—" Her eyes widened as she remembered. "Is anyone else alive?"

"No."

"Apache?"

He shrugged. "No arrows. But everyone was scalped."

She shuddered and held the man closer against her. Young, good-looking vaquero, little more than a boy. And he'd kept his hair. "How'd you find him?" Shea demanded.

That small chin thrust out in a way he was beginning to recognize. "When you were gone so long, I got worried and started down to work my way around the corrals in case you were in trouble."

"Damn it, I told you to wait! What if this man had been a scalper?"

"Well, he wasn't! And—and if anything happened to you, I'd want it to happen to me!"

Her eyes sparkled with held-back tears. Shea's anger dissolved along with the irrational jealousy he felt at seeing her fuss over the vaquero. Besides, there was too much to do.

"Let's get him under a *ramada*. Maybe you can get his fever down, dress that wound with mashed agave. Can you fetch our other gear?"

She nodded and started up the ridge. Shea hefted the youngster as gently as he could and packed him down to the *ramada* farthest from the house of death. He'd hoped to get the dead men away from the corrals before Socorro returned, but she reached them before he did, put down her burdens.

Kneeling by the raddled, stinking corpses, she made the sign of the cross over each and bowed her head for a moment. Then she picked up the food and water, hurrying to the *ramada,* at once making the man a pillow of the rebozo-wrapped food. She didn't look up as Shea passed her with the first body, but began to bathe the vaquero's face and throat with the edge of her rebozo.

On his reconnaissance of the space behind the big house, Shea had glimpsed an arroyo. Digging separate graves for all these people was pointless; the thing was to get them decently covered with the kind earth, and that quickly!

More cattle had come up and were bawling their heads off, so as soon as he'd got the remains of the second man to the shallowest part of the arroyo, Shea hauled up more water, pausing as he struggled with the bucket to see that there were dozens of the animals now. Surely Apaches would've run them off to slaughter or sell?

Cows with satisfied thirst gave way to newcomers who crowded in as fast as they could at the long broad trough and seemed to fairly soak up the water. Shea's back and arms were aching by the time the last of them were drinking. He lowered a much smaller bucket and took it over to Socorro.

"Try this," he said, filling one of their gourds. "It should taste sweeter than that *tinaja* juice!"

She thanked him but lifted the young vaquero and held the gourd to his mouth. He drank and seemed quieter. Compressing his lips, Shea handed her another gourd.

"You drink, too," she insisted.

Shea tilted the bucket and took a long delicious draught. Pure and cool, it tasted better than the finest whiskey or wine. "Stay here till I come back," he commanded.

"Eat a little first," she suggested.

He wouldn't be able to keep it down. Not with what he had to do. "Later. Use the *tinaja* water to bathe the kid."

Several coyotes faded out the back door as he entered the house. Ravens flapped out doors and the several small windows. Shea looked at the bodies and choked back vomit. Arms dragged off, feet, legs. And what was left—

Hadn't he seen a wheelbarrow out back?

Into it, breathing as thinly as possible of the tainted air, he loaded the human debris, jolted the grisly burden to the arroyo, having to stop to retrieve an arm that fell off, a head that separated from gnawed shoulders.

Nineteen people, eight of them children, and the six men by the corrals. Twenty-five human beings wiped out.

Why?

The way everyone was scalped made him think of bounty hunters. But these folks weren't Apaches.

As he placed the mother and baby on top of other corpses, Shea gritted his teeth and wished he could get hold of whatever devils, red, white or brown, who'd done it. Might they have cruel deaths and a long hell!

It took several trips. When the last bodies were dropped into the gulch, he found a shovel and ax in one of the sheds and chopped a covering of limbs and brush for the burial before he caved in the arroyo sides to add a layer of crumbled white earth.

Panting, he rested in the shade a few minutes before

he tossed and rolled rocks on top to discourage animals. Not enough, but he'd add more later.

He carried ax and shovel to the house. Iron was rare in this region. That the raiders hadn't taken such things pointed more than ever at men who'd only wanted scalps.

Sweet Jesus, give me a crack at them and I promise to cleanse your earth of as many as you give me aid to put away!

You could say the Sonoran government asked for it by granting bounty on Apache scalps. But it wasn't some high muck-amuck paying the consequences. It was people like this, working hard to scratch their living from a bleakness he couldn't have imagined from Ireland. Those women, the kids, that baby!

The long room with a fireplace at one end served all the needs of living. Chilis dangled from the beams, strings of garlic and many-colored corn. A black iron kettle on the hearth held dried remnants of beans. Either the raiders had eaten their victims' food or some animal had.

There was a trestle table with carved chairs, benches of rawhide pulled taut over wooden frames. Bridles, saddles, and other gear dangled from pegs or lay on the floor. There were several chests, opened and plundered, and in one corner a niche with Guadalupe, the brown madonna of Mexico.

In the storeroom off the kitchen baskets and clay jars had been wantonly broken, kicked over or spilled. Birds and small wild things had foraged the trove, leaving their tracks and droppings. But there was still a lot of usable food.

The other room held a big canopied bed, posts handsomely carved though the mattress was of shucks and it was covered with serapes. There were a number of straw mats and more serapes stacked in the corner. Evidently the owner of the ranch and his wife had kept a certain rough state though now they lay jumbled with their vaqueros and servants.

52

The odor of decay was thick. They'd have to stay here till the vaquero died or got better. Shea found steel and flint and started a fire from the waiting tinder and mesquite, carried good-sized branches to burn where the bodies had lain. In several places, blood had soaked the hard-packed dirt floor. He carried in shovels-ful of earth and scattered it over the stains.

The mesquite was exuding its fragrant smoke, puri-fying the foulness. It was all Shea could do to ready the place for Socorro.

Near sundown now and he hadn't eaten since morn-ing. Before they entered the Promised Land! Now he was ravenous.

Shea glanced quickly inside the other small houses, probably the homes of married vaqueros. Fireplaces, grinders, tortilla grills, a bean pot. No furniture. A few garments hung on pegs and mats and serapes were rolled in a corner.

Again he had to stifle unreasoning jealousy as he ap-proached the *ramada*. Socorro had held him, a stranger, the same way a few short weeks ago, saved his life.

Was he blithering ingrate enough to grudge this poor lad the same mercy?

Shea reined himself in sharply, but a niggling part of him *would* grumble that she didn't need to pillow that dark, probably verminous head against her breast; she didn't need to be smiling quite that sympathetically as she coaxed bits of moistened meal cake down him!

"So you're back amongst us?" Shea said, stooping down.

That smooth brown cheek had never been shaved. It was a fine lot of curly black hair that had escaped the knife. Broad, high cheekbones, a full handsome mouth if it hadn't been dry and cracked. But it was the eyes that rocked Shea.

In a small town in the Sierra Madre, villagers had asked several off-duty San Patricios if they would kill a *tigre* that was killing their stock. This *tigre* had killed off all the local dogs who'd been used to trail him. Besides, the soldiers had rifles, not worn-out old muskets! There would be a big barbecue and *baile* for them if they succeeded, floods of good mescal and lots of pretty girls!

What soldiers ever turned down such an offer?

Michael, Shea and two experienced hunters, with the U.S. Army Model 1841 percussion rifles they'd brought across the Rio Grande, set off with a rancher who took them that night to the depredating *tigre*'s home territory.

One of the hunters threw back his head and gave out a blood-curdling roar, imitating a trespassing rival male. In seconds there was an answering yowl, followed by the giant cat himself.

The *tigre* got the full load of four rifles, but still crashed after his foes till they had to run. Villagers brought torches after the beast collapsed. Hauled up by one sinewy spotted leg, hitched over a pole set between uprights, his tawny body, marked with black rosettes and spots, looked immense. He must have weighed as much as Shea and from nose to tail measured eight feet.

But Shea, in the flare of torches, had looked into fierce golden eyes that had in them all the wonder, ferocity and beauty of the wilds. He felt no pride as they glazed and he suddenly despised the exulting villagers who pelted the limp body with rocks and mud.

"What's the matter?" Michael had asked, and then, peering at his twin, shook his head disgustedly. "Come out of it, Shea! Sure, you can't blame the poor folk for wanting to keep their livestock!"

"I don't," said Shea. But those eyes had burned into him. He hadn't stayed for the barbecue and dance.

Now he looked into those same *tigre* eyes.

Lashes long and soft as a girl's closed over them. "Thousand thanks," the vaquero said weakly. "Are— are they all—?"

"Twenty-five dead. Fourteen men, three women, eight children."

The young man made an obvious effort to fit the people he'd known, perhaps loved, to that numbering.

"Todos," he said after a moment. "All." His hands clenched convulsively. "There must be a reason that I live! It must be to avenge this rancho."

"You—had family here?" Shea asked.

The youngster said dully, "Don Antonio Cantú, the ranchero, was my father, though I am called only Santiago. My mother died a long time ago."

"Then you own the ranch."

"No." The cat eyes were surprised. "Don Antonio never married my mother. She was a slave."

"Slavery is forbidden in Mexico," Socorro remonstrated.

The boy grinned feebly. "She was Apache, *madama,* stolen from her people and sold to Don Antonio when she was ten years old. She belonged to him like his horse or cow."

"Do you know who did it?"

"Yanquis!" He spat the word. "Scalp hunters. There must have been a dozen of them. They rode up from the old riverbed yesterday morning, dropping those of us who were outside and riding up to the house. I crawled into the brush beyond the corral, covering my blood."

He stopped. Tears formed and ran slowly down his cheeks. "I had no weapon. There was nothing, wounded like this, that I could do. I—I heard the women scream. I kept fainting as I bled, it was like a faraway bad dream. Some of the Yanquis came back to scalp my friends. One said he thought there'd been another body but the others hooted at him, said he was so greedy he was seeing things." The young face contorted. "They counted the money they would get, grumbling that there were so many children who were worth only twenty-five pesos. Then one said they had a fine bargain anyway, for these scalps were much easier to take than those of Apaches for which they'd be paid."

"Would you know them again?"

The yellow eyes gleamed.

"I got glimpses of the ones who came back for the

scalping. The tallest was clean-shaven. Elegant he was for a butcher's work. The other two were bearded, blond, filthy. One wore eyeglasses and was called Doc."

"That should help." The sun was setting. Almost immediately chill sharpened the air. "Let's get into the house."

Shea started to scoop up Santiago who warded him off. "I—I can walk, *señor,* with help."

"And start yourself bleeding? To hell with that!"

But the youngster would have resisted had Socorro not said with gentle firmness, "Let him do it, Santiago. Sometime he'll need you."

A prophecy? Shea's scalp prickled. What did fate have in store for the three of them met on the edge of the world at the rim of death? And what did they do once Santiago was strong enough to go with them or strike off on his own?

It was like carrying a steel-muscled but badly wounded young lion. Socorro, with their supplies and the bucket of well water, hurried on. By the time Shea reached the house, she'd piled up several of the woven straw mats in the central room and spread them with a serape.

Thank goodness, the pungency of mesquite smoke had driven off most of that other smell, and the fire in the hearth flickered welcomingly in the gloom. Strange to get such a sense of shelter, almost of homecoming, from a place so recently a charnel house. But after weeks in the desert, it *was* walls and roof, a fireplace, made and used by people.

It must seem far otherwise to Santiago. His jaws were ridged taut and tears squeezed from his eyes as Shea lowered him to the pallet. Pretending not to notice, Shea said, "Let's have a look at that hip."

He took off the pulped, peeled agave and frowned in concentration. Socorro had got rid of the maggots. Though there were pus-swelled crustings here and there, it looked like an amazingly clean wound. Perhaps they could concoct some sort of salve for the discomfort and itching that would come as the ragged hole started to close.

Straightening, Shea said, "I'll get you a new bandage, youngling." Collecting the knife from near Socorro who was, with considerable trouble, shaping tortillas from meal cakes extended with more water, Shea went out, spied the outline of an agave in the twilight, and took off a leaf. Throwing away the narrow pointed end, he peeled and pounded the rest of it.

Santiago appeared to have drowsed off in exhaustion. Carefully as he could, Shea pressed down the agave. Socorro had already trimmed away the pants leg. Later, when he woke again, they'd get off his boots.

Rising, Shea studied the proud fierce features. Out of an Apache, was he? A young eagle, whatever! Don Antonio Cantú might have had more legitimate sons, but he couldn't have got one of whom to feel more proud. And however that was, unless someone living had claim to the ranch, it just *had* to be Santiago's.

A tantalizing smell began to tease Shea's nostrils. Sniffing, he went over and hunkered down by Socorro. "Sure smells good!"

"It's only some of our jerky and meal with the chilis and garlic you brought." Socorro sniffed, too. "But spices do make a difference! And a pot to boil things in! Tomorrow we can have beans and corn." She glanced toward Santiago. "Some hot gruel and broth will be good for him, too. Is he asleep?"

"Seems so."

"Shall we take our meal, then, and feed him when he wakes?"

Shea nodded fervently. "I'm starved!"

He started to dip a tortilla into the kettle. She raised a delicately arched eyebrow and filled a gourd for him. Somewhat abashed, he sat down in reach of the tortillas which were stacked in a basket and covered with another.

Damned if the minute she got a chance, she didn't start making simple things complicated! But he had to admit that complicating unsalted jerky and meal cakes into a tasty stew was a talent he appreciated.

"Never ate anything so good in my whole life," he said after a few very busy and absorbed moments.

Socorro glowed. Her manners were daintier than his but she did away with two bowls before Santiago began to stir. She thinned down some stew and went over to feed him while Shea polished off a fourth helping and eight of the somewhat lumpy tortillas.

Sluggishly replete, worn out by the day, he was close to dozing while he sat there. With great effort he hauled himself to his knees, washed out the kettle and turned it upside down on the griddle to dry. Fetching wood for morning from the pile at the door, he put in a large chunk to hold the coals, fixed the rawhide bed for Socorro and made his pallet just outside her door.

After helping Santiago outside for the necessities of nature, Shea barred both doors, thinking that if the rancho's defenders had had time to fort up and had decent weapons, they should have been able to stand off a small army.

"We had an old flintlock," Santiago said, as if reading Shea's mind. "But I don't think Don Antonio had even time to load it."

Shea wished mightily for one of the percussion rifles, or failing that dream, any kind of firearm. All they had was a knife and the buck's horn. Some kind of distance weapon . . . He turned abruptly.

"Santiago! Can you make a bow and arrows?"

The vaquero's mouth twisted in a faint, mocking grin. "You believe I inherit such knowledge through my Apache blood?"

"I wish to hell you had!"

The young man gave the slightest hitch of one shoulder. "I've never held a bow, much less made one. But I think I can."

"Good!"

Socorro put a gourd of water near Santiago and told him to call her if he needed her during the night. Shea waited till she had prayed by the shrine and gone into the bedroom. Then he spoke under his breath.

"You need anyone, my lad, you just call me!"

The whelp damn near chuckled, cocking an amused eyebrow. "Your hands are not so gentle as the lady's. Nevertheless, I won't disturb her sleep. Nor yours either, I hope. Good night, *señor*."

But for all the boy's brave front, Shea's sleep was disturbed. He woke slowly to an unfamiliar sound, stiffened in the darkness, missing the stars, wondering for a few seconds where he was. The sound that must have waked him came again, a muffled, breath-held kind of noise.

Santiago was weeping.

He had the right.

Compassion flooded Shea. Should he say something, try to comfort the boy? No. That wild young pride would resent it. Better let him have the relief and think no one had heard.

After a time the stifled sobbing ended but it took Shea a long while to get back to sleep. He thought of Socorro in the next room, seeming so far away after the way they'd slept almost touching these past weeks. Grown right into him, she had, like part of his body, part of his soul.

She hadn't carried on today, or shirked what had to be done. But had it revived the terrors of her own disaster? How long would he have to wait before he could even kiss her, hold her in his arms?

Aching, Shea stared at the dim light of the windows. An even more unwelcome fear intruded.

Santiago *was* a kid, but hell, he was really no younger than Socorro and he was devilish handsome. She was sorry for him, too. What if—

Oh, go to sleep, you damned fool! Shea told himself. But it was what seemed hours before he did.

V

Next day Shea heaped more rocks on the mass grave and set up a cross. He added a small one. For that baby. And he prayed again for his brother Michael, Socorro's father, and all those who lay in lonely graves, though he reckoned when you got right down to it, any grave was lonely.

He found a razor and a bit of real soap in the bedroom window, borrowed Socorro's scissors to get off the worst of the beard and, with great relief, shaved.

Even though it was hard work to haul and carry the big leather bucket, Shea enjoyed watering the cattle, seeing them crowd up to drink, their dun, roan and black bodies scuffling for room.

He moved much more freely now that he had trousers, a pair he'd found in one of the chests. Too short and a bit loose on hips and waist, but still a proper garment. He'd also found a rough white cotton shirt and there'd been things Socorro could wear.

Santiago had said the cows could go three days without water. Only a small portion of the Cantú herds came up on any single day. There were *tinajas* in the hills and some cattle never came to the troughs at all.

"How many cows does the ranch have?" Shea asked at the evening meal. Santiago was awake, so the tortillas, the kettle of beans and a pot of corn soup had been moved over by him.

"This fall we branded about fifteen hundred calves which means the range carries between seven and eight thousand head."

When Shea frowned his puzzlement, Santiago explained. "Don Antonio keeps his steers till they're three

61

years old. Then there are heifers, bulls and cows. For each calf, there are about five other animals."

Shea's head reeled at such figures. "But what do they eat? They'd walk themselves poor hunting grass!"

"They like grass when they can find it." Santiago shrugged. "But they browse just about everything but creosote. They love mesquite beans and acacia and paloverde pods. And they eat quantities of cholla and prickly pear."

"Cholla!" Shea winced at the thought of the many-jointed, thousand-thorned pads. They made prickly pear look gentle. "How can they? Looks like their tongues would swell up and they'd die."

"That does happen sometimes," the vaquero acknowledged. "The lady says you come from a land that has no cactus, the thorns are mostly on roses and berries, and there is much green grass and giant trees." It was his turn to stare in disbelief.

"That's so."

"I," said Santiago flatly, "cannot imagine a place without cactus!"

"And I couldn't imagine a place with it till I got here," Shea said ruefully. "These are mighty good beans, Socorro. And that corn soup is great!"

Socorro smiled, also ruefully. "You don't speak of the tortillas."

Shea blushed. He knew how long she'd worked to grind the corn into meal, tedious hard labor she wasn't used to. And slapping tortillas into shape must be a lot harder than it looked when you watched someone who'd done it all her life.

"They're very good," he lied. "It's just that they're sort of taken for granted and——"

"Mine are lumpy," enumerated Socorro. "They have holes and heavy thick places and are raggedy. They are raw where they aren't burned!" Picking one up, she gazed at it in disgust. "I don't think I'll ever learn!"

"Many dull women can pat tortillas," Santiago said. "You have healing in your touch."

"The agave is curing your wound and water eased the fever," demurred Socorro.

Santiago shook his head. "No, lady. If *you* had not cared for me yesterday, I believe I would have died in spite of all the water and agave in Sonora!"

She looked incredulous but Shea nodded. "I *had* died when you found me."

Confused and somewhat dismayed at such testimonials, she ducked her head, took another tortilla which tore as she loaded it with beans and said dolefully, "I still wish I could make these!"

"No doubt the rose complains that it doesn't bear corn," remarked Santiago gallantly.

God's whiskers! If he framed his tongue to beguilements like that now, what would he say when he was back on his feet? Casting the brash youngster a stern look, Shea said consolingly to Socorro, "You'll learn," and changed the subject back to ranching, fascinated with the size of the herds, the size of the ranches, the vastness of everything.

Santiago told him that in the last century, Don Antonio's grandfather had been granted, for services to the crown of Spain, one *sitio de ganado mayor,* place for large animals, of about 4,330 acres. He had later acquired other *sitios,* including several to the north which had been abandoned when Mexico, after 1821 independent of Spain, hadn't been able to protect the frontiers. Don Antonio's elder brother, Narciso, had inherited the main ranch with a fine house and furnishings and now he would take over his dead brother's holdings.

"How far away is your uncle?" Shea asked.

"Don Narciso? He wouldn't like me to call him *Tio!* Oh, a day's riding would take one to his *portal.* Not that I intend to go!"

"But he has to be told about Don Antonio!"

"He'll learn in time. His grief will be soothed by controlling more land and cattle."

"Surely he'll give you part of what was your father's!"

"To 'the Apache heathen' as he calls me?" Santiago mocked. "My father always intended to give me a start when I married, but I was in no hurry for that." He brooded a moment, then laughed. "I can't do anything about the land, but I can run off some cattle, *seguramente!* What do you say, Don Patricio?" This was the style of address he had adopted for Shea. "Would you like to help me rustle cattle?"

"Where would you put them?"

"We could sell them to the presidios at Tubac or Tucson, but I think—" Santiago's glance rested a brief caressing moment on Socorro. "I think we all need a home. Why don't we take over one of the abandoned *sitios* my father owned? I have been to the one southeast of Tubac along Sonoita Creek. Good water, trees and grass. It was once a *visita,* or outpost mission, but was auctioned when the government sold off church lands."

"If your Uncle Narciso is so stingy, what'll he say about that?"

Santiago smiled lazily. "The place has been abandoned for over twenty years. I can't think that Don Narciso, who spends most of his time in Hermosillo, both from fear of Apaches and love of society, will even remember those *sitios* as long as there *are* Apaches."

"So how do you imagine we'd survive?"

"Face it, Don Patricio! No part of northern Sonora or New Mexico or Chihuahua is safe. Look at what happened here. I would prefer to die in greener country with more water!"

"What do you think?" Shea asked Socorro. "Are you sure you don't want to return to Alamos?"

"Very sure. After the *Areneños,* I can't worry much about Apaches."

"They're said to take women for slaves."

She smiled, steel beneath it. "I wouldn't be one long. This rancho, Santiago, how is it called?"

"Agua Linda. Pretty Water. But we'll give it a new name. Socorro."

She flushed. "Oh, no! Agua Linda is a nice name!"

"But 'Socorro' has greater meaning. Don't we hope the place will succor us, as you saved Don Patricio and me? Why not give it a name that will mean 'refuge'?"

"I like it," Shea said.

What he didn't like so much was that Santiago had suggested it. But after all, except for legalities, the *sitio* belonged to him.

Socorro's nursing, the agave poultices and a tough young body soon put Santiago on the mend though it looked like some clawed beast had torn out a piece of his thigh.

"If you wear your trousers tight, you'll have to use a pad," Shea joked. Socorro was outside so Santiago gave him a cocky grin.

"Just as long as I don't need a pad where it matters, Don Patricio."

"You don't have to call me Don." The boy's extreme courtesy to him was getting on Shea's nerves. "I'm not that much older than you!"

The golden eyes widened, then narrowed in a measuring way. *"Pues*, our lady respects you. I must respect her respect."

"Our lady?" Shea scowled.

The elegant raised eyebrow. "How not?"

"How?"

"Has she not saved us both?"

Not much to argue there. Shea felt confused and irritated, like a large clumsy animal maneuvered by a swift tricky one. "You ready to try making a bow?" he growled.

"Any time you bring the wood. Try to get something with a little spring, please, Don Patricio."

A mocking hesitance before the title? Shea muffled an exasperated obscenity and went out, taking the ax.

Our lady! Sounded like blaspheming.

Besides, Shea didn't like the coziness of that "our" as if he were claiming equal standing in her favor. Shea had known her first, hadn't he? Slept by her close all those nights, made her boots and bandaged her blisters and walked her out of that wasteland?

No comparison of his experience with Socorro and that of this disconcerting youngster's! Better to loftily ignore his ever-so-courtly arrogance.

Resolving to do that, Shea headed for the arroyo where the burial was and where larger trees sucked water from below as well as benefiting from the seasonal rains channeled down the gulch.

Socorro knelt by the mass grave. This must be where she came during those daily absences that seemed longer than responses to natural needs.

Our lady was praying to Our Lady. Head bowed by the crosses, she seemed the embodiment of all women who grieved, yet still hoped and did all they could for the living.

Ashamed because he burned to have her as a woman, Shea turned quickly down the bank before she could see him, swore only mildly at the acacia that caught his ankles, and forced himself to concentrate on finding wood that might make serviceable bows.

Acacia was too crooked, small and brittle, you'd do well to make darts from it. Dubiously eyeing palo-verde, ironwood and mesquite, Shea thought he might have to settle for branches from the first, but none of the three inspired confidence. The limbs were either small, or gnarled and knotted from their struggles with wind and drought.

Then, as he trudged down the arroyo, he saw another kind of tree, several of them, white-trunked and tall, with leaves that were shiny green on top and silvery gray beneath.

This was more like it! And the first tree he'd seen since leaving Caborca that stood more than twelve feet high. Most weren't as tall as he was.

Seizing a down-bent branch, he tested a suitably long limb. It had some resilience but didn't threaten to snap. A moment before he'd have taken it gladly. Now, with several trees to select from, he prowled about, testing his visual judgment by bending and feeling.

Should they arm Socorro? Shea thought of Indians, white scalp hunters and varicolored no-goods, and grimly decided she'd better have all the protection they could scrape up.

Selecting the three boughs he deemed most likely, Shea axed them off, cleaned them of smaller limbs and leaves and took them to Santiago, who was lying on his side watching Socorro as she knelt at the *metate,* bringing her weight down on the pestle as she ground.

Hard work, but it was also a sensuous moving of the upper body though she chatted away with no awareness of that.

Standing where he blocked Santiago's view, Shea offered the boughs. "Think they'll do?"

"*Alamos*—cottonwood," approved Santiago. "Probably the best thing we can get here." He hitched himself into a sitting position, thanked Shea who put a serape behind him for support. "There should be some good strips of rawhide in the storeroom. Please, if you'll bring them and the knife, I'll see what I can do. We need three bows?"

Shea nodded toward Socorro. "She'd better learn to use one, too."

He brought the lengths of rawhide to Santiago. "Have any ideas on what would make the best arrows?"

"Apaches use cane. There's a stand of it below where you found the cottonwoods."

"Cane? That wouldn't be strong enough!"

"Tell that to the men who've been pierced with cane arrows from three hundred feet away!" suggested the vaquero.

"I suppose we can try them," Shea grudged. "But if they snap when we try them on targets, we'll use something stronger."

"By all means," returned Santiago placidly.

As Shea went out, he heard Socorro say in a defensive tone, "You must remember, Santiago, that *el señor* is from another land." That smarted more than Santiago's veiled amusement.

God's whiskers! vowed Shea. *Cane arrows or ironwood, I'll learn to outshoot that little monkey!*

Through the afternoon the two men worked on weapons. Socorro brought Santiago frequent drinks of tea she'd made from an herb drying in the storeroom which she confidently said was *manzanilla,* a good tonic.

She offered some to Shea who took a sniff and shook his head though he longed for real tea or coffee. That was human nature for you! Here they were in comparative luxury and he craved more. Which reminded him.

"We've used up the jerky," he remarked to Santiago. "Mind if I butcher one of the scraggiest old steers?"

"Take your pick, except for an old roan stag who has the Cantú brand on his shoulder and a cross on his flank." Santiago glanced at his poulticed hip. "I think I can travel in another week or ten days. We'll need jerky for the trip. Those steers are skinny. Better kill two."

Shea took the knife and ax down to the well, kept an eye on the cattle who came to the trough. There were quite a few, to his eye, who qualified for slaughter. He waited for one particularly gaunt old warrior to drink his fill. As he moved back, thirst quenched, Shea waited till he was out of the way of the other cattle, then brought the ax down as hard as he could at the back of the neck, cleaved through the vertebral column deep into the flesh.

The steer fell, wound pumping blood, head lolling, dead almost immediately. Shea skinned him, then with the ax and knife carved him into quarters. He took a generous chunk of loin up to the house for supper.

"Save the head," admonished Santiago.

"What for?"

"Tatema." Santiago kissed his fingers. "Delicious!" It didn't sound that way, but if this kid was running

a bluff, Shea meant to call it. "I'll save it," he promised and went back to work.

By the time all the meat was in the house where it'd be safe from hungry birds and animals, Shea was more than ready to rest and eat. They heard snarling outside, a sharp yip. Santiago laughed.

"Someone disputes with Don Coyote. You *did* save the head?"

"Yes. Now you'll have to tell me what to do with it."

"Simple. Make a hole and line it with rocks. Build a fire and keep it going till the rocks are very, very hot. Meanwhile, you've shaped clay all around the head. This goes in the hole, you cover it with more hot rocks, then earth on top of that. Do it in the morning and we'll have a rare treat by evening."

Socorro said decidedly, *"I* won't!"

"Lady! *Tatema* melts in the mouth."

"Not in mine."

Santiago tilted his head at Shea, who choked a bit on a tough but good-flavored hunk of beef. "I'll try anything once. What do you think of the bows and arrows?"

Thoughtfully considering the weapons piled beside him, Santiago hefted an arrow. It was three feet long and a thin wedge was cut out of the cane into which was set a piece of whittled hardwood with a bone point.

"No feathers and an Apache would probably die laughing at the balance, but I shot a few out the door and I think they'll serve. The piece of hardwood will come loose if the arrow's jerked at and leave the point in the quarry."

"Hey! What if I'd been fixing to come in when you shot?"

"Oh, our lady watched to be sure that didn't happen and then fetched in the arrows," explained Santiago airily.

Shea grunted. "We'd all better start practicing soon."

Socorro's smooth brow had been furrowing. Now she

burst out impatiently. "Don't you notice something, Shea?"

He looked about, saw nothing different, studied the food which he'd been too busy eating to pay much mind to. "The beans! They're almighty flavorsome tonight, Socorro."

Ominously, she said, "They're exactly as they have been, neither worse nor better."

"Uh . . ." Trapped, he said desperately, "Your dress looks nice."

"Ay, ay! Burro!"

Dashing back glittering tears, she sprang to her feet, fled into the next room. Stifled sobs. Shea turned helplessly to Santiago. "What—?"

Santiago pointed to the basket of tortillas. "No lumps, no holes, none burned!" he whispered. "So proud she was, Don Patricio!" Jealously, he added, "She could scarcely wait for you to pick one up and notice."

Tortillas!

Shea blinked, shook his head. This girl who'd survived a massacre, snatched two men from death, found water where most people, including him, would have died—this girl who'd walked uncomplainingly through the closest thing earth had to hell was crying because he hadn't complimented her improved tortillas!

God's whiskers!

But when you thought of the hours she put in at that *metate,* the way she'd persisted in trying to flatten the small balls of dough into perfect, even rounds, the way she'd burned her fingers on the griddle—yes, Shea could understand.

Tentatively picking up one of the flat cakes, he saw that indeed it was vastly superior to the first ones she'd made. He got up and headed for the bedroom, casting Santiago a look.

Huddled on the big bed, Socorro looked very small and vulnerable. "Go away!" Her shoulders heaved. She burrowed deeper into the serapes.

Shea dropped to his knees. "Socorro, the tortillas

are—why, they're handsome! I should have noticed right away but I was too busy stuffing myself with them like a mule eating hay!"

Another snuffle.

"Socorro! Damn it, I'm sorry!"

She hitched herself up on one elbow. Slowly, her face emerged. She dashed her tears away before she gave a soft, shaky laugh. "A big redhead mule devouring my poor tortillas! Yes, that's what you are!"

He'd be any kind of mule if she'd forgive him. "Come watch me flap my ears while I eat some more?" he invited.

Her smile broke like the sun from behind clouds. "Come, then, *burro pelirrojo!*"

Though he wasn't hungry, Shea finished off the tortillas. Beneath Santiago's sardonic stare, he couldn't say much beyond "Mighty good!" but he looked at each tortilla admiringly as he lifted it, rolled it with respect and took small appreciative bites while Socorro beamed.

Somehow it all made him remember his mother, how she'd tried to give a bit of flavor and grace to their scanty meals, flowers in a broken mug, scallions and herbs from the garden, wild mushrooms, salvaged windfall apples that better-off people left for their pigs.

He understood suddenly that feeding people was a way of loving them. One of the most important ways; without food they died. And he undertook to never again have a meal without thanking in some fashion the person who'd fixed it.

Even, he thought dourly, if it was Santiago!

The *tatema* was exhumed from its pit next evening, the mud peeled off along with the hide, and the result placed hurriedly by Shea in front of Santiago.

Blissfully spooning out one of what had been the eyes, Santiago said, *"Muy sabrosa!* Try it, Don Patricio!"

Swallowing hard, Shea gingerly poked around with a tortilla and the knife they all shared at meals. *If* you could forget what it was, the *tatema* was tasty. Santiago hadn't been playing a nasty joke.

But the vaquero got to enjoy most of that special delicacy.

They prepared now for the journey north. Santiago made more arrows and they all practiced shooting for about an hour each day. Even sitting, as he was obliged to, Santiago quickly became a good marksman.

"It must be carried over from using the reata," he said when Shea swore disgustedly after his fifth miss at a gourd Santiago had hit on his first try. "Without boasting, Don Patricio, I was the best roper among many good ones. Using the eye and hand together takes training." He grinned. "Or maybe it's my Apache blood!"

It had turned out that Santiago's blood was considerably mixed. His grandfather had been an Opata captive who was raised by the Apache and had married one of their women. The daughter of this union had been captured by slave traders and sold to Don Antonio—who, back in his blue-blooded ancestry, had a Tarahumare woman whose conquistador master had legitimized his sons by her.

Whatever the blend, it had produced a splendid result, Shea thought, as he brooded on the fact that he had never thrown a rope in his life. One more thing to learn! He thought of Socorro's improved tortillas and doggedly notched another arrow.

Socorro's bow was smaller than those of the men and her arrows were scaled to it. It took her a while to learn how to hold the arrow while pulling back the bowstring, but once she got the feel of it, she shot with a kind of joy.

"I never got to do anything like this before!" she exclaimed one day as Shea brought back her arrows. Windblown and flushed, she had never looked more beautiful. "It's a lot more fun than grinding corn!"

*　　*　　*

At first it had seemed the scalp hunters had stolen the horses and mules. They must have taken the main *remuda,* but gradually ones they'd missed turned up for water and Shea got them into the corrals where he fed them with grass cut from the region where the cane grew, with cottonwood boughs, and singed prickly pear.

Remembering that his father had died because of a horse, Shea had a special feeling for them though he'd only been mounted a few times in his life, and that uncomfortably. He counted with considerable pride as three horses and two mules increased to five and six, respectively. There were packsaddles and the big box-like leather *aparejos,* or square bags, which could carry useful things, serapes, kettles, the ax, tools, provisions. And plenty of water!

"Just how do you figure we can drive that herd one hundred and fifty miles?" he asked Santiago one night.

"We won't. Cristiano will take them for us."

"Cristiano? Who's he?"

"The old roan stag I told you not to slaughter. The one with the cross on his hip."

"Now, look, youngling, I'm new to this country, but—"

"Cristiano is the leader. Before, when we've taken herds to Tubac or Tucson or the mines, he's led the way."

Santiago looked so serious that Shea believed him though he scratched his head. "How was he trained?"

"Lead steers do it naturally. Of course, Cristiano was a bull till he was five years old. As you may know, in Mexico we seldom geld cattle or horses, but Cristiano grew so fearsome, goring several other good bulls, that Don Antonio had to choose between virility for him or all the rest of the males. Gelding took away Cristiano's rages but he's still the boss."

Santiago had begun to get about a little with the aid of a stick. Several times Shea had seen him out by the crosses of the burial arroyo, but instead of being bowed, his head was thrown back as he gazed at the distant mountains. If he were praying, his prayers were mighty different from those of Socorro.

"I should tell you one thing," he said one morning as they breakfasted on corn gruel and a rabbit he'd brought down with an arrow. "Once we're settled at the Socorro, I must leave you for a time, but I'll find you some Papagos for help."

"May I inquire what's your pressing business?" Shea asked.

"I must find those scalp hunters."

"But there's no telling where they are by now!"

Santiago's lips pulled back from his white teeth. "I shall hunt for scalpers and kill any I track down till I finally get the right bunch. It won't be a waste of time. To kill any bounty hunter is a good thing."

"What if one kills you?"

The yellow eyes lighted. "So long as he's the last of them, I'll die blessed!"

Socorro put a pleading hand on his arm. "Santiago, *por favor*—"

"Do not, lady," he told her. "Do not ask me what I cannot do, for in all things but this I will serve you."

Shea remembered his father and killing the farmer so long ago. He understood the young man's bitter resolve, but it was one thing to kill a single murderer, another to tackle a half-dozen heavily armed and savage men.

"I'd go with you," he said slowly, "if it weren't for Socorro. Don't try it alone, lad. There must be other men who'd like a crack at them."

"I will not wait!" Santiago screamed as if something had snapped deep inside him.

They stared, shocked. Recovering himself though he still breathed heavily and kept his hands clenched, Santiago whispered, "The vaqueros were my friends. For Don Antonio I had respect. Doña Ana, his wife, ignored me as much as possible, but their son Carlos—he followed me everywhere. Seven years old and already good with the rope, not afraid of any bull or horse. What a man he'd have been! And there was his sister, Elena, only five, who tried to do everything he did—all of my friends, their wives and babies—"

Blindly reaching for his stick, Santiago rose and hobbled outside. Socorro followed. For once, Shea wasn't jealous.

The boy was right. He had to avenge his people. And he, Shea, would go with him in a second if there were some way of leaving Socorro in safety.

Maybe she could stay at one of those presidios, Tubac or Tucson. *We'll see,* Shea thought, and sighed.

He was sick of killing and of death. All he wanted was to settle down and make a life with Socorro. Here in the Province of Sonora in the autumn of 1847, that might be an unattainable dream. But at least they had water and food and an ally who knew the country.

Knew it? Opata, Apache, Tarahumare, Spaniard— hell, he *was* the country!

Shea heard him talking to Socorro now, unleashing pent-up grief, desolation and fury. That would help. Sighing, Shea took his bow and cowskin quiver and went out to hunt.

PART II

SOCORRO

VI

A week later they left the ranch. According to Santiago, who kept a calendar by knotting a strip of rawhide, it was, *mas o menos,* the middle of November. They needed serapes at night but the sun still heated the day, though not in the parching manner of summer or early autumn.

Cristiano, a gaunt wary old warrior of many scars, led the mixed herd of two hundred. There were a few bulls, some steers for beef, but mostly there were young cows Santiago had selected for breeding good cattle.

Looking at the pack mules was, for Socorro, like seeing a moving storehouse. Each of the six carried two *aparejos* which held up to seventy-five pounds apiece of corn, whole or ground, beans, dried squash, chilis, jerky and wheat. These hung from two loops of rawhide fastened to the packsaddle.

On top of these and the saddle frame were piled the movable things that would be of inestimable value: the iron kettles, utensils, baskets and earthenware, tools, rawhide and tanned leather, usable clothing, the luxurious down pillows from the big bed, and serapes covering each load and lashed down securely to the saddle. One mule carried things they'd need on the way: food, the ax, hammer, shoes for the mules and horses and nails to fasten them.

In the leather pouch at her waist, Socorro carried a great treasure. Two needles, carefully stuck through a bit of cotton, a pair of scissors and real thread! Her father's most elegant gifts had never delighted her so.

It was astounding what less than two months in the wilderness could do to a person. Before she left

Alamos Socorro would have indignantly rejected the notion that she'd be glad to have the shoes and garments of a dead woman, but she'd felt no compunction at appropriating anything that could be worn or used for patching.

She did, though, take Doña Ana's few treasures and bury them near the cross: a small carved chest of jewelry, tucked away where the scalpers had missed it, combs for the hair, a cobweb mantilla, a fragile blown-glass vase, as well as a wooden doll and several small carved animals that must have been the children's. She'd tried to do this secretly, but Shea had seen her and strolled up, red-gold eyebrows meeting in a puzzled frown above his straight long nose.

The brand on his cheek had faded to dull red and no longer puckered, but he'd wear it to the grave. In spite of that, with his gold-flamed hair and eyes the color of storm, he had an imperious male beauty that weakened Socorro each time she looked at him, made the deepest parts of her go soft with longing.

Yet when he looked at her in that certain, heart-stopping way, she was terrified. She had wept in his arms. He had held her kindly. But she knew instinctively, in spite of all his assurances, that she must not always expect him to play the comforting brother.

But he *was* kind. He had suffered much. It was a fresh shock each time she saw him to think of the leathery skeleton he had been, peeled-back lips baked in a snarl, the horrid bloodless wounds.

This strong handsome man, who was learning the ways of the country so swiftly that even scapegrace Santiago respected him, was very much her creation, almost as much as if he'd been her child. She'd given him life. Her love for him was mixed with tenderness, pride and awe.

If only—in imagination, his touch changed to the grasping cruel fingers that had held her by legs and arms while each *Areneño*—

No! No! She could never endure that again, the tear-

ing invasion of her body. Fear blotted out the sweetness
of the fantasy's beginning. There, by the edge of the
mass grave, she closed her eyes a moment, stilled her
panic till she could look at Shea and see him, his beloved face, banish the nightmare.

He was still frowning at the things she was placing
in the small hole by the cross. "Why are you doing that,
lass? You might as well have them. They can't do Doña
Ana any good."

"Perhaps she'll know. It's so terrible, Shea, the way
she died, her children—"

He hadn't argued, then, but had helped her fill in
the hole and knelt beside her for a while. She knew she
prayed for his brother though he must have the inter-
cession of a mother long since in heaven.

Socorro prayed for her father, Enrique, Michael
O'Shea and the folk of the rancho. And she prayed for
herself, for Shea and Santiago, that they might survive
without becoming as hard as this country and as cruel.

In spite of the horror of the massacre, leaving the
house and fireplace filled Socorro with desolation. She
couldn't see that leaving a place recently decimated by
scalp hunters for one abandoned over twenty years ago
because of Apache attacks was much of an improvement, and she had grown used to it here.

Still, she had felt almost the same way when she and
Shea left the *tinaja* where she'd found water in her ex-
tremity and had nursed him back to life.

In gathering the few last things that morning, she'd
hesitated at the little shrine. Guadalupe would be such
a comfort. Yet it seemed sacrilege to take her from
this house. After a last prayer, Socorro continued with
her packing, was tucking necessaries into an *aparejo*
when Santiago brought her the gilt and blue wooden
image.

"It's mine more than anybody's now," he said. "We
must have her in our new home." He smiled, the young
sweetness of his boyish mouth contrasting with those
tigre eyes that sometimes were frightening, though to

her he was unfailingly gentle and courteous. "She'll be Our Lady of Socorro."

It would be carping to point out that the madonna had recently smiled calmly, blindly down on rape and murder. Socorro suspected that Santiago gave not a gypsy's damn for shrines. But she herself wanted the Guadalupe very much so she didn't protest as he wrapped the figure carefully in an old shirt and tucked her carefully between two serapes.

Now, as they rode away, past the corrals and along the dry riverbed toward the northeast, Socorro looked back once at the house, hoped that people would live in it again, safely, that corn would be ground in the *metate* by more skillful hands than hers, laughter would sound by the fireplace and children be made in the great canopied bed.

Her bow, like those of the men, was fastened from the saddle horn in a rawhide sling that also held the quiver of arrows, which now had feathers, for they'd collected every feather they found in what was left from hawk and eagle kills. She could hit targets most of the time now but shrank from hunting so she'd never sighted at a moving object, except the inflated cow stomach Shea had insisted that she aim at while he moved it along a branch with a rope.

She hoped she'd never have to kill anything, but it was excellent to know that she probably *could*. Santiago was a peerless marksman, but Shea grew more accurate daily and had brought in a number of rabbits and another ancient buck which had made a welcome change from jerky.

Also, each had a knife sheathed at the waist. Besides Socorro's, Santiago had found one overlooked by the scalpers. Then, from a broken saw found in the storeroom, he'd whetted an effective, vicious-looking blade and given it a bone handle.

"Damn near a Bowie!" Shea whistled. "Better not try to eat with that or you'll slit your gullet!"

82

Santiago regarded it admiringly. "Large, perhaps, but in a fight it will be a veritable sword."

Socorro hoped there'd be no fights. She also hoped to dissuade Santiago from trying to find the scalp hunters. They'd surely kill him. Perhaps, at the least, she could get him to ask the presidio soldiers to mount an expedition he could accompany.

But first they had ten days' journey, trying to get these cattle through country where Apache might swoop down at any time, not to mention scalp hunters. Her spine chilled at the thought. She sat up stiffer in the saddle, shifting her weight, glad now that she'd let Shea bully her into wearing the trousers he'd thrust at her last week.

"Time you and your horse got used to each other," he'd growled. "And don't make a fuss about these pants, my girl! We're not on a Sunday's decorous circling of the plaza. You're going to need good balance and control of your horse."

She stared at the garment. "But it's a sin! An abomination!"

"It'll be a lot worse sin if you fall into the cactus or catch your skirts on a branch and get dragged!"

She eyed him rebelliously. His jaw hardened. "God's whiskers! I'll put them on you!" he began, then swallowed and attained calm with great effort. "Socorro, if we were being chased and those damned skirts caused Santiago and me to have to ride back for you so that we all got killed, would it be worth it? If you think so, wear your dresses."

She gave him a shattered glance, ducked her head and went inside to change. Every day one of the men saddled Castaña, the pretty chestnut mare Santiago had chosen as the finest of the gentler horses, and accompanied Socorro on a ride. From the way her unused muscles ached after only a few hours, she knew that without this toughening she'd have been a very sorry case during the days of riding ahead of them.

Castaña might have been the gentlest of the horses,

but that wasn't saying much. She, like all the others, had to be roped before she could be bridled and saddled and Socorro rode with vigilance, reins firmly held. Castaña skittered at any sound in the brush, and though Santiago explained this came from having been bitten by a rattlesnake, Socorro came to think it was an excuse for flightiness.

Santiago had a fiery black mustang he'd trained himself, and Shea rode a big roan. The other two horses followed along voluntarily. The men had decided they had all they could handle with the cattle and pack mules. If the horses came, fine; if they didn't, too bad. They had brought a couple of extra saddles and bridles on the pack mules, though, because if the ranch thrived more horses and vaqueros were going to be needed.

Flexing her toes in the stirrups Socorro threw back her head and breathed in air so clear that it seemed to sparkle.

Mountains marched all around them, barren and savage up close, like brooding Pinacate, but glowing in the distance, some purple, some misty heaven blue, some pinkish golden.

She laughed with sheer well-being, casting off her sadness at leaving the sheltering walls, turning her face toward the majestic vistas before them.

Shea, slightly behind her, urged the roan, Azul, forward. "I don't know why you're laughing, but I'm glad you are!" he called.

She dared take one hand from the reins for a second to make a wide sweeping motion. "It's just so grand and beautiful. Yes, I know it can kill! It almost killed us. But nowhere else can there be such sun, such air, such mountains. . . ."

"Such cholla, desert and rattlesnakes!" he teased.

She pulled a face at him, refused to be sobered. In her trousers, free of cumbersome skirts, riding a spirited horse into a new venture, she felt roused from a half-life limited by tradition and being a woman. She was proud that she could make decent tortillas now, but oh, this!

"They may be called, as Santiago names them, La Sierra del Agua Dulce, La Sierra Pintada, La Sierra de Sonoita, and I don't know what else! But they are all of them Las Sierras Encantadas. Enchanted Mountains."

He grinned, shielding his eyes against the glare as he gazed about. "You're right, lass! It *is* enchantment for them to look so soft and dreamy when up close they're rock and earth, so scrubbed by wind and rain that it's a brave cactus or creosote that gets a toehold and hangs on!"

He fell back to help Santiago urge on the mules. Perhaps he'd inherited his father's gift with horses. Certainly he'd taken quickly to riding, handled the big grayish red horse with firmness and understanding. With sombrero quieting that flaming hair, he looked a man of the country. Santiago, of course, had ridden as soon as he could walk. He seemed part of Noche, his black, and could direct him with his knees or pressure of his weight.

Cristiano, the pride of leadership upon him, led the cattle, and no young bull cared to challenge him. These were the small "black" Spanish cattle, by no means all black for they moved in a dust-haloed somber rainbow of duns, brindles and roans mixed with the predominant black.

These, like all cattle in the New World until the late-coming English and French brought animals, were descended from the Andalusian stock brought over in 1521 by Don Gregorio de Villalobos, blood of the proud black *toros* of the bull ring.

Their wicked-looking horns spiked forward and they were wild as deer, but they could live off browse and cactus. They'd all been driven near the troughs that morning and most had drunk. Santiago said they should reach Sonoita next day and water at the river of that name, which they'd follow through the Sierra de la

Nariz, then take the southern branch till it ended at the Sierra de Cobata, a journey of about three days.

Santiago said they'd depend then on wells at Papago *rancherías,* though they might find a little water at the far end of the Altar River, during the four or more days it would take to cross more desert and rugged mountains to the Santa Cruz River. This important river ran north past a few abandoned mines, missions and the presidios of Tubac and Tucson, Mexico's only defense against Apache in that immense region.

They'd find the Santa Cruz only to leave it at Calabazas, following Sonoita Creek westward between more mountains for the final day which should bring them to Agua Linda, or Socorro, as the men insisted it must be called.

Ten days. By then she might not think those mountains so enchanted unless by evil witchcraft. A cow was lagging, stopping to munch cholla. Socorro shooed her back with the herd.

Santiago had explained that ordinarily there'd be vaqueros at both sides and a couple at the end to urge along the "'drags.''

"It is strange," he'd laughed, "but cattle are much like humans! The leader leads because of something inside him and the others follow. Why? Cristiano has led thousands of his kind up to slaughter at the presidios. Has he never wondered why they didn't follow him back to the ranch? Did none of these at his tail now never miss companions who'd gone with him? And cattle always keep a position, unless they're hurt or sick. Some stay in front, some the middle, and others are forever at the end, dropping out, loafing."

"It's the same in armies," Shea grunted. "I was in both United States' and Mexican and can vow there are a hell of a lot more drags than leaders!"

"God's wisdom," returned Santiago. "If there were more leaders, we'd have more wars than we do!"

They had a long nooning in a shaded dry wash, giving the cattle time to graze on thin clumps of scattered grass and bite off joints of cholla which dangled thornily from their mouths as they chewed.

The three people drank thirstily of tepid water from the leather jugs of which each horse carried two tied to the back of the saddle next to the rolled serape. Socorro sparingly wet the edge of the rebozo she wore beneath a sombrero and wiped her face of dust, much refreshed by this small thing.

"The poor burros!" she said.

The cattle were free to browse and the horses had been unsaddled and hobbled so they, too, could make the most of this rest. But the mules still carried perhaps three hundred pounds apiece.

Santiago shook his head. "I regret it much, lady, but you saw how long it takes to do the loading. Tonight, when the packs go off, they'll be the more grateful."

Was that what God thought about lightening people's burdens? Socorro's thought was so irreligious that she tried to push it away, but it persisted and she decided that God shouldn't have given her a mind capable of such ideas if He didn't want her to have them. At least the mules were browsing, making the most of their burdened leisure, while the humans exercised their teeth on jerky and coarse ground corn mixed with a little water.

After about three hours, they saddled and pushed on. Socorro had insisted on saddling Castaña during the journey. She planned, though she hadn't told the men about it, to learn to do everything they did except hunt and butcher. So long as they were around, she had no necessity to do either, and if they were gone, she'd live without meat. The only way she could eat it now was by refusing to think of the living creature it had come from.

Castaña, as Santiago had warned was her habit, puffed up when, after putting on the *tiruta,* a white and black woven blanket, Socorro hefted the saddle, near stirrup raised to keep it from flopping, onto the mare's back.

Following his demonstration of that morning, Socorro pulled the cinch as tight as she could, waited till the mare relaxed and yanked again, hard. This brought the cinch several inches tighter, doing away with the danger of the saddle turning later. Socorro hung the bow and arrow sling over the saddle horn, tied on the water jugs.

"We have to understand each other," she told the mare who turned her head to give an affronted look. Socorro, clucking softly, gave the mare a scant handful of corn, rubbed the whorled spot on her forehead. "I'll be much nicer to you than the vaqueros were, but don't try to play me for a fool."

Santiago gave a shout and Cristiano led off. The cattle sorted themselves out, dropping into their preferred places, and the mules plodded stoically at the rear.

They were another animal brought in by Spaniards, Socorro realized. In fact, all the important domesticated creatures of Mexico and the Southwest had come from Spain. Strange, for they had become so much a part of the country. Goats, sheep, cattle, mules and horses.

Her father, in his youth, had gone with a merchant of Chihuahua on a trading journey to San Antonio in Texas, which at that time, of course, was still owned by Spain. Settlers from the United States had been coming in, though, bringing stock descended from English and, occasionally, French cattle.

Their crossing with Spanish horses and cattle had produced larger, different animals than those in Sonora. Her father had laughed about the mixed-breed cattle, all imaginable hues, with great long horns that grew in fantastical ways, some almost straight up, others angling back, most forking from the sides with a few arching curves before tapering to vicious tips.

Longhorns, the Texans called these weird creatures, and rightly so. Don Esteban said the spread from tip to tip was usually four to five feet, but six or seven feet was common, and he vowed he'd seen one beast encumbered with horns spreading fully ten feet, though

Socorro suspected *aguardiente* had something to do with *that* figure.

As Socorro mounted, blessing the freedom of trousers, she noticed Santiago didn't vault into the saddle as he had that morning. His leg must be paining, she thought. He still limped, perhaps always would, for though the bone was intact, he'd lost a mass of nerves and muscles. He was so graceful and lithe, however, that even his limp had a glide to it.

The afternoon grew hot. A good thing it was mostly at their backs. Hundreds of hooves churned up white dust, powdering burros and packs, sticking to Socorro's face and lips.

Her body ached. She shifted her weight frequently and was almost glad when a cow strayed, for the diversion of chasing it back. She wouldn't ask for a halt, though. If Santiago, with his barely healed wound, could manage, so would she.

When they finally stopped at twilight in a broad dry wash, her spine felt like bruised agony and she was numb from the hips down.

Dragging the saddle off, and the blanket, she rubbed the mare down with a scrap of fleeced sheepskin Santiago had given her for that purpose, removed the bridle with stroking and praise. Castaña gazed at her a moment, then joined the other horses who were rolling in the sand, powdering their sweated backs with great enjoyment.

At last the burros were unloaded and ambled off to luxuriate in sand-bathing and browsing. Socorro liked the furry little beasts with their long ears and sleepy manner.

No fire was kindled for fear of bringing down Apaches or other raiders. "One thing about jerky"—Shea grinned, leaning back against his saddle—"it makes your jaws tired enough to match the rest of you!"

"Tomorrow we can have a fire at Sonoyta," Santiago assured them. "And it'll be all right when we camp at inhabited Papago *rancherías*."

"Can we trust the Papagos?" Socorro frowned. "The *Areneños,* the Sand Papagos, certainly rob and kill when they have a chance!"

Santiago knew about her father's death. He didn't know what the *Areneños* had done to her, though possibly he guessed. "Oh, far back they were related, but living in those dunes and craters, always hunting food, has made them very different from other Papago who are peaceful farmers and herdsmen. You need have no fear, lady, of most Papago or Pima."

"Pima?" asked Shea.

"Farmers and friends of the Papago, but they tend to live near water and among trees whereas the Papago have always kept to the desert."

Darkness had fallen though there was a new moon. An owl called. Some thought this an evil omen, but surely they hooted every night. Socorro liked the cry, so long as she wasn't alone, and the distant singing of coyotes which sounded as if they were serenading each other from various directions.

Relaxed against bedroll and saddle, she felt too sleepy to get up and go properly to bed, was trying to nerve herself to the effort when a frightful braying scream pierced the air.

She sprang up to follow the men, in the dim moonlight seeing that Santiago had grasped his saberlike knife. The riding horses were hobbled but other animals were loose. The burros set up an incredible racket, horses neighed in fright, and the cattle began to stir restively.

A shadowy figure heaved up from the ground, sprang into the air and came down viciously on a spitting, snarling shape twisting on the earth from which the burro had risen. Again and again the infuriated burro lashed his hooves into his enemy with all his force and weight. He stopped only long after there was no movement from the mass on which he vented his rage and fear.

"A lion!" Santiago spoke to the trembling burro,

went over him cautiously. "He got his death, not his dinner, old one! But you'll carry no pack for some days."

"Is he hurt?" asked Socorro, shuddering as she passed the huddled silence and scratched the burro between his ears.

"The lion jumped on his back but failed to instantly break Viejo's neck. Too bad for *Señor León!* A mule may seem a meek beast, but when something or someone he doesn't want there gets on his back, he hurls himself down and rolls." Santiago shook his head regretfully. "Viejo has some deep wounds on his shoulders and flanks. He may die, for all his courage."

"Can't we do something?"

"Some split pads of prickly pear will help staunch bleeding. Apart from that all we can do is share his load among the other mules."

While Shea dragged away the mountain lion, Socorro helped Santiago skin several cactus pads, pound them to astringent pulp, and apply them to where the vicious claws had raked.

"Poor little brave one," she murmured, rubbing the white muzzle. To Santiago she said, "He should have water to make new blood for what he's lost."

Santiago hesitated, then shrugged. *"Bueno.* There's plenty of water at Sonoyta and we'll refill our containers there. But after that, he'll have to manage like the other animals."

He poured water into one of the big leather *boletas* or buckets and held it for Viejo to drink. "Won't the blood draw another cat?" Socorro worried. "Please, let's have him hobbled close to us."

"So some lion can have us for dessert?" teased Shea.

"Lions avoid people, though if one were hungry enough I suppose he'd take a bite if he could." Santiago urged the burro forward. "It can't hurt to keep Viejo near us and if it makes you happier, lady, we shall do it!"

So Viejo was hobbled where he could graze close to

the bedrolls. Socorro slept in the middle with Santiago a few yards away on her right and Shea a similar distance to the left. It seemed a long time now since he'd lain close to her. She realized, with a certain desolation, that now they were no longer alone, they'd never sleep that close together again—unless they married.

She wanted the closeness but not what it would bring.

VII

Viejo survived the night. Socorro brought him water, put fresh cactus on his wounds, fed him some peeled pads and even a handful of corn. As they traveled that day the little beast fell behind, though he tried valiantly to keep up, and Socorro stayed back far enough to keep him in sight. He'd be easy prey now for coyotes.

During the long noon stop she watered him again, fetched him clumps of grama grass and more prickly pear pads. "You killed the lion," she told him, caressing his neck. "If you're that strong, you can get well if you try!"

He lagged badly that afternoon, and several times he simply collapsed. On the last fall, he didn't get up. Socorro reined back, held Castaña's reins and tried to coax Viejo to his feet. He struggled and gave a lugubrious bray, but his legs refused to obey him.

"Maybe I should cut his throat and end his troubles," Shea said, riding alongside.

"No!"

"But, *chiquita,* if he can't keep up—"

"He'll be stronger tomorrow! I know he will. If he can just last today!" Tears stung her eyes as she looked at the little animal who'd kept going so long in spite of its mangled shoulders and flanks. "Please, Shea, can't you help him up?"

He started to argue, saw her face, and threw up his hands. "I can get him up, doubtless. But his staying that way . . ." Swinging from the saddle, he gave her Azul's reins, put his arms beneath the burro's middle and lifted.

"Come on, warrior!" he encouraged, panting. "Come on, lad!"

The small creature tried desperately but could not raise himself. Santiago had dropped back. He tied Noche's reins to a paloverde, limped over to join his efforts and exhortations to Shea's.

"Please!" Socorro whispered. "Please, Viejo! If you can't get up, they must kill you!"

The burro seemed to gain resolution and new strength from the men's will to help him. At their next concerted lifting, he scrambled his legs beneath him and slowly, shakily gained his feet.

"Muy valiente!" Santiago applauded.

But the burro didn't move forward, only stood swaying. "Maybe we could rig a kind of sling beneath him," Shea suggested. "Fasten our ropes from one saddle horn to the other, passing under his belly."

Santiago squinted at the westering sun. "We can try it for the rest of the day but if he's not sufficiently restored by tomorrow, we'll leave him at Sonoyta. Some Papago family will be glad to have him."

"Well, let's at least get him there!" Socorro entreated.

The men each fastened a braided rawhide reata to a saddle horn, crossed them beneath the burro and secured the end to the long rawhide tie strings behind the cantle. Santiago pointed out that he'd better stay loose in order to herd the cattle, so Castaña was opposite Azul with the burro borne up between them. Not much of his weight was on the sling. The idea was to support him if he started to go down.

Socorro lost track of the times they had to pause till the little animal collected himself and strove onward. The herd was out of sight except for dust. But Viejo *was* moving.

Just before sundown, Shea pointed. Socorro, whose attention had been anxiously fixed on Viejo, glanced eastward to a broad long valley.

Fields, *ramadas,* small huts! They seemed a veritable city.

"We're there!" Socorro called to the flagging burro.

The cattle were still drinking when Shea and Socorro rode up to the river. "That's a *river?*" Shea demanded. "Faith, it can't be more than a foot deep and twelve wide!"

"Enjoy it!" Santiago advised, laughing, as he unloaded a burro. "It's the most water you'll see till the Santa Cruz!"

Socorro helped undo the ropes. Viejo sank to the ground, so after she'd unsaddled Castaña, she brought him water. He was meditatively wisping up clumps of long coarse grass. She felt much relieved about him. Since he hadn't died, he must be getting better and he could be left at this settlement if he weren't fit to travel next day.

Leaving him to enjoy his grass, she unpacked a kettle and was putting jerky and corn in it to cook over the fire Santiago had kindled, when a half-dozen Papagos approached.

Fear chilled her. Though these men wore loose white trousers and shirts instead of loincloths, for a moment their dark faces seemed to be those of the *Areneños.* She could feel those sinewy hands again, brutal thrusting pain, hear the laughter and bestial labored breathing. Then Santiago and Shea stepped forward. The Papago spoke in friendly Spanish and Socorro's evil nightmare faded.

They had just finished their harvest and had plenty of beans, corn and melons. They asked if the travelers needed food. Here, as a gift, were melons, tortillas and a jug of honey.

Santiago thanked them with great courtesy, explaining that they didn't need corn and beans but would be glad to trade for more honey.

He and Shea brought out some of the equipment and clothing salvaged from the Cantú ranch, and after some discussion, the Papago selected several shirts, a pair of boots, and an old saddle. One man went back for the honey but the others lingered though they refused to join in the meal.

"We have already eaten," one old man said. "You have far to go so we will not use your provisions. But to sit for a time at your fire . . ."

Invited, they did so, while Socorro offered tortillas to Shea and Santiago which were soon put to vigorous use in scooping up the thick stew.

"Have other strangers passed through?" Santiago asked. "Six white men, about three weeks ago?"

The old Papago's eyes veiled. "These are friends to you?"

"No." Santiago's lean cheeks corded. "Men I must kill."

"May Elder Brother aid you!" said the wrinkled ancient. "Our *rancheria* has too many men for their liking, but ten days ago a woman came to us who'd escaped slaughter at La Nariz by hiding in the fields. Except for her, the white men killed everyone in the settlement and took the scalps. Thirty-one of them."

"And there was no pursuit?"

"By the time the woman came to us, they were far away," excused a younger man. "Besides, they had good rifles. But we went to La Nariz and buried the dead."

No use chiding Papagos for not behaving like Apaches. After all, if they were fierce and warlike, they'd have killed the travelers and kept their livestock instead of bringing them melons and honey.

Santiago stared somberly at the fire. "If this cursed leg of mine hadn't held us back! Thirty-one more!"

"We'll get them, lad," growled Shea.

"It's not your quarrel."

"Hell it's not! Can't have two-legged wolves running around the country like that ripping people up!"

After a long hard look at the Irishman, Santiago nodded. "First we get our lady settled. Then . . ." His hands clenched.

The Papago who had gone for the honey returned

with several earthenware jugs of it, sealed with melted beeswax, and a generous supply of the sweet stored in baskets lined with corn husks. What a wonderful difference that would make! Socorro didn't know what she craved most, something sweet or something salty, but it was luxury to have either.

Santiago cut open the yellow-fleshed watermelons and their guests ate of these since there were plenty and melons were too heavy to carry on a journey.

Socorro thought nothing had ever tasted so delicious as the cool juicy crispness. Though at first she'd wished the Papagos would take themselves quickly back to their village, she was glad now that they'd stayed till she'd had time to watch them, see them as individuals.

As they talked, answering Shea's questions, it turned out that the settlement hadn't always been so peaceful. Once there had been a mission here, a church and convent, but during the Pima revolts of less than a hundred years ago, the Papagos had killed the priest, burned the mission, and taken over the livestock which had produced the animals grazing beyond the village.

Then it was their turn to ask questions of Shea. Did they believe there was a country such as he described, green with much water? They listened gravely. Probably what he told them of the war between the United States and Mexico seemed as removed and incredible as Ireland, but the tales would be something to repeat and marvel over.

It was late when they finally rose, wished the travelers a safe journey, and returned to their village. Socorro took Viejo part of a melon which he greedily devoured, making ecstatic sucking sounds as he tried not to lose a drop of the juice. He'd been up moving around a little, so she hoped he might be able to go with them tomorrow.

Weary as she was, Socorro went down to the river, took off her dusty clothes and bathed. The water was cold and she didn't stay long, but she felt much refreshed as she slapped her body dry before resuming her dress.

Back by the dying fire, one of the men had spread her pallet. They were so good to her!

Stretching to ease her aching muscles, she was almost instantly asleep.

She woke next morning to see a shawl-wrapped figure sitting by the dead fire. Starting up, Socorro choked back a scream. This was no ghost, no *La Llorona,* but a slender young woman, almost a child, whose broad, handsome face had a small nose that somehow gave her the look of a cat. Her hair was blacker than her shawl and so were her eyes.

"Who are you?" Socorro demanded. "What do you want?"

"I Tjúni." The girl's voice was soft but there was a guttural sound to her Spanish, and she spoke it haltingly. "Your men seek scalp hunters. I go with them."

Shea and Santiago were both sitting up now, staring at their uninvited guest. "You must be the one who escaped from La Nariz," guessed Santiago.

A nod of the covered head.

"Do you know where the scalpers went?" asked Shea.

"No."

"Then it's best you stay here, child," Shea said kindly. "Santiago and I will have all we can do to look after ourselves. But you can be sure we'll catch up to those rascals. Your people will be avenged."

"I come."

"It's daft," Shea argued. "You could get yourself killed. Then what would be the good of getting away the first time?"

"To kill scalpers!" she said, rocking slightly. She did not cry but her eyes blazed. "To kill them!"

Santiago stirred. His feelings after the Cantú slaughter had been the same as this girl's so he must sympathize. "Surely you desire to have the scalpers dead. You might slow us down, keep us from getting them."

Fiercely, she shook her head. "I follow anywhere—
lead! I one of Desert People! All family dead now. Parents, brothers, sisters, grandparents, cousins, man I
would marry. Whites say they travelers. Ask for food.
Get down from horses, pull rifles, shoot men." Her face
twisted. "I in field for melon. Hear shots. Hide behind
fodder stacks." She shuddered. "They not kill women
at once."

"Tjúni—" Socorro began.

"Some women snatch up knives, fight. These shot.
Scalpers rich, for leave knives in hands. Find mother
like that. Small sister, not yet in *hoholikaki,* house of
seclusion. Now she never go for rites of becoming woman or have child."

Santiago's golden eyes burned into her dark ones.
"You'll come with us. But afterward . . ."

"You may stay with us," offered Socorro. "But the
ranch where we're going was abandoned because of
Apaches. It will not be safe."

Tjúni laughed. "No place safe! My people not wolves,
like Apache, but we fight! Not let them drive from
country. Spaniards, Mexicans, they fell back. Never sent
enough soldiers to check Apache." She remembered to
whom she was speaking, stopped and muttered, "Pardon, lady, but is true."

Socorro, jarred at hearing her own complaint on the
lips of a Papago, only said, "I wish you would call me
by name. I am Socorro."

Tjúni didn't answer.

She'd brought another melon. They had this for
breakfast along with jerky cooked in corn and a mouth-
ful of honey apiece. Socorro saved some melon for
Viejo who seized the rinds as well.

"Should we leave him?" she asked Shea, who turned
from saddling one of the extra horses for Tjúni. "He
seems better now but there's so far to go!"

Shea studied the little beast, scratched him between
the long ears. "Why don't we let him decide? Leave him

99

here by the river where there's plenty to eat. If he follows, it'll have to be because he feels like it!"

Pausing as he finished tying a pack, Santiago nodded. "We can trust Viejo's judgment. Burros are sagacious."

"Sagacious!" Shea echoed.

"Absolutely yes! I love horses, amigo; they can be loyal and brave. But the smartest horse is not so intelligent as the dumbest burro."

Viejo twitched his ears and munched watermelon rind with a placidity that belied Santiago's praise. When the herd moved off behind Cristiano, the burro watched as his heavily laden brethren followed, dropped his head and continued to feed.

He's staying, Socorro thought in relief tinged with regret. She had grown fond of the small creature but of course it was better that he stay here than die exhausted in an attempt to keep up.

The river soon failed and they followed its dry course as it wound southeastward. It was twenty-three miles to La Nariz, a two-day journey. They had a dry camp that night, but ate well because Santiago had brought down a javelina, or wild pig, with an arrow. Though the meat was rank, when rubbed with chilis and roasted it was a welcome change from jerky.

They put their fire out before twilight when it might betray their presence, and went to sleep early, fatigued by the unusual lateness of the night before.

Socorro, as usual, slept between the men but Tjúni, though invited to share that protected spot, took the serape they'd given her and slept some distance on the other side of Shea. Perhaps she selected his proximity because he was older and called her "child," but Socorro wished the handsome girl had chosen Santiago's side.

At nooning next day Socorro roused from a nap to hear a rending of grass close to her head. Opening her eyes slowly, she gazed at a white muzzle, gray-brown head and eyes outlined with white.

"Viejo!" she cried, sitting up. Getting to her knees,

she hugged him. "You caught up with us! You must be strong again!"

"Stronger than if he'd come with us yesterday," Santiago observed. "He had another day of water and good forage, probably started after us well before dawn this morning." At Socorro's look of silent entreaty, he said, "Yes, I'll give him water! We can fill up our containers at La Nariz."

Late that afternoon they could see the long dark mountain which looked like the profile of a face with a snubbed nose from which it got its name. Tjúni said there were ancient fortifications along the side and designs on the rocks made by Those Who Came Before, a vanished people who had much skill in making pottery and tools.

No one was interested in viewing such antiquities, however, nor did they linger at the *ranchería* longer than was necessary to water the herd.

The men of Sonoyta had, as Tjúni explained was Papago custom, buried the dead with their belongings, sitting up in holes dug in the ground, covered with mesquite or paloverde poles from their houses. These burial pits were heaped over with stones. Thus even the village was gone except for a few *ramadas* and heaps of mud-daubed ocotillo that had been the walls.

Standing near the stone heaps, Socorro prayed for the slain. Shea and Santiago joined her. But Tjúni, face stony as the dark mountain, only stared eastward after the murderers.

The "river" forked here and next day they took the southern branch which ended at a deserted *ranchería* at the foot of the Sierra de Cobota. From there it was four days to the Santa Cruz.

Twining a way through the rugged maze of the Sierra del Pajarito was the worst part of the whole journey and it was fortunate Tjúni was along for she knew the passes which time had dimmed in Santiago's memory.

When they came out of this range onto level land

where mountains marched on all sides of them, Santiago took off his sombrero, gave it a wild flourish that sent Noche dancing.

"The Santa Cruz tonight," he shouted. "Socorro tomorrow."

That night they crossed the shallow waters of the Santa Cruz and camped beneath the ruins of what had been Calabazas. According to Santiago it had been first a Pima village, then a *visita* of Mission Guevavi where Jesuits held services. When the Pimas died in an epidemic, Papagos setttled there, and when the Jesuits were expelled from all Mexico, gray-robed Franciscans took over and Tumacácori became the mission headquarters for *visitas* in the area.

During those years of the late 1700s, Apache raids depopulated Guevavi and much of the region. After Mexico got its independence in 1821 Spanish troops were withdrawn and most of the Spanish-born Frandemic, Papagos settled there, and when the Jesuits predecessors had been fifty-four years earlier.

The Apache renewed their raids. Thousands of settlers fled and thousands more were killed. Calabazas was abandoned like nearly every ranch or settlement that wasn't very close to either Tubac or Tucson, the last presidios in all that wild country.

Gazing up at the ruins on the east bank of the river, Socorro shivered. If this place, with its long history of Indian and mission occupation, hadn't survived the fury of the Apache, how could they hope to withstand it at the old ranch?

She straightened her shoulders. Better risk this savage land with Shea than return to the captive life of Los Alamos or ask her unknown *hidalgo* cousin to take a violated woman for his bride. The truth was that she couldn't imagine life without Shea though she very well knew such a man couldn't forever sleep chastely beside her.

Sighing, she got out food for the evening meal. It was too dark now to start a fire for fear of Apaches, so dry jerky and corn must feed them, though they could each have a sweet taste of honey.

What a difference being able to cook these staples made! The jerky, well stewed with chilis, was quite good. Added to corn, it made stew. And the corn could make soup, mush and tortillas.

When they got to the ranch, within the shelter of walls, they'd risk fires, of course. It was where they were going to stay and they had to take certain chances if life were to be worth living. It came to her suddenly that home, in this region, wasn't a place of safety so much as a place where people decided to take the chances of being permanent, the pleasures and the perils.

Taking a handful of corn down to Viejo, whose lacerations were starting to slowly heal, Socorro patted him along the black cross marked on spine and shoulders. It was supposed to be Christ's cross, bestowed on the ass because it had carried Jesus on the flight into Egypt and again into Jerusalem on Palm Sunday.

"Why, *burrito!*" she said, laughing. "Your lineage is more ancient and honorable than that of any grandee! Yet you bear our burdens."

She imagined that Carlos would be most upset at such a notion and in that moment ceased to be troubled by his presumed standards or those of Alamos society. The *gente de razón,* from her experience, had more pride than reason, pride in things she could no longer consider important after her struggles in the desert.

The breeze lifted her hair as she walked back to camp. If, to have a home, she must dare light a flame that might call down Apaches, couldn't she risk the fire of her love for Shea? Must she huddle in dark fearful cold because he had a man's hands and a man's body?

In the moonlight she could see Tjúni watching Shea and a tide of jealousy rose in her. The girl was beautiful in her wild way and, set as she was on avenging her family, she still hadn't endured that shameful agony which had branded Socorro as viciously as the iron searing Shea's cheek.

I'll always have the scar, Socorro thought, *but it needn't be a wound.*

As if called by her resolve, Shea came to stand by her, his bright head a glory that she yearned to touch. His eyes were shadowed but his voice was deep, husky with controlled violence.

"Tomorrow, lass! Tomorrow we'll reach home. You'll have a hearth again, a bed. . . ."

She heard his breath catch. Her own blood raced painfully. Caught between dread and desire, she forced a laugh.

"And a *metate!* Back to grinding corn!"

"We'll make a mill for you," Santiago promised. "But we haven't lost a cow, a horse, or, thanks to you, lady, even that old burro! And more than likely we can increase our herds with cattle and horses that have run wild since the ranches were abandoned."

Tjúni's voice slashed like a knife through these dreams and plannings. "You have sworn to find the scalp hunters."

"True," said Santiago. "First we do that."

Shea nodded. And though Socorro slept between them that night, she felt as if they had already gone away.

VIII

Agua Linda, or Socorro, as Santiago insisted they call it from the start, came in sight late the next afternoon after a journey down the valley through which Sonoita Creek flowed. Towering red cliffs and mountains on either side were softened by huge trees, some of which were black walnuts that had dropped their nuts which lay darkening on the ground.

White-trunked sycamore and silvery gray cotton-woods were losing their yellow or browning leaves among red-leafed maples and elms, while farther from the stream on the flatter, dried land were large oaks and the smaller, more densely growing ones.

On the mountainsides changing leaves were brilliant against the deep green of pine, fir, spruce and cedar.

Squirrels were busy, an antelope bounded away, and they glimpsed a bandit-masked raccoon washing its food as a woodpecker thumped resoundingly.

The grass grew thick and high, a feast to all the desert-reared animals. There was no cholla and little prickly pear though agave and yucca still jutted from the hill-sides and impossible-seeming niches along the rugged cliffs. It was an altogether greener, softer, more luxuriant region than Socorro had ever seen, for though Alamos was rich in shady trees and flowers, it was still part of the desert.

The valley widened into a broad plateau that stretched to rolling hills with sharp-toothed mountains beyond. Sun turned crumbling adobe to warm gold, touched bleached, gray-white corrals, the remains of several *ramadas* and sheds, sunflowers growing thick around them.

"Rancho del Socorro!" called Santiago, reining back so that Noche pranced beside Castaña. "Is it not a beautiful place?"

It was, in spite of the desolation. Gazing at the house located safely above any floodings of the clear sparkling stream, Socorro said, "The people must have hated to leave it."

"They feared Apaches more," Santago brooded, hawk's eyes smoldering. "Some fled to Don Antonio's and lived another twenty-five years only to die at the hands of those scalpers!"

"But they had twenty-five years first," Socorro reminded him.

He shrugged. "I think no mortal can escape his fate."

"Yes," agreed Socorro ironically. "No doubt hardheaded daredevils are fated to die sooner than other people, and in more interesting fashions!"

He only laughed at her and rode off to push along some stragglers who were trying to eat all this marvelous grass before it vanished into desert and cholla.

It was spine-tingling to watch the cattle stop when Santiago rode up front and signaled to Cristiano that his duty was done, that now the herd could spread out up and down the valley, water when they would in the flowing creek.

The burros were driven up to the buildings to be unloaded. When this was done, they joined the unsaddled horses in rolling sweat off their backs and stiffness from their bodies. Only Viejo lingered near the people who entered the old ranch house to survey its disasters and possibilities.

The roof had fallen in but the walls, though eroded by wind and rain, were five feet thick and basically sound. Leveling off the uneven top and adding new adobe shouldn't be too difficult, and most of the roof poles seemed sturdy and unrotted.

There were three rooms, as wide as the roof poles had been long, about twelve feet. The longest room was in the middle, perhaps twenty feet long, with adobe benches built along the walls. It shared a fireplace with what had probably been a bedroom, the fireplace built facing where the inner wall left off to form a passage.

The kitchen had a fireplace, too, and more adobe benches on either side of it as well as niches conveniently made in the wall to hold cooking needs. A *metate* and *mano* and the heavy stone griddle for baking tortillas had been left, doubtless because of their heaviness.

What woman had used them last? Socorro wondered. Where was she now? But there was little time for fancies. She said to the men, "If one of you will make a fire, I'll get a stew going."

Santiago accepted that chore and went off to collect wood. Shea brought up fresh water and started taking things from the packs, leaving the food, jars and baskets for Socorro to put away. When Tjúni saw the baskets of corn, she put some in the *metate* and started grinding with graceful, practiced skill that made Socorro extremely rueful about the progress she had, till now, been proud of.

Socorro put jerky, chilis, corn and water into the big kettle. The meat and corn could be softening even though the fire wasn't ready. She tried talking to Tjúni but the Papago girl answered in monosyllables so that Socorro was glad to leave the kitchen and was clearing out rubble and parts of fallen roof, wary of snakes and rodents, when Shea's hands closed over her eyes.

"Come here," he ordered. He brought her forward, then let her look. In a niche above the door stood the blue- and gold-robed dark madonna, standing on the crescent moon, her lips parted in a gentle smile.

Socorro's throat choked with tears. She was happy and sad, hopeful and fearing all at once. Shea's hands dropped to her shoulders. She tried to meet his gaze but the depths of his blue-gray eyes made her feel she was sinking into them, drowning.

He tilted up her face. "Welcome to your home, my love, my lass!" His lips were cool and hard and very

107

sweet. Socorro had no strength; she lay in his arms while his kiss possessed her.

His breath caught in. He crushed her against him, mouth pressing fiercely on hers, burning to her throat. "My God!" he groaned. "My God, I need you!"

She scarcely heard; that wild melting in her changed to terror. She fought him, striking out, writhing, weeping. He pinioned her, holding her close. He must have done this for some moments before her mind cleared and she understood what he was saying, knew him again.

"Is it that bad, *chiquita?* Don't tremble so! I'd rather die than hurt you, don't you know that?"

"Oh, Shea!" She clung to him, sobbing. "I—I love you! But something happens—something awful!"

He stroked her shoulders, her back, soothing her till her tears stopped. "I love you," he said simply.

"And I love you! But—"

He hushed her with fingers on her lips. "We love each other. We're home. Think how lucky we are, my girl, and don't worry about the 'buts'!"

Somewhat comforted, Socorro dashed the tears away, caught up his hand and kissed it, pressed it to her face. "You are too good to me! I—I'll try—"

"Not right now," he teased. "Aren't you going to put something on that fire Santiago's built?"

Making a face at him, she hurried into the kitchen and put the stew on to cook. Tjúni was still grinding, the coarse cotton of her shiftlike dress pulling back against her breasts in rhythm with her motions. Her eyes followed Shea. She smiled very slowly. If Shea kissed her . . .

Socorro closed her mind against the tormenting vision, energetically continued putting things away, placing them on the earthen benches or hanging them from pegs, while Shea and Santiago took over the clearing out of debris and remnants of roof. Santiago made a broom of strong sacaton grass tied to a palo-verde branch and swept out everywhere but the kitchen where the dust would have gotten in the food.

By the time Tjúni had a basket of tortillas ready, perfectly thin and round to Socorro's great envy, the stew was bubbling, giving off a tempting odor. Shea brought the sleeping mats for them to sit on and they attacked their food with hungry relish, grateful for the warmth and light of the fire as night deepened. They were at a higher altitude now. It must have been nearing the end of November, and the air cooled instantly when the sun dropped behind the mountains.

When the meal was finished, Tjúni's dark eyes traveled from one man to the other. "When do we hunt the scalpers?"

Santiago's gaze joined hers, fixing on Shea. "We've got to get some men and at least one woman to stay here with Socorro while we're gone," he said. "We should put the roof on and bring in some game or kill another steer."

What he planned, Socorro knew, was to leave her situated with the ranch in working order so that, if he didn't return, she could try, if she were so minded, to hold the land and herd, make this place her home.

"You don't need to bother with the roof," she said. "If you find some vaqueros for me, they can fix it, or you can when you come back."

Shea's eyes probed her. "You're sure?"

She didn't tell him that if he didn't return, she'd need no roof, that without him, she would not live. "I'm sure."

He raised his broad shoulders in a half-shrug. "Well, then, tomorrow Santiago can ride to Tubac and try to bribe some trustworthy vaqueros into throwing in with us. I'll go hunting."

"Just in case you get nothing"—Santiago grinned—"I'll try to bag something on my way home."

Tjúni gave Socorro a patronizing look. "Plants are different here from those of the low desert, but I know some of them from food-gathering trips to the mountains. Shall we hunt that sort of food, lady, while *El Señor* hunts meat?"

Socorro knew the other young woman would not call her by name; it was her way of maintaining distance. Socorro regretted this. It would have helped to be able to pour out her confused despair to another woman, talk about and try to conquer the irrational panic that flooded her at a man's touch, but she was too proud to persist in breaking down Tjúni's reserve.

"I'd be glad to learn about wild foods," she told the girl.

Santiago frowned. "If you're going to be roaming about, I'll leave my bow with you, Tjúni. You can shoot?"

"Better than my brothers," she boasted, before she remembered what had become of them and her pretty mouth twisted. "Let me show you in the morning."

Santiago got to his feet, wincing the slightest bit. These long days in the saddle must have pained his mutilated thigh, but though he sometimes cursed, he never complained.

"Well, let us hope I can find some foolhardy vaqueros at Tubac and not have to ride on toward Tucson! I can reach Tubac tomorrow, but Tucson must be fifty miles farther north."

"Setting up excuses already in case you meet a pretty woman!" Shea growled.

"Pretty *and* willing," Santiago retorted. "At least I can promise the vaqueros that changing the brands on our herd won't be onerous. The C needs only another curve to form an S!"

He picked up one of the mats and drifted into the next room. In a moment the others followed, except for Tjúni who said she preferred to sleep in the kitchen. Socorro paused before Guadalupana and asked her blessing on them and their new home. When she turned, Santiago and Shea stood beside her, heads bowed.

She put a hand in each of theirs and they stood like that, joined by her body, their closeness saying what none of them could put in words.

They had each survived a kind of death, had saved each other's lives and sanity. Closer and deeper than lovers, they were bound together.

"Do not fear, lady." Santiago's voice was earnest. "This will be our home for many years. I *know* this."

"May you be right, my friend!" She gave him an impulsive kiss on his smooth boy's cheek, then, too late, remembered Shea.

To him, wanting her as he did, a kiss like that would be an insult. She touched his cheek and said good night, miserably aware that it took iron control for him to keep his hands from her.

She must, *must*, get over her terror. Before he found solace in Tjúni or visited Tubac for the women used by the soldiers.

As she made her pallet in the roofless moonlit room, she wished she could carry it in, sleep close to Shea, even as close as they'd been on the journey. But walls were between them now, would be till she found a way to escape that stronger, crueler wall within herself.

Help me, she prayed. *Blessed Mother, let me show my love when Shea comes back. But most of all, bring him back, and Santiago and Tjúni, though I cannot like her. Let my love be safe. Then, if I cannot give him what he, as a man, must have, help me accept his turning to another.*

She managed to mean the prayer while she breathed it, but seconds later she imagined Shea holding Tjúni as he had held her, uncovering that lithely curved warm body.

I can't bear it! she thought as sharp blades seemed to twist through her body. *I'd want to kill them both!*

Somehow she must teach that wailing mindless dread within her that Shea was her love, kind, tender. But when she tried to school herself through how it would be with him, how he would kiss and caress and hold her, when his hands touched her secret body they became the brutal gripping fingers of those laughing men who'd held her for each other's rutting.

Sitting up, she stared at the high white moon till the horror faded, then wept convulsively.

Next morning early, Santiago was off for Tubac, Shea went hunting, and the women started on their food gathering, armed with rawhide and woven straw bags as well as bows and arrows slung in rawhide cases over their shoulders, and knives sheathed at their waists.

"We're too late for acorns," Tjúni regretted as they crossed the creek and started for the mountains. "But when there's more time, the piñon nuts should be ready higher up." She pointed at cattails growing in a marshy place. "We can get those later. Be sure to slide your hand down in the mud beneath the root because that, and some of the stalk, is all that's good to eat this late in the year."

Next she touched a low thick bush with jointed, slender stems. "That makes good tea and helps when one cannot pass water or when that hurts. The Pima powder it to put on all kinds of sores and it's supposed to be a cure for syphilis, though I think the best cure for that is not to get it in the first place!"

They passed several large black walnut trees since they were near the house and the nuts would keep. The wild grapes had been devoured by birds and animals; Tjúni muttered that the squawberries seemed to all be gone, and Socorro began to wonder if they were going to find anything for their bags. Well, at least there were cattails, tea, walnuts and sunflower seeds!

"Ah!" gloated Tjúni, stopping abruptly beside a vine-like plant that had numerous small straw-colored lanternlike fruits. *"Tomatillo!* If we find enough, these will make a very good preserve!"

Socorro found another bush and a little farther on, they found more. Tjúni was delighted that a shrub with thick, leathery leaves still had a few nuts on it. "Roasted and ground, *jojoba* makes a good coffee," she said, going over the bush with great care. *"El Señor* must like coffee. All the blue-eyes do."

112

"I like it myself," said Socorro, though she much preferred chocolate.

Their next discovery kept them busy for over an hour, a dense mass of hackberry bushes. The birds had taken most of the easily reachable fruit but there were many of the small orange globes tucked deep down among the thorny branches.

Socorro popped a few in her mouth and enjoyed the sweet taste though the seed was so large there wasn't much flesh. Some berries were shriveling but Tjúni said to pick them anyway since, dried, they could be ground for a meal that added flavor to corn or gruels.

By now it was afternoon and they had traversed the sides of several small mountains, twining deeper into the wilderness. The berries had kept them from getting too thirsty but they were glad to find a spring breaking from a hollow in the side of a cliff. The spring trickled along the rocks, then plunged downward with a miniature roaring as if it fancied itself an awesome waterfall indeed.

But there seemed to be some other sound.

Straightening from her drink, Socorro listened. Tjúni was already peering over the ledge, keeping herself hidden by rocks and bushes. This time there was no mistaking the scream.

Or man laughter.

The sounds brought back to Socorro how it had been with the *Areneños*. Fighting back the sickness that twisted through her, she looked downward.

The spring ran through a small green basin protected on three sides by cliffs. It must have seemed a safe place to the Indian women, five of them, till the men appeared.

Two old women were already dead, throats sliced, kicked aside like refuse to make room for sport by the dead fire. Six men were busy with the three women they'd kept alive, holding them down for each other's convenience or taking their turn.

113

One woman lay as if unconscious or dead, one screamed and fought, and the other endured without a sound though the blond on her was huge, thrusting as if he were trying to split her open.

Socorro gripped Tjúni's arm, but Tjúni already had her bow strung. "Have arrows ready!" she hissed at Socorro. "Which you think you able to hit? Big yellow-hair? Maybe also one just getting up? You shoot them till you hit, then try for silver hair if I not got him!"

"But—what if we hit the women?"

"No matter." Tjúni spat. "Apache! Hurry!"

Socorro's hands trembled as she readied the bow and nocked an arrow, sighting on the hulk of the blond, but then she steadied. If only someone had killed the *Areneños* when they were raping her, she would have gladly died at the same time. Besides, the scalp hunters would certainly murder their victims once they had their pleasure.

Help me, Mother! It didn't seem sacrilegious to ask the Virgin's aid.

Two arrows hummed almost as one. Both struck. Tjúni's arrow took her man in the throat. He clawed, staggered backward, fell to his knees. By the time he was on his face, Tjúni's next arrow had toppled another of the standing men.

She aimed next for the bearded rangy one who had been holding the blond man's prey and now was springing up, running for the rifles stacked against a boulder. It took two arrows to bring him down and still he kept crawling.

"Finish him later," Tjúni ordered. "Good, you finally stretch out the yellow-hair! Try not to use three arrows on the redhead!"

This man and another were running for the trees, not even trying to pick up rifles. They must have thought the women's men had returned, that they were surrounded by warriors.

The first silver-haired man ran in a zigzag. Tjúni was calling fervently on Iitoi, Elder Brother, but it took her fourth and last arrow to pierce him between the shoulders. He pitched forward and was still. Socorro hadn't been able to hit the redhead.

"Stop wasting arrows!" Tjúni panted, taking one from Socorro's sling.

She dropped the man before he reached the trees. And there was one arrow left for the man still wriggling on his belly toward the rifles.

"Too bad you throw away so many arrows!" Tjúni grunted. "Now we go down, cut Apache throats. But," she added, gazing down at where one woman still lay as if dead, one lamented, and the other was slowly dragging herself to her feet, "they not give much trouble. And we kill little vermin in cradleboards so they no grow up to plague us!"

Leaving her bow by the food bags, Tjúni started carefully picking her way down crumbling rock overgrown with shrubs and small trees. Socorro, recovering from paralyzed shock at the other's intention, chose a more precipitous route and blocked her way.

"We aren't going to kill them!"

"What?" Now it was Tjúni's turn for shock. "Not kill Apache?" She shook her head in contemptuous wonder. "You crazy! Really crazy!"

As if brushing off a persistent fly, the Papago girl started on. "We will not do it!" Socorro sobbed, horror at the way they had just killed the men weakening her knees till she thought she was going to faint. "We're going to help them!"

Tjúni only laughed.

They were at the bottom of the cliff now. She was slipping the knife from its sheath. Socorro did the same. Planting herself in front of Tjúni, she said desperately, "You'll have to kill me before you kill them!"

Tjúni's pupils contracted. She stared at Socorro a long tense moment. "You crazy," she shrugged at last. "Not much use. But I not like try tell *El Señor* why I alive when you dead!" She added venomously, "You be sorry when little babies now make warriors, come raiding!"

Ignoring the Apache women, Tjúni, back stiff with outrage, set about salvaging arrows and stripping the men of knives, valuables and usable clothing.

The woman who hadn't screamed was young and comely, dressed in finest buckskin though it was now bloody and soiled. "You kill bad men?" she asked in Spanish that was at least as good as Tjúni's.

Socorro nodded and motioned toward Tjúni. "The same men killed her family."

The Apache woman said in scorn, "Cheap trick, sell Papago scalps for Apache!"

Dangling a gold watch from its chain, Tjúni glanced up. Her eyes glinted dangerously. "Except for this Papago, you be dead!"

"You have right." Apache faced Papago and Socorro understood, chilling, that they embodied implacable hostilities going back hundreds of years, existing long before her own Spanish ancestors set foot in this country. "We owe you life, Desert People woman," continued the Apache. "I, Luz, swear men of our band never harm you."

"That," retorted Tjúni, "like saying one wolf out of many leave you alone!"

The other looked as if she'd say something, checked it, and came to kneel by the victim who had screamed. Socorro was already holding the girl gently, coaxing her to drink from a gourd that had been nearby. It was easy to see why she'd lacked the stoic control of the older woman. She was scarcely more than a child.

Luz spoke to her harshly. The girl's weeping dulled into wrenching gasps as she struggled for control.

"Be grateful you too young to conceive by those devils!" Luz admonished in Spanish.

Accepting the cloth Socorro ripped from her skirt, Luz wet it from the gourd and began to wash the child's scratched and bloody legs, speaking softly now in Apache, hands deft and careful in spite of the pain she herself must be feeling.

Socorro moved to the unstirring body just beyond, tried to lift the woman. Her neck was broken. Socorro pulled down her skirt, turned at a squeal from a cradle-board.

Thank heaven the babies, three of them, were unharmed! Then she sucked in her breath. On the other side of the boulder where the rifles were, two small bodies lay like broken toys.

Running to them, Socorro groaned, leaned on the rock to vomit. The two naked boys, three or four years old from the size of them, had been dashed against the boulder. Their thin skulls were cracked. Brains oozed over them and the ground.

Tjúni, returned from recouping arrows from the men who'd almost reached the trees, stared down at the children without expression.

"The man who run fast, he gone. Smart. Stay on rock, leave no trail." She shrugged. "No matter. He die with that arrow through him." She surveyed the rifles with gratified approval, nodded toward the trees. "Horses and pack mules back there. We load on rifles, good things, go home!" She laughed exultantly, gave the stripped body near her a kick that sent it flopping. "Now my people rest quiet! My little sister have peace!"

"Yes."

Socorro's numb horror must have shown in her face for Tjúni scowled. "You not glad? If not for revenge, so men now not need go hunt these?" She gestured at the grotesque sprawls.

True. Now Shea and Santiago wouldn't have to go after the scalpers. Relief lifted some of the weight from Socorro's heart. She felt as if she breathed again.

Moving back to Luz and the girl, Socorro said, "Do you want to come to our house?"

"Why?" returned Luz. She had washed and held

herself proudly. Her broad forehead and high, pronounced cheekbones gave her face wild, hawklike beauty. "Our men will come here."

It didn't seem right to leave her and the girl like this. "Let me at least help you with the bodies," Socorro said. "There are the children—"

"Yes. They belong Suni, she of broken neck. It her husband's right decide where to bury them." She prodded with her toe the huge blond man Socorro had killed. "It be good for warriors whose wives or mothers dead to have these carcasses to carve on."

That thought sickened Socorro. "We'll go then," she said.

Luz stepped after her. "Where you live, that I tell our men to spare it?"

"It is the ranch once called Agua Linda, in a broad valley above the creek."

Luz nodded. "I know it. You safe at least from Mimbres who follow Mangus Coloradas. He my uncle."

"Mangus! Your uncle?" Tjúni, who'd come over to collect some of her piles of booty, stared transfixed.

Even Socorro, in Los Alamos, had heard of the giant Apache who was the terror of his enemies from the northern mountains and New Mexican settlements to deep into the Sierra Madre, from Durango to Sonora.

"My uncle," said Luz pridefully. Unable to resist a jab at the Papago girl, she added, "He not one wolf of many! None like him, not even Cochise of Chiricahuas who is married to one of his daughters. Even where he not chief, he important, for gave another daughter to big Coyotero chief, Cosito, another daughter to Navajo headman."

Tjúni had nothing to say to that. She only gazed at Luz with a mixture of awe and loathing, then turned brusquely to Socorro.

"You bring food down? Then we go, get home by dark."

"Wait!" cried Luz. "Our men come!"

IX

Laughing and jesting, a dozen Apache came out of the trees. Each wore a breechclout with buckskin leggings tucked into boots that reached variously from hip to thigh and most had buckskin shirts though a few wore cotton ones. The long black hair of some of them fell below their knees and all wore headcloths. Four of them carried a deer, tied by its legs to a pole.

Dragged and shoved among the last was a prisoner. He tried stubbornly to keep his feet and made no answer to taunting howls and plans of how they would amuse themselves with him.

"Shea!" Socorro cried and ran forward in the same moment that Tjúni gasped, *"El Señor!"* and the warriors saw the dead scattered about.

One gave a stricken cry, ran to the crumpled small bodies beside the boulder. Another made a sound of smothered outrage, whirling on Shea, knife upraised.

Luz shouted. The warrior with the knife froze.

"He's ours!" Socorro cried. "If you're grateful for this day, save him, Luz!"

There was confusion, some men dropping beside wives or mothers, others already hacking the scalp hunters' heads off, cutting away their privates.

Luz stood shieldingly in front of Shea and told her husband, a tall young eagle, what had happened. Tjúni's fear of the Apache men drove her to join Socorro and Luz.

Then amid the mourning and sounds of vengeance, silence fell. An Apache who towered over Shea by several inches came into the clearing. Luz left her husband and hurried up to him, speaking urgently.

His glance swept the basin, seeming to note each body. A muscle jerked in his dark cheek when he saw the broken children, seemed to relax a trifle when he saw the undisturbed babies in their cradleboards. His dark eyes came back to Socorro and Tjúni.

"You saved my niece, the girl, the babies," he said in Spanish. "I give you your man and protection for your rancho and anything you own. I cannot, you understand, speak for all Apache, but I will make it known to all, Pinal, Mogollon, Tonto, Mescalero, Gila and Coyotero, that Mangus will look at a raid on you as one on himself."

In that ravaged country, his promise offered more safety than any presidio. With his own hands, he untied the rawhide cutting into Shea's wrists, said with a half-smile, "As well as your life, Hair of Flame, you also get to keep your deer!"

"You have it," Shea said. "I'm glad to leave its carcass instead of my own."

Mangus's lips didn't flicker at the absurdity of anyone making a gift of game to his peerless marksmen. He thanked Shea gravely, turned as a warrior led up two of the pack mules, speaking to Mangus in Apache.

Turning, Mangus said to Shea, "It is right that you have the animals and belongings of these dogs, but we would keep some of the rifles and any scalps they may have taken."

"You're welcome to the horses and mules, great Mangus, and everything else *except* the scalps and rifles." Shea spoke in a firm, pleasant way, though he was bruised and marked by his recent handling.

Mangus didn't remind Shea that he was in no position to deny his recent captors anything. "Why do you say this?"

"You would use the rifles for raiding."

"Ah," laughed Mangus. "What if we promised to use these guns only for hunting or to defend ourselves, for instance when we are asked to parley with the whites? White hospitality to Apache has often been like that given Juan José, who came before me as chief of the Mimbres. A supposed friendly trader invited him and his people to come for gifts. The gift was a loaded howitzer. Johnson, the trader, collected the bounty on twenty-five scalps."

"We need three rifles," Shea said. "You are welcome to the others if I have your word they will be used only for hunting—and when you accept invitations from the whites."

"I will give that word," said Mangus. He looked bemused by Shea's incredible boldness, rather like a mountain lion defied by its prey. "And the other rifles shall go only to men who will swear the same." His eyes glinted. "We have not done badly, after all, at keeping out the whites with lances, arrows and a few old flintlocks. Besides, Hair of Flame, there will be other whites with other good rifles!"

Shrugging, the Irishman said, "That's as may be."

Mangus's face hardened. "Why do you want the scalps? To collect the bounty? In my own camp, you've told me what I cannot do, and now I say to you surely that these scalps, which must be of my people, shall not be sold for money!"

"If they were of your people, you should have them," Shea agreed. "But unless these men made a fast trip to Hermosillo, most of the scalps came from a Mexican rancho and a Papago *ranchería*." He indicated Tjúni. "Her family was killed. So were the family and friends of my partner. We may not be able to tell which scalps are whose, but all of them will be buried with respect."

"We will have a look," said Mangus, striding toward a mule and starting to undo the pack. "If the hair looks Papago or Mexican, we don't want it."

Tjúni's eyes flashed but Socorro laid a warning hand on her arm. "Apache hair is much longer than most Mexican or Papago," Mangus went on.

"He should know!" hissed Tjúni under her breath.

121

"I do know, little Desert Woman," returned Mangus equably.

Her breast heaved a moment and then she muttered to Socorro that she couldn't bear to watch an Apache handle her family's scalps, so she would go after their food bags and bows.

The pack and *aparejos* of the first mule held food and equipment, but in a bag in the pack of the second mule were many scalps. Mangus pulled them out, laying them carefully on the grass, assessing each with a practiced eye.

"Strange," he said at last, staring down at the grisly pile. "I had thought I could tell at once an Apache scalp from Papago or Mexican, but while it is true that some of these could not be Apache, many of them might be! No wonder the Mexican officials are so often cheated into paying bounty on their own kind!"

"How many are there?" Shea asked. "At the rancho, there were twenty-five, and from the *rancheria*, thirty-one. Fifty-six in all."

A musty smell came from the scalps as Shea and Mangus counted. "Sixty." Shaking his head, Shea got to his feet and his hands clenched. "My God! On just one excursion!"

Mangus said harshly, "Do not forget, without your women, there would be eleven more scalps in that bag. You may keep them. It would seem only four scalps were added to those of the Mexicans and Papago. Maybe Apache, maybe not, but you have said they will have respect."

Mangus kept the horses, three rifles and some of the provisions, but he told his women's rescuers to take the mules and the clothing and supplies the Apache didn't need.

"Also," he said, with a slight twinkle, "you need some decent arrows, some with quills. If you have to protect a camp of mine again, I prefer you be equipped to do it properly!"

Several dozen arrows were collected and added to

the bloody ones in the women's slings. Warriors re-arranged the packs, including the food bags Tjúni had fetched from the cliff, and fastened the deer to the more lightly loaded mule.

Socorro wanted to tell Luz goodbye, but when she looked around for her, trying not to see what was happening to the scalpers' bodies, Luz, with great enjoyment, was cutting off the genitals of the blond who had raped her.

The camp resembled a butcher's, a *carnicería,* quarters of men scattered about, heads impaled, the hats placed on them. Already some of these were being used for targets.

Shuddering, Socorro turned away, plunged into the trees, knowing only that she had to get out of this place. With a long stride, Mangus was beside her.

"You hate this, my sister, yet your heart was strong to save. I know the Desert People woman would have gladly killed my niece and the others. That is fair enough. I have killed her kind often, and will again. You do not belong to this country. Get Hair of Flame to take you to some gentler place, some country far from raiders and blood."

"You are kind, great Mangus." She lifted her head and looked him in the face, finding him savagely beautiful, all virile male, one she could have acknowledged as her master, though till now she had pitied the beautiful Mexican captive he had taken for a wife and by whom he had the daughters he had so strategically married off. "But all of us have met disasters in our own places. With the help of God, we will make a home here."

"You will find my protection greater than your God's in this land, sister. Go in peace, then. May you live long and well."

As he faded back, Shea said, "You are always welcome at Rancho del Socorro, Mangus." At the other's amused glance, he grinned and corrected himself. "So long as you're not raiding our neighbors!"

"I will remember," Mangus said. Then he was gone from sight.

They were beginning to worry about Santiago when he rode in on the fourth day after his departure, dejectedly saying even as he got out of the saddle that no vaqueros from around Tubac or Tucson would join him for any consideration. More, the commanders at the presidios had told him roundly that if he and his friends were crazy enough to settle in that abandoned region, they needn't expect help from the military who already had more than they could do to defend settlers located near them.

"Cowards!" jeered Tjúni. "Wait till they learn we have the protection of Mangus Coloradas! The presidios will want to move here to share *our* safety!"

"What is this?" Santiago frowned.

Even after they had explained, he was still dumbfounded. "*You* killed the scalp hunters?" he demanded, looking dazedly from Tjúni to Socorro. "The ones who murdered my people?"

"Tjúni killed all but one," said Socorro.

Shea's mouth quirked down, pulling his scarred cheek. "*Chiquita,*" he said whimsically, "I do not think that even here you must apologize because you're not good at killing!"

"I have a thing to say." Tjúni drew herself up proudly. "I wait so Santiago hear, too. I want kill Apache women, babies. *She* say no." The confession was difficult. Tjúni gulped before she went on. "Do as I want, when Mangus come with *El Señor,* we all die." The girl turned to Socorro. "You no good at many things but I not call crazy again!"

Shea cast Socorro an astonished look. She hadn't told him, seeing no reason to make herself sound falsely heroic. She hadn't for a moment really thought Tjúni would kill her and how could she possibly have let the girl kill the maltreated Apache women?

"It's over," Socorro said quickly. "Let's forget the whole awful thing—except that Mangus is our friend."

"We wait for you to bury scalps," Tjúni told Santiago. "Maybe you want to see if you know some?"

The happy surprise washed from his face. "No. Let us do it quickly."

Socorro made him eat first. Then they all went out to find a proper place for burial. It troubled Socorro, the sad remnants of so many human beings being interred at the ranch. She hoped it was no portent of things to come. But she was glad that Santiago and Tjúni would know their people's scalps weren't decorating some official's office or exhibited as curiosities.

Tjúni chose the eastern side of the long hill behind the house. Since there was no way to tell what scalps were whose, except for some curly ones that Santiago recognized, Tjúni and Socorro had wrapped all of them in a soft rebozo.

The men were looking for a place where the rocky soil looked possible to dig when Tjúni cried, "Here's a little cave! Let's use it."

Santiago placed the bundle in the shallow grotto. Tjúni put in some late sunflowers and Socorro added sweet grasses. The men rolled a boulder in front and they all added rocks till nothing could penetrate the barrier.

Santiago dropped to his knees. Shea and Socorro knelt beside him. "Will you say something? Out loud?" asked the young vaquero.

It was important to him, so Shea, though embarrassed, spoke clearly, "O God, you have all these Your children in Your keeping. We pray the Holy Mother will play with the small ones and hold them in her arms, for they were very young. And we pray You comfort those who mourn and do not let us become stony of heart because of how and where we live."

He led a Hail, Mary!, Santiago and Socorro joining. But Tjúni didn't kneel. She gazed instead toward where the scalp hunters' heads must be rotting on their posts.

There had been coffee beans in the scalpers' packs, hard brown sugar *piloncillos* and very salty fat bacon as well as beans and corn meal. The bacon had to be used and provided much needed grease, but the coffee and sugar cones were hoarded against some future feast.

Another treasure, disdained by the Apache who'd culled the packs before they were turned over to Shea and the women, was the woolen socks and there were some pretty blue beads which the men must have used to entice women when it was inexpedient to rape, kill and scalp them.

Tjúni asked for these and Socorro was glad for her to have them though strangely she never wore them. Maybe they, too, were being saved for a fiesta. The cooking things would be useful as would the serapes, clothing and extra horseshoes and nails.

But the great windfall was, of course, the rifles. All were 1841 percussion and Shea, handling one in amazed delight, explained its superiority.

"First place, it has a grooved bore which spins the bullet. That makes its flight straighter and longer. But the real joy is getting away from those damned flint-locks! When it's raining, or the powder's wet, you're out of luck."

"Of course." Santiago frowned. "How else can it be?"

Shea held out one of a number of linen-wrapped objects packed into a metal box. "These percussion caps are the secret. They're waterproof, full of powder that kicks off at the impact of the trigger. A whole new world in shooting, lad!"

Santiago's eyes lit eagerly and he picked up one of the rifles, handled it as if it were a mysterious, exquisitely desirable woman. "You will show me this?"

"Yes, first time we hunt." Shea viewed the stack of percussion cap boxes with satisfaction. "We have a good supply but eventually we'll have to get more. Better use our bows as much as we can. But, God's whiskers! What a difference these would make in a fight!" At the looks on Tjúni's and Santiago's faces, Shea flushed and sucked in his breath. "Sorry! I forgot—"

"*De nada.*" Santiago shrugged. "One cannot always look over one's shoulder at the past. We have fine rifles now and they will serve us well." He went on meditatively, "I wonder if the Yanqui soldiers who passed through Tucson last December had such weapons."

"If they were like Taylor's army, some did and some didn't," grunted Shea. "I'm glad those damned Yanquis went on to California and it's hoping I am they'll never come back!"

The war was over. He'd the same as seen it end with his own eyes when the flag was run up at Chapultepec and the last San Patricios were left dangling. But what the terms were, how much land the United States would exact from its beaten adversary, probably hadn't been settled yet and might not be for some time. It was a long border between the two countries, much of it Apache-dominated wilderness.

"Surely the Yanquis will never claim Sonora below the Gila!"

"They will if they want it!" Shea said gloomily.

"The talk in Tucson was that this Captain St. George Cooke had orders to find a wagon road route to California," was Santiago's uncomforting remark. "His men were ragged and very tired; they came from some fort far east of Santa Fe, near the other end of the merchant caravans' Santa Fe Trail. And they were called Saints! Did you know such men in the army?"

"Sure never knew any saints! Did these live up to their name?"

"They behaved very well. The commander of the presidio took his command and left till this Cooke and his Saints, nearly four hundred of them, moved on after a few days." He shook his head reflectively. "The men were not supposed to drink or use tobacco. They were not even permitted, by their religion, to take tea or coffee. Further, they may have as many wives as they can provide for! Have you ever heard of such a thing?"

"Most men can't handle one female. Listen, youngling, I think the folks at the presidio took in earnest what the soldiers told them for jokes!"

"You mean the force you were with wasn't like that?"

Shea thought of his sergeant who never went to bed sober if he could possibly avoid it, chewed tobacco constantly, and raised hell with the cook if plenty of strong black coffee wasn't always ready. "Laddie, I was in both armies and I haven't yet met a soldier who didn't drink!"

"The Saints didn't play cards or swear, either."

That was too much. "Didn't swear?" roared Shea. "Now I know you're making it up or those Tucson people lie like tinkers! No one can be a soldier and *not* swear!" He had to swallow hard to force back a demonstration.

Santiago grinned wickedly. "I'm sure you swear magnificently," he soothed. "I look forward, when we're working the cattle, to learning many new words!" He sobered. "It was also said that Mangus Coloradas parleyed with Cooke's commander, a General Kearney, near the Santa Rita mines a few months before Cooke brought his men through Tucson."

"What happened?" Socorro pressed. The huge Indian had captured her imagination and in spite of his fearful deeds, she had an unwilling sympathy for him.

"Mangus is supposed to have suggested that he form an alliance with the Americans to fight the Mexicans."

"What?" gasped Shea.

With a lift of one shoulder, Santiago said, "It must have seemed reasonable enough to Mangus. He knew the United States was fighting Mexico. What he couldn't understand was that the war would end, it wouldn't go on for hundreds of years like the one between Mexicans and Apache."

Shea's eyebrow climbed. "And what did this General Kearney say to that?"

"He told Mangus he wanted peace with the Apache but that Apaches couldn't raid New Mexicans anymore without getting American soldiers after them. He tried to tell Mangus that New Mexico had been conquered by the United States and was now part of it."

"God's whiskers! What Mangus must have thought about that!"

"Yes. He told the general that the land belonged to *his* people, that they were willing to be friendly with the Americans so long as they themselves were unmolested, but that they would never make peace with the Mexicans."

Shea said grimly, "Never's a long time."

There was much to do before winter, the most important thing being to get the roof on the house. Since it would take adobe weeks to dry properly, the men salvaged serviceable mud bricks from several sheds and mortared them to build up the house walls to their former height. While they did this, the women gathered ocotillo to use on top of the roof poles before long coarse sacaton grass and a final covering of liquid adobe were added.

Tjúni and Socorro were also busy gathering food, both to eat and store. The deer Shea had killed had been sliced for jerky except for what would keep fresh. For a few days they feasted on venison and then were quite ready to live on corn and beans varied with wild foods.

The men, in fact, took to eagerly saying, "What's new today?" though the *tomatillo* preserves, made with honey and the hulled fruit, were much more popular than a mush of grass seeds.

Roasted and ground *jojoba* nuts extended with browned corn meal made a pleasant morning drink and though the joint fir tea had a sort of smoky flavor that took getting used to, it was quite good with honey.

Out among the sunflowers they'd found a few volunteer pumpkin and squash, starting to shrivel a bit but still all right for cooking and drying. They saved some seeds for spring planting but dried the rest, roasting the pumpkin seeds along with those of the sunflower, some of which were ground into meal.

"Let's have some *pipián*," Santiago suggested when he saw the drying squash seeds.

The only lard they had was rendered from fat bacon. Putting some of this in a fry pan acquired from the scalpers' packs, he added chilis, seeded and torn into bits, chopped garlic and the seeds, frying them till the seeds were toasted. He mashed this mixture, then added honey, water and sunflower seed meal.

"If you'll stir this till it's thick," he told the women, "it'll make that old javelina I shot yesterday taste nice as young suckling."

It almost did.

Socorro was astounded at the different ways to eat the cattails they collected, groping deep in the mud to secure all the root. These had to be kept damp for peeling so each woman carried her harvest in a rawhide bag of water.

"Where'd you get potatoes?" Shea demanded that evening, sampling the crisply browned fried chips and then eating them with relish. He could scarcely believe the tasty dish came from cattails. "And they're even salty!" he exclaimed. "I don't like fat bacon much, but it sure helps as flavoring." He sighed. "I'll bet those scalpers had salt in their provisions, but I guess Mangus just couldn't part with it."

"He did leave the coffee," Socorro pointed out.

"I'm not complaining," laughed Shea, and reached for more fried root.

The women also made flour from the peeled, dried roots, chopped and ground fine with the stringy fibers removed. "In the spring, new leaf tips good," explained Tjúni. "Then green bloom spike. Later, pollen." She smacked her lips. "Pollen sweet, rich. Good in cakes or mush or soup."

Socorro shook her head in wonder. "It's lucky you know all this!" she said. "It helps us save our beans and corn and tastes different and good."

"How I not know?" demanded Tjúni. "My people in this country since Elder Brother make and put us here."

She had said nothing about leaving. Though she and Socorro were almost constantly together, the Papago girl treated Socorro with polite distance. She made no more belittling remarks but continued to call her "lady" or nothing at all. Though she seemed to be trying to school her eyes not to follow Shea, rest on him when he couldn't notice, Socorro still caught flashes of longing in Tjúni's expression and there was no mistaking the way her voice, matter-of-fact if not aggressive to Socorro and Santiago, warmed and softened when she spoke to the tall Irishman.

He treated her like a child, which, Socorro thought with unwilling sympathy, must be absolutely maddening.

After the heavy roof poles were mortared in place, the women handed up ocotillo stalks to the men who stood on crude ladders. The closer these were placed, the better, and it took several days. Next the women handed up bunches of sacaton grass, and after that was evenly spread, adobe soft enough to be molded was spread over the top and pressed down hard with hands and pole ends.

"I think we've earned coffee!" Shea announced, stretching as he got down from the ladder after the adobe was on.

Later, after it had dried, a thinner mixture would go on to fill the cracks and even the level so that there'd be no hollows to collect water and turn the adobe back to mud. The main chore was done, though. They had a roof.

X

And their first celebration. It was as if they'd been running hard and could ease up a little.

The men went hunting and brought back a deer and several quail. Tjúni plucked the birds, cleaned them, stuffed them with seeds and herbs and baked them in a layer of clay. The men laid aside the tenderer cuts of venison and jerked the rest, saving the brains for tanning and stretching the hide to dry beside that of the one Shea had almost lost to the Apaches.

Socorro roasted a handful of coffee beans, ground them fine and carefully scraped every grain to go into the coffee pot, also from the scalpers' trove of exotic goods. Though coffee had not been habitually used in her father's home, it was kept for entertaining visiting merchants who'd acquired a taste for it among the Yanquis.

How good some chocolate would be, whipped to froth and spiced with cinnamon! Would she ever taste it again? Socorro laughed in surprise at the sudden intensity of desire for such a fleshly, trifling indulgence.

"What's funny?" Shea asked.

His deep blue eyes danced and she guiltily realized there was little merriment in the house except for what Santiago created. Laughter was good medicine. She must try to bring more of it into their lives. But it was hard to joke or act foolish with Tjúni watching.

"We have a roof, enough food, plenty of water," she explained. "When we were in the old volcanoes, any of these would have seemed a wonder. Today is the first time I've really craved chocolate which must be because we're having coffee!" She shook her head, smiling ruefully. "It must be that the more one has, the more one wants!"

He said nothing. Had she made him angry, did he think she was complaining? She glanced up to be pierced by the hunger in his eyes. As if he couldn't help himself, he sank to his knees beside her, set his hands on her shoulders, even in that moment compelling himself to keep a distance between their bodies.

"I want you, *chiquita*. More of you, all of you—there can never be enough. There could never be more."

His mouth took hers, but in his desperation there was no kindness; his lips bruised and, with a hoarse groan, he caught her against him, holding her so close that her breasts ached against his hard chest, his pounding heart.

That heart seemed to enter her own body, sledging, throbbing. Hammering like that invasion when she'd been spread-eagled, helpless, and men had laughed. And thrust, battered . . .

She was back in that nightmare, struggling, trying to scream. Maddened, she no longer knew who held her, only that she was gripped by hands and arms of steel, forced against a male body that would savage her, rend her apart. She couldn't stand it again, never, never!

Slowly, she became aware of hands shaking her. "Is it always going to be this way?" She recognized Shea's strangled voice. "If it is, before God and the devil, I can't endure it! To feel you turn crazy scared like that, have you fight me! I can't bear it, my love!"

He had released her, risen wearily to his feet. Shattered at the implication of his words, she sprang up, laid a pleading hand on his arm, flinched when he moved away as if her touch seared him.

"But, Shea, it's only when——" She broke off, confounded by what she'd been about to say.

"When I hold you?" His eyes, sad, angry, yet cherishing, traced her face, her throat, lingered on the pulse there. "When I treat you like a woman?"

She hung her head, unable to meet those eyes, confront his baffled pain. His breath escaped in a heavy sigh. "What I told you once, Socorro, that I could be with you without having to take you—it isn't true. No use deceiving ourselves. I thought that as time passed, as you knew me better, you'd change."

"Shea! I love you!"

He smiled but it didn't reach his wintry eyes. "How? Like a brother? A father, maybe?" He shook his head. "It won't do, *chiquita*. I'm not blaming you, God knows! You're brave and wonderful, you brought me back from the dead. I owe you my life, it's yours for the asking." She would have moved forward, protesting. He stopped her with a strangely gentle, rejecting hand.

"Will you believe that, no more than you can help your fear, if I stay around you, the time will come when I can't help myself? I'll take you!" His voice dropped. "And then I would want to die!"

A thrill of pity mixed with marvel was in Socorro as she realized the power of this need of his, the amount of will it had taken all this time for him to control it.

He was right. It couldn't go on. Even had he been willing to try, she wouldn't ask it now that she understood. Closing her eyes a moment, she reached to the depths of her love for him, her will to live and forget the past, found the strength to ignore his warding hands, step forward and rise on tiptoe to kiss him.

He kept his body stiff, his mouth unresponsive. Forcing her away, he said tightly, "What is this? What are you trying to do?"

"To *show* I love you."

His eyes grew so blue they were almost black. Huskily, he said, "Oh, my sweetheart, but there's more to it than that!"

"I—I know." She took a long breath, feeling she must crumble at his feet if he didn't take mercy on her soon. "Please, I want to be your woman. Can you—

take me and yet do it so I can know you, remember who you are?"

The rigidity of his face dissolved, even the scar looked less raised and livid. His arms were around her, no matter now that her knees had given way, and his face was in her hair.

"I can be patient, little love. I can be gentle. It'll be sweet agony to woo you from one delight to the next till you finally want me as much as I want you now! But are you sure?" He kissed her eyes, the curve of her cheek. "It's not that I've blackmailed you into this?"

She laughed shakily, leaning back to caress his face, luxuriating in permitting her fingers to trace that long mouth, his eyes, the scar that ran from shadowed cheekbone to lean jaw, the places where his hair fell over his forehead enough to leave the skin fair in contrast to the red-gold flame above and the sun-darkened expanse beneath. She touched his hard-muscled neck, the place where the collarbones angled on either side.

"I have so much to learn about you!" she murmured.

He turned up her face. "No tricks! Is this because I said I'd go away?"

"Well, of course it is, redhead burro!" She scowled ferociously. "It made me know I can't live without you, that I don't want to!"

He shook his head, the amazed joy in his face dimming. "To have you grit your teeth, accept me in spite of how you feel—that would be worst of all."

"No. The worst would be for you to stay and run yourself nobly, silently mad because of my foolishness." She stroked his hair, reveled in the way it felt curling to her fingers. "I don't want to be trapped forever by what happened, *querido!* Help me."

"We'll help each other," he said huskily. Were those tears glinting at the back of his eyes? "But I want to make you my wife."

Touched, amused more than dismayed to realize how far they were from conventions or the means to observe them, Socorro said, "But, love, it's hundreds of miles to a priest! Santiago said both Tumacácori and San Xavier del Bac at Tucson were abandoned years ago!"

"Then we can go to Hermosillo. Or your old home, Alamos," he said stubbornly.

Her mouth dropped open. "Are you mad? Risk our lives, spend months in traveling the desert, and for what?"

"Why, the blessing! To show you honor!"

"Thousand thanks," she said dryly. "But I'd rather stay alive!"

His brows knit and his jaw set stubbornly. "Listen!" she adjured before he could argue. "Have we not buried people without the church? Your brother, my father? All the others? Don't you believe God can allow for our circumstances? I've felt closer to Him in the desert, and all these weeks we've risked our lives, than ever I did at Mass in the cathedral! I'm glad there's no priest, no ritual, no easy habit, to stand between me and my God."

"But what can we do?" he growled, troubled. "Someday there'll be towns and priests—all of civilization, damn it! We can be proper married then, of course. But before, if someone hinted you were just my—" He swallowed. "I'd kill them!"

"You won't have to!" she promised. "We can be married at our feast, under our new roof! Santiago and Tjúni will be our witnesses. And when a priest finally dares come back to this country and we can get caught up on marriages and christenings and the other sacraments, he'd better not reproach us for what his kind's dereliction has made us do!"

"When?"

His voice was soft, almost inaudible, but it sent quick, bright terror through her. What had she vowed? What had she done? Maybe in a week; maybe a month—

She checked the skittering of her mind. Time enough had passed. Too much, perhaps. More wouldn't help.

"Tonight. Before our feast." She made her tone happily confident. "It will make a fine memory to have our marriage marked by a roof on the house!"

But after he was gone and she heard the joy in his voice, though she couldn't hear his words as he told Santiago the news, she was full of panic.

Married without a priest? Married without family? Married without a beautiful dress?

Ridiculous to care, after all she'd been through, but she felt like crying when she remembered the painstakingly hand-stitched pearl-encrusted gown and veil which must have fallen to shreds long ago on some *Areneño*.

Married at all . . .

She threw back her head. She wouldn't think of that, what came after the plighting, after the feast. Only that she loved him, and, loving him, it was unthinkable to let him go on as he had.

Though some of the Cantú ranch women's clothes, like the dress she was wearing, were in better condition than the tattered one she'd worn in the desert, she preferred to use it. After all, she'd been wearing it when they met—and weeks afterward, too!

It was clean and she'd already mended it as best she could. Their bed? Shea would simply move his pallet in by hers. It would be a comforting thing to sleep beside him again, worth enduring those moments when they weren't.

Tjúni came in while Socorro stood there trying to think of any other preparations she should make. "So you be *El Señor*'s woman," Tjúni said without a flicker of expression. "No time to ferment *tulbai*, corn liquor, but I make some good thing with this!"

She got one of the treasured *piloncillos* from the peg-hung bag where it was stored, gazed at it like an artist considering how to use a rare and wonderful pigment. "Go wash hair," she told Socorro crossly, sounding almost like Great Aunt Teresa Catalina. "Bathe in creek. No need you here! I make food."

Grateful that Tjúni knew, that she herself wouldn't

have to tell her, Socorro thanked the Papago girl, got the dress she meant to wear, some yucca root, and escaped. Tjúni had the right to some time alone to get used to the idea.

It was late afternoon and sun still kissed the water, tempered the brisk sparkling air. Picking a place shielded by willows, downstream from where they got drinking water, Socorro slipped off her dress, chemise and the sandals Shea had made for her when she'd rubbed that blister onto her foot.

Water had rounded the many-colored pebbles, trickled over them like molten crystal. Catching in her breath at the chill sting, Socorro moved into the deepest part which came only slightly above her knees.

Gooseflesh prickled her arms, made her nipples stand out, rosy beige, and as she scrubbed with the soapy root, she tried to repress an imagining of Shea fondling and kissing those tender budlike tips.

But why shove thoughts away?

He would be her husband! Better that she think of him as she washed, smoothing thighs, waist, between her legs, better think of his touching the same places and with that cleanse the taint of those other hands.

"Shea," she murmured. "Shea, how I love you."

But the water was too cold for languorous fantasies. She washed her hair, rinsed it and splashed swiftly out, shivering as she rubbed her body to warm glowing with her old rebozo, dried her hair and, bending over, tossed the long black tresses till they began to dry. A good thing for her the *Areneños* hadn't been selling scalps to anyone and had left hers in place!

Slipping into her old dress, she wished she had perfume or scented creams, told herself she had a brush, which was much more important. As she started for the house, she met Shea with clean clothes over his arm and a piece of root in his hand.

Late sun turned his hair to glory as he blocked her path, laughing, and gathered her into his arms, wet rebozo and all. "Someday I'll buy you gorgeous gowns and jewels, my lovely almost-Mrs. O'Shea! But I'm glad you'll wear that dress while we're getting married. Did I ever tell you that when I first saw you after my fever broke enough for me to know anything, I thought myself in heaven with the Blessed Mother herself tending my poor baked hide?" He chuckled, playing with damp tendrils of Socorro's hair. "I remember thinking it strange, though, that God couldn't get His mother a decent gown!"

"Shea!" She put her fingers on his mouth though she couldn't help giggling. "That's sacrilege!"

"Not so much as the thoughts I got, even weak as I was, when the tears in your dress gave me tantalizing glimpses of things the poor angels wouldn't know what to do with!" said Shea unrepentantly. "I expect that's why I decided to get well." His lips brushed hers. In the sunlight, in the flush of laughter, she welcomed his kiss. His arms tightened possessively. "My God! I can't believe it!" He held her back, searched her eyes. "You're sure, *chiquita?*"

"I'm sure. Just—oh, Shea, please help me!"

He held her gently, smoothing her hair. The steady strong rhythm of his heart seemed to enter her own and calm it. "Now let me get bathed before that sun dips and you have a frozen husband!"

The last light of the sun was a shaft of gold slanting through the small high window in the back of the *sala,* illuminating Guadalupana's smile, the moon beneath her feet, the touches of gold on her blue robe.

Socorro and Shea knelt, silently praying, dedicating their spirits and will to this marriage, as well as their hearts and bodies. Then they rose, facing each other, and Shea took Socorro's hand.

"Before God and these friends, Socorro Quintana y Montez, I, Patrick O'Shea, take you for my wife. I promise to love and honor you all our years. All I have or will ever have is yours, as is my life."

Looking up at him, she said clearly, "I, Socorro

Beatriz Elena Maria Quintana y Montez, take you, Patrick O'Shea, for my husband. I will love and honor you through the years God gives us, with all my being and all my will and all my heart, saving only the worship that belongs to God."

And perhaps that, too, may the Mother who would understand intercede for me! she thought as he bent his head to kiss her.

They knelt again and, with hands joined, said an Our Father. When they rose, solemn and a bit uneasy, Santiago, with his almost unnoticeable limp, came over. He gave Shea an abrazo, thumping his back harder than necessary.

"You are fortunate above all men, Don Patrick! You scarcely need my felicitations. With such a bride, how can you not be joyous?"

Turning to Socorro, he bowed over her hand. His lips touched her skin lightly, briefly, yet they seemed to burn, and as he straightened, the torment in his eyes made her flinch. It was gone so quickly that she told herself it was only a trick of the light on those golden *tigre* eyes.

"My lady, if you have even half the happiness you deserve, you will be blissful beyond words. Like Don Patrick, I owe you my life. If you permit, I will serve you all my years."

Gravely, she kissed him on the cheek. "Thank you, Santiago." She wanted to add that she thought of him as the brother she'd always longed for, but suspected that was about the last thing he'd care to hear.

The sunlight was gone when Tjúni stepped forward. "I no have pretty words like Santiago. But I serve wedding feast." She gestured about the long empty room. "Eat here, not in kitchen. *El Señor* light fire, Santiago fetch mats."

By the time Shea had the laid fire going, Santiago had arranged the mats and Tjúni had spread the food on one of them, refusing Socorro's help.

"This one night, you sit, watch others work." She almost smiled. "Bride only one time."

And it's clear that though you accept it, you don't like it a bit. Ironic that their witnesses must be the two who felt deprived by the union. Socorro smothered a sigh. Santiago was of the age and temperament to fancy himself in love with any pretty woman he met. It was the group's total isolation that kept him focused on Socorro, that and the fact that Tjúni had given him no encouragement.

Tjúni. This time the sigh escaped. How tangled their relationship was! Tjúni worshiped Shea. Her unspoken conviction that Socorro was too incompetent and soft for being his mate, living beside him in the wilderness, was one that Socorro often came despairingly near to sharing.

But again, if there were other men around, enough of them, surely the beautiful girl would attract one determined enough to lay siege till he won her. Just as Santiago was bound to find a woman to capture him if he met enough of them.

The ranch would need vaqueros. If some were young and unmarried, if others had daughters . . . Smiling at the play of flame on flame as the fire gleamed on her new husband's hair, Socorro was so happy that she wanted everyone else to be too.

Tjúni had prepared a feast. Besides succulent baked quail with flavorsome stuffing, venison and tortillas, there was *pipián,* toasted sunflower and pumpkin seeds, corn soup and frijoles mashed and fried with chilis. Socorro didn't care much for the strong coffee, nor did Tjúni, but Shea and Santiago, when they saw the women didn't want more, zestfully tippled away the whole pot.

"At least no one will be *crudo,* hung-over, tomorrow," Santiago laughed. "But it's a shame we have no wine, or at least mescal or *tiswino!*"

Tjúni nodded agreement to that and went to bring the special treat she had concocted with the *piloncillo.*

It was candy, small squares of dried pumpkin boiled repeatedly with sugar in the pumpkin's soaking fluid and at last rolled in finely grated bits cut from the cone.

"I'd forgotten how such things taste!" murmured Santiago, eyes closed to better savor the confection. "Don Patrick, my lady, may much of your marriage be sweet as this, and the rest as good and strong as the other food we've eaten."

When it came time to clear away, Tjúni again refused Socorro's help. "Only one night you bride."

"Thank you, Tjúni. It was a wonderful feast!" Socorro hesitated, wishing there were some way to reach the other young woman. "When you marry, I'll serve your feast."

Tjúni's face was stone. "I think no," she said. "I think if I marry, you no be there." Head high, heavily laden, she departed for the kitchen.

The remaining three looked at each other in surprise. "She must be thinking of going back to her people," Shea decided finally. But from the glance Santiago gave Socorro, she knew he'd interpreted the words as she had—that the man Tjúni wanted would only be available at Socorro's death or departure.

It was a wretched notion but after the first shock, Socorro reacted by resolving that Tjúni was going to have an extremely long wait.

She smiled with sudden brilliance at Shea, slipped her hand in his. His face paled beneath its tan. With an intake of breath, he lifted her in his arms, and carried her through the door into their bedroom.

He didn't undress her or himself, but held her against him, head on his shoulder. Stroking her hair, her neck, her back, he murmured love words, soft words, till she relaxed against him, made a soft sound and snuggled closer.

"Shea, my husband, my life, I love you!"

"And I love you, *chiquita*." His voice was husky against her ear. "But this is only our beginning. We'll love more and better as we learn how." Light from the small window gave his head a shape but she seemed to feel the intensity of his gaze as his long lean fingers followed the contours of her face, lingered on her throat.

"Lass, tonight, any night, I want no more than you can give; but I want every bit of that! Perhaps you won't have to tell me, maybe I can tell from your body, but don't let me blunder on when you want me to stop."

"But, Shea—" How to tell him that she doubted there'd ever come a time when the core of her didn't turn to dark freezing at the moment he tried to enter her?

"Promise, wench," he whispered with mock ferocity. "Or I'll stop this minute and you'll miss some things that are nicer than pumpkin candy!"

"Can that be?" she teased, trying to steady the rising beat of her heart. "Did a woman tell you so?"

"Dozens of them, Mrs. O'Shea! Lucky you are, getting the benefit of my education." He sucked in his breath as if someone had hit him in the stomach. "What a fool I am! That's the way!"

"What?" she demanded.

"Why, I can pleasure you without using that part of me which I'm so attached to and that you, poor child, wish I didn't have!"

"But that wouldn't be fair!"

"It would," he corrected sternly. "The sooner you learn to enjoy being a woman, the sooner I can enjoy you. I'm being very selfish, my girl, so you stop arguing and just feel my hands and lips. I promise there won't be anything else. It would be a help, though, if we could take off that dress." When she hesitated, he coaxed tenderly, "Please, my love. It would pleasure me so to touch you without getting tangled up in skirts and bodices!"

Ashamed to deny him that, she sat up and he helped her slip out of her things though he stayed fully clothed. His hands were trembling when he began to caress her, moving from face to throat, then slowly, fleetingly, to her breasts.

She gasped as mixed signals of alarm and anticipation spread through her. This was Shea; Shea, her husband; Shea, her love! He kissed her mouth lightly, the pulse in her throat, stroked her lightly, exquisitely, till she moaned, pressed closer to him.

At last, his warm hand found the place that had been all these months to her like an unhealed wound. But he touched it as if it had been a rose, a delicate flower he wanted to bring to bloom without damage. When she tensed involuntarily, he kept his fingers still, spread comfortingly upon that old mutilation.

Warmth curled through her lazily from that quietness. She seemed to feel another heart in her very depths, throbbing softly to begin, then increasing in beat till she arched against him, wanted the hand to move, wanted—needed, oh, must have—some end to the crescendo.

Something fiercely primitive also wanted this first time to be with him, too, not something done for her with him holding back.

She reached to stroke the hardness straining against his trousers. He groaned. "Oh, lass, don't!"

"But I want you!" she whispered. "All of you! Oh, love, fill me!"

He took her in a way that lanced the remains of the abscess, cleansing her with the vigor and beauty and fire of his loving. Then, exhausted from their ecstasy, he who had been her man lay on her breast, suddenly her child.

"Our marriage was blessed," she told him, nestling her face against the curling hair that was damp near the roots.

He said sleepily, chuckling as he patted her rump, "If it wasn't before, it sure is now! I hope I won't go to hell, lass, for saying I prefer this ceremony!"

"If you do, I'll go with you," she whispered, holding him close, marveling.

The splendor they'd made with their bodies! A dazzling of lightning and fireworks, spinning away into vastness where one rested in a sort of ocean, buoyed by it, feeling its rhythm that beat for eternity whatever happened to the separate waves.

"Can it ever be that way again?" she asked. "Ever be so wonderful?"

"Mrs. O'Shea!" he told her, and now he was her man again, gathered her in his arms, resting her head on his chest. "You'd better sleep while you can! That wasn't anything compared to what we're going to do!"

There was a sound of hoofbeats. Shea tensed, relaxed as they faded. "Poor Santiago's trying to ride off his devils, I guess. Needs a woman of his own. Do you reckon Tjúni—?"

"No." How blind men were. "We'll need vaqueros in time. You must find one Tjúni would like and one with a daughter who'd be right for Santiago."

"How about a wife?"

"You're terrible! Shea, honestly, if you don't—Oh, Shea! Yes, *querido,* yes!"

This time she couldn't believe she had ever feared his body.

XI

Breakfast was a little awkward next morning. Socorro couldn't help but wish she and Shea could go on touching, laughing, kissing, felt inhibited from even smiling at him very long.

Both Tjúni and Santiago must be having enough trouble concealing their feelings without open displays between the newlyweds. But Socorro was tremulously conscious of Shea, so filled with grateful happiness that she wanted to sing and dance and, most of all, lose herself in her husband's arms.

Munching a tortilla and leftover venison, Shea asked Santiago what he thought about hiring some vaqueros. "When they know what Mangus has promised, they shouldn't be afraid to come."

Santiago considered for a while. Though he was no older than Socorro, he'd known frontier ranch life from babyhood, and Shea, his senior by ten years, was always ready to defer to his judgment on matters concerning the operation of the ranch.

"I think," he said at last, "that instead of asking those who were afraid, we should wait till spring, hoping that bolder men will hear of us and seek us out. They will work better if they choose us."

That made sense but did nothing about producing a suitor for Tjúni or a girl for Santiago. "Can we manage till spring?" Shea frowned.

Santiago shrugged. *"Pues,* you and I can't do as much as if we had help. But unless it's an unusually hard winter, we won't have much cattle work till spring when we may have to midwife for the few cows that have problems, and keep coyotes and lions off the new

147

calves. From then on, we'll need help. If we get a hundred and fifty calves next year, and we should, because for our herd I picked mostly heifers and young cows, we'll almost double what we have. And of course all winter and spring, Don Patrick, you and I will be on the watch for wild cattle descended from those left here when the ranch was abandoned."

Shea shook his head in bewilderment. "Hundreds of cattle, thousands of acres! Seems like a dream to a poor man from Ireland!"

Santiago grinned. "And to me it sounds like a dream when you talk about grass so thick and rich and fast-growing that a cow can stay fat on an acre or two! The grass here is much better than at the Cantú home ranch where we figured a cow needed sixty acres for browse. But we can think it excellent if twenty-five to thirty acres carries a cow."

"Think your uncle might try to take over when he learns that your father's dead and you've reestablished this ranch?"

"Without doubt—provided he could inherit the protection of Mangus. He hasn't even kept his mines running since Mangus wiped out the Santa Rita miners to the west."

"When did he do that?" asked Shea.

Santiago's brow furrowed. "It must be about seven years ago, in 1840, but the story begins before that." And he told how, in the '20s, the Santa Rita copper mines, which must be nearly two hundred miles east, were under constant pressure from Apaches. The first American fur trappers to travel along the Gila, a father and son named Pattie, stopped at the mine, after earlier talking with Apaches who said they had no quarrel with the Americans, only with the Mexicans. The mine operator, Juan Unis, asked the Americans to stay on as guards and when they weren't interested in that, he suggested that they rent the mines for $1000 a year.

The Patties agreed and the elder stayed on for a time, parleying with the Apaches and getting them to promise not to raid the mines. In return, the miners were not to establish a permanent settlement or bring in families. Even after Sylvester Pattie left, the agreement was fairly well observed by the Apaches though miners had brought in their women and the village had four hundred people and a plaza.

When it became a hangout for scalp hunters, Mangus Coloradas accused the miners of violating their promises and in 1840 the truce broke.

The mines depended on supplies from Chihuahua which were brought in by the long mule trains, *conductas,* that also took out the copper. Mangus ambushed two of these supply trains. There was no stored food in the village since the regular plying back and forth of the *conductas* had furnished a steady supply.

Within a few weeks, even though miners went hunting, the people were on the edge of starvation. They didn't know what had happened to the *conductas,* but it was plain they weren't coming. So, loading pack mules and wheelbarrows with their belongings, carrying all they could on their own backs, four hundred men, women and children started the long trek to Chihuahua.

As they passed through a narrow gorge, Apaches attacked. The ones who escaped that onslaught were wiped out in the next defile except for five or six who managed to escape with their terrible news. The mines had been deserted since then.

"And so have been Don Narciso's, forty miles west of here," concluded Santiago.

Small wonder, thought Socorro, and in spite of Mangus's promise, she felt cold.

Now that the house was livable, the men began cutting wood, taking dead limbs off mesquite and thinning the *bosques,* thick groves of the trees, which gave shade for the cattle in hot weather. Socorro and Tjúni collected walnuts, dumping them in a corner of the *sala* till the darkening hulls dried enough to be taken off more easily.

All of them went on the piñon expedition, taking

Viejo to carry their supplies for they'd spend three or four days in the mountains. They found several thick stands of the short-trunked pines and there, in spite of foraging squirrels and chipmunks, they collected quantities of the small fallen nuts.

Where piñons grew mixed with juniper, their harvest slowed, but the clear cold air, the smell of pine, and sudden vistas that stretched away across mountains and valleys to more mountains, purple, pink or dark or soft blue, according to distance and vegetation, were a tonic change from the lower country, pleasant though it was.

They all felt on holiday and one time when the afternoon sun had warmed pine needles to give off an even heavier aroma, Shea's eyes met Socorro's in a way that sent her pulse leaping. In a few minutes they wandered off together, found a sheltered sunny place and made love.

"It's our wedding trip," Socorro laughed, idling her fingers on his collarbone.

He kissed her slowly, sweetly and with appreciation. It was one of the special things that made her love Shea so much more all the time that she could scarcely believe she'd dared call love that vague, timid, contradictory feeling she'd had before marriage.

Shea never just turned his back and went to sleep. The hunger and fierceness with which he took her melted in their passion but his loving didn't. He held her close while they rested. Then he always kissed and caressed her again, making her feel not only desired but tenderly loved. Cuddling her against him now as he sat up, he gazed across the vast country.

"It's a grand place, *chiquita,* magnificent past words."

She tightened her arms around him at the sad note in his voice. "Do you miss your green island, my husband?"

"Yes. But my mother is buried beside my father under its sod, my brother's bones are in the desert, and there is no going back." He cupped her face in his hands. "My life is here with you. My life *is* you."

Their lips met, the fire kindled.

They gathered piñons steadily the rest of that day to make up for their truancy. Socorro was sorry to start down from the high country next day, but it was well they did, for snow began in flurries, diminishing as they descended and stopping entirely before they reached the valley.

To keep the piñon nuts from decaying or getting wormy, Tjúni showed Socorro how to roast them in baskets with live coals. The trick was to shake the basket so that it didn't scorch while the nuts were roasting. Stored in baskets and jars, the parched nuts made a rich and tasty addition to their food stores.

The husks of the walnuts had turned black. Now they could be trampled till the pithy covering flaked away, leaving the tough shell. These were hard to break. Santiago or Shea cracked some outside between two stones each evening. These were placed in the center of the mats by the fire and, after supper, the four used yucca spikes to pick out the meats. The shells were so thick that the meats were small, but they were excellent food, good alone or added to bread and soups.

Santiago saved the husks. "Soaked with a little water, these make a good medicine for cleaning wounds or getting rid of lice on cattle and mules," he explained. He grinned at Shea. "And should you want to disguise that fiery mane of yours, Don Patrick, the juice would give you nice brown hair."

Shea lifted an eyebrow at Socorro. "Would you fancy that?"

"No!" she said vehemently. "But I may use it when I start going gray."

"Wouldn't worry about that yet," Shea said.

They told stories on these nights by the fire. One of Tjúni's was of Earth Magician, born during chaos, who separated earth and sky, thus causing the birth of Iitoi, Elder Brother. This son of earth and sky helped Earth Magician make the sun, moon and stars and by the light of these, they continued to create.

151

From two drops of sweat Earth Magician made two spiders who crawled four times around the world, laboriously webbing earth and sky together at the edges. Next the creators made people, but these fought each other and were so bad that the makers destroyed them. The next lot were just as evil. Four times man was shaped and done away with. Earth Magician's last crop of people were so misshapen that he went off to the underworld and stayed there, and Iitoi at last made some humans in his own image that he was satisfied with, but on some he dropped blood and these became Apaches.

His people killed Iitoi, though, four times they killed him, but he was always alive the next day. He was a fine singer and made the deer, birds and other animals as well as trees bearing fruit. Coyote helped with this, when he wasn't playing tricks.

"And Iitoi lives on Pinacate?" Socorro asked.

"Yes, and at Baboquivari, maybe three days' journey northwest of here." Tjúni looked at Socorro in the flickering light. "Now it's your turn, lady."

Socorro told of La Llorona, the horse-headed night spectre with an enticing woman's body. Men who followed her died of fright when she revealed her countenance. Once she'd been a lovely woman whose nobleman lover deserted her and their children. She killed her children and herself and since then was doomed to wander the earth, wailing for her slaughtered babies.

"That's a sad tale, lass," muttered Shea, but his were just as sad though lit with the glow of myth and heroism.

Deirdre of the sorrows, Cerridwen's cauldron which restored dead men to a sort of terrible life without soul or mind, Cuchulain betrayed and dying bravely. There was the bright proud victory of Brian Boru over the Danes, but the later history of Ireland was far sadder than its days of warring tribal kings.

What could touch the horror of Drogheda when Cromwell's soldiers killed thirty-five hundred men, women and children, then sent thousands more to slavery in the West Indies and Virginia? And there was Wolfe Tone's revolt, put down by that same Lord Cornwallis who'd been defeated at Yorktown by George Washington. Wolfe killed himself in his cell rather than meet the dishonorable fate of hanging.

Santiago sang *corridos* or ballads, and songs of love. His stories were short, usually fables with a commonsense moral, but he told one haunting story of Godmother Death.

A peon besought Death to be godmother to his son. She consented and taught the boy many secrets of healing so that often, as he grew into manhood, he was able to save those his godmother would have otherwise taken. She had told him it was all right for him to treat people so long as she hadn't entered the room, but if she appeared, he must leave the patient to her.

He fell in love with a beautiful girl. They were very happy, till she fell sick. The young man did everything he could for her but she grew worse and at last he looked up to see his godmother at the foot of the bed.

He refused to yield his girl to her. Forgetting all Death's kindnesses to him, he called her fearful names and defied her. She looked on him silently, then left without a word.

His wife lived but his healing power left him. From then on, he was as any peon.

"I think he did right," Socorro breathed, glancing at Shea. "What good is power without the one you love?"

Santiago's tawny eyes held hers. "You are fortunate, lady."

She bowed her head and dug intently at a nut. It wasn't comfortable, being so happy with Shea, sleeping every night in his arms, when Santiago and Tjúni had no one. But at least more vaqueros must be found by summer and that should change things. There'd be more people around, at any rate, so the four wouldn't be so totally dependent on each other for company.

153

Still, even with the undercurrents, there was a sharing and companionship about that winter that Socorro knew wouldn't have happened with other people around. It was a special bond, even with Tjúni, who kept herself aloof from friendship with Socorro, though she'd been neither spiteful nor insulting since the day they encountered Mangus.

Along with their mingling of songs, stories and talk, Shea suggested that he teach them English. "If the Americans make a road through Sonora—and you can just bet they will—next, there'll be soldiers and towns." The brand on his cheek contracted as he set his lean jaw. "I don't like the idea of trading with them but we'll damned well have to! If you don't understand what a man's saying, it's easy for him to cheat you."

So they made it a habit to spend an hour or so in English practice each night. Tjúni learned more quickly than the others. Either she had a better ear or she wanted to outdo Socorro and bask in Shea's praise. Which she did.

After enough wood was stacked outside the house for winter, the men repaired corrals and *ramadas* and the women helped at making adobe bricks. When enough of these were cured, another building was started at a right angle to the house. This would house the vaqueros they still hoped would present themselves before spring.

The women also learned how to use the rifles, though again Tjúni proved a much superior shot. Santiago also engineered the mill located a discreet distance from the creek. An elevated floor standing on four legs had been made of roughly hewn pine and a small house about six feet high was built on this eight-foot foundation. It had taken a lot of hunting to find just the right millstones, broad and smooth and round.

It took so many hours to chip, bore and drill holes in them that Socorro shook her head. "Really, Tjúni and I don't mind grinding the corn."

"No use spending half your day at it," Shea grunted. One millstone was fastened to the floor. A wooden shaft was set in a socket in a rock beneath the floor and protruded through the first stone. The lower end of the shaft, beneath the floor, was equipped with three-foot-long horizontal paddles. These paddles were turned by the force of water guided against them by a small trough formed in the end of several hollowed-out half-trunks of big cottonwoods that fed water from the creek.

When, after immense labor, all was ready, the women were invited to bring as much corn for the grinding as would keep for several weeks.

With a flourish, Santiago poured kernels through a hole in the upper stone, and Shea opened the sluice. With tremendous groaning, the stones turned. Gradually meal began to spill out from between stones, falling to the platform.

Within minutes the mill had ground as much as the women, working steadily, could have done in several days. When, at a shout from Santiago, Shea closed the sluice, Tjúni and Socorro began scraping the meal into baskets. Tjúni had such a frown that Socorro asked what was wrong.

"Not right way to grind corn! *Metate* better."

"Why, the meal looks the same!"

"Won't be," said Tjúni dourly. She glanced with loathing at the millstones. "How *that* do anything but smash corn?"

"I'm glad it can," retorted Socorro. "I can certainly find things I'd rather do than kneel slaving at a *metate* for hours a day!"

"Papago girl who grinds good much wanted for wife. If all get meal from such thing, how tell good wife from bad?"

"There must be other ways." Socorro laughed.

It was clear that the mill struck at deep roots in Tjúni's tribal heritage. Though the tortillas from its grinding tasted as good to the others, Tjúni grimly maintained that she could tell a lot of difference and was sure the mill-ground meal was neither as tasty nor as healthy.

Since they were close to the marsh, cattail roots and stalks continued to be an important addition to their cooking, a blessing since, as Tjúni pointed out, they'd been too late to collect stores of mesquite, cholla buds, or acorns.

"But we can roast agave in winter," she said, and gave one of her rare smiles. "No need make bake pit, already one not far from corral."

"You mean that big rock-lined hole?" Socorro had noticed it, but all Tjúni had said at the time was that it looked like something Apache had used.

Tjúni nodded. "Pit much larger than what we need. Made to bake dozen, two dozen agave hearts. We bake maybe two, use one side only."

On the morning of their expedition Tjúni left Socorro to make the breakfast tortillas, a chore she delegated more and more out of disgust for the mill-ground meal, while she went off to start a fire in the baking pit.

She borrowed Santiago's machetelike knife. Socorro had her own, and right after breakfast, equipped with a long woven mat for carrying the agave hearts, the women started out, passing the pit which was about ten feet wide and three deep. The fire blazed against one wall, sending out a pungent scent of juniper and mesquite, a curl of blue-gray smoke that reminded Socorro of Shea's eyes.

They were so happy. A woman, according to Great Aunt Teresa Catalina, had to endure her husband's appetites; she wasn't supposed to enjoy them, but of late Shea had begun to stare at her with teasing incredulity.

"God's whiskers, *chiquita*, you're wearing me out!" he'd whispered last night when her fleeting delicate touches had waked him while rousing another very independent part of him. "I'll have my revenge, though!"

Gathering her in his arms, he tantalized and teased till she was quivering, arching against him. There came that wonderful moment, that always new, heart-stopping instant when he entered her, sometimes in one joyous thrust, other times with a deliberation that made her intensely aware of the sensation flowing through her blood and nerves at his sinking deeply, sweetly, ever more completely, into her.

She loved those pauses best, when he filled her and they lay quietly, feeling the secret internal pulses of each other, till one or the other could bear it no longer and they loved with a violence increased by earlier control.

Last night had been their longest, wildest, deepest joining yet. She felt the glow of it on her like a film of liquid sunlight. Though she managed not to skip or sing, there was a lilt in her step.

"You have baby?" Tjúni asked abruptly.

Socorro stared. "Why, no. No, I don't think so."

"I think one started," Tjúni persisted. Her dark eyes studied Socorro's face but it was impossible to read her own. "Next fall, about time for ripe acorns, I think you have child."

Shea and Socorro were too busy discovering each other to want children yet, but of course they expected them. Socorro was especially desirous of a small Patrick with eyes like his father's and hair as vibrantly flaming. And if in last night's loving they'd begun a child, it should be a strong one, full of life and hungry for more.

"Well, if it's true, I should know before long," she said. Though Tjúni had brought up the subject, she could scarcely enjoy it. Scanning the area between them and the hills stretching behind the house, Socorro remarked that there were few agave of any size.

"They grow slow. Apache make pit, roast all agave they find close except 'men' plants."

" 'Men' plants? What are they?"

"The ones with no flower stalk in spring. 'Woman' plant with stalk very sweet. Life run into stalk that grow inches every day. Leaves wilt. Everything in stalk. Then dies."

Socorro had seen agave, of course, including the withered stalks and leaves of dead plants. It was from agave that mescal and pulque were made, the first a fiery intoxicant, the last a milder drink sometimes given even to babies.

It was new, though, to consider it as a food. She felt as if she'd been blindly walking around in a food storehouse all her life and was only, since her time in the desert, discovering the keys.

Tjúni stopped beside a large agave that must have measured five feet from the tips of the outthrusting leaves. Another almost as large grew a short distance away.

"Raw agave poison," Tjúni warned. "Juice sting skin, be careful. I do this plant, you start other."

She showed how to begin with the largest leaves at the bottom of the plant, cutting where they broadened and began to turn white where they joined the core. Avoiding the dripping juice, Tjúni tossed the leaves on the fiber matting.

When Socorro thought she knew how to proceed, she started on her plant, cutting as deeply and firmly as possible. It was slow, hard work. In spite of her caution, she got juice on her hands which reddened the skin and stung ferociously, and she got more than one prick from the sharply pointed leaves which hurt long after the contact.

At last the core was stripped. While Socorro moved her aching shoulders back and forth to ease them, Tjúni loosed the earth about the core with a pointed stick, then pushed it over with her foot. Collecting grass to protect her hands, she picked up the heart and placed it on the leaves, added the second, and they started for the pit, each carrying an end of the mat.

The fire had burned down, leaving smoldering coals. Tjúni asked Socorro to bring water while she picked more grass. With the water, they washed the agave hearts and wet the grass which was thrown on top of the coals.

Some leaves came next, then the hearts and more leaves, Socorro going back to fetch the one they'd not been able to bring the first time. More bear grass was put on, a layer of earth, and then, using the mat to protect her hands, Tjúni covered the exposed sides and top with hot stones she'd banked up near the fire. More earth went over these.

"Now," she said, rising from her labors, "no more work till we fix leaves tomorrow, have feast!"

Socorro and Tjúni went down to the creek and washed off the juice with powdered yucca root before starting the midday meal. When the women entered the kitchen, Shea and Santiago warned them away from the *sala*.

"Just stay out of here till we say you can look," Shea admonished.

For days now he and Santiago had been busy with axes and adzes but Socorro had supposed they were preparing door and window poles for the vaqueros' quarters, which were almost ready for them.

Wondering what they were up to added a pleasant spice of curiosity to the rest of the day. When supper was almost ready, Shea and Santiago told the women to shut their eyes and not open them till they had permission.

There were bumping sounds, shuffling, and then Shea's arm went around Socorro. "Look!" he commanded jubilantly. "No more sitting on the floor while we eat! And you can do a lot of your cooking now without kneeling or bending over!"

The table was rough-hewn oak, slabs from two large trees joined together with pegs, the legs fitted tightly into the thick top. It was eight feet long and what it lacked in beauty was made up for by its ruggedness.

"It'll take whatever you do to it," Shea said proudly. "Pounding, hacking, hot kettles. Could even have a baby up there! And that's not all!"

He and Santiago were back in a moment with a bench, a log smoothed only on top, grooved to fit the slab legs. "Now if we put the table with one side close to the benches built out of the wall, and this bench on the other side, we could have a pretty fair bunch of people for dinner and all sit at one table!"

"It's splendid!" praised Socorro.

She was sure from Tjúni's silence that the Papago girl didn't like it, but they put on the food and settled down without any open storm. Tjúni did sit on the adobe bench beside Santiago. It was as if she took comfort from still being close to a sort of earth even if it was elevated and kept her from sitting in the way that was natural to her.

Next day when the roasted agave heart and leaves were taken from the pit and carried to the house on the mat covered with fresh grass, the golden mushy hearts were placed in a big earthenware bowl.

"Now we scrape pulp from leaves," Tjúni said. Spreading grass on the large flat stone they used for food preparation, she ran a broad-bottomed stick along the leaf, pressing to force out the yellow-brown pulp.

"That would be easier on the table," Socorro decided. Doggedly, Tjúni continued where she was. They had discarded some burned leaves but there were enough to yield well over a quart of syrupy pulp.

Tjúni regarded this with great satisfaction. "Grind sunflower seeds and piñon nuts to mix with some," she said. "Rest we boil to syrup after boil leaves for rest of juice. Syrup good in mush."

So it was an agave feast they sat down to that night: the sweet soft heart eaten with wooden spoons Shea had made, the nut confection, corn mush sweetened with syrup, and, for scooping up with tortillas, there was the wild turkey Santiago had brought in and cleaned that afternoon, cut in large sections and simmered in a sauce of chilis, ground walnuts, cattail root and syrup.

Everyone ate with gusto, enjoying the new tastes and variety. This was the first festive meal they'd had since Shea and Socorro's wedding, the day they celebrated the roof's completion.

"I've heard about roasted agave," Santiago said. "But I didn't think it'd be so good! Mmm! Just like *piloncillo* melted down!"

"Mighty good!" agreed Shea. He grinned ruefully

at the women. "All you've done the last two days is get this meal ready! Doesn't seem right that we sit here and gobble it up in half an hour."

"There's enough for tomorrow, too," said Socorro.

"Syrup, nut-seed candy for two week, maybe three," added Tjúni.

"All the same, I think we should save agave for special occasions or if we're short on other food," Shea said. "Next time Santiago and I can help, too, roast enough to make a lot of syrup."

Tjúni sniffed. "You want to be like Apache, make big party out of it! Next thing you want to make cross of cattail pollen on biggest agave heart before it goes in pit!"

"Why not?" laughed Shea. "We need some festivals!" Taking Socorro's hand beneath the table, he lifted his gourd cup of joint fir tea. "My good companions, let's drink to our first, but not last, agave feast!"

They all did. Even Tjúni smiled.

XII

Snow stayed on the Santa Rita peaks to the northwest most of the winter, reached to the hills on occasion, but only two or three times was the valley white-blanketed, and that not thickly or for long. Socorro never tired of gazing at the march of mountains surrounding the long fertile valley that followed the creek.

The Santa Ritas were the highest, of course, but across plains, valleys and the foothills to the east was a jagged sawtooth range, and south, beyond a long stretch of smaller hills, lay the Huachuca and Santa Cruz Mountains, stark savagery tempered by distance to azure and heaven blue.

The roof was on the vaquero quarters now and the men had made a cedar chest for storing clothes and serapes and two large chairs with rawhide bottoms which Tjúni would not sit in.

"Mill first," she grumbled to Socorro, out of ear-shot of Shea whose feelings she continued to spare. "Then table, bench, chair! How people move around with such things?"

"They don't, at least not often," Socorro explained.

"Not good, tied one place. Better, able move right away! Not like Santa Rita mines people all loaded down, easy killing."

"We don't want to move," Socorro said. "We want to stay here all our lives."

"And get more chair, table, chest!" grunted Tjúni. "More buildings. More cows, mules. More everything!"

Remembering her home in Alamos, Socorro repressed a chuckle at Tjúni's condemnation of this "luxury."

163

"Of course we'll accumulate more things," she said. "What's wrong with that?"

"*They* own *you!*" Tjúni said darkly. "No go where you want when you want. Someone might steal things. Or must find way to take them. Great nonsense."

There was truth to this but Socorro had no longing to return to the state in which she and Shea had come out of the region of dead volcanoes.

She was glad of the cooking ladles, the spoons and plates the men had made from oak. And she enjoyed the woven rawhide and post bed now filling a corner of the bedroom. Though anywhere she could sleep by Shea was better than the finest bed without him.

The men had also fixed up an abandoned cart. Its wheels were three feet high and four inches thick, made from cottonwood slabs fastened into one piece and cut to rounds. It was all wood, including the axles, and this first vehicle of theirs was sheltered under a *ramada,* for Shea said he wasn't working that hard to let the result warp and rot in the weather.

No one had been ill all that winter till Shea got a cold and an extremely sore throat late in February. Socorro caught it next, and in a few more days both Santiago and Tjúni were snuffling. At Shea's first complaint, Tjúni took Socorro to hunt for *canaigre.*

"Good plant to know," she said, stopping by a plant with long slender leaves and short reddish stems. "Root helps sore throats, sore gums, heals bad skin. And young leaves, like now, healthy to eat."

The leaves needed three changes of water to get out their bitterness, but they were a welcome addition to the dried staples. Shea dutifully chewed the root several times a day.

"It's either helping or it's paralyzed my throat," he grimaced.

Socorro, soon chewing in turn, could scarcely force herself to swallow the acrid dose, but it did seem to ease her cough and inflamed throat. No one got sick enough to go to bed and by the time their coughing stopped, spring was tinting the valley a soft new green.

"Time to plant corn," Tjúni said. She frowned anxiously. "No one of corn brotherhood to sing proper songs. Hope it grows!"

"We grew corn without songs," Santiago assured her.

They planted close to the mill to get the runoff from the grinding stream. Delving holes in the earth, they dropped in the seed and covered it with a heel. Then Shea opened the sluice and small ditches carried the water through the patch.

A few weeks later they planted squash, pumpkins, beans and chilis. All of them had worked at making an ocotillo fence around the crops, cutting off the stalks and thrusting them close together in the ground where they would root and form a strong, thorny, living barrier.

Socorro had never planted before. She loved the smell of turned roots and sod, dropped the seeds and covered them with an awed sense of their magic. Out of these hard tough kernels would come plants, springing into the sun and air from buried darkness. The plants would fruit and die, but they left seed for the next crop.

It was all the more miraculous to her because Shea's seed in her was making a child, she was almost certain, though she hadn't told him yet. If she missed her next flow, too, the baby should be born in October.

She tried not to worry that there was no midwife. Tjúni probably knew about such things. For that matter, if Shea had to help some of the young heifers with their calves, he should learn something from that! She chuckled at what he'd say to that indelicate thought, noticed that the others had stopped planting and turned to follow their gazes toward the creek.

Horsemen were coming, four of them. They wore sombreros so at least they weren't Apache, but the rifles were in the house. *At least,* thought Socorro, heart beating fast as the riders approached, *we all have our knives.*

"Santiago!" called the man in the lead, splendidly mustached with a hawk nose. "Can it be you? It must be, with those *tigre* eyes! We thought you dead with all at Don Antonio's rancho but it must have been you who buried them and set up the cross!"

"Don Firmín," acknowledged Santiago courteously. "It was not I who buried the dead, but my good friend, Don Patrick O'Shea. Without him and this lady, his wife, Doña Socorro, I would have died of my wound."

All the mounted men bowed in their saddles and swept off their broad-brimmed hats.

"Apaches?" asked Don Firmín.

"Yanqui scalp hunters. You may tell Don Narciso they are dead."

The Mexicans' eyes widened with admiration. Santiago laughed. "It is not as you think. Tjúni, this woman of the Papago, and Doña Socorro killed the scalp hunters as they were murdering women and children in a camp of Mangus Coloradas."

"I killed only one," demurred Socorro.

"But you saved us all," interrupted Tjúni. "If I kill Apache women, baby, then Mangus kill Don Patrick and us, too."

Shea grinned ruefully. "All I did that day was get myself and the deer I'd shot captured by Mangus. Fortunately, they decided to take me back to camp for their entertainment. I owe my life to the valor—and mercy—of the women."

Again Don Firmín inclined his head to Socorro and, somewhat grudgingly, to Tjúni. "Then that is the root of the tale that has reached even to Hermosillo and Don Narciso's ears."

"What tale is that?"

"That Mangus Coloradas has given his protection to a few people at the Agua Linda ranch, that he has sent word to all his allies that he will avenge any attack on these friends of his." His teeth flashed beneath the full mustache. "You are much envied throughout Sonora, Chihuahua and New Mexico!"

"Will you not come into the house and have some food?" invited Socorro. She looked appealingly at Shea. "Perhaps you and Santiago could talk with our guests while Tjúni and I finish planting?"

"Almost done. I finish," said Tjúni.

So the others washed in the log trough and while Shea and Santiago helped with the horses, Socorro stirred the simmering stew of venison, corn, cattail stalk and wild greens, including lamb's quarter and *quelite* or pigweed.

The tortilla griddle was already hot, sitting over coals at the edge of the hearth. Socorro's tortillas still couldn't approach the even thinness and regular shape of Tjúni's and she sighed a little as she mixed water and meal, kneaded it and began to shape the balls from which she'd pat out the tortillas.

What did Don Firmín want? Had he been sent to evict trespassers? He certainly wouldn't have ridden hundreds of miles through Apache country except on an errand of importance.

When the men came in, she brought them joint fir tea and placed a small bowl of the precious agave-nut-seed candy on the table. There were only four drinking gourds so she gave Santiago and Shea their tea in the tin cups of the scalp hunters which were seldom used. A man's cup is more reminiscent of him than a frying pan or coffee pot.

"Don Narciso will rejoice that one of his brother's blood escaped massacre," said Don Firmín after he had thanked Socorro with great effusiveness.

"Do you think so?" inquired Santiago, dark eyebrow climbing above his golden stare. "I wouldn't think my proud uncle would care to acknowledge our relationship."

"But you evidently feel you have some entitlement, Santiago, to have taken over Agua Linda."

"It is now Rancho del Socorro," corrected the young man. "Yes, I felt I had a right to it. Don Antonio had promised me land when I married and I think you know I served him well."

Don Firmín puffed up his cheeks. "Well, now your claim can be regularized. Don Narciso has sent me to offer a partnership."

None of his companions had said a word, except to murmur thanks for their refreshments. Two were young, one short and chunky, the other lean with a pitted face. The third was older, barrel-chested, with incongruously slender waist and hips. They seemed ill at ease at being waited on and kept their eyes on the table.

"What is this of a business partnership?" asked Santiago lazily.

Don Firmín made a pyramid of his fingers, rested his chin on them. "As you know, your uncle's mines were deserted after the workers learned what had happened to the four hundred people of the Santa Rita mines. The land grants up here, the Agua Linda, El Charco, San Manuel—what good are they with Apaches running loose? Don Narciso has plenty of land and cattle in the south where it is at least somewhat safer. But he liked the cash from the mines. He misses it."

"Knowing his tastes, I can believe that." Santiago smiled. He watched Don Firmín with polite, but not eager, interest.

"I am empowered to offer a proposition to the people who have the protection of Mangus." Don Firmín leaned forward. "If you will assume nominal ownership of the mines and assure Don Narciso that Mangus will not raid them, Don Narciso will supply workers, *conductas,* supplies, management—everything. He asks only for your name."

Santiago's lips twitched. "I have had no family name. How laughable that a part-Apache bastard's name should now be of value to my good uncle!"

"Of value to you, also, my son. Listen! If you can win safety for the mines, you will get a quarter of the proceeds and he will give you clear title to not only

Agua Linda but the other *sitios* as well. A hundred thousand acres! It is a kingdom."

"It is a wilderness. Ruled by Apache. Come, Don Firmín! The Cantús' ownership of these lands is empty. We can use them at will. I do not think you would care to put us off and remain to battle the Apaches."

Turning to Shea, Santiago drawled, "What do you say, Don Patrick? Shall we see if Mangus will spare the mines?"

Shea smiled at Don Firmín. "You will understand we must ask the women. Mangus's gratitude is to them. But if they do consent, it would seem our share, after the mines' expenses are paid, should be a half."

"Half!"

Shea lifted one shoulder. "Half is surely better than nothing." He considered for a moment. "I suspect we may have to offer Mangus some trade goods to dispose him to agree. Such gifts, of course, would be part of the expense paid before the profits are divided."

"Ay!" groaned Don Firmín, shaking his head. "Can I go back to Don Narciso with such an offer?"

"I expect he told you to offer a quarter and settle for up to two-thirds," suggested Santiago smoothly. "Would I be right in believing that you hoped to squeeze some share for yourself?"

"What a thought!" reproached Don Firmín sorrowfully. "Have I not served your uncle all my life?"

"All the more reason not to love him," returned Santiago imperturbably.

Tjúni had come in. Very shortly, the food was on the table. Socorro was glad of the wooden plates. She didn't much mind dipping from a common bowl with her friends, but she didn't care to eat after strangers who looked and smelled none too clean.

When the dishes were done, the women joined the men again. Santiago had accepted tobacco and cornshucks from Don Firmín and only Shea wasn't smoking. He looked from Socorro to Tjúni.

"You've heard the proposals about the mines. Shall we see if Mangus will allow them to be worked?"

"You choose," said Tjúni indifferently.

"I think it would be well to have legal claim to the land," Socorro said. "At this time it may not matter, but surely the region will not always be so wild."

"It's stayed wild in spite of all the efforts of Spain and then Mexico for over three hundred years," Santiago shrugged.

Don Firmín tucked down his full red lips. "The Yanquis will soon be pouring across to California. You've heard about the gold?"

"Gold?" they all said at once.

Savoring their attention, Don Firmín smiled with the superiority of one who has important news earlier than those who'd be most affected by it.

"A cousin of one of our vaqueros rode hard all the way from Lower California to bring his relatives the tidings. So they could go to make their fortunes before a tide of Yanquis arrive. Late in January gold was found at a sawmill site in the Sacramento Valley. *Californios* are swarming to stake claims. It will not be long before gold-seekers pour in from all the world. Tucson is directly on the easiest southern route and you aren't far below it."

"Surely Apaches will keep them out!" Shea growled.

The *mayordomo* shook his head. "Apaches will kill some, others will die of thirst and exposure, but these will be small obstructions in the path of a flood. American soldiers will come to protect the travelers; there will be forts and settlements. What has not been done in the last three hundred years will be accomplished within ten, twenty, thirty years. Certainly by the end of the century. The Yanquis will not be denied."

"The war is all over?" questioned Shea. "The terms agreed?"

"For sure the war is over." Don Firmín grimaced. "Over long before hostilities were formally ended at the close of February. Early in February, so Don Narciso heard, a treaty was worked out in Guadalupe Hidalgo, a village near Mexico City. Now the American government, and ours, must approve the provisions."

"And these are?" probed Shea impatiently.

"In one thing, at least, I wish the Americans luck, though they are biting off what will give them sore jaws before they chew it, if they ever can! They have promised to keep the Apaches who fall within the territory they've stolen from raiding into Mexico. They are guaranteeing to pay for damages the Indians cause Mexican citizens! Is this not a fascinating prospect?"

Santiago gave a long slow whistle. Shea's jaw hardened. The livid D stood out on his cheek. "And this territory? How much are the Americans taking?"

"Naturally they insist on the original bone of contention, the land Texas claimed between the Nueces and Rio Grande. The Rio will be the border with Texas. From there, the Americans take New Mexico and the line follows the Gila west, the Colorado north, then passes between Upper and Lower California to the Pacific."

Shea sighed with relief. "Then the Americans won't get Tucson, let alone this area!"

Santiago scowled. "That battalion of Saints that passed through Tucson over a year ago, Don Patrick, they were charged with marking a wagon road. Travelers will naturally stop at a settlement, especially in the desert, rather than camp in the wilderness because of the boundary of a nation they've just defeated."

Puffing out his cheeks, Don Firmín nodded. "So long as there was not much in California, apart from land to draw them, the Yanquis didn't go in numbers. But when they smell gold, *válgame Dios!* They will swarm like bees to honey, and the shortest way!"

Shea got up abruptly and went outside. Socorro followed him. "My love," she said softly. "Must the Yanquis trouble you so much?"

He gazed around at the marching mountains, rounded, jagged, fierce, undulating, all different, all lit

171

with sun and shadow, then gazed along their valley, the stands of cottonwood, walnut, sycamore and ash, the giant mesquites.

"This has been our Eden," he said at last, putting his arm around her. "But it seems the worldly serpent is about to enter!"

"Shea! You've said yourself Americans would settle near us sometime!"

He sighed. "I know, lass. Just hoped it wouldn't be so soon."

Because she loved him even more than this home they'd made in this place she'd come to consider her world, Socorro swallowed hard and murmured, "If you really hate the Americans so much, we could go far enough to be sure of being south of the boundary."

He gathered her to him, pressing his face against her hair, stroking her shoulders. "God's whiskers, *chiquita,* I'm not that selfish! Or maybe it's selfish I am, being bound to hold what we've worked for!" Tilting back her head, he kissed her till she stopped worrying about whether those inside were watching. Huskily, he whispered, "The only trouble with your being so sweet is it sure is hard to wait till night! You suppose we could go down to the creek—?"

"I do not," she said primly, though her blood was singing. The most beautiful man in the world except for that cruel brand which she seldom noticed anymore because it was part of him. "We must go in and be properly businesslike while you tell Don Firmín, if Tjúni agrees, that we will try to win Mangus's protection for the mines in return for half the profits and title to the ranch." She furrowed her brow. "But the lands should really be in Santiago's name."

"He insists that you and I are equal owners. Won't budge from it." Leaning through the door, Shea called, "Santiago, Tjúni! If Don Firmín will excuse you, will you come here for a moment?"

Santiago stubbornly refused sole ownership of the properties. "I would not be alive without you," he argued. "Nor, with Mangus as close as he was that day, do I think we'd all still be alive except for what the women did."

"But—" began Socorro.

"We've shared our dangers, we should share our good fortune!" Santiago included Tjúni in the sweep of his arm. "Is this not how things happened? Doña Socorro saved you, Don Patrick, but she says herself she couldn't have walked out of the volcanoes without you. You know what you did for me. We brought Tjúni with us but without her shooting, no offense, Doña Socorro, the scalp hunters would probably have added your beautiful hair to their trophies!" He paused for breath. "Again, though, if Doña Socorro hadn't pitied the Apache women, Don Patrick and doubtless all of us would have been killed. We should be owners equally!"

Tjúni's eyes opened wide. "Me?"

"Yes," nodded Santiago and Socorro again regretted the two handsome young people hadn't fallen in love.

"Papago no believe *own* land. Use it, move around on it." Tjúni's gaze looked far beyond them, then focused sharply. "No want name on white man's paper. So Spaniards, so Mexicans took land not theirs. Enough if I not bothered when use land I need."

Santiago looked a bit deflated at this rejection of his offer.

Shea frowned, then, as the girl met his stare unwaveringly, he said with grudging approval, "You must do what you feel is right. But the rest of us will always know and honor the right you and your family, when you get one, will have to the land."

So Don Narciso was told the grants should be conveyed to Patrick O'Shea upon news that Mangus would allow the mines to operate. The *mayordomo* was taking Alejandro, the short, heavy vaquero, back with him, to return with Narciso's answer.

The other two asked for work: Belen, the thick-chested, slender-hipped Yaqui, and Jesús, or Chuey, the lean, pockmarked one who looked even younger than Santiago.

"We have more men than we need," said Don Firmín. "If you could use more vaqueros, I will inquire and see if a few more would like to return with Alejandro. Pedro Sanchez was born here and still laments the abandonment under dread of Apache. He's older than Belen but expert in all things, and I think his two sons would follow him."

"Has he daughters?" asked Socorro.

"Daughters!" Don Firmín closed his eyes ecstatically. "How that bandy-legged little monkey produced those delectables only God knows." He grinned at Jesus who dropped his head and studied the floor. "Did you gather wild flowers for the tall stately one or was it for the younger, that pretty little soft quail?" When the vaquero seemed unable to answer, Don Firmín shook his head and gave a mock sigh. "Was it that you picked the flowers but dared not offer them?"

"Don Firmín!" protested the miserable young man.

"Your luck may improve if Pedro brings his family up," said the *mayordomo.*

"We'll need men," said Shea. "If at first they'll work for food and shelter, they'll be paid a share of what we sell our cattle for."

"What does a vaquero need but food, a hut he can build himself, and now and then some clothes?" asked Don Firmín.

The look in Santiago's eyes made the foreman get to his feet somewhat hastily. "Don Narciso wished me to make all speed. There are six hours left of daylight. Alejandro and I will be on our way."

He refused to stay the night but was grateful for the leftover tortillas Socorro gave him. Santiago took Chuey and Belen to the vaqueros' quarters where they left their pallets and saddlebags. They would do their own cooking, they said, but would be very glad if the ladies would supply the tortillas.

After such a long time of there being only the four

of them, it seemed strange, even slightly uncomfortable, to have strangers at the ranch. But Belen and Chuey were quiet and unobtrusive. That afternoon they rode out with Santiago and Shea to see if any cows were in trouble with calving. When they returned after twilight, Santiago reported that Chuey was incredible with the reata.

"I think he could cast a *mangana* on a mosquito!" Santiago marveled. "The way he brought down that bull that charged us! And Belen is very skilled with cows. A young one could not give birth; the calf was turned the wrong way, but Belen reached in and brought it around, helped the worn-out little cow expel it. A fine baby bull."

"They're good vaqueros," Shea agreed. "Now if this Pedro Sanchez brings his family, we can really chouse out strays. Reckon we could sell some this fall?"

Santiago laughed. "You want to get rid of wild ones like those that charged us today? A good idea. We should cull off the meanest, skinniest ones, build up our herd from those carrying the best flesh."

"We're really getting started!" Shea's exultant laughter died as rapidly as it had begun and Socorro knew he was thinking of his dead brother who could not share his luck, or of his starved mother. Aching for him, Socorro took comfort from thinking that the child she carried would help him look forward, not at the cruel past.

"How will we ask Mangus about the mines?" she questioned.

"We'll have to find him. Which may not be the safest thing in the world." Shea thought for a moment. "I must go for sure since this red hair will be easy to recognize."

"I'll go with you," said Socorro.

"No, love. We might be killed long before we found any sign of Mangus. I won't risk you."

"Then I won't risk you!" she flashed.

"Mangus doesn't know Santiago," Shea pointed out.

"I no hunt Apache!" said Tjúni in positive tones.

Socorro held Shea's gaze. "If it's important enough for you to go, I'm coming! If it isn't, let's forget the whole thing. We have enough to eat and a start of cattle."

"We have no legal title to this land," Shea pointed out. "We'll need more as our herd increases."

"And with money we could buy good breeding stock, horses and cattle," put in Santiago. His eyes glowed and he put on swagger as he strolled about the room. "Ay, it would please me to show Don Narcisco that his brother's Apache bastard could become a big ranchero!"

"You think Don Narcisco will agree to the half-share?" Socorro asked.

"*Seguramente sí!* He needs cash for his frolics in Hermosillo and Mexico City. Some is better than none."

"Then I think," said Socorro, turning to her husband, "that we should start tomorrow and look for Mangus."

"Maybe you took a fancy to that big Apache," growled Shea. "Maybe you hope he'll keep you for a wife!"

"If I did," she said sweetly, "I'd hunt him by myself! Don't try to go off without me, Shea. I'd follow you alone."

"Not alone, lady," corrected Santiago.

With a surrendering shrug, ruefully eyeing his wife, Shea said briskly, "All right, we'll leave in the morning. And will you pack a bit of honey since there seems to be none on your tongue?"

She made him change his mind that night in their bed, loving him with great skill and sweetness, driving him to wildness that wasn't spent in one embrace for he woke her in the night, already aroused by his caressing so that their meeting was swift and violent though they lay tenderly afterward, holding each other.

"My stubborn *hidalga!*" he chided, touching her face, her eyes, her throat.

176

She bent her lips to his hand. "No, Shea. It is that I could not live without you. If you go to danger, I would rather be with you."

"I'm ten years older than you," he teased. "If you want ardors like those of this night, *querida,* in twenty years you'll have to get rid of me and find a new husband!"

"Burro!" She nipped his ear hard enough to make him yelp. "If you think you can retire in twenty years, you're badly mistaken!" But as she snuggled against him, feeling infinitely safe and loved in the circle of his hard strong arms, she knew she'd rather be like this, resting with him, even if that was all that could ever be between them, than enjoying the most virile and imaginative lovemaking of anyone else.

She could not, in truth, imagine anybody else. Shea was her lover, brother, father, child. She prayed with sudden ferocity that she would not be condemned to live after he was dead.

XIII

To hunt an Apache!

Who might be anywhere in these hundreds of miles of mountains and plains ripped by cañons, arroyos and dry riverbeds. Tiúni had said this was the month for gathering cholla buds, the principal food available in early spring, and the Apaches would not be higher than the cactus grew. So Shea and Socorro twined their way across the plateau through the jagged Whetstone range, moving eastward.

Neither Santiago nor Tiúni knew that region, except that the San Pedro River cut through it north and south and the Chiricahua Mountains reared like fortresses south and west of the abandoned Santa Rita mines in New Mexico. Further east, three hundred miles from Rancho del Socorro, was the Texas border city of Franklin, sometimes called El Paso del Norte, Pass of the North, with Santa Fe and Albuquerque several hundred miles straight north.

A vast country. The small adobe settlements west of the Pecos in Texas till one came to the old towns on the California coast were tiny scattered candle flames almost invisible under the blazing desert sun.

Shea must have been having the same thoughts. When they stopped that evening on the banks of a dry wash, hobbling the horses and Viejo in the best grass they could find, Shea turned slowly, gazing at the mountains that rose from the desert on every side of them, the north and eastern ranges flushed crimson by the last light of the vanished sun.

"If there's gold in California, enough to keep calling, there'll be a road through here," he said. "Army posts to defend it, whores, sutlers and saloons for the soldiers, little cockroach clusters where people will stick. But right now it doesn't seem there's anyone here but God."

"And Apaches?" she suggested with a thin laugh, for it was a dangerous thing they were doing.

There were many bands, split again in groups small enough to forage a living. Mangus's word might not have reached them all. It might be disregarded. Or the pair might be set upon and killed before their identity was known.

"I expect Mangus will find us, not the other way around," Shea admitted. "But we won't have a fire tonight."

It was chilly. They sat close together on their bedrolls, serapes around them, and munched jerky and parched corn pounded with the last of the walnuts. Tjúni had fixed several bags of this for them; they had their bows and Mangus's arrows for silent hunting as well as rifles. The most important of their supplies was water, the only thing that Viejo carried in addition to the water bags slung behind both saddles.

"We found no water today," Shea said. "If we don't find some tomorrow, we'll water the horses from Viejo's load, and if we don't hit some by noon the next day, we'll just have to start back. We don't kill our animals —or ourselves—over this."

Weary from the long ride, they went to sleep as soon as they'd eaten, bedrolls made up together. "It's been a long time since we slept out," Socorro murmured, head on his shoulder, arm across his chest. "Look, *querido!* How bright the stars are!"

"Mmm. Roof turns the weather but it also hides a lot of other things." He stroked her hair. "Reckon we should sleep outside now and then just so we won't forget."

"Let's do! Sometimes let's leave the house and let it be the way it was when we first found each other—no, not when you were so weak, but after, when you were well, when we were all alone! Can we, Shea?"

"It's a fine notion, lass," he chuckled. "We'll do that! If the ranch grows and Americans come and there's a road and towns, we can still go back to our beginning when it was just the two of us in the beauty and death of the desert. It'll be our special feast."

And then, though they had both thought they were too tired, they loved each other beneath the stars while coyotes called and wind stirred the tall grass.

They found water next morning, thanks to Viejo, who persisted in following a dry wash to a place where he lifted up his voice in a shattering bray and began to scrape at the sand with his hoofs. In a few minutes, the sand darkened with moisture.

Shea and Socorro dismounted, got sharp sticks, and dug, too. Water began to seep into the hollows. By the time Viejo was straining up what he'd uncovered, Castaña and Azul were crowding in, snuffing. Shea knelt. With his hands he scooped out the wet sand, rapidly enlarging the hole till the horses could drink.

Several times they had to be held back while Shea dug more and the hole refilled, but at last the three animals were watered. Shea and Socorro dug another hole and filled their empty water bag from it.

To help spot the place on the way back, they tied a strip torn from the bottom of Socorro's chemise to the highest cholla they could find. Short of rain or wind, they should be able to follow their tracks fairly well, but they didn't want to take a single unnecessary chance about water.

By midafternoon they were threading their way into mountains, keeping to the arroyos as much as possible. At a narrow pass between two yellow-white cliffs an Apache slipped out of the rocks and said to Shea in Spanish, "Why do you come here, Hair of Flame?"

Socorro couldn't be sure, but she thought he was one of the warriors who'd been with Mangus. Her heart came into her throat as she saw other men appearing along the ravine, some with bows, a few with rifles.

"I would speak with Mangus Coloradas," Shea said calmly.

"That is good." A flicker of amusement showed in the Apache's dark eyes. "He would speak with you to know why you have left your place to come into his."

Turning, he led the way.

The camp was in a meadow ringed by cholla-covered slopes and watered by a spring that trickled down from the mountains. Conical brush shelters, about a dozen of them, were set up near mesquites grown large and wide-branching because of the water. Naked children dodged about with squeals and laughter.

Mules and horses grazed at the edge of the meadow, and older boys were practicing with bows and arrows, wrestling or, on horseback, charging imaginary foemen with lances clasped in both hands, controlling their mounts with their knees and legs.

Girls of that age helped their mothers with the cholla bud harvest, some collecting buds, knocking them into baskets with forked sticks, others rolling them about in baskets with small bits of sandstone in order to clean off the innumerable thorns, and a large number busy at large pits where they were layering, on top of a bed of hot coals, saltbush, cholla buds, hot stones, buds, hot stones, and so on till the top of the pit was covered with a very thick layer of saltbush with earth on top.

Buds that had already been through this baking lay drying in the sun, protected from dirt by more saltbush. This had been the next food chore that Tjúni had planned. It looked even more laborious than preparing agave.

As Socorro took in all this, she was watching intently for Mangus. He was not among the warriors who'd followed them in and now stood lazily about.

"May we water our animals?" Shea asked their guide. The long-haired warrior nodded and took off Viejo's pack while Shea and Socorro unsaddled. They were watering their horses, Viejo slurping blissfully beside them, his still hairless scars from the mountain lion vibrating up and down, when a giant figure strode down a slope.

He had a deer over his shoulder. When he reached the camp, he let it drop. Several women came up to take charge of it while Mangus looked carefully at his guests.

"Why have you left your valley, Hair of Flame?"

Shea's eyebrow shot up. "I had never understood that we could not leave it, Great Chief."

Something glimmered in Mangus's eyes. "No. But you are safer in the place known to be under my protection." His massive shoulders made a dismissing gesture. "Now you are in my camp, you are safe as if at your ranch. Come, rest, have food and drink. Your woman will sit with us. She is valiant and to be honored."

They sat on fiber mats beneath the largest mesquite. Luz, Mangus's niece, her face even handsomer now that it was no longer bruised and bleeding, murmured a greeting as she brought *atole*, corn gruel, and gourd bowls of a fermented drink so fiery that Socorro took one swallow and choked.

"*Tiswino*," Mangus explained, looking somewhat hurt at Socorro's involuntary reaction. "Good brew, this, with much brown sugar from Chihuahua."

Socorro didn't want to think of how he'd got it and was glad when he appropriated her portion and Luz came back with joint fir tea.

"Now, Hair of Flame," said Mangus. "Why have you come?"

He listened quietly. When Shea finished, he said, "If only miners came and took the ore, it would not matter. But they would bring families. Soon there would be a fort, bad white men selling poison liquor, maybe even a refuge for scalp hunters as the Santa Rita mining village was."

"If you allow the mining," Shea countered, "I will

183

undertake that no families are brought in, no whiskey-selling riffraff. And you may have gifts from the supplies. Cloth, brown sugar, wheat, serapes."

"Guns? Powder and ball?"

"Can you promise they would be used only to hunt or to defend?"

Mangus made an exasperated sound between his teeth. "Can I promise the sun will shine just enough to bring the crops but not burn them?"

"You may have any other goods of the *conductas*. And the miners will have only a few guns for hunting. They will know they are in the country only by your favor."

"You admit that?"

Shea laughed. "How can it be otherwise?"

"I will talk to my people," Mangus said. "Tonight you will have your answer. Tomorrow you may go." He rose, considered for a moment. "Come with me, Hair of Flame, to answer questions. My niece and wives will see to your woman."

"Thank you," said Socorro. "But I would just like to watch what's done with the cholla buds so that Tjúni won't find me so useless when we gather ours."

"That woman of the Desert People?" Mangus asked, benignly looking down at Socorro from his great height. "Her name means 'saguaro fruit' but she is more like the spines!"

Smiling at his own joke, he went off with Shea toward a knot of men.

Socorro watched the work at the baking pit awhile. Now and then a woman glanced curiously at her. Socorro would smile. Usually they smiled back. Not always.

One unsmiling woman had a mutilated nose. Socorro had heard that, or death, was the punishment for an adulterous woman. Unnerved, Socorro moved next to where the buds were being dethorned in the baskets where they were rolled about with sandstone.

Just watching the tedious labor made her sigh. She

secretly hoped Tjúni wouldn't insist that they prepare vast quantities of buds.

Surely their crops would produce enough to lessen dependence on wild foods. It was priceless to know what these were, where to find and prepare them, but when they made up most of the diet, a woman's life was filled with simply locating and preparing them. In the desert so much time and effort went into the struggle to get enough food that there wasn't much energy left for other things.

Ruefully turning away, Socorro stared with shock into gray-blue eyes that watched her from the brown face of a small girl with yellow, yellow hair. Dirty as it was, the color shone through. On her back she carried a cradleboard which barely cleared the ground and into this was laced a big dark-skinned baby with the same startling eyes.

They couldn't be Apache. Well, the baby might be mixed, but the girl—she was certainly American or of Europe. Socorro was no good judge of children's ages, having not been much around them, but she guessed this one at six or seven.

Scrawny, dirty, dressed in a cotton rag so filthy that it had no discernible color, the child had something arresting about her, a toughness, a defiant sadness, that touched Socorro.

Testing the English Shea had taught her, Socorro asked softly, "Who are you?"

The girl's eyes dilated, then narrowed to pinpoints. She whirled away but she couldn't move fast because of the cradleboard and Socorro was beside her quickly.

"Do not be afraid." Socorro tried desperately to think of the right words. "I want to be your friend."

"Why?"

"You don't look happy."

No response. "Brother?" Socorro asked, pointing at the baby who watched her out of those strange pale eyes. His hair was black and straight, his skin coppery.

"Yes, brother," said the girl, adding in a burst of

pride, "He's very good when I take care of him." Her words were hesitant as if it were hard to remember them.

"That is a big help to your mother."

The thin shoulders jerked. In a choked voice the girl muttered, "She's dead. It was in the mountains."

"I'm sorry."

"I'm not. Juh's wives can't hurt her now."

This was not a child to cuddle and croon over, though her very prickliness and unseasonable maturity made Socorro long to do that. "Do you know who you are?"

The girl shot her a scornful blue glance. "Of course. Mama told me to say my name every day, my brother's, too, and practice talking so I wouldn't forget." She sighed a little. "Sometimes I don't but most days I remember."

"Will you tell me your name?"

"Talitha. Talitha Scott. I was born in 1840." As if saying it warmed her and caused pain at the same time, Talitha's voice softened. "My brother is James." She looked at Socorro. "Mama always hoped some white people would come help us get away. Will you?"

"I will do all I can." Socorro vowed silently to take the children even at the risk of life. The little girl wrenched her heart. "I'm sure my husband will, too."

"He's that lovely red-haired man with Mangus?"

Socorro laughed and for the first time dared to lightly touch the girl's hair. "He *is* lovely, isn't he? And kind." She sobered. "What if Juh will let you go but wants to keep your brother, his son? Would you come?"

The child shook her head, moved quickly away. "No! I won't leave James!"

A sullen-looking woman called something at the girl who broke step with Socorro but gazed wistfully at Shea. "I *think* my daddy looked like that." At a shriller order from the woman, Talitha moved away, but her eyes clung to Socorro's.

"We'll find you," Socorro promised. "Take good care of James."

The woman who'd called the girl took the cradle-board and propped it against a tree, sent the baby's sister running off on some errand. One of Juh's wives who'd been unkind to Talitha's dead mother?

It seemed wise to learn as much as she could before taking her request to Mangus, so Socorro looked around for Luz who was out gathering buds.

At Socorro's questions, Luz frowned and concentrated on knocking a formidably thorn-guarded bud into her basket. "Juh's wives would be glad enough to be rid of the children, even the boy who is his son. But I do not think Juh will let the boy go. He was very fond of the mother and her blue eyes, perhaps because his grandmother was a blond Spanish captive."

"The little girl loves her brother. I think she wouldn't leave without him!"

Luz's glance said eloquently that was none of her concern and should be none of Socorro's. "What do you know about the mother?" Socorro persisted.

The white woman, whose hair had been fair as her daughter's, had been captured a year ago last fall, shortly after many soldiers with wagons marched from Santa Fe, the same ones that had stopped at Tucson and passed on through the land of the Yumas even further west, who could know where?

It was thought the woman's husband was with the soldiers but no one really cared. The two older men with her were killed and Juh claimed the woman. He valued her though she cried a great deal, even after her fine baby was born, and even though she was impossibly clumsy at cooking and other chores. Juh's wives were sorely tried with her and treated her as viciously as they dared without attracting Juh's attention.

"I will talk to Juh's wives for you," Luz offered. "Perhaps they can persuade him that the little boy, who is not a year old yet, is likely to inherit his mother's poor health and be a problem, especially if something happened to his sister who spends her time caring for him. Juh almost sold the girl last winter to a white slave trader who liked her hair."

"*Sold* her?"

"Why, you must know that children—and others—are sold," shrugged Luz. "Apache children, women stolen to sell to Mexicans, the same with Navajo. And Apache, Navajo, Ute, Comanche—all sell Mexican captives."

"Then perhaps Juh will sell the girl and let her brother stay with her."

"Perhaps," said Luz, and went back to her work.

Socorro waited nervously by the huge mesquite till the council broke up and Shea came to her. The taut lines of his face relaxed and he gave her hand a squeeze.

"I think they're going to agree, *chiquita!* They'll talk it over and give an answer tonight. Looks like we're going to be part owners of a copper mine!"

"There's something more important," she said, and told him about the little blond girl and her half-brother.

"God's whiskers!" Shea breathed. "Juh was in that bunch I talked with. A real hawk. I can't see him giving his flesh for a white man's rearing."

"Talitha won't come without him."

Slowly, Shea asked, "Are you sure she's unhappy, lass? I've heard that often captives come to like the wild life and refuse to leave it when they have the chance."

"Not this one. She remembers her mother's pain. And she's not wanted by Juh's women."

"Sure, then," he said, flashing the smile she loved that deepened the cleft in his chin, "we must take her with us. Somehow. Guess I'd better go talk to Juh. That's him, with Mangus."

"I'll come with you."

He shook his head. "If Juh gets mad, I don't want you mixed up in it."

"But, Shea, we must convince him we'd take good care of his son. He needs to know what I'm like."

188

Shea frowned. "Maybe you're right. But if he gets ugly, stay out of it."

"We have to get those children."

"My love, we'll do our best, but we can't *take* them in the teeth of this whole boiling of Apaches!" Reading her thought, he said grimly, "Can't steal them, either. The women saw the girl with you. She disappears with the baby, they'd figure that out. Mangus couldn't save us after such a trick, and, as far as Juh's boy's concerned, I couldn't blame him!"

Juh, a stocky man of middle years with an imperious manner even around Mangus, didn't speak much Spanish, which may have been fortunate. Mangus's eyes narrowed as Shea asked for the children.

Before the chief could refuse, Socorro stepped forward. "Great Mangus," she pleaded, "the girl was almost sold to a slave trader. Why can she not be sold to us?"

"The girl is not the trouble. How can you ask an Apache to give up his son?"

Socorro swallowed hard. Mangus loomed above her, Juh's eyes glittered, and she was cold with terror. "The girl loves her brother." It was hard to move her stiff lips. "He's still very small. Juh's wives cannot love him equally with their own children, look after him as well. He might die without his sister."

"Then she must stay."

It took all Socorro's strength and will to persist. "Great Chief, I beg you for this."

Their gazes locked, wrestled. At last, unwillingly, Mangus said, "Your heart is too soft. But it was soft for my people. You would have fought for their lives against the woman of the Desert People. You mean this thing. But it is very difficult."

"Juh could see the boy whenever he wanted to," Socorro offered desperately.

"We would give Juh our own share of the mine profits till he was satisfied with the price," Shea offered.

"*If* there is a mine," reminded the chief.

"If. But we'll be selling some cattle this fall. Juh can have the share of my wife and myself."

"A man does not sell his son." Mangus considered. "The only way would be if he thought you would give the boy more chance of living." The chief's eyes came again to Socorro. "Would you promise to let the boy come live with his father when he's old enough, learn the Apache way?"

"I think we must consent to this," Shea told her softly.

"What is old enough?" Socorro asked.

"Will you bargain on the rim of hell?" Mangus laughed harshly. "When the boy is seven—eight, old enough not to need a woman."

"Supposing he doesn't want to grow up Apache?" Socorro dared. "He is, after all, born of a white woman."

"I will not even say that to Juh," remarked Mangus dryly.

It seemed the most they could hope for. Socorro flinched inwardly to think of explaining to Talitha that she couldn't keep her brother always. But by then the girl would be thirteen or fourteen, changing to woman, ready in a few years to marry. James might have become more aggravation than joy.

Anyway, there was no better hope.

"You will give up the boy when he is asked for?" insisted Mangus. "Without this word, I would not ask Juh such a thing."

Shea's eyes helped Socorro. "Yes. We will give him."

Mangus turned to Juh. He spoke rapidly, lifting a hand when Juh recoiled, swung toward the guests. Mangus's raised voice checked the warrior who listened reluctantly.

When Mangus paused, Juh hurled an angry response, would have spun away, but Mangus called him back, rapped out several questions.

Juh scowled. The muscles in his jaws worked, but at last, with ill grace, he muttered something which

Mangus seized upon. After a few minute, Mangus explained to the O'Sheas. "Juh says he has beat his women but they indeed do not like the boy. One nursed him under threat for a time after the mother died, but then claimed she had not enough milk for the white woman's child and her own. The boy would have died, Juh admits, if his sister hadn't fed him ground piñon nuts in water with honey, the way Luz showed her. He knows the boy may die without a mother but that might be better than giving him to whites."

"He's a strange father," Shea said levelly, "to prefer a dead baby to a healthy seven-year-old."

Mangus must have repeated this almost exactly for Juh's eyes blazed. He stared at Shea, hating, measuring. At last he gave a bitter laugh, spoke quickly and watched Shea with malice.

"He says he must know if his son's foster father is a brave man," said Mangus. "He says, Hair of Flame, that the brand on your cheek is sometimes given to cowards."

The scar stood out whitely as the muscles in Shea's jaw contracted. "Does Juh want to fight me? I will, any way he chooses."

Mangus frowned. "You are a fool! If he picked lances—"

"I'll show him in any manner he wants that his son will not grow up with a coward."

Again, Mangus faced Juh. After a few exchanges, Juh smoothly proposed something that brought angry remonstrance from the other. Juh shrugged stubbornly, repeated some gutturals and waited.

Mangus spread his hands, turning to Shea. "Fighting is easy. He would have another thing. If you will be branded again, bear a brand for his son, you may keep him till he is old enough to join his father."

"Branded?" Socorro gasped. "No! That's cruel; there's no sense in it!"

Juh smiled stonily at her, enjoying her distress. Mangus stood broodingly, his gigantic presence a force immobilized by his conflicting loyalties. "There has to be another way," Socorro entreated Mangus.

"It is Juh's price."

Shea had listened as if stunned, blue-gray eyes dilating. Now they narrowed. He braced himself as if drawing strength from the hard earth. "Where's the iron? Let's get it done."

Mangus jerked as if his own flesh had been seared. "My friend, don't do this! The cub's not worth it, not to you! Do not forget he'll come back to the Apache. He cannot be your true son."

"This should not be asked," cried Socorro. "My love, it's too much! We must just hope Talitha can raise him."

"It's she who must come with us," Shea said, glancing toward the little girl who had edged up with her brother and the cradleboard so much too large for her. "And she won't leave him." He smiled and dropped on one knee, smoothing back the tangled yellow hair. "Get your things together, colleen, and your brother's. We'll leave in the morning."

Her face crumpled. "They—they'll burn your face!" Hampered by the cradleboard, she turned as quickly as she could to Socorro. "Go without us," she begged fiercely. "Please, I can take good care of James! We'll stay here!"

"Get your things," Shea ordered. His big hand clasped her thin shoulder, sent her toward the shelters. He said then to Mangus, "I'm ready."

XIV

The broken horseshoe glowed dull red in the flames. Socorro's mouth was parched as she watched, unable to look away. There were no branding irons in an Apache camp, of course, and almost no metal.

One man suggested a musket barrel be heated but that idea was scorned because it might ruin the gun. Someone, though, had the old horseshoe and someone else had made primitive tongs from the fork of a willow strong and flexible enough to grip the iron firmly.

Juh held the tongs. Most of the warriors and many of the women and children had gathered. Luz came up to Socorro, gave her some chunks of pulped, peeled agave leaf.

"Use them quickly. I will have ready a tea that will dim the pain and help him sleep."

Socorro had been too numbed with horror, too full of revolt against this useless torture, to accept that it would be and plan to ease Shea afterward. Luz jolted her back to reality and how to minister to his wound. It was something to hold to.

Brands *did* heal. Shea had survived one along with a flogging; he'd survived the thirst and despair of the desert. This was terrible; she wished she could bear his agony herself, but he'd live.

When Talitha came close beside her, though, she detested the girl and the brown-skinned blue-eyed baby. This was her fault—and hers, for asking Shea to help them. "You shouldn't see this," she told the child. "Go away!"

But Talitha only hunched her shoulders as if expecting a blow and looked up at Socorro with sorrowful eyes. "He's doing it for us. I—I wouldn't ever have asked to go away if I'd known this would happen."

Socorro's heart melted. "Poor little one!" she said. Kneeling, she put her arm around Talitha, cradleboard, James and all. "It's not your fault. It's Juh. But my husband's strong, the brand will heal, and in time it'll be only a mark of courage."

But now, *now* was Juh's gloating face, the rough crescent of glowing red. Mangus strode over to take the tongs from Juh. "I will do this," he said.

Juh snarled but Mangus's gaze quelled him. That was a mercy, at least. Juh might have purposely bungled, held the iron too long or used it to blind and maim. Mangus would brand, but quickly.

Arms crossed, Shea stood with his head thrown back as Mangus approached. Socorro saw Shea's fingers bite in on his elbows, convulse at the sizzling. The smell of burned flesh made Socorro's stomach twist. She broke into cold sweat and only held on to consciousness by a great effort of will.

Then it was done.

With a shuddering sob, Socorro released the children and hurried to Shea, covering with pulped agave the livid arc that interlaced with the old brand. Sweat stood out on him and his skin looked gray beneath its tan. But he hadn't cried out or retreated from the iron.

"Go to my wickiup and rest," Mangus told him. "You are brave enough to rear an Apache!"

The tea Luz brought put Shea into a sound sleep. "He may have strange dreams with strange beasts and colors," said Luz. "Too much of this can kill. But used with care it dulls pain and brings rest. I'll give you enough to get your man through the next bad days. And I'll see that the children are ready in the morning." She paused at the entrance of the wickiup. "The men will decide about the mines tonight. I think they'll all say yes because your husband is so brave."

Socorro thanked her, but looking down at Shea who

moved in his drugged sleep and moaned, she loathed the thought of the mines because they had led to this.

Except for an old woman who noiselessly kept to one wall like an aged spider content to slumber in its web, Mangus's household yielded the wickiup to their guests. One of his wives brought food, a gruel of corn, seeds and meat, and Luz fetched some honey for Shea, which she helped Socorro feed him, propping him up so that he wouldn't choke. They gave him joint fir tea, also.

"Be sure he drinks a lot," Luz advised. "It will help keep away fever." As she was leaving, Mangus entered, squatting down at once because of his height.

His lips curved in a sardonic smile as he glanced from his niece to Socorro. "Well, this is the way of it, men hurt each other and women try to heal the wounds. Though I have known some women who enjoyed the wounding, too! When Hair of Flame wakes, you may tell him we accept his offer. The miners can work without hindrance so long as they don't bring in families and erect forts. We ask for a tenth part of each *conducta*'s supplies and agree to take no ball and powder so long as the miners are supplied with only an amount reasonable for hunting."

"Those are good terms," Socorro said, though because of Shea's branding she was now feeling revulsion for the whole enterprise. "You must have argued for my husband."

"Until he took the brand for an Apache child, what I did for him was, in truth, for you." With a curious lightness, Mangus touched Shea's hair which even in twilight was dusky flame. "Now I will call him friend for his own sake."

A hard-bought name. Socorro's eyes filled with tears. When she could see again, Mangus was gone.

The long sleep restored Shea as nothing else could have done. "Some dreams I had, though," he grumbled as Socorro bandaged agave pulp to the burn with a strip of her chemise, finding it difficult to fasten in place without covering one eye. "God's whiskers! Horses with wings, all shades of the rainbow, some with men's faces! And the women!" He grinned, winced as that tugged his cheek. "Lass, you wouldn't believe those women!"

"So that's why you moaned all night!" Socorro scolded. "And I was feeling sorry for you!"

"Skin like velvet," he teased and the devilish gleam in his eyes reassured her that he would be all right. "And their breasts!" He made an expressive gesture with his hands, chuckled at her look of outrage. "Only trouble was, some had three and others four! Confused me something awful!"

"After such a night, can you ride today?" asked Socorro with a sniff.

"My head feels like it might float away." Shea touched it with caution. "Mangus gave me the iron as lightly as he could but it still hurts like hell. Rather ride than sit around, though. Guess I'd better find out if we get to work the mines."

"For a tenth part of the *conductas* and the safe-guards you mentioned. You should talk with Mangus, but let me bring you some food first." She added severely, "I don't think I'll let you have any more of that special tea if it's going to make you dream of beautiful hussies!"

"Let's save it for night," he agreed wickedly. "Can't enjoy such delights properly on horseback."

Relieved that he was well enough in body and spirit to joke, Socorro took his face in her hands and kissed him. "Oh, my love! You were brave." To hold back the tears that threatened to come, she laughed softly, ran her hand over his chest. "Should you moan pleasurably tonight, *mi hombre,* I'll take advantage of your dreams of those so opulent ladies!"

He rested his bright head between her breasts, touching them lightly. "You have just the right number and shape of these, *chiquita.* We'll have to be chaste on the way home because of the children, but wait till I get you in our bed!"

They stayed like that a moment, more a part of each other than they had ever been, and then were lost in a kiss when Luz called from outside that she had brought their breakfast.

Talitha had a worn rag doll her mother had made before their capture, a tattered *Book of Mormon* and a pair of moccasins Luz had given her. For a blanket, she had what looked like an old roan cowhide.

Besides his cattail-down stuffed cradleboard, James had a leather ball and a small gourd rattle that he liked to flourish. Luz had equipped him for the journey with a supply of the soft inner bark of the cottonwood to place between his legs so that he wouldn't foul his cradleboard, and there was a supply of piñon nuts and honey with which to concoct his "milk."

Absurdly small, Talitha sat behind Shea, clasping his waist as best she could. James was on Socorro's back and the cradleboard was such a convenience, leaving her arms free, that she decided she'd have something like it for her baby.

She'd seen very little of babies but James didn't howl as the others had all seemed to, and he watched what went on with alert interest when he wasn't sleeping. A baby must like this closeness to its mother and being in the middle of things.

With Viejo behind them, they said their farewells and left the Apache camp.

Talitha, during their stops, changed James's linings and fed him. Both children had lice but Socorro was too weary to do much about it even had she known a remedy. When they got home, they'd all have to sleep outside till they got rid of the tiny gray pests. Meanwhile, imagination made her feel that she was crawling with them.

Shea thought the burn might heal faster now without a poultice so she only applied a little mesquite gum softened with water and made his tea from the crumbled white flowers Luz had given her. He drank this after their meal of pinole and jerky. Socorro had been too tired and absorbed in Shea to pay much attention to the children but when she saw that Talitha, cuddling James, was sitting a long way from camp, a lonely little figure in the deepening night, she felt a wave of contrition.

Going up to her, she knelt and put her arm around the thin shoulders. "What's the matter, child? Surely you don't already want to go back to Juh?"

Those blue eyes caught enough of the last light to confound Socorro as the girl put James down on the cowhide to kick in happy nudity. "Do you wish we'd stayed?" she asked bluntly.

"No!" Shamed, Socorro hugged the child against her. "You're our family now!" When Talitha's body stayed rigid, Socorro teased gently, "It's wonderful to get children who're already here. Much less trouble!"

"But we *were* trouble," Talitha whispered. "You— you must hate us! The way they burned him—"

"Hush!" Socorro stroked the matted hair, letting the child cry. "Shea is now James's father in a very special way."

"He didn't do it for James." Misery almost stifled Talitha's voice. "I heard him. He did it for me."

"He thought you were worth it," Socorro said, but Talitha clung to her and sobbed as if her heart would break.

Astounded and dismayed at the tempest that had been building up in the girl, Socorro let her cry, casting about for a way to ease her burden. When Talitha's weeping gradually subsided into hiccoughs, Socorro said softly, "Would you like to know a secret?"

Talitha peered up. "A—a secret?"

"Something even my husband doesn't know," Socorro assured her.

Talitha scrubbed an arm across her face and sat up, beguiled. "What?"

"I'm going to have a baby. Next fall. I hope you can love it half as much as you do James, and help me take care of it. Will you?"

"A baby?" Talitha echoed, shrinking away. "Then you won't need us at all!"

"Didn't your mother need you more than ever when she had James?"

"Well . . ." Talitha considered.

Socorro pressed her advantage. "My baby's lucky to have both a big sister and brother. Wouldn't you have liked that?"

"I don't know. I think I like being oldest."

"A good thing, since you are!" Getting to her feet, Socorro said briskly, "It's time we went to sleep. You and James had better sleep between us so you won't roll off into some cactus!"

Remembering that lice were supposed to be decimated by ants, she found an anthole and put the cowskin over it. Shea was already asleep when she spread out a blanket and put James closest to his broad back. Talitha lay between Socorro and her brother.

"Mother used to kiss us good night," the girl said.

"And I'd like to. May I?"

Talitha held up her arms, but only allowed herself an instant's cuddle before presenting James who wriggled sleepily. "He needs the most loving. He's little."

And half-Apache, promised to go back to Juh in six or seven years. As well love a wolf cub destined to return to the wilds. But he *was* little and the only mother he had was Talitha who needed one herself.

Socorro held the baby in her arms till Talitha sighed with contentment and nestled against her, too. Soon they were all asleep. And if Shea dreamed of extrabreasted women that night, he didn't moan voluptuously enough to wake anybody up.

They reached Rancho del Socorro at noon the third day. Chuey, Belen and Santiago were just riding in and

199

Santiago raced forward, pulling Noche up soon enough to keep from scaring Castaña and Azul.

"You come safe!" he cried joyously. "But, Name of a Name! What has happened to your face, Don Patrick? And what is that you have?" He sprang down, with his gliding limp, to hold their bridles.

Belen, unbidden, came to help Socorro, taking the cradleboard so she could dismount. "What is this?" He echoed Santiago's last question, broad face hardening as he stared disbelievingly at the baby in the Apache cradleboard.

Talitha, set on the ground by Shea, ran up to claim her brother. She probably hadn't understood the Spanish, but there was no mistaking what the bandy-legged Yaqui thought. He yielded James to the fierce little yellow-haired girl and turned to Shea in bemusement.

"It has blue eyes but that is an Apache cub. What will you do with him?"

"He will be our son." Shea's long hand curved around Talitha's shoulder. "And this is our new daughter, Talitha."

Briefly, he explained. Tjúni had come out in time to hear and looked even more disapproving, if possible, than Belen. "Girl of your blood," she said. "That Apache—he never anything else!"

Santiago laughed challengingly, dropped to one knee beside Talitha and offered the baby his finger. James laughed and gripped it, smiling sunnily up, those pale eyes so strange in his coppery face beneath the black shock of hair.

"I'm almost as much Apache as this child," said the vaquero, tawny eyes sweeping from Tjúni to Belen and Chuey. "He will be my godson. A good vaquero."

Shea slowly shook his head. "Don't count too much on that, my friend. The father let us take him only if we would give him back when he's old enough to manage without a mother."

Santiago still kept one arm around Talitha but he

slowly withdrew his finger from the baby's clutch. "Better you had left him."

"The girl wouldn't come without him."

Looking at her puzzled, frightened face, Santiago asked, "Does she know? That her brother must go back?"

Socorro gave a cry of shock, realizing that probably Talitha did not since she seemed not to understand Spanish, and that had been the parleying tongue. Unthinkable to let her believe she'd have James always. She must be told, soon.

Tjúni's eyes had never left Shea's brand. "Your face?" she demanded. "Why?"

Shea flushed. "I—Mangus—" He couldn't bring himself to tell of Juh's price, so, defiantly facing Tjúni, Socorro did.

The Papago girl trembled with outrage. "You—you let your man take hot iron for that?" she hissed, spitting toward James.

Shea said sternly, eyes like blue flame, "There was no *letting,* Tjúni. It was the price. We'll talk no more about it! The children are ours now and though James may not stay that way, we'll treat him so." His glance flicked from her to Belen and Chuey. "Anyone who cannot accept this had better leave the ranch."

Santiago, still kneeling, again proffered his finger, chuckled as James seized it. "Ay, godson, from now on I shall call you Jaime which is easier to say! Hurry and grow big enough to swing a rope!"

Only then did Shea say that their journey had been successful, that Mangus would allow the mines. When Alejandro returned with Don Narciso's almost certain agreement, that message could be taken back and the mines could reopen. It was exciting but Socorro felt somewhat dazed as she carried James into the house while Talitha kept close to Shea.

For so long, there'd been only herself and Shea, Tjúni and Santiago. Now, suddenly, there were vaqueros, a mining operation, two children, and next fall she'd have her own baby! She hoped she could keep up with it all.

As they entered, Shea stopped her, turning her to meet his kiss. "Welcome home, my love," he said. The look in his eyes brought a rush of warm honey through her. He added under his breath, "God's whiskers! It's more than time we got back to our own bed!"

She blushed but her blood sang. He was her love, her husband, the very heart of her existence. Starting from that, all other things fell into place, so it was really very simple. She bent to kiss Talitha and welcome her to her new home.

Talitha, with her bright hair now washed and brushed and her swift little birdlike body, soon became a favorite of all the men though it was Shea she clung to like a shadow when she wasn't helping the women. Even Tjúni had to grudgingly admit that she never shirked as they collected, dethorned and roasted cholla buds, then dried them further for storing.

She still carried James around, and the cradleboard banged her thin shanks, but as she gradually came to trust Socorro and saw that Tjúni, though dourly unaccepting of the baby, wouldn't hurt him, she was usually content to leave him in their care when her duties were finished and she could run off to find Shea. She was learning Spanish now and Belen, who plainly adored her, was teaching her some Yaqui. No one suggested that she practice Apache though it might well have been useful.

"We have to tell her that Juh's going to take James," Socorro worried to Shea as they lay one night in the tender exhaustion that follows lovemaking.

"It's six or seven years off, *chiquita*. Maybe the ugly bastard'll get killed before then. Or have enough full Apache sons to forget about this one."

She touched the puckered scar ridged across the earlier one. "We can hope that," she sighed. "But she ought to know."

"Borrowing trouble," Shea grunted, fitting Socorro into the curve of his shoulder. "Never mind, then! I'll try to find a way to tell her."

It was next day while Tjúni and Socorro were gathering the inner leaves of cattails to use the tender white lower part, when Talitha came running, splashing heedlessly in the marsh.

"Is it true?" she panted, catching at Socorro's skirt. "Is it really true?"

Socorro dropped her leaves in the basket and led the child to solid ground. "It's true that the only way we could get James at all was to promise Juh might have him later."

"You—you had no right!"

"We had to do something. Would you rather have stayed with the Apaches?"

"No, but—it's not fair! Juh hasn't got any right to my brother!"

"According to Apache ways, he did."

Talitha huddled into herself for a moment. Her mouth twisted and when she looked up at Socorro, her eyes gleamed with unshed tears. "Then Shea—" (for some reason she refused to call him Father) "was branded like that for *nothing?*"

"It isn't nothing that you're here," Socorro said firmly. "And you must know that James has a better chance of growing up."

Talitha was quiet for several minutes. Then she said savagely, "I hope Juh dies before James is big enough to go to him! Every day I'll ask our mother to make that happen!"

"Talitha!" Shocked at such implacability in a child, Socorro tried to put an arm around her but she resisted, tiny face severe.

"I—I don't blame you or Shea," she said at last, rubbing splattered mud off her arms. "You did the best you could."

"We did," agreed Socorro, indignant when she remembered Shea's ordeal, though she also felt for this strange little girl, forced to grow up much too fast. "It's a long time till James is seven. Juh might keep him a short time and decide he isn't a very good Apache, let him come back to us. Anyway, let's take good care of him now."

Talitha nodded. As she trudged away, her thin shoulder blades thrust against the dress Socorro had made for her from one brought from the Cantú rancho. The bruises from the kicks and pinches of her foster mothers had faded and applications of diluted juice from black walnut hulls had rid both her and James of lice, but there was no way to give her back her childhood.

That evening Socorro was surprised to hear her talking to James in what was neither Spanish nor English. "What are you telling him?" Socorro asked.

"I'm teaching him Apache."

"Surely it's a bit early to worry about that!"

"I'd forget if I waited." Talitha gave Socorro a straight blue look. "I don't want him to be like I was, not knowing what's being said, getting cuffed around when he blunders." She added grimly, "But I'm asking Mother to get rid of that nasty old Juh!"

When Socorro told Shea, he laughed admiringly. "She'll manage, that one! The Apaches don't have a chance!"

Socorro frowned and sighed. "It's not right for a seven-year-old to be so hard, so *tough*."

"She didn't have much choice if she wanted to live and look out for her brother."

"I know, but—"

"She'll be all right. Laughs and skylarks with the men, loves horses. Belen's even teaching her to rope." Shea kissed Socorro's throat and eyes, nuzzled her ear. "Stop fretting about her, *chiquita,* and pay some attention to me."

Alejandro had brought back Don Narcisco's agreement on the mines and executed documents conveying the northern *sitios* to Shea. Returning, he carried back news of Mangus's terms so before long the mines, abandoned for two decades, should be back in operation about forty miles southeast.

Following Alejandro by a few days had been Pedro Sanchez, the vaquero formerly so attached to this region. A small wrinkled monkey, he and his billowingly endowed wife, Carmencita, had somehow produced two exceedingly pretty daughters. Anita, small and delectably rounded, whom Chuey immediately began to court with wild flowers and languishing; and Juana, tall and slender, with a face as tenderly sweet as the madonna's in the shrine above the door.

The youngest of the two sons was Natividad, called Tivi, gangling and not yet at his full growth though he was a good vaquero. Tivi had very white teeth, a broad face and broad smile, and exuded an air of good-natured innocence in contrast to his slightly older brother, Güero.

Güero had to be the result of some passing foreigner's seeking comfort with Carmencita, though all the Sanchezes treated him as fully one of them. His red-gold waving hair and green eyes were arresting against his brown skin and he moved with arrogance. When his family presented itself to their employers, he swept off his sombrero before Socorro but his eyes were speculative and his mouth curved as if with a secret derision.

She was glad he wouldn't be living at the main ranch. In order to better keep track of the cattle and gradually claim the many wild ones foraging within the far-flung boundaries of the ranch, they had decided to establish another center at El Charco on the south. The Sanchezes would live there, Pedro as foreman or *caporal* for the area, though the vaqueros would, of course, shift around as needed.

"It's good to know there are other people, especially some women, not terribly far away," Socorro remarked to Tjúni after the Sanchezes had departed for their new location. "We won't see them much but just knowing they're there makes a difference."

Tjúni looked dour. "That Güero has bad eyes, Natividad is stupid, and those women—" She snorted. "Glad they gone!"

That didn't sound very promising for the hope that the Papago girl might find a husband among the vaqueros. Belen was old for her and Chuey enamored of Anita. As for what Santiago had thought of Juana, it was impossible to tell.

Whether matchmaking prospered or not, there were enough men to at least start to pull in the wild horses and cattle. This fall as much of the stock as possible would be branded and the scraggier specimens culled for the drive to market.

And this fall Socorro's baby would be born. She had still not told Shea. There was much work to do and she suspected that he'd try to pamper her.

Cactus was in bloom now, and Tjúni said that in the lower desert saguaro would be wearing the white flowers that looked so ridiculously small perched on their great tubular growths. When the flowers ripened to red sweet fruit late in June, it would be worth a trip to gather them.

The crops were growing well and sometimes they had green shoots of corn stewed with tiny squash and *nopales,* the tender young pads of the prickly pear. The green bloom spikes of cattails could be boiled now and Tjúni said that before long they'd be covered with the thick rich golden pollen that could be cooked by itself with water or mixed into mush, soup or bread. "Strong food," she called it. "Very sweet."

In June, when the *conducta* reached the mines, the manager, Don Elizario Carvajal, rode to Rancho del Socorro to invite the proprietors to come and select what they wanted.

"Mangus Coloradas was waiting on us," Don Elizario admitted with a flash of teeth beneath his neat mustache. He was such a mountainous man that one felt sorry for the horse that carried him, but his bulk was hard, not flabby. "As agreed, we gave him a tithe of everything but powder and ball." He chuckled. "The savages seemed pleased, though I think they missed the zest of ambushing us and winning their luxuries by force."

Shea grinned. His second branding was a darker crescent over the white seam of the D. "We'll be mightily glad to get our sugar and wheat without a fight!" he assured the manager.

He and Santiago accompanied Don Elizario back to the mines several days later and returned with two pack mules laden with what amounted to treasure: salt, cones of hard brown sugar, wheat, needles, thread, bolts of heavy material for making trousers, bolts of blue and red cotton for dresses, iron pots, two saws, two hammers and nails.

There were also things that Shea had especially requested: the chocolate that Socorro missed so much with cinnamon to stir into it and a grooved wooden whirler to make it froth; coffee, the only thing he'd liked about the U.S. Army; hand-crafted boots for Santiago, and the softest of fine wool rebozos for Socorro and Tjúni, Tjúni's a rich golden-yellow, Socorro's heaven blue to replace the one used so rigorously during their ordeal in the desert.

That seemed so long ago and yet it was less than a year. Socorro realized with shock, as she reveled in what came out of the packs, that a year ago, sheltered in her father's comfortable home in Alamos, she would've taken all these now-luxuries for granted. It also seemed to her that she hadn't been alive.

Part of that was because she hadn't met Shea but more of it was because, surviving first in the desert and now in this high valley, she'd learned to live on what was available, had confidence that she could meet challenges that would have terrified the pampered merchant's daughter.

She smiled at Shea as he wrapped the blue shawl about her. "We're so lucky," she murmured. "So lucky!"

He thought she was speaking of goods from the

conducta, tightened his embrace. "Just wait, Mrs. O'Shea!" he promised. "One of these days, you're going to have rings on your fingers, jewels at your throat, satins and silks——"

"Burro redhead!" she broke in laughing, then clung to him as suddenly, within her, she felt the baby move, like the stirring of a hand.

It wasn't the way she'd planned to tell him, in the middle of day, in front of the others, but the quickening of the child made real what had been only her secret. She wanted him to know. Bringing his head down, she whispered in his ear. He put her away from him, staring.

"Our baby moved? What baby?"

"The one that will be born in October. Oh, Shea, let's have a boy with your eyes and gorgeous hair!"

"You're bringing me in on this a little late, madam, to be so fussy," he growled before he yelped with consternation. "God's whiskers! Here you've been riding horseback, lugging James around, bending over those marshes, working in the crops! Maybe"——his eyes widened in horror——"maybe what you thought was the baby quickening was the start of a miscarriage!"

"You *are* a redhead burro!" she flung at him. "I never felt better in all my life! I *have* been careful! Did I ask to go along to pick out things from the *conducta?*"

Tjúni said decisively, "Women of Desert People work till baby come, work again next day. Woman making baby not invalid!"

"My mother worked, too, but it sure didn't help her!" Shea bent a stern look on Socorro. "Promise me clear that you'll stop lifting heavy stuff, bending over, stretching up——"

He paused for breath and she glared at him. "Anything else?" she inquired dangerously.

"That you'll rest when you're tired!" he finished. He appealed to Santiago since Tjúni was watching him with wonderment and scorn, "Can you think of anything else she shouldn't do?"

"I can think of several things you'd better stop!" Santiago chuckled. But his golden eyes softened as he said gently to Socorro, "I would agree that your husband, señora, *is* a burro and indisputedly a redhead! But should you not humor him? It is, after all, his first child. So far as we know."

Socorro had to smile reluctantly and Santiago went on coaxingly, "The first child born at Rancho del Socorro is special to all of us. *Por favor,* lady, guard it well for your friends." He added piously, "In return, we'll pray that the merciful God will bless the baby with your looks, not those of your ugly husband!"

She gasped with indignation, saw from the gleam in Santiago's eyes that he was deliberately arousing her in behalf of Shea, and subsided in a helpless sputter. But Talitha confronted Santiago like a small yellow wildcat.

"Don't you call Shea ugly! He—he's beautiful!" Whirling to Shea, she caught his arm. "I'll watch Socorro for you, be sure she doesn't hurt herself! Don't worry, Shea. The baby will be fine!"

The grown-ups blinked. Then Shea said gravely, "Thank you, Talitha. I'll depend on you. And that reminds me. . . ."

Shaking out one of the lengths of cloth, he produced a doll dressed elegantly in dark blue silk, wearing a lace mantilla and holding a fan. There was a tiny gold chain about her neck and the head was china, carefully painted in lifelike tones, rooted with real black hair.

Talitha gazed at it in disbelief, didn't move to take it even after Shea held it out to her. "It's yours," he said, puzzled. "Don't you like her?"

"My—my hands are dirty," she stammered and then ran to wash. Only then would she take the doll. She held her with reverence while Shea unearthed one last indulgence, a jug of mescal, and proposed they all drink to the coming child.

"To the heir of Rancho del Socorro!" toasted Santiago.

Shea shook his head. "No. That will be your son."

"What son?" shrugged Santiago and his gaze veered, as if involuntarily, to Socorro, before he grinned at Shea. "We've shared the dangers and work. We own the land equally, the share from the mines. No need to divide yet, so long as all are content. But Mangus's debt to Socorro is the only reason we're still alive, that we hold this ranch. Her child has claim to the home place."

"No!" she protested. "That's not right, Santiago!"

"It *is* right. My children, if I have some, can have El Charco."

"And mine?" asked Tjúni.

Both men looked blank. "Why, you'll be staying with us, won't you?" fumbled Shea.

"No." Tjúni's face was expressionless as she glanced at Socorro. "I stay till you have baby, till you strong again. Then I move to western side. Maybe a few Papago families settle near." Her slim brown hand, flattened, moved in rejection. "Furniture, Apache brat, mines, lots of people—no place for me now!"

"But Tjúni!" Socorro objected. "You can't just go off by yourself!"

"Can."

"If you won't stay with us, at least let us get you settled with your own people," Shea argued.

The Papago girl smiled suddenly. "Yes. You do that! Find two, three, four Papago families to live on my land." She nodded. "I like that."

Santiago said feelingly, "It would save much trouble if you married one of the Sanchez brothers."

"Not marry to save you trouble," she told him coolly. To Socorro, she said, "True my people no own land. Move on it with seasons. Belong everybody like sunlight, like air."

Her face tightened and her dark eyes included Shea and Santiago, flicked to Talitha and little James who stared back at her from his cradleboard which was hung on a stout peg. "New time. New people come. I want place not to *own* but for not be driven away from."

"You'll have it," Shea promised. He offered more mescal but the others refused. The celebration was tainted now with the knowledge that their lives were separating, that they had lost the unity of that first isolated season when they depended completely upon each other and were each other's world.

Socorro, Talitha helping, was gathering ears of corn that afternoon for making green corn tamales when she noticed something yellow-gold on the hillside by the burial of the scalps. Tjúni.

Since the other woman's announcement that she meant to live apart, Socorro had felt oppressed and troubled. It wasn't that she was truly fond of Tjúni. She was perfectly aware that the Papago worshiped Shea and saw his wife as a useless encumbrance. But Tjúni was so much a part of their life that it was hard to imagine the ranch without her, a sort of dour, often disapproving teacher-guardian of the wild country, the ageless ways.

It was true that Tjúni had been irritated by developments that outraged her sense of what was right: the mill, furniture, partnering the mines, bringing in more vaqueros, adopting half-Apache James. But Socorro still felt Tjúni's decision was triggered by the fact that Socorro was to have Shea's child.

"You stay with James," she told Talitha, who, faithful to her word, dogged Socorro in a way that would have been maddening if it hadn't been so devotedly earnest and amusing. "I want to talk with Tjúni."

Approaching the slope from the side, she climbed gradually around to the burial grotto. She hadn't been there since the interment though she remembered the rancho and Papago victims in her prayers.

Clearly, Tjúni had been, for the blue necklace she'd claimed from the scalpers' packs lay in one crevice— for the young sister who had not yet become a woman

211

when she was violated and killed?—and there were several bowls and gourds and an offering of bright wildflowers placed in the shallow cave.

Tjúni was staring westward, sun lighting her face in its sullen beauty. She didn't hear Socorro till a rock grated underfoot. Whirling, the Papago girl's eyes glinted briefly with tears before her features were composed again, closed and impenetrable.

"Why you come here? These not your dead."

"I came to see you." Taking a deep breath, Socorro tried to pierce the invisible barriers between them of race, beliefs, rearing, but mostly the deep-rooted hostility of a woman who craves the man of the other. "Tjúni, I hate to think of your leaving. Is—is it because of the baby?"

"Baby?" Tjúni's slim eyebrows raised. "For long time now I know that! Remember, I told you when we bake agave!"

"Then why?"

Tjúni stared at Socorro. It seemed she wasn't going to answer when at last she said harshly, "I think when you big with baby and after it come till you strong, Shea need woman, take me." She swallowed, disappointment and hurt pride making her voice even jerkier. "He worse now! Think on nothing but you! Most men need more than one woman!" She ended fatalistically.

"He different. For him, you only."

So it was said, out between them at last. "I'm sorry for how you feel," Socorro said carefully. "But I'm glad my husband loves me. Wouldn't you have more chance of meeting a man you could care for, Tjúni, if you went to live in one of the Papago settlements?"

"I care for man. No want other."

There was nothing more to say. But as Socorro turned to go, Tjúni's words came after her. "After baby safe come, you no need me. One year, all seasons, I teach you plants, getting food. You know now."

Socorro looked at her, accepting that because of

Shea they could never be friends, yet feeling a deep bond with Tjúni, as strong in its way as love or hate.

"Yes. You have taught me." She tried to lighten the moment. "But you still make the best tortillas."

Going down the hill, Socorro faced the westering sun, the Santa Ritas towering above the valley, the blue, distant mountains. It was the blooming time.

Yellow, white, blue and crimson wild flowers were everywhere and prickly pear and barrel cactus drew bees with yellow, rose and orange blossoms. Along the creek, the reddish willow bark had vanished behind new green and the white trunks of sycamores only showed in spots through new leaves of maple, elm, ash and walnut. Quail were thick in the high grass and a flutter of doves winged up before her.

They reminded her of the birds that had led her to water in the dead volcanoes and lava flows, water that had helped her save a stranger whose flaming hair had seemed the only living thing about him.

He strode forward now to meet her, that hair still a glory, eyes eager and loving. Socorro smiled at him and the child within her stirred as if to greet its father.

PART III

TALITHA

XV

Talitha slowly came awake on her pallet in a corner of the *sala,* luxuriating in the awareness of Shea and Socorro in the next room. James, who slept at the end of their room near the door, was stirring.

If Talitha hadn't roused, one of the grown-ups would have gone to James, seen to his needs. Instead of being hated and neglected as he'd been in Juh's lodging, here he was loved and cared for. Knowing this made Talitha feel as if a weight much heavier than the cradleboard had been eased from her shoulders.

James would be all right now. Even if something happened to her, he'd be all right. Till Juh claimed him?

Mother, Talitha prayed, gazing at the doll Shea had given her which sat enthroned in a niche above her bed because it was much too grand and delicate for play, *Mother! Make Juh die or have him forget all about James. Please keep him away from us. Amen.*

The doll looked a lot more like Socorro than blond Judith Scott, but it was comforting to call her by that name and believe that something of her mother could be reached and kept through the doll. Talitha didn't ask God to deal with Juh, partly because she suspected it was wicked to desire another's death, but more because she didn't think it would do much good.

God was too busy to worry about people, or why would He have let the Apaches shoot her grandfather and uncle full of arrows? Or let mother die when James needed her milk? Either God was too busy or He didn't care. Mother, if she was able, would joggle His attention or do whatever she could, so Talitha pinned her

217

hopes on the human love she'd known rather than divine love she'd heard about but never seen.

She was confused about God anyway. She could remember Nauvoo, the holy city of the Mormons, built on the Mississippi in Illinois. This town, where Talitha was born, quickly became the largest in the state, neat well-built houses with abundant gardens spreading out from Temple Square. Talitha remembered that shining white temple rising on the hill above the river like something in a dream.

But it was never completed. When the prophet Joseph Smith, a man who'd seemed to four-year-old Talitha like a smiling blue-eyed giant, had smashed the press of a newspaper that had been criticizing him, he and his brother had been jailed in Carthage and killed there by a masked mob, in 1844.

Since Mormons didn't use tobacco or drink alcohol or even coffee and tea, they already seemed peculiar to their Gentile neighbors. They had their own militia, the Nauvoo Legion, and the Danites or "Avenging Angels" were feared by outsiders. Hard work made Mormons prosperous and a target of envy. When Smith declared it was righteous to have more than one wife, Gentile hostility swelled till Brigham Young, Smith's successor, started a search for a land far from civilization where the Mormons could build their own kingdom.

The winter Talitha turned five saw Nauvoo turned into a huge wagon-making center because it was going to take twelve thousand of them to move the Saints. Each family was to have a wagon, oxen, two cows, three sheep, a tent, rifle and ammunition, a thousand pounds of flour, twenty of sugar, farm tools, utensils and bedding, when they started out that spring.

But the more violent Gentiles wouldn't wait. They destroyed property and threatened till the people of Nauvoo fled for their lives in bitter February weather, crossing the iced-over Mississippi. They camped in the snow that first night, sleeping in the wagons, and Talitha wept bitterly for her kitten which got lost in the confusion.

During that month, camped about nine miles from Nauvoo, the refugees sold their Nauvoo property for giveaway prices and prepared to travel to a better wintering place. Talitha still remembered how a white flag signaled that Brigham wanted to see all the men; a blue one meant only the captains need gather.

Her father, Jared Scott, had been captain of a hundred, which had made her small chest swell with pride since her friend Samantha's father, though much older, was only captain of ten. Dividing the thousands of people into smaller units, each leader answerable to the one above, with final authority in the Council, made what could have been a tragic disaster into a surprisingly orderly exile.

Some families had escaped Nauvoo with nothing and shared the tents and food of others. In spite of the bitter cold and scarce food, the band played each evening, and Talitha watched her parents, young, lithe and merry, whirl and dip to the fiddler in the blaze of the campfires.

> "I got a gal in the head of the hollow,
> She won't come and I won't follow. . . ."

That music, laughter brave as the fires against the piercing wind, the swirl of her mother's skirts and her yellow head against Jared Scott's reddish one . . . this was one of Talitha's most treasured "remembers." Mother had explained it to her. In order not to forget where you came from and those you loved, you called places and people up to you, closed your eyes and tried to fill in the sounds and smells, brightness of sun, or darkness of night.

"No one can take that from you, Tally," Judith Scott had said before she died. "Remember your father and me. Remember our God. And tell James—"

I'll have to start doing that, Talitha told herself as

she slipped off her pallet and hurried to get James before he woke Shea and Socorro. *Though I don't know what to tell him about God. I never understood much of that. I'll tell James about the temple, I guess.*

Shea's arm was around Socorro and she lay with her face tucked against his shoulder, looking too small to carry the baby that thrust her belly against the coarsely woven coverlet. Seeing them like that gave Talitha a strange, lonely feeling.

They made each other's world. They didn't need anyone else. Talitha had come to love Socorro, but she idolized Shea. When he took the brand for her brother, he became the center of her life. She longed to be necessary to him, do something to make up for what he'd suffered for her sake. So she guarded Socorro, saved her as much bending and stretching as possible, and prayed, also to her mother, to protect Shea and someday let her repay him.

Socorro had made James some diapers from old clothes and a worn sheet from the Cantú rancho. Talitha carried James to her pallet to change him, tossed the diaper in the soaking kettle outside the kitchen door, put a clean long shirt on him, also made by Socorro, and perched on a stump to feed him his mush and watch the faint rose of the eastern sky change to flaming crimson and gold. She had been careful, while getting the cold mush, not to rouse Tjúni who slept in the kitchen.

Tjúni scared Talitha who was very glad the Papago woman was leaving after the baby came, and it wasn't because she was Indian. Except for Juh's wives, most of the Apache women had been kind enough to Talitha, and Luz had actually helped her. But there was something frightening about Tjúni.

There were sounds of breakfast being made now and Santiago came out of the vaqueros' quarters with that gliding limp that made him distinguishable from a long way off. He dropped to one knee, offering a finger to the baby who clutched it tight and laughed with glee.

"Hola, ahijado!" chuckled Santiago. "Godson, you have a grip that will let you rope the wildest bulls and hold them to your dally!" He looked at Talitha's hair with mock horror. "The good God gave you such hair and you don't comb it? Have a care or it'll get so tangled you'll have to be sheared like a sheep!"

"I comb it every day," she told him with dignity. "But James was hungry and I had to feed him first."

"Well, let me take him while you unsnarl that pretty hair." Swept to the vaquero's shoulder, James squealed and drummed his bare heels on Santiago's chest. "You think I'm a horse?" laughed the young man. Holding James securely, he gave some gentle bucks and carried him inside as Talitha ran off to comb her hair and fetch water, her before-breakfast chore.

Late summer was time to plant a second crop of corn, more squash and pumpkins. The small yellow-fleshed melons that ripened faster than they could be eaten were buried in sand which would preserve them for months. After being sun-dried, chunks of squash and pumpkin hung from yucca fibers in the kitchen above the ollas and baskets of corn and beans. Strings of red chilis darkened to maroon as they hung from the *vegas,* the protruding roof logs, and the stock of wild foods grew almost daily. It was too bad they didn't have a cat, though, to get rid of the mice that found their way into the stores.

Reddish-purple prickly pear *tunas,* singed of their spines and dried, were stored in jars. Tjúni had wanted to make an expedition to the northwest to collect saguaro fruit, but had been overruled.

"No use taking a chance of Apaches," Shea said. "Away from the ranch, you'd seem like any Papago. And we've got enough food."

Tjúni had sulked. Gathering the dark red fruit was a high point of the year for her people. The seeds were dried, the pulp boiled down to syrup, and at the end of the harvest, each family contributed juice to be made into wine.

"Use *navai't* in three days or no good," Tjúni explained. "Men very drunk."

"And the women?" teased Shea.

"Women drink some," Tjúni told him austerely. "But stay sober. Look after men."

There were plenty of other foods to be gathered, though. *Jojoba* nuts were roasted and eaten like that or ground to stretch the coffee. Long, curving yucca fruits were roasted in hot ashes, peeled, and the baked pulp spread to dry in the sun. They were sweet-tasting and Talitha never tired of them though they were eaten raw, boiled and baked during their time of ripeness.

Socorro was able to help harvest mesquite beans and hackberries. She insisted they leave some beans for the livestock and wild creatures, but bushels were spread out to dry on the roofs. The men built a small adobe granary where a storehouse was planned, and the cured beans went into this while those that had wormholes or didn't look as if they'd keep were ground into meal for earlier use.

Tjúni and Talitha brought home baskets of small acorns which were stored with layers of ash to prevent worms, and went along the mountainsides to find tiny red squawberries covered with whitish sticky fuzz. These took a long time to gather and Talitha thought they were a lot of work over nothing till she savored the difference they made in joint fir tea, lending a tart tanginess to the rather oily, musty taste. This higher land also yielded currants and chokecherries, while elderberries and grapes could be brought from lower washes and streams.

Talitha had helped Apache women gather many of these wild foods so Tjúni had little chance to scold her. They worked in silence, mostly, companions through necessity, though Talitha already spoke Spanish as well as Tjúni. Talitha was always happy to hurry home and hug James, who was left with Socorro during these excursions.

So autumn came on. Walnuts began to drop. Soon

it would be time to go up in the mountains for piñon nuts, but Shea didn't want Tjúni to be gone overnight till after the baby came, and he and Santiago worked close enough now to get home by sundown.

"I'll be glad when we can have a real rodeo," Santiago grumbled, helping himself to more acorn stew made rich with chilis and beef. "Start from all sides and drive the cattle to that high plain between here and El Charco where they could all be branded and marked at once. A fine sight, Don Patrick, to see the cattle together!"

"Even our little bunches look like a lot of cows to me!" Shea grinned. "We're sure chousing a lot of wild ones out of the brush, and horses, too."

"We'll break some of those this fall," Santiago said. He squinted at Belen and Chuey who, since they didn't talk much, had started their third helpings. "You've been giving Don Patrick or me all your *señales?*"

Both vaqueros nodded. *Señales* were the bits of ear taken out when cows were earmarked and branded. From the early days of the Conquest, cattle owners had been required to so identify their animals and register the marks with the nearest official.

Socorro had told Talitha that the first branding in New Spain had been done by Cortez who burned three tall crosses on his slaves as well as livestock. The Cantú C was registered in Ures, the Sonoran capital, but there seemed no point, during the present chaos, to make that long and hazardous trip in order to make the S and ears notched near the bottom legally recognized.

"The old branded cows of these *sitios* are dead, *naturalmente,*" said Chuey. "We must be branding their grandchildren and great-grandchildren!"

"As well as the descendants of our neighbors' cows," grinned Belen. "But that matters little since the neighbors long ago fled southward or were killed by Apache."

Shea furrowed his brow, pulling figures from his mind. "We've branded about one hundred fifty calves from the herd we brought from the rancho. Figuring some losses, call that bunch three hundred twenty-five. We have *señales* for over five hundred wild ones, and the Sanchezes will have branded some more since turning in their last tally." He paused in disbelief. "We have well over a thousand cattle!"

"Don Narciso has twenty thousand," shrugged Santiago. "But it's a decent start. And there are still lots of wild ones."

"With calves each year," added Belen.

"And to make sure those are good ones, we're culling out the unthriftiest cows and bulls and holding them at El Charco," Santiago said. "When we're through branding, we can sell the scrubs to the mines or Tubac. I hope we don't have to drive them to Tucson!"

Talitha thought of Nauvoo and Temple Square, the comfortable houses with their neat gardens and shady trees. Was Tucson like that? Santa Fe certainly hadn't been. She remembered it as a sprawl of mud buildings around a dusty plaza. Even the Governor's Palace and the cathedral were adobe and Judith Scott had been inexpressibly shocked at the way women bared arms and shoulders and smoked cornshuck cigarettes.

Belen's barrel chest heaved as he laughed. "I wouldn't mind going to Tucson!" he said. "But better I don't. My money would go to cards and drinking."

"Mine wouldn't," said Chuey piously.

"Seguramente!" teased Santiago. "It's going to take more than flowers to convince Anita Sanchez."

"It's not Anita!" Chuey defended, squirming.

His pockmarked face gave him a fierce look, but Talitha had learned that he was kind. Once when she fell off the corral and skinned her knee, he dusted her off and gave her a piece of brown sugar. More importantly, instead of telling her girls didn't belong around vaqueros, he, with Belen, was teaching her to rope.

"Now that Pedro Sanchez is in charge at El Charco, he thinks his daughters should marry better than plain vaqueros," Belen explained. He shook his big head sympathetically. "So my poor friend Chuey will save all his wages and perhaps, when he's seventy, he can marry that pretty little quail."

Glancing at Santiago, who nodded, Shea said, "We think it's fair for you men, who're waiting for your pay till we get some money, to have a bonus. From now on, you can put your own brand on every twentieth one you find. Of course, when they calve, you can brand the yearlings."

Chuey's dark eyes widened. "*I* can have cows?"

Though Shea laughed, there was an undertone of old bitterness in his voice and Talitha remembered that he'd been very poor in that green distant island where he came from. Though how could people be poor in a place where there was water and crops would grow?

"If *I* can have cows," he told the vaquero, "why not you? It's all by the grace of God and the wrath of the Apache."

"Have you thought on this?" Belen asked gravely. "With three Sanchez men branding, they'll get a lot of cattle. And, *patrón,* it would be only human to take a few more or at least to pick the best cattle."

"That's up to you men," Shea said. "Santiago and I think you'll be fair with us, as we are trying to be with you."

Dazzled by the prospect, Chuey dreamed aloud. "Why, I may be a ranchero myself! Anita's father couldn't look down his nose at me then!"

"You'd better stay right where you are," cautioned Belen dryly. "Under Rancho del Socorro's protection, till the Apache are tamed, which may be never!"

"If you marry, we'll build you a house far enough from Belen so his snoring won't bother your bride," offered Santiago. He grinned. "It may be that by the time you're ready to start your own ranch you'll have enough fine sons to spare a couple to work at Socorro."

Shea turned to Belen. "Don't you have a woman you'd like to bring up here?"

Belen's swarthy face creased as he seemed to ponder. "There is no woman—now," he said. "With permission, until there is a change, I'll brand my cows for the *doncellita.*" This was his special name for Talitha. It meant "little maiden."

"No need for that," frowned Shea. "Talitha will have equal shares with our blood children. James, too, if he doesn't stay with the Apache."

Talitha had never thought about such things, or about what would happen to her when she grew up. She didn't want things to change. It was wonderful to live with Shea and Socorro and have James so young that nasty old Juh wouldn't try to take him away.

"I don't need any cows," she said almost desperately. "I just want to stay at the ranch forever and ever!"

Shea laid his big hand soothingly against her cheek, gave a surprised chuckle. "Why, for sure you'll stay, Tally, as long as you want though it won't be many years till you'll draw men like a lode of gold."

She shook her head. There'd never be a young man she'd love as she did him, no face that could have for her the beauty of his branded one. Life without him would be like never seeing or feeling the sun again. She would die in darkness.

He laughed with perplexity, raised a shoulder and let it drop. "All the same, till Belen wants to brand for himself, take what he offers. It won't hurt to have your own herd building."

The next evening Belen, as he came in for supper, produced two narrow inch-long bits of what looked like short-haired leather. "Your first *señales, doncellita.*" He bowed, presenting them to her. "I didn't brand forty cows, but Don Patrick added one so you'd start with a pair."

Talitha stared at the pieces of ear which each represented a cow. It gave her a strange feeling, gratifying, yet with a kind of heaviness, to own something, especially something alive. Shea grinned down at her.

"You're on your way to being a *patrona,* Tally. Your Cross T went on the two best heifers we roped today."

With a bit of charcoal he showed her how the brand

looked, a T with the cross bar lowered slightly. "Like one of Cortez' crosses," remarked Socorro.

"The notch is cut out of the very tip of the ear," added Belen. "When you see one like that from the unbranded side, you'll still be able to tell it's yours."

Tally looked at the *señales*. "If I'm going to have cattle, I should learn to work them. I need to help Socorro till the baby comes, but next fall I want to help with the branding."

"*Doncellita!*" Belen choked with laughter. "Will you wrestle a steer down then, hold him to the ground?"

"I'm not big enough for that yet," she said gravely. "But I can cut *señales* and learn to brand."

She swallowed at the last words, remembering again how the iron had seared Shea's face. But it didn't hurt animals much when properly done, Santiago had assured her, singeing off the hair and burning the thick hide just enough to leave a mark. She straightened her shoulders and gazed up at the three men. "I should learn to do everything. James will be too little to help for a long time and the new baby will be even younger."

"There's going to be plenty for you to do in the house," began Shea, but Santiago cut him off.

"*Bueno!* But such a *vaquerita* must have her own horse." He considered her, challenge mixed with admiration in his golden eyes. "And will you learn also the taming of horses?"

She found the mustangs frightening, But, having decided that if she were going to be treated as a true child of the O'Sheas she must deserve it, Talitha gulped and said, "I'll learn the best I can."

"No one can do more," the vaquero assured her. "Well, then, when we're through with branding, you and your horse can learn together."

"Thank you," said Talitha.

Going into the *sala,* she stood on tiptoe and put the *señales* in the niche beside her doll. Her first cattle!

* * *

All through the winter the men would make sorties into the cañons and mountain valleys to look for more offspring of long-strayed cattle, but by October they'd finished the principal branding. There were thirteen hundred head wearing the S and Tally's pile of *señales* now numbered eight.

The mines wanted a hundred head, and the Sanchezes, with Shea along so his fiery hair would identify them as Mangus's protected whites, drove the other hundred culls to Tubac where they were eagerly purchased. At three pesos a head, there were six hundred silver pesos, and even after the vaqueros were given their back pay, there was a rich clinking in the leather bags stored beneath Shea's and Socorro's bed.

Shea was far from happy, though, with what he'd found at Tubac. "Yanquis!" he growled, as if he didn't look like one himself. "A whole column of U.S. Army dragoons! They say they're just passing through on the way to California, but you can bet they'll be back, or more like them!"

Socorro paled, hand flying to her throat. "Soldiers! Did they—"

He shook his head. "The commander was drunk and trying to seduce a couple of girls. Besides, one thing about Juh's little present, it's blotched the first brand till no one could guess what it was. Guess I can thank him for that since it looks like we're going to have the U.S. Army on the prowl."

"So the presidio was garrisoned?" asked Santiago.

"Mostly with Pimas and Apaches *de paz,* in fact out of the two hundred forty-nine people living around Tubac, I'd guess there to be two or more Indians to every Mexican. While the dragoons were there, this Apache chief from around Tucson gave all the Indians quite a speech about how they must not steal from the Americans or give them any trouble."

"You sound annoyed that the chief didn't urge a massacre," teased Santiago. "Were there any Mexicans or soldiers at Tumacácori?"

"Not a one, but the Pimas are taking care of the church. Poor devils! They must wonder why the Faith was sent to them if they're to have no help in keeping it."

"I wish we could see a priest, too," Socorro said in a way that caused Shea to put his arm protectively around her.

"I wish so, lass, but for the past four years or so the priest from San Ignacio, far to the south, has ridden up when he could get an escort and once or twice a year baptizes and marries people at Tumacácori, Tubac and Tucson. I gave a cow to an honest-looking Pima at Tumacácori and asked him to bring us word next time the priest comes."

Her eyes lit like candles. "Thank you, *querido*. It is true we're married before God and in our hearts, but I wish it could be done by a priest and written in the parish archives. Especially when we will have a baby."

Unnoticed, Talitha blinked at these puzzling words. People couldn't have babies, surely, unless they were married? But she didn't understand the religion of her new family. Catholics, apparently, didn't have enough priests, but among the Mormons, every man in good standing was a priest.

Talitha felt sad and vaguely angry that her adoptive parents seemed to need something from their church which it demanded yet didn't furnish the means of getting. She suddenly decided that she wouldn't tell James very much about the Scotts' religion. Religion just seemed to make life harder. Mormons had been killed and hounded out of different places because of their faith, persecuted by people who had a different one.

But Shea was telling how the presidio feared attacks and how fifteen Tucson soldiers had been killed last summer at a watering hole. It had been two months before their bodies were brought in for burial.

"What you mean is that things are normal," Santiago

shrugged. "I do not love the Yanquis, but if they could stop this raiding, I could wish them here permanently."

"They'll be here soon enough," Shea said grimly and his fingers went to the blotched D on his cheek.

Talitha knew she was American and that her father had belonged to the army which had burned Shea on the face. That had been a wicked thing and she was guiltily ashamed.

How mixed it was! She had to tell James about Nauvoo and Winter Quarters, how pretty Mother had looked dancing. But the man she'd danced with wasn't James's father. And if Jared Scott had been in Mexico he might have been one of the soldiers who'd had to hurt Shea. Talitha was glad that at least that hadn't happened!

So later that day she told James how in March of '46, after fleeing Nauvoo, the Mormons moved on in snow, mud and rain, wagons miring down, axletrees breaking.

"Mother had to sell our feather beds," she said to her dark-skinned blue-eyed brother who lay on a cowhide playing with a cornshuck while she ground mesquite beans for stew. "She traded her big bowls and pretty cups to a farmer's wife for some corn. The people in Iowa were nice, not like the bad ones in Illinois, and they liked to hear our band play. It sounded so pretty, James! Maybe someday you'll get to hear a band."

She thought about that awhile, sighing as she wondered if she herself ever would again, or hear a fiddler, or dance. How lovely to whirl and dip and laugh as Mother had with Daddy! But more and more, when she tried to recall Jared Scott, she saw Shea instead.

"And then, James, after taking a whole month to wade a hundred miles of mud, we came to Mount Pisgah. The main party went on but some of us stayed there and planted inside a big field Daddy helped split rails to fence. There was a big arbor of brush and poles. And that was where Mother danced the last time with Daddy." She paused, frowning with the effort of remembering. "You see, an officer came wanting five hundred of our men to join the army and go fight the Mexicans. Brigham thought that was a good idea since the pay could go to the church and help the Saints get to the Promised Land."

General Kearney had already left Santa Fe when the Mormons got there, but Major Philip St. George Cooke had been sent back to command them and lead them in finding a possible wagon route to California.

"Mother got sick in Santa Fe," Talitha mourned. "And Major Cooke said lots of the men were too old or puny to soldier. He left over a hundred of them in Santa Fe. My uncle and grandfather stayed and when Mother got well, they said we should go with the other Mormons back to Iowa, but Mother cried and said we could catch up with the Battalion it we hurried."

Talitha choked off, seeing again the broken burned bodies of her uncle and grandfather. "Mother didn't dream what would happen, James. You mustn't blame her! She just loved Daddy so much and wanted to find him—"

Which made Talitha wonder. Had her father reached California? Where was he now? The war was over. He'd try to find his family but the most anyone could tell him was that they'd left Santa Fe following the tracks of Major Cooke's wagons.

Talitha felt dimly sorry for Jared Scott but didn't want him to look for her. He belonged to that life when he and Mother had danced. Now Mother was dead and how could her husband want the son of Juh?

Blinking, Talitha cracked more hard mesquite beans and ground them savagely. "James," she said so sharply that he tensed and gave her an inquiring stare. "I'll tell you about our mother and Nauvoo and Mount Pisgah. But not much about Jared Scott. Or that mean old Juh! Shea's your daddy! You don't need anyone else."

XVI

Santiago and Chuey had lassoed the dun *potro* or gelding, got the horsehair hackamore or *haquima* on him, and forcing his head around to his thigh, Chuey took a rounded club and hit the bent neck repeatedly.

Talitha sucked in her breath and slipped into the corral. "Santiago! That hurts him!"

"Get back!" Santiago told her.

He and Chuey pulled the gelding's head the other way and used the club again. Belen, who was watching, put a hand on Talitha's shoulder, steered her back outside the corral gate.

"Listen, *doncellita,* they make the neck sore in order to control the horse more easily. The hackamore, as you see, has no bit, just a noseband. Don't you think a vaquero needs a little help?"

"But—"

Belen led her to his tough little roan who was hitched near the corral. "See, he's rolling the *rodaje* or little wheel with his tongue. It entertains him when he's waiting for me. But look at what's on the other end of the little roller." Belen pried open the roan's mouth to expose the bit, a mouthbar with braces holding what looked like a small spade.

"This is a spade bit, *doncellita.* If one is heavy-handed, it cuts a horse's mouth terribly so we accustom him slowly. He is ridden with first a heavy hackamore, then a light one, till he handles well and learns to work cattle. This may take a year or more. Only then does he have a bit, and that's introduced with great care." Belen released the roan who rolled his eyes at him and went back to tinkling the wheel. "The hackamore reins

233

are tightened some and fastened to a band running around the *potro*'s withers so that he has to arch his neck. The bit is put in his mouth but the reins to it are left loose. He wears the bit about half an hour the first time, and next day keeps it longer. After a while he gets used to the feel and starts playing with the *rodaje*. Only when he's used to the bit is he ridden with it, and the hackamore is still worn for control, its reins tighter than those of the bit, till he can be reined easily."

Talitha shuddered. "I don't want to beat my horse on the neck! Or cut her mouth." She pointed at the dun gelding who was being led around the corral. "He's a grown-up horse, Belen. Wouldn't it be easier to teach a colt?"

"Who has the time?" shrugged Belen. "A horse needs to be about four years old before he's ridden much. He's strong enough then to carry a man's weight and use for roping cattle." Belen grinned at her, touching her hair with his brown hand, scarred from the reata and missing a fingertip. That had happened when the finger got caught when making a turn around the saddle horn with the rope when there was a big steer at the other end. "When a horse is small enough to be handled without trouble, he's no good for riding, and by the time he is, little Tally, remember well that he's dangerous on both ends and uncomfortable in the middle!"

Talitha hunched her shoulders. "I—I think I could get my horse to know me. Then I could train her without a club."

Grunting, Belen said, "How will you exist on a ranch, *doncellita*? Horses and cattle are gelded. The cattle are sold for slaughter. If you feel such things too much, how will you live?"

"What's all this?"

Shea had come up and his eyebrows quirked in that way Talitha loved. What if he thought she was silly, too? But his eyes, blue and kind, yet piercing, demanded the truth; or, rather, she would always have to tell him truth whether she wished to or not. So she did.

There was a strange, remembering look in Shea's eyes. "My father was a rare hand with horses and though I don't remember him, much less how he did it, I have seen horses gentled in quite another way than this. But, Tally, ranch horses are pretty wild, even after breaking. You know Azul, Noche and Castaña have to be lassoed before they'll let themselves be bridled and saddled. In Ireland, and also with the U.S. Army, horses can be walked up to, usually, and haltered or bridled in the field. Whether a mustang could get like that . . ." He frowned dubiously.

"Couldn't I try? Get a young horse and make friends?"

"Friends!" snorted Belen. "With a horse, there must be a master, and the sooner he knows it, the better for both of you!"

"That's true for the wild ones," Shea agreed. "But if we spent some time with the colts, leading them, getting them used to humans, it might settle them down faster in the long run." He grinned at Talitha. "We can sure see what happens! Have you picked out your horse?"

Talitha shook her head, but Belen started for the other corral. "With permission, Don Patricio, let me show you a filly I think will be right. Though I fear you may let Tally spoil it!"

As she peered through the gate, Talitha caught her breath. There were five or six horses in the corral, but the one that entranced her was rich cream with a tail and mane that glinted like moonbeams. She had dainty hooves and great dark eyes, so beautiful that she seemed like a horse from a dream or fairy story.

Too wonderful for her. That one should be for a fine lady, a commandant's wife at the least. Talitha dragged her gaze from the small mare and glanced at the gray gelding, a sorrel filly, a handsome black with a white blaze on the forehead. These were obviously the pick of the horses gleaned from the wild ones.

"The golden one," said Belen. "She is young and, though spirited, is not vicious."

Shea glanced down at Talitha. "Do you like her?"

Breath squeezed tight in her chest. "I—I *love* her!"

Shea nodded. "Good. We'll see what we can do with her."

The training of Ladorada, as Talitha named the filly, was a point of argument among the vaqueros, though as she responded to Shea's caressing firmness, even Belen began to take a grudging pride in the way she would come up to Shea or Talitha and no longer have to be roped.

Shea rode the filly till it was plain that she wasn't a bucker, roller or biter. Then Talitha took over, wearing trousers from the hoard of Cantú clothing. Shea or one of the vaqueros always went with her, but Ladorada's disposition was as sunny as her color and the lightest pressure of the reins was enough to turn or halt her.

The filly's training was so successful that Santiago used the same methods on the blaze-faced black colt, and when a promising young horse was spotted, it was given a chance to tame gently before the rougher ways were used. Castaña's colt by Azul, a bright steel gray, was haltered and led about when he was a month old.

It was during this period toward the end of the rodeo that the twins were born. Tjúni grumbled that, properly, Socorro should retire to a place of seclusion to give birth and be purified, but it happened that Socorro's sons were born under no roof at all.

Her pains began one afternoon when she and Talitha had been gathering wild grapes and, enticed by finding always another vine a little farther along the creek, they had gradually drifted several miles from the house. Talitha was putting a handful of grapes in the basket when Socorro gasped and her face contorted.

"We—we'd better start home," she said as Talitha stared at her with frightened eyes. "Those funny small fingers that have been crawling up and down my back—now they are a great fist squeezing—"

If anything happened to Socorro! Talitha caught her breath in a whimper. She loved Socorro for herself as well as Shea's beloved. "Maybe you should stop here. I'll run for Tjúni!"

Socorro nodded, gripping a willow branch as another pain wracked her. Her teeth bit into her lip and a fine dew stood out on her forehead. "Bring Shea, too, if you can find him. I'll keep walking. Maybe I can get to the house."

Talitha didn't know if that was a good idea, but there was no time to be lost in argument. Putting down the grapes, she ran as hard as she could, dodging roots and bushes, till she reached the long valley and could skim through the flatter grasslands above the creek. Her heart was bursting.

Blood hammered in her ears. But she didn't slacken pace till she found Tjúni gathering squashes while James watched from his cradleboard propped among some rocks.

As Talitha gasped out her news, Tjúni turned with maddening deliberation, went into the house and collected old cloths, a serape, a knife.

"Boil water," she told Talitha.

Putting James down in the corner, Talitha built up the fire and put on a kettle of water, saw Tjúni poking about in her collection of herbs and roots and cried imploringly, "Oh, hurry! Please! The pains were strong!"

"First baby," returned Tjúni placidly. "Take a long time. She probably get to house first."

After what seemed forever, the Papago woman started out and Talitha began to hunt Shea, calling his name.

Catching up Ladorada, Talitha climbed up on the corral and mounted bareback, almost weeping with anxiety. Where, in all this expanse of hills and trees and cañons, could she find Shea? The only thing she could think of was to give Ladorada her head and hope she'd pick up the trail of Azul and the vaqueros' mounts.

At first Ladorada followed the trail to El Charco, then veered off at a silted dry wash. Talitha saw hoof tracks, fresh horse droppings, and breathed easier. Urging the little mare on, Talitha could soon smell burning hair, heard shouts and commotion.

Where the wash widened into broad plain, Chuey and Belen were guarding several cows, one of whom lowed angrily. Near a fire where several irons heated, Santiago held a yearling down by forcing its head at an angle and pinning its shoulders with his knee. Shea brought the iron down onto its hip.

A steamy hiss; the calf bawled frantically. Shea cut the ears, slipped the reata off the hind feet. The yearling heaved itself up, gave a mighty shake, and fled to his mother who sniffed him over and began to lick the brand.

"Shea!" Talitha called. "Socorro—the baby—"

He whirled, seeing her for the first time. "She's all right?"

Talitha nodded, swallowing. "Tjúni's gone to her. The pains started down on the creek."

"She's not at the house?"

"No." As if it had been her fault, Talitha hung her head.

Shea had reached Azul in several long strides, swung into the saddle, and was off without a word to the vaqueros. Talitha went after him, but not before she had seen how Santiago's tawny eyes followed Shea with something like hatred before he ordered Chuey to rope the next cow.

Talitha was worried that James might be screaming in his cradleboard, but at least he should be safe, so she rode down the creek. Shea was already kneeling by Socorro by the time Talitha reached them. Tjúni had got the serape under her. It was no more than a mile

238

to the house, but even Talitha saw that Socorro couldn't walk. The pains gripped her every few minutes and though she held Tjúni's hands and strained, nothing was going forward.

Her long dark hair was damp with sweat and her lips were bloody where she'd gnawed them, but she managed to smile at Shea. "Your son, *querido!* He must be a big redhead burro, too, taking so long to come!"

In Tjúni's stead, he took her hands, braced as she strove, fell back in exhaustion. He turned to the Indian woman, pale beneath his sun-browned skin.

"Can't we do anything?"

"She do."

"She can't keep this up—trying so hard." Shea gritted his teeth as his wife's body convulsed. "There must be some way to help!"

Tjúni lifted a shoulder as if to say Socorro's deficiencies in childbirth were no fault of hers. "Something wrong. Baby's head not in right place."

"Well, can't we move it around?"

"May kill baby."

"Damn it, we can make another child!"

Tjúni said nothing. "Your hands are smaller than mine," Shea said. "You won't hurt her as much. Try!"

Socorro pressed down again and panted, "Don't hurt my baby! Please, please! Oh, Shea, help me!"

"My hands are little," said Talitha, astonished to hear her own voice. "I'll try if you'll tell me what to do. But my hands are awful dirty. Let me wash."

She ran to the creek and scrubbed with sand and water. Kneeling between Socorro's arched legs, she saw the strange quivering opening that expanded during the next pain, thought she glimpsed something inside.

"I go make strong tea," said Tjúni. "She need drink. You feel around," she added grimly to Talitha. "If you find head, try move it down against birth opening."

She moved off. When the pain came next, Socorro screamed. The way Mother had when James was born. Juh's women would have been glad for her to die with

239

the child locked in her, but Judith had wanted to live to protect her daughter and at last James had come out and breathed and lived. Though mother had not—

Mother, help me! Talitha prayed.

Trembling, though she moved as delicately as she could, Talitha slipped her fingers into the distended canal, feeling slowly at what seemed a confused mass of arms and legs, until she encountered a firmness that was rounded and seemed covered with short wet hair.

The head. It could be nothing else. But she wondered in cold terror if the baby could be a monster, for it seemed to have more hands than it should.

One shoulder was wedged against the opening. Talitha tried to shift it, terrified of breaking a bone or doing some lasting damage. Socorro bore down again. The shoulder wedged even more awkwardly. It had to move or both baby and mother would die.

Taking a deep breath, as soon as Socorro relaxed, Talitha, with the desperation of knowing there was nothing to lose, fitted her other hand around the baby and pulled. The shoulder slid around, the head dropped into place, and at the next contraction, as Talitha withdrew her hands, the head pressed against its gateway to life.

"The head's in place," Talitha whispered to Socorro who lay with her eyes closed. "You can bring him if you try hard now."

Socorro's lashes fluttered. "Him?"

"I don't know if it's a boy," Talitha confessed. It was no time to say that it seemed to have at least three hands.

With the next spasm, Socorro bore down, and her cry was more like that of one in battle than in labor. The head looked as if it must burst through, but the swollen flesh restrained it. Maybe if Talitha held the lips wider . . .

Socorro screamed again. Talitha put a hand on either side of the baby's head, tried to ease it through the straining portal. The flesh tore, but the black-thatched skull thrust part way out.

"Push!" Shea pleaded. "Push! He's coming!"

Socorro groaned and thrust. Talitha guided the head. Another pang expelled the shoulders and the rest of the small red creature came in a rush, landing in Talitha's arms.

Talitha stared at the pulsing thick cord connecting the baby to his mother. What did you do with *that?*

Shea looked equally helpless, but then he said, "Must be like any creature!" and cut through that vibrating cord with the knife. "There should be some stuff to come out," he muttered. "But first—"

Taking the tiny wriggling creature, he held it up in the last rays of the sun. "Our son." His laughter was hoarse with relief. "Look at that black hair! Just like yours!"

"But he should have red hair!" Socorro protested. She grimaced. "I—I don't feel as if he'd been born! There—there's still *something!*"

"Afterbirth," Shea told her.

"No," said Tjúni who'd come back unnoticed. "More baby." She stooped to Socorro, held a small jug to her mouth. "Drink this. Make strong. Other baby want to come quick."

"Twins?" growled Shea. "My God, is this what our mother had with Michael and me?" Handing the baby to Talitha, he chafed Socorro's hands. "Lass, lass, I'm sorry!"

After she'd drunk Tjúni's brew, she'd lain back, eyes shuttered, but now she looked up at him with a scolding smile. "Sorry we'll have fine sons? You *are* a burro redhead! Now let me push against you. . . ."

Within minutes, the second boy emerged. Tjúni helped bring out the afterbirth which she thrust deep in the hollow of a tree and covered with rocks. She made Socorro drink more tea and then Shea carried his wife homeward while Tjúni and Talitha followed, each with a baby wrapped in old shawls. The second had red hair.

Wouldn't Tjúni have helped Socorro? Talitha wondered, glancing sideways at the Indian woman. *Maybe
she didn't know how, but neither did I.*

It was twilight when they reached the house, walking because Socorro couldn't ride. Santiago moved out
of the shadows at their approach as if he'd been waiting, and his limp was pronounced as he passed in front
of the door.

"Doña Socorro? She's safe?"

She laughed hazily, "There are twins, Santiago! And
one can be called Hair of Flame!"

"If they were deformities, being yours they would
still be beautiful!" Santiago returned fervently. "You
should eat now. You must be strong to feed that pair!"
His voice cracked. "I was ready to hate them for your
pain, lady, but it seems for your sake I must love them."

Frowning down at the babies, he extended a finger
to each, grinned at the ferocity with which he was
seized. "*Ay,* what ropers they will make! Nothing will
escape them!"

Chuey and Belen came shyly forward, murmuring
good wishes to Socorro and peering, fascinated, at the
twins. Telling them to fetch the horses from the creek,
Shea carried Socorro to the bedroom, and soon she
had a child at either breast, mouthing hungrily, though
of course she wouldn't have real milk for a few days.
They seemed happy with the thin pale liquid that
dribbled from their lips, though.

Shea brought a candle, a luxury from the *conducta,*
and lit it. In spite of her ordeal, Socorro looked lovely
with her children in her arms, their small downy heads
nuzzling against her. She smiled at Shea.

His blue eyes were dark with something that made
Talitha feel like an intruder. She went to the kitchen
and filled bowls with *posole* which she carried back to
them. Shea and Socorro thanked her, but their gazes
never left each other.

Shrinking within herself, Talitha collected James
from Santiago, bent over him as she spooned gruel into

his eager mouth. Shea and Socorro had their own children now. They wouldn't have much time to bother with a pair of waifs.

But I'll take care of you, James! Talitha promised silently, blinking back tears. *I'll love you enough to make up for your not having anyone else!*

Strong brown hands scooped James out of her lap. "Eat your own supper, little one, and let me feed my godson!" commanded Santiago.

Belen handed her a scrap of thin hide. "Another cow for you, *doncellita*."

Chuey produced a dark feather that glinted with gold in the firelight. "From an eagle," he said, and gave it to her.

Talitha's heart swelled, crowding out the tight unhappiness. Why, the twins would need care; she could help with them! And James would be their big brother. She loved Shea and Socorro best, of course, but Santiago and the vaqueros were also her family. With two new babies to love and play with, life would be better than ever!

For a while, the twins had limpid deep blue eyes that seemed a mixture of all colors, but gradually Miguel's turned hazel while Patrick's were bright blue. When the fine baby hair dropped off, Miguel's new curls were black but Patrick's shone rich deep red. They looked much alike except for coloring, though Patrick was thinner and bigger.

At first it hadn't seemed possible that anyone as slight as Socorro could nourish two babies, but she had plentiful milk. Shea made her rest and eat till she protested, laughing, that she was getting fat, and insisted on resuming more of her work.

When the twins were a month old, Tjúni abruptly announced that she was leaving, going to her promised part of the westerly San Manuel *sitio*.

"But we'll have our Roof Feast next month," Shea reminded her after the startled silence that greeted her words. "That'll mark a year since we got good shelter. You should wait for that, at least!"

"More than a year since I meet you at Sonoyta," she answered. "Piñon time, agave roasting, cholla budding, corn and squash planting, time of cattail pollen, *tunas* and grapes—through all seasons I with you. Your *roof* mean nothing to me."

Shea started to argue but Socorro intervened quickly. "You must take plenty of food and all the other things you'll need," she said. "And this is your home, if you ever want to come back."

"*Your* home," countered Tjúni. She looked straight at Shea for a moment before she said as if to herself, "But I make own house."

"I'll go with you," offered Santiago. "There's a fairly sound building that I can help you thatch and I'll butcher a cow for you." He grinned. "Would you like me to find you a likely man in Tubac or Tumacácori?"

"I choose man," she said curtly. Talitha wondered why Socorro's face was suddenly so still.

Tjúni departed riding a mule while another carried a pile of household goods and necessaries. Talitha was glad to see the last of her for Tjúni had never laughed except scornfully and there was a sort of brooding about her that made Talitha uncomfortable.

Santiago and Chuey went with her, returning four days later with the news that Tjúni's abode was thatched, a supply of wood amassed, and the meat of three cows was drying for jerky, for as if on signal, the day after the party arrived at the old San Manuel outpost, two Papago families had appeared, distant relations of Tjúni, driven from their home fields by Mexican bandits pillaging northward. So Tjúni wouldn't be alone and there'd be more men to help with the cattle and in case of trouble.

In December, while Talitha and Socorro were preparing special foods for the Roof Feast, Shea said early one morning that he was going to Tubac and would be back next day.

Socorro knit her brow, suckling a baby at either breast. "I wish you wouldn't! With Apaches and bandits out, it's surely best to stay close to home."

"I have business there," Shea teased mysteriously.

She sniffed. "It had better not be business with skirts!"

"My love!" He chuckled, playing with a lock of her soft hair. "How can you think I'd have the energy?"

It turned stormy and cold the next day, adding to Socorro's worry, but Shea rode in before sundown, leading Viejo whose *aparejos* were laden with what looked like dead branches but proved to be small trees with roots still embedded in soil.

"Pomegranates and peaches," Shea explained as he leaned them against the wall just inside the door. "I thought it'd be nice to plant them on our Roof Day." He shook his head grimly. "Don't feel much like celebrating after what I saw in Tubac."

Socorro's frightened eyes lifted to him and the vaqueros frowned. "Apaches," Shea said. "They struck a few days ago, ran off the cattle and horses and promised they'd be back. The people who survived are gathering up their things and making for Tucson."

"But the soldiers!" protested Socorro.

"Often there's only five or so fit for duty," Shea said wearily. "When I passed through Tumacácori on the way home, the Indians were taking the saints down from their niches and packing the vestments. They're going to Tucson, also."

The adults all looked at each other and Talitha shivered because these people, her safety and to her so powerful, looked devastated. Socorro's head drooped.

"We had little to do with Tubac or Tumacácori," she said. "Yet knowing the people were there made it seem as if we weren't completely cut off."

"They hope to come back in the spring," Shea encouraged. But next day their Roof Feast was haunted by the knowledge that the nearest people of their kind were in Tucson, eighty miles away.

Even so, there was a solemn joy binding the group that knelt before the madonna in the *sala*. Shea thanked God for protecting them and besought His grace for all homeless ones, especially those driven so recently from the Santa Cruz Valley. Talitha squeezed her eyes shut and said her own prayer. *Mother, don't let anything happen to my family here and don't let mean old Juh ever get James!*

It looked as if it might snow, so as soon as the noon feast was over, they went outside to plant the trees. Socorro, bundling up the twins, selected spots where she wanted the pomegranates and peaches and the men were digging when Belen straightened.

He pointed, face a mask. From the west a lone rider was coming. Shea said quietly, "Santiago, why don't you and Chuey get in the vaqueros' quarters and have rifles loaded? Socorro, you and Talitha stay inside."

"It's Mangus," said Talitha. She'd seen the chief so often that even at this distance, she recognized the set of his huge body. Her tongue stuck to the roof of her mouth. She caught James's hand, started to scoot him inside despite his indignant howl. "If—if Mangus wants James, say he's dead or something!" she entreated, then hustled her sturdy little brother to the bedroom.

He shrieked that he wanted to see "Man-us" but Talitha cuffed him and said if he didn't keep quiet the big Indian might eat him.

James's garbled reply, deciphered, was that he didn't want to be eaten and he was a very good boy. Talitha hugged him close, stricken at the big tear rolling down his blunt little nose. "I'm sorry I hit you, honey," she whispered. "But sometimes you have to do what Tally says right away. Now stay there while I peek out the window!"

Dragging up a bench, she stood on tiptoe and watched Mangus nearing the men. When he was close enough for his features to be recognized, Socorro went out, and stood with her babies to receive him.

Talitha couldn't hear what they said, but Mangus

seemed to ask permission to hold the twins. Neither showed any fear of the huge Apache. Patrick reached up to touch Mangus's face. After a moment, he gave them back to their mother's arms. Turning to the pack behind his saddle, he brought out a cradleboard—a very wide one.

Talitha blinked and saw that it was made for twins. Soft buckskin lacings, a canopy that ran the width of the top of the board, with turquoise, feathers and other charms fastened to the top. When the boys were older, it would be a heavy load to carry, but would still be a convenient way to tuck them out of harm's way when Socorro was busy.

So the visit was friendly. Probably through the miners, Mangus had learned about the twins. Talitha took a deep breath, then caught it in, as Socorro turned to the house and Mangus and Shea followed.

The Apache ate of the plentiful food of the feast, relishing the pumpkin candy, *pipián,* wild turkey in mole sauce, and innumerable tortillas and tamales. When he had consumed enough for four men, Mangus for the first time turned his attention to Talitha who had come to help serve him.

"Where is the son of Juh?"

Talitha cast Socorro and Shea a pleading glance. Shea said gently, in English, "Bring James in, Tally. Mangus only wants to be able to tell Juh he's well and alive."

Reluctantly, Talitha went to the bedroom. She'd been able to make James stay there only by saying there was a bad man in the kitchen. Now she had a hard time convincing James that the man wasn't bad *today,* but at last she bribed him with the promise of more pumpkin candy.

"And don't you cry in front of him!" she adjured her seventeen-month-old brother. "You knew him when you were a little baby so try to show him you've grown up!"

James clung to her skirt till they crossed the *sala,*

but when he saw Mangus he did something that made Talitha's scalp tingle. He stopped a judicious distance from the giant and greeted him in the Apache tongue, the words Talitha had grudgingly taught him in case her prayers availed nothing and James had to live with Juh.

Mangus gave her a swift, penetrating glance. He returned James's greeting and watched him curiously as the child went over to examine his foster brothers' elegant double cradleboard.

"So you have taught your brother the tongue of the Din-eh," Mangus observed dryly. "Do you then so miss the sound of it?"

The taunt brought back her despair and anger, the terrifying loneliness after her mother died. Trembling with outrage rather than fear, Talitha hurled words at him with the wish they were fatal arrows.

"I have taught *my brother* what he may need to know, but I pray every day that Juh will die before he can take James away!"

Shea put his arm around her soothingly, but Talitha glared ferociously at the massive Indian, no longer afraid though her body continued to shake.

"You are brave. You hate well. And you are clever." Mangus gave her a long stare. "Maybe it is you we should have claimed rather than the boy."

Rising lithely, he watched James patting Miguel and Patrick. "I shall tell the father of your brother that he is well," he said to Talitha with the hint of a smile. "You have fine sons now, Hair of Flame. I hope they never fight my people. When they are old enough to understand, tell them they were carried in a cradleboard of the Din-eh."

He stooped to clear the doorway. For a moment his great shadow darkened it and then he was gone.

XVII

It was a cold winter with blowing snow, but somehow Chuey managed to ride often enough to El Charco to convince Pedro Sanchez that Anita could be safely entrusted to him. The problem of a priest was solved by Shea's assuming civil power as the head of a settlement and performing before the madonna in the *sala* a brief ceremony which was followed by a long feast.

Santiago and Belen took up lodgings in the *sala,* leaving their quarters to Anita and Chuey till the couple's house was finished. James now slept on a pallet close to Talitha's in the kitchen. A long storeroom was added that spring, forming a right angle with the kitchen. The ranch structures were beginning to form a rough square around a space where most of the fruit trees were planted. Socorro intended to plant wild flowers and herbs there, too, and Shea said they'd dig a well so the women wouldn't have to go to the creek for water.

That would be a big help in winter, though in summer Talitha rather enjoyed taking laundry to the creek, sudsing with powdered yucca root, and scrubbing stubborn spots with fine sand.

James was toddling into everything, endlessly curious, and had to be watched. The twins required most of Socorro's strength and time. So, with Tjúni gone, it was fortunate that Anita took over much of the cooking and cheerfully helped with the other work. So delighted was she with her new husband and a house of her own that she sang while she bustled about the kitchen. She would frequently insist that Socorro rest with her feet up and make them both gourds of frothy chocolate from the *conducta* supplies.

Talitha and James had chocolate, too, at such times. James was such a special pet of Anita's that Talitha was sometimes jealous but she never showed it, remembering that a year ago only she, in all the world, had cared what happened to the dark-skinned blue-eyed little boy—except for Juh, of course!

Early that summer Talitha saw dust rising to the east, ran hastily to alert the men who were gentling horses so each would have a number of mounts to use during the cattle gather.

Coming out of the corral, the men ran for their rifles and the main house. Talitha sped to the creek for water in case they were besieged for several days. When she panted up the slope with both buckets, Shea met her and scooped them from her.

The dust churned nearer. Talitha strained her eyes. "Cattle!" she gasped. "Shea, there's hundreds of them!"

"Looks it," he nodded, urging her through the door and barring it as he set the buckets down. "What I want to see is who's driving them!"

"It's the wrong direction for Apaches," Santiago observed. "Going straight east, there aren't any ranches between here and Texas."

"Going west, there's not much left except Papago and Pima *rancherías,*" added Shea. "We're pretty much an island, Tucson to the north and the other Sonoran towns south."

Belen peered cautiously out a window. "Me, I don't guess where those cows come from or who drives. But *diablo!* They are big cows with very big and funny horns!"

Shea leaned over the Yaqui's shoulder. "God's whiskers! Longhorns! I saw them in Texas, every color of the cow rainbow!"

"Why, it's as my father said!" Socorro breathed, also gazing out. "The horns grow every direction and some spread longer than I am tall!"

"What're they doing here?" Shea marveled. "And how could they ever have come through all these miles of Indian country?" He grinned and slapped his leg. "Maybe they've got some of those Texas Rangers for herders!"

"Texas Rangers!" Socorro whispered, grasping him. "Shea, would they bother you?"

His hand went to the confused double brand on his cheek. "Don't see why they should. Texans aren't really Yanquis, *querida*. The ones I knew were always bragging about having been a free republic after they broke loose from Mexico and most of them still act like they come from a country all their own."

"Here comes a man," called Santiago, who had positioned himself in the bedroom.

Anita huddled by Chuey, Belen was with Santiago, the twins were suspended from a roof support pole in their fine cradleboard, and James squirmed among the adults like a puppy, vainly trying to see what was happening outside.

"If he's Apache, he's got on white man clothes," grunted Shea, disengaging himself from Socorro's anxious hands. "I'll step out and see what he wants."

"Take your rifle," warned Santiago. "I'll come with you so he'll know you're not alone."

"Both of you stay close to the house," Socorro insisted. "You can get back in quickly if there's trouble."

Talitha stood at the edge of the window with Socorro and watched as the stranger jogged slowly up. There was a rifle in his saddle scabbard, guns at each hip, a great sheathed knife, and his hair and eyes were the color of sand, lighter than his sun-burned skin.

"Howdy!" he called in English. "Damned if it ain't good to see someone 'cept them thievin', murderin' Apache devils!"

Shea laughed. "If all you did was see them, you were lucky!"

The sandy-haired man spat tobacco expertly to one side. "Not all that lucky! They picked off three of my men, ran off cattle four different times. We've been pushin' hard." His eyes wandered to the creek, strayed along the broad grassy valley. "Sure would be obliged if we could rest here a few days, let the cattle graze and water good. I've heard the way to California's even worse than what we've come through."

"California!"

The stranger offered his plug of tobacco, cut himself a hunk when it was refused. "Why, sure, California! Big prices out there for beef! He grinned. "Them as want to pan for gold are welcome to it! I'll make mine out of sellin' these old longhorns that you cain't hardly give away back home!"

Shea and Santiago exchanged glances. They'd been planning to sell their culls to Tucson that fall. Shifting in his saddle, the Texan said, "If we can stop here, I'll pay you in cattle. We sure need a rest."

"You're welcome," Shea decided. "Spread your herd west. Even if they mix some with our cows, they're different enough to sort out! Then you and your men come along and eat with us."

"Say, that's mighty kind of you." Climbing down from his patient roan, the lanky man shook hands with Shea, and, after a moment's hesitation, clasped Santiago's hand, too. "We'll manage our own grub after this, but it would sure be fine to have a meal that's not scorched where it ain't raw!" He grinned. "I'm Will Thomas, late of the Texas Rangers."

Santiago looked incredulous and Shea chuckled. "I just thought you might be. A Ranger, I mean. I'm Patrick O'Shea and this is my partner, Santiago Cantú. When you're ready to eat, you can meet the rest of the family."

Talitha ran down to the marsh for more cattail roots to put in the stew while Socorro made more *posole* and Anita patted out her thin, perfect tortillas.

"I think it'd be good to send our cattle with him, if he's willing," Shea told Santiago. "Even giving him a third of the profit, we'd still more than triple the money we'd get in Tucson."

"And quadruple the chances of getting no money at all," Santiago argued. "It's far to the gold fields. Even if this Señor Thomas makes the drive, what will ensure his remembering to stop at Rancho del Socorro when he's traveling with a heavy purse but no herd that needs graze and water?"

"Hell, Santiago, everything's a risk!"

"To be sure. But let us see a little more of these Texans before offering a deal."

Shea gave his younger partner a blue-eyed look of disgust. "I never meant to propose it till we got his measure. Just wanted to know what you thought."

"So now you do," grinned Santiago. Shea gave him a grumpy look as the Texans paused outside the door, taking off their dusty, wide-brimmed hats.

Socorro invited them in. They looked at her as if she were a dream, trying not to stare, and bowed deeply as Shea introduced her. She blushed, slim as ever though her body was more gracefully rounded and accented by motherhood.

"You are welcome," she told the men in her careful, pretty English.

Shea named Anita, Chuey and Belen, then dropped his hand to Talitha's shoulder. "This is our daughter, Talitha. Our son James is peeking at you from around the wall, and that pair in the cradleboard are our twins."

"Quite a family!" Will Thomas complimented. His pale brown eyes warmed as he smiled at Socorro. "You seem much too young, ma'am!"

"James and I aren't really hers," Talitha forced herself to blurt, though her heart had swelled with pride at being called the O'Sheas' daughter. "We—we were Apache captives, but Shea and Socorro talked Mangus into letting us go." *And that's why, Texan, even if you cared, you couldn't make out the D beneath the crescent of that old horseshoe.*

"Mangus!" Thomas regarded Shea with fresh respect. "If you talked that heathen out of anything, mister, you've got more blarney than the rest of the Irish together! Wouldn't be surprised if it wasn't his bunch that killed my hands." His eyes narrowed in suspicion. "Say, you keep him in guns and ammunition? That why you're settin' here on this good land when everybody else seems to have been run right out of the country?"

Shea stiffened. "I don't arm Mangus. But we are friends. And if that bothers you, Mr. Thomas, you better move on."

After a clash of gazes, Thomas ground his heel sheepishly in the hard-packed dirt floor. "Reckon I was out of turn. No offense."

"Then none taken." Shea gestured toward the table. "Find a place and help yourselves!"

The Texans eagerly obeyed, each pausing long enough to nod as Will Thomas gave their names. "That butterball with the towhead is Lefty Wright. The bandy-legged little rooster is Dallas Payson, and the one just as ugly as me is my kid brother, Joe."

There wasn't room for everyone at the table so the vaqueros and Talitha and James filled their plates and sat on the adobe bench built as part of the wall.

"But surely there are cows in California!" Socorro was protesting. "My cousin's family had thousands! And there are many ranchers!"

Will Thomas shrugged. "Somebody says when the missions were taken over by the Mexican government, most of the mission herds were slaughtered just for hides and tallow. The remaining stock hasn't multiplied fast enough to take care of the Gold Rushers. After last December, when President Polk said in his annual message that there was sure enough gold in California, seemed like everyone who could crawl, walk or ride started west. Some say there'll be one hundred thousand new people there by the end of this year. And they'll need food." He filled a tortilla with spicy stew, devoured it and sighed happily before he squinted at Shea. "Like

254

I said, we've lost three men. If you can spare a couple, I'll pay 'em good wages to come along."

Shea rubbed his chin. "Might be we could work something out. What do you think, Santiago?"

"That it would be fine to get Gold Rush prices for some of our beef." Santiago turned to the Texan, speaking slowly in English, hesitating over some words. "Maybe two of us could help you, Señor Thomas. If you wait for us to round up some cattle and throw them in with yours."

"How long?"

"Perhaps a week."

"It's a deal," said Thomas heartily, giving his hand first to Shea and then Santiago. "You get full price on your own cattle, and I'll still pay top wages to whoever comes along."

"I'll go," decided Santiago, gold eyes lighting. "Chuey? Belen?"

Anita put a protective arm through Chuey's, for even though most of the conversation had been in English, the gist of it was fairly evident. Chuey grinned and shook his head.

"With permission, Don Santiago . . ."

"I'll go," Belen growled, "if none of the Sanchezes want to. Is it that we gather cattle and go with these *Tejanos* to California?"

Santiago nodded. "We'll start to brand and cull this very afternoon. And get the Sanchezes started."

"We'll help," said Thomas, who seemed to understand a good deal of Spanish though he didn't attempt to speak it. He smiled gallantly at the women. "I'd chase cows all day for a meal like this!"

"Then you must eat with us all the time you're here," Socorro urged.

With the four Texans helping, as well as the Sanchezes, there was no question as to where a certain nine-year-old was most needed. Sighing, Talitha got down the twins who were starting to fret, changed their diapers and persuaded Socorro to lie down and rest while she fed them.

The next days passed in a rush. It seemed to Talitha that the Texans would surely consume all the food in the storeroom. No sooner were the breakfast dishes washed than it was time to start a noon meal to be carried wherever the men were working, and Talitha scarcely returned with *those* dirty dishes when supper had to be put on to cook. After six days, during which the Texas herd browsed happily and enjoyed the water, a hundred head of S cattle were ready to go. There would have been more but some of the late yearlings looked too puny for the long drive. Güero Sanchez had volunteered to go, so it was he and Santiago who rode off with the Texans, though Shea, Chuey and Belen helped gather the herd and start them out of the valley.

Cristiano bellowed, puzzled and angry that a herd was moving without his leadership, but finally seemed to notice that most of his companions remained. Over these, he exerted mild tyrannies till his self-esteem was restored.

Will Thomas left twenty head of *Chinos* to breed with the ranch stock and produce larger, beefier animals. They had shed their long curly winter coats and their brown underparts looked sleek and bluish.

"You'll have one of their first calves, *doncellita*," promised Belen, squinting at a young cow. "By using them and culling out the unthrifty, Don Patricio will have the best cattle between Texas and California!"

Talitha laughed. "When the Indians have run off most of the herds in between, that's not much praise!"

Belen shrugged. "I haven't seen the beasts of the *Tejanos,* except for this herd, or those of the *Californios.* But I can tell you this rancho's cattle are already better than those of Don Narciso."

"Why is that?" frowned Talitha. "Santiago says the Cantús have been raising cattle for over a hundred years."

"Which doesn't mean Don Narciso has learned anything," grunted Belen. "He wants to hear he has thousands of horned cattle and if their bones clank together, he never listens."

Shea came to stand beside them, his hair blazing in the sundown. The unscarred side of his face was toward Talitha. He was beautiful in a harsh male way, but it was the sight of his scars that stirred her to a passion of worship. It was as if her heart had been branded along with his cheek. Her life belonged to him. James ran up now and grasped his foster father's leg.

Swinging him to a shoulder, Shea gave his head a shake of wonderment. "Still doesn't seem real, lass. Four years ago, I was in Ireland, watching potatoes rot in the field while my mother starved. Three years ago I was in the United States Army camped down on the Rio Grande. With Michael, God rest him——"

His voice trailed off. Talitha took his long brown fingers, pressed them to her cheek. "You have Miguel now," she reminded him. "And Patrick."

He bent to sweep her close in a hug that embraced James. "And I've got you two and Socorro. Life's dealt me fairer than I deserve, Tally. That's why it hurts to think of Michael and my mother who neither one had much."

"They had you!"

"Like I said," retorted Shea. "They didn't have much!" He chuckled at Talitha's indignant outcry, but she didn't stay to chide him. It was past time to be helping with supper and the twins.

Talitha wasn't strong enough to wrestle down a cow, but she learned to press the red-hot iron firmly against the hide, long enough to mark but not sear the flesh beneath. And, setting her jaw, she could do the earmarks now, and hand the *señales* to Shea.

Ladorada was a good roping horse, and, using the skills Belen and Chuey had taught her, by summer's end Talitha could make the underhand *mangana* that caught a horse's front feet, or the *peal* which caught an animal's hind feet in a double loop like a figure eight. She could bring the rope swiftly around the saddle horn, letting the calf throw itself by its own weight braced against that of Ladorada, but she could handle only the smaller, scrawnier ones.

"Don't rope more than you can hold, *doncellita!*" Belen scolded, scooping her up after she'd been yanked from the saddle, hauled over Ladorada's laid-back ears, her palms skinned from the burn of the *reata* as the yearling she'd failed to throw kicked himself free of the double noose and vanished into a mesquite thicket. *"Por Dios!* Another foot and you'd have landed in the cactus!" He gave her an admonishing but careful shake. "You're sound? Nothing broken?"

The breath was knocked out of her, her palms stung ferociously, and she'd skinned her elbows but Talitha blinked back tears and scrambled up. "I'm all right, Belen! I—I just wish I'd hurry and grow till I could really do my share."

"You do enough," he said. "Besides, as you grow, you become a woman, not a vaquero. So do not put too much of your heart into this thing, *doncellita.*"

Disregarding his proffered help, she gripped the saddle horn with her grazed hand and climbed into the saddle, grateful that Shea was out of sight down the arroyo and hadn't seen her tumble. She helped Belen chase the yearling out of the thicket and when he roped and threw it, leaped down to hold it near the branding fire, she put the S on it and deftly slit the ears.

One more for Shea and Rancho del Socorro.

It was that July, while she was gathering currants and chokecherries, that she followed a cañon into the mountains and found the hot springs. Bubbling from the rocks into a shallow natural basin, the water overflowed to lose itself in the stream that sparkled its tortuous way down the gorge.

Talitha was hot, and this seemed a wonderful place to bathe. Tugging off her dress, she bent to wash her face, made a surprised sound.

Warm water! Cool water would have done as well or better that afternoon, but except in full summer, unlimited hot water would be worth the walk.

Socorro would love it! They'd bring James and the twins and wash their hair, let them splash in the big rock hollow! Delighted with her find, Talitha clambered into the smooth giant bowl and luxuriated in cupping water in her hands and letting it trickle down from her shoulders.

She wore her dresses short, so from midcalf her legs were brown as her face and hands, but the rest of her was creamy pale. She made a face, wishing she was dark all over, scowled at the small pink points on her chest.

Some day they would be breasts that would hold milk for babies. She hoped hers would be more like Socorro's than Anita's which were so big that they were the first thing one noticed about her. Talitha wanted babies some day, but that took a husband and she didn't want to marry anyone, ever, and go away from Shea.

She might have to, though, when she grew up.

She didn't want to think about that. It was a muddle. She wanted to get bigger and stronger, able to do the full work of man or woman. But she didn't want to leave the ranch. Or for Juh to claim James, which he could do in five more years.

Sighing, she stood up and stepped on dry rock, shaking herself, standing in the sun till she was dry. Then she pulled on the faded blue cotton dress, cut down from one of Socorro's, slipped into the sandals Belen had made of cowhide. Picking up her half-filled basket, she followed the cañon till it broadened into a high basin with piñon- and juniper-studded cliffs rising stark on all sides. Grass carpeted the clearing and water gushed in a small waterfall from a crevice in the rocks above.

A lovely place. And there were lots of currants scattered along the stream that trickled through the basin till it vanished in a vast rockslide above a side cañon. Strange that Socorro and Tjúni hadn't found it.

Bending to pluck the small red fruits, Talitha's foot stirred something almost buried among the leaves. Something white and hard. A nudge sent it rolling down the incline, fetching up with a splash in the water.

Hollows stared at her from what had to be a human skull. As if it conveyed to her some horrible knowledge, she suddenly recognized, here and there in the grass and bushes, what she had dismissed as stones.

Slowly, she confirmed her suspicion. Five skulls, two of them still impaled on sticks hidden in the grass, arrows jutting from the eye sockets. But she found no other trace of the dead except a few bones wedged among the rocks. Animals and birds must have dragged off the rest.

A memory of Luz echoed, Mangus's niece saying how she, her sister and three babies had been rescued from scalpers by a white woman and a Papago, and how the Papago had wanted to finish what the scalpers had begun.

Staring at the skulls, Talitha felt a thrill of awe. So this was why Mangus protected Rancho del Socorro. And why Socorro chose not to come here, even for the fine currants.

Talitha wanted to run. She'd lived long enough among Apaches to absorb some of their fear of the dead, of hovering spirits, and these men must have been mutilated in a way that would give them no peace in the afterlife. But that was heathenish, thinking that way! And if Tjúni and Socorro had been brave against the living marauders, she mustn't run from them dead.

Her lips were stiff; her mouth and throat very dry. Swallowing, she worked her way among the bushes, including those close to the skulls.

Only when she'd gathered every ripe currant she

could find did she leave the basin she would ever afterward think of as the Place of Skulls.

She told Socorro and the others about the hot spring but she said nothing about the clearing and what waited there. Several times that summer Talitha visited the hot spring with Socorro, Anita, the twins and James. They used orris root to wash from hair to feet, and went home much refreshed. If Socorro realized how close they were to the fateful basin, she never betrayed it.

Tivi Sanchez, bringing supplies from the mine's *conducta,* had more bad news about Tubac. Some Missourians heading for the gold fields had stopped at El Charco and he'd accompanied them up the Santa Cruz Valley, hoping to find Tubac repopulated and a market for beef. Some of December's refugees must have come back, for Indians had raided only hours before the Missourians rode into the smoking ruins. Tivi had helped them bury the dead.

"And this time I think no one will come back," he concluded, his broad, boyish face somber.

Socorro crossed herself and turned to Shea. "Sometimes I almost wish Mangus didn't shield us! I feel guilty, that we're alive, while others—"

"Hush!" he said roughly, putting his arm around her, bowing his bright head protectively against her dark one. "We came here at the same risk anyone does. Few but you, my darling, would have pitied Apache women."

"My pity would have been useless except for Tjúni's arrows."

His broad shoulders moved resignedly. "Tjúni has her reward."

"Not the one she wanted," retorted Socorro. She glanced anxiously at Tivi. "The Papago at San Manuel, how are they?"

"Gathering saguaro fruit when I rode by. By now they're all drinking *navai't.*" He grimaced. "Though why they claim it must be used up in a day is beyond me. It tastes awful any time. Makes even Güero vomit."

"You're managing without him?" Shea asked.

"Better without than with," Tivi said with surprising grimness. "*Mamacita* misses her blond one, of course, but father, Juana and I would as lief he stayed in California." When Anita shook her head reprovingly at this younger brother, he said hotly, "Don't be a hypocrite! No doubt you love your Chuey, but you wouldn't have been quite so ready to leave home if it hadn't been for Güero's fits and tempers!"

Brushing a kiss on her plump cheek, he said he couldn't stay for supper since his mother worried every hour he was away, but he did accept a couple of tortillas wrapped around plentiful helpings of beans and meat. As he rode away, Talitha watched the O'Sheas look toward the west and north, in the direction of Tubac, caught a chilling intuition of how alone they must feel. Mangus, because of his towering personality and shrewd acquisition of sons-in-law, had some influence with bands other than his own *Mimbreños,* but there was no telling when some party might decide to loot the ranch and let Mangus avenge it if he could discover the guilty. And he might die at any time.

Shea said, "We'd better keep plenty of water, and food sealed as tight as possible against rats and mice, in the *sala* at all times—be ready to fort up if we have to. Anita, can you shoot?"

Shrinking back like a frightened soft brown quail, she shook her head. "Then we'll teach you." He studied Talitha and sighed. "You'd better learn, too. In a siege it doesn't matter who's holding a rifle as long as they can shoot."

Belen nodded. "True, Don Patricio. Apaches don't like to lose men. If we were ready for them, they'd probably forget about us and run off all the cattle and horses they could handle. They don't want the land, except as something to range over, as wild things do. In this, they are not like white men."

"Where white men are, the land is well soaked in blood," Shea agreed wryly. "That's because each one wants as much as he can get to fence and use as his own."

"So the white man is tied to his land. It winds up owning him."

"Like marriage," Shea grinned, shrugging, "it goes both ways!"

XVIII

So Talitha learned to load and fire one of the percussion rifles inherited from the scalp hunters, leaning it on a window ledge or one of the firing niches. She staggered when it kicked back against her shoulder, but was soon aiming much better than Anita, who squeezed her eyes shut when she pulled the trigger, letting the barrel flop down.

"We just have to hope you'll do better than that when your life depends on it!" Shea told the young woman after a week of daily practice. "Can't keep on wasting ammunition." More cheeringly, he added, "Anyhow, you should be able to hit a horse if it came in close, you don't have to pick off the rider!"

Socorro shuddered. "I hope it never happens!"

"My dear love, so do I! But we need to be ready."

Sycamore and cottonwood outlined the creek with yellow, glorious against the mountains and evergreens. Santiago and Güero hadn't returned and Socorro began to fret, saying they should be back by now. Maybe they had died of thirst. Been killed by Indians. Murdered by lawless Gold Rushers.

"Maybe they met pretty girls and stayed awhile," countered Shea. "Or decided to try for the gold themselves. Who knows what a young single man may do?"

But Santiago rode in a few days before the twins' first birthday, and something he carried in a basket in front of him was received with almost as much delight and wonder as the gold he carried—between three and five hundred dollars for each of the ninety head that had survived the trek.

Over thirty thousand dollars!

Will Thomas, for all his sensible talk, had caught gold fever and, with his Texans, had stayed in California, as had Güero. "I'll ride to El Charco tomorrow and let his mother know." Santiago's black brows knitted. "For my part, I hope he stays. If Will Thomas hadn't kept his men in check, they'd have killed that fair-haired swaggerer, or at least have mauled him."

"You rode all the way back *alone?*" Socorro demanded fearfully.

"I'm alive, my lady." His golden eyes smiled, lingering as if starved for sight of her. He came down from the saddle, gracefully in spite of his damaged leg, and handed Talitha the basket. "Besides, I wasn't really alone. This soft creature snuggled in my blankets at night and purred most of the day."

A cat! Talitha sucked in her breath, tingling with astonished joy. She'd had a kitten, back in Nauvoo, but it had vanished during the flight across the river. Thinking back now, she realized that she hadn't seen a cat since leaving Fort Leavenworth.

This cat was gray and yellow and black and white, almost as if she'd been pieced from the skins of her most distant ancestors. Around her golden eyes was a black pirate's patch, and the other eye was green. She appraised Talitha lazily, stretched, yawned and sprang lightly from the basket, strolling soft-pawed and stately into the house as if to see if it was good enough for her. Within a moment, a startled squeal indicated that she'd already taken up the ancient vocation of cats, catching rodents.

"What's her name?" Talitha asked.

"I've called her Chusma—that means 'ragtag.' But she's yours, little Tally. Call her as you will."

"Chusma's all right," Talitha said after some thought. "It sounds like 'choose me'! Oh, Santiago! I love her! And so will James and Patrick and Miguel—"

"And all of us!" added Socorro. "I'm sorry for the little mice with their bright eyes and soft fur, but it's been terrible to have them always in our grain."

"That's how lots of people feel in California," Santiago laughed. "Anyone with cats to sell can get sixteen to a hundred dollars. I paid twenty dollars for this one and thought her a bargain."

Chusma still rubbed often against Santiago's legs, but she slept in the bend behind Talitha's knees. If Talitha wasn't up early enough to suit her, Chusma tugged at her hair, first gently, then with more claw, or swatted her briskly on the cheek. If Talitha, trying to escape these summonings, pulled the cover over her head, Chusma could usually insinuate a paw inside, or, failing that, would *stomp* up and down on her till Talitha surrendered.

The cat's increased girth was attributed to all the mice and rats she devoured, but one night she didn't curl up by Talitha and frantic searching didn't locate her. James cried for his fascinating new playmate and Talitha, after comforting him, sobbed herself to sleep.

Had a mean old coyote or javelina, wolf, fox, wildcat or even bear made off with Chusma? It couldn't be! Not after Santiago brought her all the way from California! Talitha hunted and called and hoped all the next day but there was no trace of the familiar patchwork or pointed ears, no meowing or plaintive rubbing at the ankles. Talitha's heart seemed to swell with heaviness, and when Shea tried to comfort her, she dodged away as soon as possible.

No one loved Chusma as she had. They couldn't understand.

Then, the fourth day after her disappearance, Chusma came noiselessly in as they were having supper, something black dangling limply from her mouth.

"A—a kitten!" shrieked Talitha.

Recovering, Socorro got to her feet. "She must want to bring them in from wherever she hid to have them. Come, Tally, let's make her a bed."

Chusma accepted their efforts, part of an old blanket nestled among the grain baskets, and within the quarter hour, she was nursing her striving, mewing offspring, grooming them with her rough pink tongue.

"A black, a white and gray, and one that looks like her!" Talitha crooned, kneeling by them, but not venturing to touch the tiny things with their closed eyes and sealed-looking ears. "No, James! She won't like you to play with them yet. Just watch. But isn't it lucky? There's one for you and one for each twin."

James's blue eyes glinted in his round dark face. He squatted on his heels and, fascinated, watched the kittens. "James get the black one?" he inquired hopefully.

"If he's the one you want. Patrick and Miguel aren't old enough to play with kitties yet."

James spent most of his waking hours during the next few weeks with the cat and her family. He fetched fresh water for Chusma and brought her tidbits. It enthralled him to watch the kittens gain their legs and wobble about.

Chusma relaxed her first nervous protectiveness after about a week and watched benignly but with vigilance as the kittens explored James as part of their territory, scrambling over his legs and into his lap. She seemed to accept him as a suitable nurse for her offspring because she soon resumed her hunting forays, shaking the kittens from her as she rose.

After a patrol of the storehouse and an hour's stalking about the yard and buildings, she returned to her brood, tail gently swaying instead of twitching as it had been when she sprang up to flee.

James didn't drag the kittens about or handle them roughly, but held them if they wanted to sleep. Once Talitha heard him crooning an Apache lullaby she'd taught him, cuddling the black one against his small hard belly.

"What are you calling him?" she asked.

"Muchacho. 'Boy,' like James."

That was shortened to Chacho. As soon as he was weaned, he started sleeping with James though the two little females slept as close to their mother as she'd now allow, which was at Talitha's feet.

Chacho developed into a large cat, princely of carriage, green of eye, and aloof from all humankind except James. The gray and white cat vanished that autumn, prey of some bigger predator, but on the day of the Roof Feast in 1850, Chacho and his sister Niña had produced two kittens, one black and white, the other multicolored. The twins were as intrigued with them as James had been with the first litter and each claimed one as his personal pet.

James was above all that. He had his incomparable Chacho, and besides, since his third birthday, Santiago had begun his tutelage as a vaquero.

Viejo, grizzled now with age, shoulder still bearing the scars of the lion, was James's first mount. He progressed to Ladorada who, because of her training and nature, was extremely gentle, though spirited. On his fourth birthday, celebrated in mid-July since Talitha didn't know the exact date, Shea gave him Azul's and Castaña's colt, a steel gray so dark he was almost black, three years old now, and gradually tamed by Shea and Talitha.

James had to climb into the saddle from the side of the corral, and he took his falls, but Santiago was very pleased with his godson. He roped corral posts, the *vegas* protruding from the walls, three stumps, wheelbarrow handles, and eventually cast his rope on Chusma. Talitha rushed out in time to save the spitting, scratching cat from strangling, and, arms and hands tracked with blood, put her small brother over her knee and gave him his first spanking.

He was so scared by what he'd almost done to Chusma that he didn't struggle or cry out. When, shaking, Talitha set him on his feet, he gazed at her with his deep blue eyes, so strange in the Indian face, and blinked back a fat tear, patting her cruelly marked hands.

"James sorry. Tally, James so glad you get Chusma loose!"

"So am I." Sighing, she pulled him against her. "I love you, honey! But your rope's not a plaything. Save it for calves and horses, and don't practice with anything alive unless Santiago or someone's around."

He frowned. "I wish I could practice on something that moves."

"Well, you can try to catch me sometimes," Talitha suggested. "Just let the loop fall, though. Don't jerk it tight!"

Shea, coming upon this game, pronounced it too dangerous, but he did rig up a moving target, a post secured in a broad slab of wood, that could be jerked about by a rope. James would work at lassoing this as long as he could get someone to move the target, and he was soon amazingly accurate.

The twins liked to pull the target, but they usually got tangled up in rope or ran too fast or barely scooted it at all, so most of James's practice time they watched and laughed and, in their not quite two-year-old patois, they promised each other that next year Santiago would give them ropes, too.

Patrick and Miguel couldn't have looked more different and still have come from the same parents, much less be twins. Patrick's red curls had darkened slightly. His blue eyes were like a summer sky, not the stormy shade of James's. Miguel was taller and thinner with dark lashes, his skin was golden, and his black hair was straight and silky. They trotted worshipfully after James and he was usually indulgent of them, though he seemed fonder of Chacho and his horse, Tordillo, than he was of anyone except Talitha and Santiago.

Shea and Socorro were kind to him, but he called them by their names and somehow never turned to them as parents, perhaps because he was used to Talitha, perhaps because the twins were born before he'd been long at the O'Sheas' and had necessarily absorbed most of Socorro's time and Shea's attention.

However it was, Talitha was worried. She longed for James to love Shea as a father, to appreciate what he'd done for him. Now that James was outside most of the time, Santiago's shadow, she seldom had a chance to carry out her promise to her mother and tell James about the Scotts and their religion.

On the rare occasions when she told him about Nauvoo and the temple, Joseph Smith's martyrdom and Winter Quarters, about the Battalion's march westward and their mother's captivity among the Indians, he listened, so long as she kept it simple, with the interest he paid to any story, but he didn't seem to connect any of it with himself. In a desperate attempt to reach him, to make him know what he owed Shea, Talitha one day told him what she never had before: that the crescent brand on Shea's face had been the price of James's release.

As James stared with widened, troubled eyes, Talitha wondered if she'd made a mistake. But James needed to know it sometime. "You remember the great big Apache who brought the cradleboard for the twins?" she probed. "That was Mangus. He held the iron to Shea's cheek."

"Why?"

Talitha had never explained his parentage. Maybe now was the time, so it wouldn't be a sudden shock when he was older. But, feeling as she did about Juh, it was hard to explain the truth. She loved James better than anyone in the world, yet he was, in blood, the son of the Apache who'd helped kill her uncle and grandfather, who'd held their mother in bondage.

Struggling to master the grief and rage that still flooded her at that memory, Talitha captured her brother's warm brown hand and held it between hers.

"Shea was branded to prove he was brave enough to have you in his keeping. Because you—we—sort of belonged to an Apache called Juh." The dark blue eyes stared into hers, puzzled, questioning, and Talitha saw there was no way to tell the story of the brand without telling James of his origins. Catching her breath in a gulp, she said flatly, "Juh's your father."

James's smooth brow wrinkled. "Like Shea is Patrick's and Miguel's?"

It's not the same, it should never have happened! "He's your blood father," Talitha said carefully. From the expression on James's pondering face, she wished desperately she'd never begun the revelation. Santiago could have done it better; perhaps even Shea or Socorro.

"Shea won't give Patrick or Miguel away?" James asked. "Not even if someone was branded for them?"

"No. But Socorro and Shea belong together." Talitha drew James to her and hugged him. "Our mother didn't belong with Juh, you see. She belonged with my father."

"Then why wasn't he with her?"

"He had to go to California with the soldiers."

"He's not my father?"

"No, dear."

"Then I wouldn't belong with him even if our mother did. I remember the big Apache. I wish he were my father. Is Juh like him?"

"No. Anyway, James, I took care of you after mother died and I'm your sister, that's certain! You belong with me!"

James didn't argue with that, but he seemed to be thinking cautiously about all of this. "Will my real father come see me some day?"

"Yes." Talitha swallowed, glad James couldn't know that she prayed every day for this not to happen. "When you're older, Juh may want you to go with him. We had to promise that in order to keep you while you were little."

"So he didn't give me away for good." James sounded much relieved.

"You won't want to be an Apache, James! And when he knows that, Juh will let you come back to us." Talitha cried out her hope, holding her brother close.

His body was warm and sturdily sweet in her arms, but he didn't speak again.

Each fall the mine manager, Don Elizario Carvajal, bastard of Narciso Cantú, big and bearlike except for his thin waxed mustache and bleak eyes, came to the ranch, heavily escorted, to pay the agreed half of mine profits after the *Mimbreño* tenth was deducted.

He also brought news garnered from messages from his father and the men of the *conductas*. There had been a plague of cholera in Sonora last year. Over a thousand people died in a month in the province of Altar alone. But that was over now. A new plague was approaching. The Yanquis.

Since the end of the war, Mexico had been trying to strengthen its northern frontier and keep it from slipping into American hands. In 1848 Sonora had decreed that military soldier-colonists would take the place of garrisons at Bavispe, Fronteras, Santa Cruz, Tucson and Altar, and though most of these were more on paper than actual, a Captain Gomez from Fronteras had settled in Tubac with a small group of soldiers and civilians and was hoping to build it to a point where it could withstand both Apaches and U.S. soldiers.

A group of Southern Mormons had wintered at Tubac last year and Gomez had tried to induce them to stay, but though they'd done some planting and irrigating, they evidently decided opportunities were better elsewhere and had gone their way that spring.

In the summer of 1851 the commandant general of Sonora himself had led a combined force of military colonists and presidial soldiers as far as the Gila, fighting Apaches when they could find them. But Apaches never fought large numbers when they could avoid it, which they usually could. As soon as the expedition dispersed, scattering to the far-flung presidios, the Apaches flowed back like a river momentarily diverted by a fragile earthen dam.

In a desperate hope of colonizing its northern region, Sonora granted to a group of land and mining speculators all vacant lands and mines from the thirtieth parallel to the Gila. Sixty thousand square miles to the French *Compania Restauradora de las Minas de Arizona!* The national government declared the grant unconstitutional, but there was no end to the plans of foreigners trying to make a fortune out of Sonora's unhappy plight. In order to get settlers, the province was willing to make almost any concession to French, Swiss or Germans—any entrepreneurs so long as they weren't Americans.

Meanwhile, the Joint Boundary Commission, set up in the Treaty of Guadalupe Hidalgo to establish the southern boundary of the United States, had surveyed one that the United States refused to ratify because it left a strip west of El Paso, vital to a future transcontinental railroad, as a part of Mexico.

"If the Americans want the land west of El Paso for their railroad," Shea said, "they must surely prefer the route marked by Cooke's Battalion. That passed through Tucson."

"But of course," shrugged Don Elizario. "The Yanquis desire much when one remembers that they haven't been able to stop the Indians, on what is now *their* territory, from raiding into Mexico. They agreed to that in Article Eleven of the Treaty, but they haven't done any better with Apaches than did Spain or Mexico."

"Do you think there'll be another war?"

"Who knows? The people of Mesilla, which is in part of the disputed area, moved west of the Rio Grande in 1850 exactly in order to escape American rule." He settled more deeply into a chair and accepted more coffee. "Mexico cannot win a war with the Yanquis, my friend, not now. The Yanquis will have what they want."

Boundary commissions and quarreling governments seemed far away from the ranch which sold its beef in Tubac and Tucson after that one drive with the Texans. Men couldn't be spared for the long drive and besides, according to travelers drifting back from the gold fields, prices had dropped by 1851 to fifty to one hundred fifty dollars per head, and were going lower.

Returned from selling cattle in Tucson that fall of 1852, Shea said the place was full of riffraff, drifters who had either not found their gold in California, or who'd been run out of even the rough mining communities. And the bandits of Sonora preferred the frontier so long as there were enough travelers to pluck.

But a different kind of people were beginning to appear along the Santa Cruz. Army officers, often topographical engineers with the Boundary Survey; mining engineers, some of them educated at prestigious German mining schools; and a new kind of settler.

Calabazas, the old *visita* just south of where Sonoita Creek joined the Santa Cruz, had been taken over by some Europeans under a contract made with the former governor of Sonora, Manuel Gándara, who claimed the land, having bought it at auction in 1844 after Santa Anna's decree that all temporal church lands should be sold. That spring of 1853, Gándara began to stock the hacienda with six thousand sheep and goats, a hundred cows with calves, a hundred brood mares, oxen, mules, and horses for riding.

"I like him, that Federico Hulsemann," reported Santiago, who had ridden over to see what was happening. "He's German, has traveled the world, and came here from California. He and his helpers are making the church into a ranch house and building a barracks. Gándara has sent up workers and they're making it into quite a place."

"Can they hold off Apaches?" Shea demanded.

Santiago grinned. "No doubt they'll get a chance to try."

That chance came sooner than anyone expected. Not long after Santiago's visit in mid-April, a group of Americans led by a dark-haired man named Andrew Gray, who were surveying a possible railroad route, stopped overnight at Rancho del Socorro, sleeping outside but elated at being offered tasty, well-prepared food. One, an artist, Charles Schuchard, made a sketch of the house and gave it as thanks to the O'Sheas who wouldn't accept pay for their hospitality.

Socorro gazed after the eleven men, proudly holding the picture. "Yanquis," she said softly, lifting her hand to Shea's grim face. "But they were nice, *querido!*"

He seemed to give himself a shake, forced a smile. "Not all can be bad. Since it seems we're to have them here in spite of Mexico and Apaches, I guess we may as well get used to them. But I don't like it!"

"Of course not!" She raised herself on tiptoe to kiss him, laughing softly, looking very young though she was expecting again. "You are my redheaded burro, after all! But let us find a place for this beautiful drawing!"

"Better put it in the chest," he said. "Then it won't get rained on when the roof leaks."

She frowned. "I want it on the wall. Where I can see it!"

"When you can see the real thing just by stepping outside?" But he smiled indulgently and helped her find a wall that seemed not to trickle during the rainy times.

It was late that morning when the artist came riding back, brought his horse to a trembling halt by the corral where Belen was accustoming an especially fine young horse to the bit while the men watched and gave advice.

Everyone whirled at the horseman's approach. Shea caught the horse's headstall and soothed it. "Anything amiss, Mr. Schuchard?"

"Apaches!" cried the artist. "We met a couple hundred of them making for Calabazas!"

Shea's mouth pinched tight. "They killed your friends?"

Schuchard shook his head. "They had only bows and arrows and you know we've got Sharps carbines and dragoon six-shooters. Besides, they said they weren't bothering with Americans. One of them named Romero spoke Spanish which our Peter Brady understands.

Romero says they intend to destroy Calabazas, kill the Mexican men, and take captive their women and children. The Apaches don't want Mexicans starting to settle again in what they call their own country."

"So what's your party going to do?" Shea asked quietly.

Schuchard gave him an astonished look. "Why, ride on and help Calabazas if we can! Will you come, too? You have rifles."

Socorro, Anita following, had come out in time to hear what was happening. Her gaze met her husband's. "Of course you must go," she said.

"It may cost us Mangus's protection."

Her chin came up. This pregnancy was weighing on her early, though she carried her full share of the work. "We can't let others be slaughtered."

Shea brought her hands to his lips. "Bless you, love!" He turned to the men. "Will you come?"

Anita gasped and caught Chuey's arm. With a shake of his head, he put her from him. Santiago was already catching up Noche. "Ride fast as you can to El Charco," Shea told Talitha. "Get the Sanchezes to come here and fort up till we're back, just in case any Apaches stray over this direction. Then you'd better warn them at San Manuel."

So Talitha, skirts kilted, rode south while the men went west.

El Charco had gained two men in spite of Güero's continued absence. Last Christmas all the Sanchezes came to Socorro so that Shea could, in a measure, solemnize the marriage of Juana to Cheno Vasquez, a vaquero of Don Narciso's who'd come north because he couldn't forget the tall quiet girl with the tender eyes and mouth. Francisco, his younger brother, had traveled with him and had been welcomed to help work the increasing herds.

The whole family was working on the young married couple's house when Talitha reined up Ladorada and gasped out her news. Pedro Sanchez pushed back his sombrero and his monkey face wrinkled even more deeply.

"Ay, *señorita,* we come at once. Shall I send some-one to San Manuel?"

"No, I'll go," said Talitha, slipping down and lead-ing the golden mare toward the watering tank.

Even in her anxiety and rush, Carmencita, Pedro's wife, brought Talitha a gourd of water, thrust some pumpkin candy into her hand. "Your legs are shaking, child! Eat this while you ride!"

Talitha hadn't seen Tjúni in the two and a half years since the Papago woman had left the main ranch, but there was no change in that handsome face with its short nose that gave it an almost catlike look. With the several Papago families that had settled at San Manuel, she was roasting agave in a large pit at the base of the mountain that lay south of the huts, *ramadas* and cir-cular granaries of the *ranchería.*

"Calabazas?" Tjúni's eyes widened. In the sunlight they looked dark amber. "Don Patricio thought he must aid them?"

"Of course he had to!" said Talitha hotly.

Tjúni gave her a glance of vast scorn, then shrugged. "I think Apache not come this way, but we set watch, hide in mountain cave if we see them. Cave good and big, spring right beside it." With pride, she went on to explain that everyone knew what do to do in case of alarm—snatch up food and weapons and make for the natural fortress.

She didn't offer refreshment and turned back to the pit, helping spread on a layer of bear grass. At a few words from her, a boy of about Talitha's age ran to position himself on a hill facing the Santa Cruz Valley.

The sun was slanting toward the mountain peaks. It would be dark before Talitha could get home since she'd need to keep to trails running from San Manuel to El Charco and thence to Socorro. But Tjúni didn't suggest sending someone with Talitha, and she wouldn't ask what the woman wouldn't offer.

Returning to El Charco in the twilight, Talitha watered Ladorada and got herself a drink from the bucket inside, also appropriating a piece of jerky. As she started on in the increasing darkness, the thoughts she'd kept at bay crowded up and tormented her.

What had happened at Calabazas? Was Shea all right? Belen, Santiago, Chuey? Had the Apaches been beaten off so that they were now hunting a new target? Were those at Socorro safe?

The darkness seemed full of terrible questions. Sobbing with exhaustion and fear, Talitha urged Ladorada onward. When, after what seemed an endless time, she saw soft light shining from what had to be the ranch house, she cried even harder, this time in relief.

XIX

The men rode in that night long after the Sanchez family had shared itself out between the vaqueros' quarters and Chuey and Anita's house. "You should rest," Talitha urged Socorro after things from the evening meal had been cleared away.

Socorro put an arm around Talitha who was now the taller of the two. For an unsettling moment, the older woman seemed almost to lean on the girl before she kissed her and straightened. "Perhaps I will lie down for a while after I get the twins to bed. You're not too tired to watch?"

"I don't think I can sleep till they come home," Talitha whispered, trying not to cry. Socorro certainly felt as bad as she did; it wasn't fair to worry her.

"If they're forted up inside the church, the fight could go on till the Apaches give up," Socorro pointed out, never admitting that it might not be Apaches who lost. "We can't stay up all night or we'll be useless tomorrow."

She went to her bedroom with the twins. James had already collapsed on his pallet near Talitha's; Chacho nestled against him. Chusma leaped into Talitha's lap, purred and yawned.

"You don't have to wait for me, cat," Talitha murmured, scratching behind the ears, but she was grateful for the comfort of the soft warm body. She was starting to drowse, jerking her head up each time she nodded off, when Socorro came back and said gently, "I've slept all I can. Lie down, Tally. I'll call you the minute I hear horses."

"I'll wait just a little longer." Talitha, holding Chusma, went to stand in the door, feel the cool night breeze drive away some of the sleep.

A distant sound made her stiffen before it faded; she couldn't be sure she'd really heard anything unusual. Stepping outside, she listened with her breath held. In a moment she detected it again, the far-off rhythm of hoofs.

"Horses," she told Socorro. "Shall I wake up the Sanchezes? Apaches never travel at night if they can help it, but——"

"Better they get up and not be needed than die in their sleep."

It always surprised Talitha when Socorro showed grim humor, but then neither could she imagine her shooting a scalp hunter. Putting Chusma down, Talitha hurried to the vaqueros' house to wake Pedro and the younger men, then called the women who were at Anita's.

Socorro had extinguished the lamp but she had carbines ready for the Vasquez brothers who had none. She, Anita and Talitha took their weapons. The doors were shut. Each window and niche was guarded.

It was very still in the house as they listened to the nearing sound of horses. Pedro Sanchez sighed with relief.

"Not many horses. No more than three or four. I think it is Don Patricio."

Socorro gave a soft glad cry but added swiftly, "Let us wait, all the same, till we're sure."

Squinting through her rifle niche, in the pale light of the waning moon, Talitha could discern looming shapes. Then she separated them into three distinct forms and, as her heart pounded with joy, she recognized the way each man rode.

Shea. Santiago. Belen. They were safe!

Just as she started to call out to them, Shea hailed the house. In a twinkling, rifles were leaned on the wall, the door was opened, and everyone went out to welcome the men who had returned.

Relaxing with coffee and food, minor wounds anointed and dressed, Shea and his companions told what had happened. "By the time we got there, the fight was on," said Shea. "We really weren't needed. Seems a captive of the raiders had managed to escape and get to Tucson. Captain Hilarión García and Antonio Comaduran had brought sixty lancers and forty Apaches *de paz* and were waiting for the attack. Must have been at least two hundred on the raid, Pinal and Coyotero most likely."

"García's men charged while the raiders were still a mile from Calabazas," put in Santiago. "The lancers brought down scores of them and the tame Apaches finished them off. Don Federico Hulsemann and his partner were *muy valiente,* coming outside the walls to fight."

"And the ears!" Belen exulted. "A string almost three feet long to go to the capital at Ures!"

Santiago chuckled. "One of Señor Gray's men thought they were dried apples till he noticed the copper and shell earrings that were still fastened to some of them!"

Socorro stifled a sound of protest. Shea drew her to him, leaning his head against her breast. "I think my wife has heard enough. We'd better all get to sleep." He said to the Sanchezes, "I appreciate your coming."

"It was for our safety also," demurred Pedro.

Shea glanced at Talitha. "You warned Tjúni?"

"Yes. She sent a boy to stand guard. They have a cave in the mountain. She thinks they can stand off any raiders that come that way."

Shea looked startled, but his mouth firmed and he said no more, leading Socorro off to their room. The others lingered for a few minutes, Belen whispering how the head of Romero, the interpreter who'd talked with Gray's party, was fastened to a spike near the door of a room used as a mess hall.

Seeing Talitha's face, Santiago gave her cheek a comforting touch. "And Señor Hulsemann gave us some excellent mescal! But it's over, God be praised, the Apaches have had a stiff lesson—and now let's all sleep for what's left of the night!"

The Apaches left Calabazas alone for the rest of that summer, but in June they attacked La Canoa, a ranch ten miles north of Tubac, killed four post-riders and another man, took captives and slaughtered oxen.

Tubac's new commanding officer, Andrés Zenteno, managed to wangle thirty-eight muskets and ammunition for the thirty-six peaceful Apaches who, with eighty-two of their women and children, volunteered to settle down at Tubac in mid-July. Because four yoke of Tubac's oxen had been killed the month before, leaving only two yoke for all the colonists, and because there were no extra plows and it was getting late to plant, Zenteno had to supply his Apaches *de paz* with wheat while his distant superiors exhorted him to see that no supplies were wasted and to make his allies self-supporting as soon as possible.

"Commander Zenteno wants to lead an expedition against the hostiles," reported Santiago who seemed to have found something at Tubac to engage his attention, for he visited the presidio every week or two, sometimes accompanied by Belen. Talitha wrinkled her nose at the way they smelled when they returned, of tobacco and some heavier, muskier scent. "He asked the Tucson garrison for men but was told no one could be spared because everyone was busy in the fields and provisions were short." Santiago chuckled. "You could hear Zenteno all over the presidio! He wrote at once to the governor. You can be sure the very paper smoked!"

That didn't save Don Ignacio Iberri of Santa Cruz who was ridden down a few days later by a half-dozen Apaches and killed within sight of Tubac's wall. But at least there was a garrison and the German partners continued to manage their sheep and goat ranch at Calabazas. The people of Rancho del Socorro no longer felt so isolated.

It was a long summer for Talitha, 1853, though it must have seemed even longer to Socorro who expected her baby in September. The twins wanted a sister like Paulita, the baby girl Anita was fondly suckling, and Socorro, earnestly admonished by them, promised to do her best. Her feet were swollen, she moved awkwardly, and Talitha worried about her, remembering the twins' birth, though she kept assuring Shea, who was also troubled, that this time it would be very different. Carmencita, who had delivered Anita so competently and often served as a midwife, would come to stay at the house several weeks before the probable time. There should be no difficulty.

Yet Socorro's condition weighed on Talitha for her own body was undergoing changes that both bewildered and pleased her. Anita had placidly explained the spots of blood that had so frightened Talitha.

"You're a woman now, *chiquita!* Every month, until you're my mother's age, this will come. Unless you have conceived." She cast a sympathetic look at the girl, lowered her voice. "Has Doña Socorro explained about that? None of our men would molest you, of course, but strangers . . ."

Talitha wasn't sure exactly how it was with men and women, but she'd seen bulls mount cows and stallions breed mares. She knew the tiny appendage on James and the twins would grow with them and someday be capable of entering a female. But when a flickering half-picture of Shea with Socorro edged into her mind before, shamed and terrified, she could banish it. She knew she couldn't bear to be like that with anyone, not unless he was just like Shea. And there was no one like him.

So she mumbled something to Anita and made her escape. There was no escaping the inexorable shaping of her body, though, the strange conflicting moods that stormed through her. She needed to be alone. Often that summer she went to the hot spring. She scarcely ever thought of the Place of Skulls.

One day in August she'd been gathering acorns and stopped by the spring to bathe and wash her hair with the orris root she kept in a crevice near the stone basin. Her dress smelled of sweat—only in these past few months had it had an odor—and she stripped it off and washed it, rinsing it well before she hung it to dry on a manzanita. Then she climbed up the rocks and slid into the basin, holding her breath as she settled in water up to her shoulders.

It felt so good! Weariness flowed out of her. After lying there a few minutes, reveling in the gentle push of the water against her naked flesh, she sat up and made lather with the root, sudsing her hair, rinsing it where the water flowed over and down. She washed her body next, scrubbing her elbows and feet with special diligence, then cleaning her fingernails.

Splashing out the used water with her feet, she sank down, leaned against the polished stone, and luxuriated as the spring filled up the basin.

When she reckoned her dress must be almost dry, she stretched and got to her feet, throwing back her head, fluffing her hair. She froze as a man's voice—not Shea's, but a stranger's—said in English, "A nymph in the wilderness!"

She couldn't reach her dress. In her startled anger, it seemed better to stand calmly, pretend there was nothing to cover, than clutch at herself with inadequate hands.

How had he approached so quietly? Even the sound of the spring shouldn't have covered all warning of his approach. She was as furious with herself as she was with him. What if he'd been a hostile?

Fear gripped her then as she stared down into eyes like frozen water barely reflecting the sky. He might be as dangerous as any Apache. He had dark eyebrows and lashes and as he moved closer, resting a hand on the edge of the basin, she saw that the shafts on his clean-shaven face were black though his hair was vibrant

286

silver. His hat and vest were trimmed with silver conchos and he had a revolver holstered at his belt.

He laughed softly. "A mute nymph? One who couldn't chatter? Or scream?" He seemed closer though it must have been a trick of her dilating eyes. "That would be too good to be true! Come, pretty, what's your name?"

She ignored that. Memory, leaping back, produced that face, those eyes. In Mangus's camp, long ago. Unable to check a sharp intake of breath, she saw in the same moment that he'd recognized her.

"That child the Apaches had!" His eyes went over her so that in spite of her resolve, she instinctively brought one arm over her breasts, shielded with the other hand that triangular patch of bright gold hair. "You've grown," he said, laughing again. "Oh, beautifully you've grown! But I remember those big serious eyes and yellow, yellow hair."

"And I remember you." She spoke through stiff dry lips.

"Then that makes us old friends," he said easily. "I'm Judah Frost." Freeing her dress from the manzanita, he handed it to her. "Come out of the water, my dear, and tell me your name and how you come to be here."

"You aren't my friend." There was a cold passionless evil in him that she discerned along with his beauty. "You tried to buy me." But she was glad of the dress and pulled it quickly over her head, retreated to the ledge above, well out of his reach.

"Of course. I intended to try to locate your family, restore you to them. Did they find you, then?"

"My mother died. She was an Apache captive."

"And your father?"

She shook her head. "He went to California with the Mormon Battalion. That's all I know."

"I'm lately returned from California. Perhaps I met him." He frowned as if trying to recapture something. "By jingo, there was a Mormon I met in 'Frisco! Said his wife and family had been left in Santa Fe, and when he went back for them, they'd vanished. He looked in Salt Lake, too, and there someone told him the wife and some male kin had left Santa Fe by wagon, trying to follow him."

"We did." She thought of her mother, subjected to Juh, the drudge of his wives.

"But you didn't get far," finished the stranger, not unkindly. "Wouldn't you like to be with your father now?"

Jared Scott, tall and red-haired, who'd whirled his wife in the light of the campfires. Jared Scott, who'd gone off with his Battalion.

"No," said Talitha.

Dark brows met above a straight, finely shaped nose. "No? Just like that?"

She didn't want to explain, but he evidently had no intention of going away. "My brother's part Apache," she said baldly. "I doubt my father would want him. We're doing very well at our foster parents'."

"And who are they?"

Something deep rooted beneath her conscious mind made her hate to give this man any knowledge, any power, but since he was in the region, he was almost sure to find the ranch. Besides, though he hadn't tried to come closer, it wouldn't hurt for him to know that she lived close by, had protectors.

"The O'Sheas of Rancho del Socorro got my brother and me away from the Apaches." Nor did she think it a poor idea to add: "Mangus protects them."

For an instant, those chill light eyes turned almost black. "Why does he do that?"

"Doña Socorro and a Papago woman killed scalp hunters who were attacking some of Mangus's women."

"Did they indeed?" He looked incredulous.

"If you don't believe me, go on up the cañon. You can see the skulls." Talitha reached for her sandals. "I must be getting home. They'll wonder why I've been gone so long."

"Then let me escort you," he said. "I'd like to meet these remarkable O'Sheas."

He picked up her basket of acorns, held out a tanned, slender, strongly muscled hand to help her down. Avoiding it, Talitha came down in another place. She didn't see how she could refuse to walk with him, but she'd have felt just as comfortable if her companion had been a handsome, intricately marked and quite deadly rattler.

"Don't you have a horse?" she asked.

"I left him at the mouth of the cañon, hobbled so he could browse while I explored."

"What are you exploring?"

"A multitude of things." His eyes didn't warm though he smiled at her. "I'm a very curious man. And you still haven't told me your name."

"Talitha. Talitha Scott. Are you looking for a railroad route? Or do you want a mine?"

"You're curious, too," he chuckled. "Well, Talitha Scott, I want a railroad and a mine. A ranch, of course. And a freighting company wouldn't be a bad notion."

"Did you find *that* much gold in California?"

He laughed briefly. "Enough. Now, Talitha, what do *you* want?"

Taken by surprise, for she wasn't used to thinking about it, Talitha started to say she didn't want anything, then realized that wasn't true. She wanted James to stay at the ranch, not go to the Apaches; she wanted Socorro to be safely delivered of her baby; she wanted all things to go well for Shea.

"Well?" the stranger prodded. "I told you what I'd like. Aren't you going to swap?"

"No."

She couldn't see his face. The way was too rough and narrow for them to walk together. He didn't speak for so long that she grew nervous, slightly ashamed of being rude. She was relieved when he broke the silence, pleasantly, as if he hadn't been rebuffed.

"How old are you, Talitha?"

That he could know. "Thirteen."

"Ah. Young. But old enough to want a good many things, I'll be bound!" She didn't answer. There was a laugh in his voice as he persisted. "Don't you want rings on your fingers and bells on your toes? Maybe you're dreaming already of a husband, a house of your very own where you could do exactly as you pleased—"

"I do as I please!"

"Really? You please to get hot and scratched gathering acorns then, and wearing a raggedy dress that was once too big on you and now's too small?"

She stopped abruptly. "Give me my acorns! And you—you go on ahead! I don't want to walk with you!"

"But I want to walk with you." Unruffled, he put the basket out of her reach behind him. "Believe this, Talitha: when I want something, I get it."

She made a frantic lunge for the basket, heard him laugh. His hand clamped on her forearm. "Shall we walk, Talitha?"

Fighting tears of rage, she met his mocking smile. It maddened her past endurance. She sank her teeth into his arm, brought her knee up at what she knew from vaquero talk was the most vulnerable part of a male.

He dodged. She heard the basket drop, the acorns hit rocks, clamped her teeth tighter. Suddenly there was inexorable hurting pressure on her jaws, digging at the hinge, forcing her teeth apart. She felt his blood on her lips, fought him savagely, but with both arms and hands he held her, and then with his body as he pressed her against a great rock.

Panting, she couldn't move.

"So little, fierce and lovely," he sighed. "Let's see what else you are!"

His mouth took hers as he held the back of her head in his hand. She could not escape. But she kept her lips tight closed against his though she was trembling, near panic in her fear of what he might do.

After what couldn't have been a long time, though it seemed so, he lifted his head. "You'll give me nothing but the taste of my own blood? But your prim-tucked mouth told me what I most wanted to know. You haven't been tumbled by some vaquero or soldier. No man has kissed you."

"Shea has!"

"Your foster father. Scarcely what I meant."

Releasing her, he studied his wrist, marked in a bloody crescent by her teeth, neither helping nor hindering as she knelt and began to salvage acorns. When she had all she could find, she started down the cañon again.

He followed. Unable to believe his presumption, she threw back over her shoulder, "Go on ahead and get your horse! Ride to Tubac or whenever you're headed! You can't go home with me now!"

"But of course I will." His resonant voice was smooth with irony. "I must meet this foster father you prefer to a husband, see this fabulous rancho where you do exactly as you please!"

"Shea will kill you!" she choked, whirling. "And Belen and Santiago, too!"

"Please!" he begged. "You wouldn't have me killed three times!" His caressing tone angered her more than abuse would have.

"I would if I could!"

"No doubt. But alas, small Talitha, we're all limited by the possible. Much as you'd like to see me shot or horse-whipped, you won't tell anyone that instead of giving you the spanking you deserved, I chose to kiss you." He unrolled his sleeve till it hid the marks of her teeth.

"I will tell! Unless you leave us alone!"

He shook his head as if grieved by her stubbornness, then asked briskly, "Is your Shea an expert with firearms? Or those others you mentioned?"

"They can shoot! They hunt. And just a few months ago they helped beat the Apaches who were attacking Calabazas."

"I see. Perhaps every week or two they aim at

something. That doesn't put them in my class, Talitha.
I have, at times, made my living by killing men. And
I practice. Every day."

Before she could follow the motion of his hand, he
had drawn the big gun, cocked it and fired. Sound
echoed among the rocks. A squirrel fell from a tree just
before them, its head blown away.

"A man's much bigger than that," the silver-haired
man remarked. "Would your foster mother like it for
cooking?"

"No," whispered Talitha. She was used to branding
and castrating, had herself helped clean deer, javelina
and other game, but she was sickened at this wanton
snuffing out of a bright-eyed, frisking little life.

That was when her real fear of Judah Frost began.

His horse, a big gelding, was the color of fog, with
a silvery mane and tail. "Think you could ride him?"
Frost asked as he put on the bridle and slipped off the
rawhide hobbles.

"I don't want to."

He gave her a mild look. "Well, probably you
couldn't. Selim has a mind of his own and still needs
a strong dose of quirt and spurs occasionally." He
swung into the silver-mounted saddle which had a rifle
scabbarded at one side. "Shall I carry your basket?"

"No."

"Talitha. I would advise you to practice courtesy with
me. Just as I practice the gun."

"Why?" Her lips curled. "Will you shoot me if
you don't like what I say?"

He threw back his head and laughed, but it wasn't
a pleasant sound. "What a child you are! No, my dear.
Indeed I won't shoot you. But if you're surly to me
in front of your people, they're bound to wonder why."
He added silkily, "Questions could prove unfortunate—
for them."

Scanning his face, she realized that this was someone far different from anyone she'd ever encountered,
someone completely ruthless with a corruption in his

nature that made Apache cruelties she had seen appear crude and of almost childlike simplicity.

If it came to a fight between Frost and the men of the ranch, she believed they could kill him. She also was sure he'd kill one or two of them first.

"Why are you doing this?" she cried desperately. "What do you want?"

"Why, Talitha," he said, gravely smiling at her. "I want you to be happy."

That frightened her more than anything else he could have said. Feeling like a captive, she trudged for the ranch while the gray horse, firmly controlled, paced along beside her.

Frost put himself out to be charming. Only Belen took himself off immediately after the evening meal. Talitha, as soon as the dishes were done, offered to put the twins to bed, but they set up a howl, wanting to see more of the intriguing stranger who'd beguiled them with sleight of hand tricks.

"Here, now!" he chided. "Have a knee apiece, you rascals! I'll sing you all the verses I know of 'Sweet Besty from Pike' and then you're off to sleep without a murmur!"

Talitha shook herself, angrily feeling bewitched, as the deep rich voice finished the adventures of Betsy, Long Ike and their oxen, hog, Shanghai rooster and small yellow dog. How could this man, so helpfully delivering the sleepy-eyed twins to her, be the same person who'd coolly threatened to kill the men if she told what he'd done in the cañon?

His eyes met hers, searing, like fire-ice, to her bones. Hastily, she swept Patrick and Miguel away. Once they were asleep, she'd intended to go to bed herself, but the things Frost was saying were too interesting to miss.

Grudgingly coming back into the kitchen, she settled in a far corner and began picking over the acorns she'd collected that day, cutting out wormy parts. There'd be a delicious acorn stew tomorrow. Chusma came, purring, to curl up by her. That compensated a little for James's utter enthrallment. At six, he was too big for knees, but he perched on the bench near Frost's chair, Chacho a gleaming black mass in his lap, and hung on tales of mining and travel.

Laughing, Frost recited "The Miners' Ten Commandments," beginning with "Thou shalt have no other claim but one," and ending with "Thou shalt not covet thy neighbor's gold nor his claim . . . nor move his stake . . . nor wash the tailings from his sluice's mouth. . . ."

He told about a Biblically inclined partner he'd had in one "diggins," who, menaced by claim-jumpers who disputed his tape-measured stakes, put away the tape, brought out his rifle, and told the intruders that if they aimed to set pick in earth, they'd better first make peace with God because he promised them he'd send their souls to meet Him. "And that bunch of hard-cases looked at his rifle a minute and went off like a bunch of shorn lambs," Frost concluded.

His most important news was that U.S. President Franklin Pierce had sent James Gadsden, a South Carolinian railroad promoter recommended by Secretary of War Jefferson Davis, to Mexico that summer to negotiate for a larger cession of land. Northern Sonora was a crucial part of this coveted territory since the best apparent southern route for a transcontinental railroad ran through it, the way searched out by the Mormon Battalion.

"Gadsden's work is being kept pretty secret, though," Frost continued. "A lot of Mexicans aren't happy with Santa Anna. If they knew he was bargaining more land away to the Americans, he'd have a revolution on his hands."

Shea gave his guest a measuring look. "If it's such a secret, how do you know?"

Taking no offense, Judah Frost smiled. "My dear sir, I'm an investor in Gadsden's rail interests. I naturally hear a few things that aren't general knowledge.

Which is very useful, let me tell you, in putting capital to work."

Talitha had heard the grown-ups discussing what they should do with the money that was beginning to accumulate from cattle sales and their percentage of the mine. They had bought some sheep and goats from the Calabazas settlers and the *conductas* had brought up pigs and chickens as well as household needs. The pigs had survived fairly well, providing tasty *chorizo* or sausage as well as bacon and ham. But the chickens were all gone in a matter of days in spite of the ocotillo fence put around them. A coyote and skunk dug under it, hawks and eagles swooped down for a picnic, and that was farewell to Socorro's longing for eggs.

If the country ever grew safer, Shea wanted to travel east and buy some good beef stock, Durhams or Herefords to breed with the hardy native stock. Addition of the Texas *Chinos* had helped, but the meat of these tough little cattle was stringy and flavorless. Shea planned to bring back a fine stud, too, and some blooded mares, again to breed to the best of the present animals and improve the strain. But Texas was the closest place fine stock might possibly be bought, and it could be necessary to go a lot farther.

So when Frost mentioned ways of using money, Talitha could feel Shea and Santiago's immediate interest. Politely, with a shade of disbelief, Shea asked, "You wouldn't be looking around here, would you, Mr. Frost, for a place to invest your capital?"

"I'm always on the watch." Frost's laugh was disarming. "My mining partner, Marc Revier, a Freiburg-trained engineer, is down at Ures right now negotiating for some land near Tubac which he says has great mining potential. And it's high time someone went into the freighting business."

"Freighting?" Santiago echoed. "Why, who would they freight to?"

"Tubac and Tucson."

At the incredulous stares, Frost chuckled and went

on persuasively, "Not great markets just now, I'll grant! But when the United States acquires this region, as it will soon by war or purchase, a lot of those topographical engineers running surveys, a good many army officers, are going to start mining along the Santa Cruz. And of course the United States will have to establish posts. Bound to be one at Tucson and I expect at least one down in this area."

Shea nodded somewhat glumly. "I take your meaning. Where there are miners and soldiers, there'll be merchants, and merchants need supplies."

"Exactly. Why, Louis Jaeger, who runs a ferry at Yuma Crossing where the U.S. has a fort, has gone into freighting and will make a fortune if another Yuma arrow doesn't finish him off." He told how the Yumas at that strategic crossing of the Gila River had long ago killed the Spanish soldiers and Franciscan priests who'd tried to settle among them, and now were sometimes friendly, sometimes hostile, to travelers coming from or going to California.

"One of the funniest things I ever heard was how the governor of California sent an expedition to punish the Yumas for doing in Joe Glanton. The militia lost one little fight to the Yumas and then settled back to eat up their food. California's still paying the bills."

"Who was Glanton?"

Dark eyebrows rose toward Frost's gleaming hair. "Never heard of him? He was the worst—or best, depending on your view—of the scalp hunters. When the Sonoran government began to suspect he was selling them more Mex scalps than Apache, he wound up at Fort Yuma in 1850 and helped run a ferry. Got into a fight with the Yumas who had another ferry a few miles away. Kicked the chief and took a club to him."

Shea shook his head. "Doesn't sound very smart."

"It wasn't. The Yumas killed eleven of the ferrymen, and the chief personally split Glanton's head open with a hatchet." Frost said quickly to Socorro whose face had gone pale, "I beg your pardon, ma'am."

Deftly changing the subject, he added that freighting supplies the one hundred eighty miles from San Diego to Fort Yuma had been so expensive that the fort had closed for a time. After an attack on Jaeger in 1851, the fort was reestablished and efforts to supply it by water proved successful last December when the *Uncle Sam,* a paddle-wheeled steamboat, navigated up the Colorado to the Yuma crossing.

"But *Uncle Sam* ran aground and sank this spring," said Frost. "So mules are bringing in supplies for the fort, and the freighter's making a pretty penny, you can bet!" He shaped his graceful long fingers into a pyramid. "If the Mexican government would establish a port along the northwest coast of Sonora, goods bought in California could be freighted here much more cheaply than from the port of Guaymas, farther south."

Shea studied Frost with considerable respect and a touch of wariness. "You certainly seem to have investigated the possibilities, sir!"

"Why, that's the fun of it, looking for a chance, taking the gamble." Frost shrugged disarmingly. "I've lost as much as I've won, I'd reckon, though I've never kept track."

For the most fleeting of seconds, his eyes rested upon Talitha. That burning shock went through her again and she got up quickly to discard the wormy bits of acorn, keeping her face averted till the flush left her cheeks. "When I see something I want," Frost's pleasant voice continued, "I go after it with all I've got. So far, I've always won though the victories may have cost a lot more than the prize was worth. To anyone but me."

Socorro said abruptly, her dark eyes searching his, "And did you keep your prizes, Señor Frost?"

He gave her a look of admiring respect. "Usually not, ma'am. The fun was in the getting. But I'm older now, more discriminating. I think the prizes I desire are ones I'll hold to." He patted back a yawn. "A most enjoyable evening! But I'm sure I've kept you from

297

your rest and I'll admit I'm weary. If I could spread my bedroll in your kitchen . . ."

Talitha winced at the thought of his sleeping in the next room, and was relieved when Shea said heartily, "There's an extra bed in the vaqueros' quarters since Chuey moved out. You're welcome to it and our table, Mr. Frost, as long as you care to stay."

"You're kind indeed."

The smooth hypocrite! Talitha longed to shout accusations at him but that could lead to disaster for these people she loved. She bent her face to Chusma as Frost thanked his hosts and said he would very much appreciate their hospitality for a few days.

XX

He left on the third morning after his arrival, riding west along the creek on the big gray horse, turning once to flourish his silver-flashing hat in farewell. In his saddlebags he carried at least half of the ranch's accumulated gold and silver to be invested in railroad shares and form part of the capital for a freighting enterprise in which the O'Sheas and Santiago would be partners with Frost.

He'd insisted on leaving them duly signed papers and guarantees though Shea had laughed at this. "If you're honest, we don't need papers, and if you're not, they won't matter!"

"Thanks for your confidence," said Frost dryly. "But I've learned it's best, in financial matters, to have it all in writing, fair, firm and easy to read!"

Santiago nodded. Though neither of them had said so, Talitha sensed that neither he nor Belen really liked Frost.

"He's promised to have his associates in California watch out for your father, Tally," said Socorro, as they turned back to their work. "If he's found, he'll be told where you are and that you're safe. And he'll send word to my cousin Carlos, telling him why I never got to California."

Talitha didn't for a moment believe that Frost cared about relieving her father's worry. "I wish Judah Frost would mind his own business!" she said violently.

Shea stared at her in surprise. Socorro, understanding at least some of Talitha's feelings, gave her a soothing hug. "Don't be troubled, dearest! After all this time, your father probably wouldn't make you live with him if you chose not to. But how joyful he would be to learn that you're alive!"

"And that mother's dead and bore an Apache child?" James was already at the corral so Talitha could vent her bitterness.

"It would be better than thinking you were all dead," Socorro said reasonably. "Besides, it's better to know what happened, however bad it was, than to always wonder, always try to find out."

"That's right." Shea's tone allowed no argument. "Whatever you think about it, Tally, your father has a right to know."

Smarting at his manner, Talitha wanted to cry out that Judah Frost was bad, that she didn't trust him. But if she told about that forced kiss and his threats, either Shea would ride after him and there'd be shooting or the O'Sheas would think she was exaggerating a playful whim into an assault. Either was unbearable, especially her fear that Shea would be killed. Talitha clenched her teeth, got a large basket, and went to gather mesquite beans.

She wasn't worried about the ranch's money, though. Frost wouldn't steal it because for some inexplicable reason he had decided to ingratiate himself with the O'Sheas. And Talitha had no doubt that he was going to have his railroad, his ranch, his freight company and mine.

But he's not going to have me.

And then she mocked herself for that thought because surely his kiss that day had been an impulse. He'd probably already forgotten it. Still, she hated him, for setting that first male kiss on her like a brand. She felt as marked as Shea though Frost's sign was invisible.

Frost's visit provided conversation and speculation for several days. Anita sighed dreamily that she was sure he was *muy fuerte y amoroso,* strong and passionate. And James went about whistling "Sweet Betsy."

Talitha found it excruciating. She wanted to forget, as much as she could, that the tall silver-haired stranger had ever set foot in the house, been accepted almost as one of them.

Because he wasn't! He was no more like Shea and Santiago than a blood-grooved Bowie was like a knife meant for honest work.

Estranged from the family because of what she knew about the man they trusted, also because she felt dirtied by his handling, Talitha found enough solitary outside work to keep her busy. She ranged widely, gathering wild currants and grapes as well as acorns and mesquite beans, restoring herself with golden air, and the changing shadows on the mountains.

"A coyote ran right up to me today," Santiago said one night at supper. "Acted blind and staggered. I guessed he had hydrophobia, so I got my rifle and shot him."

"Wonder if he'd got to any of the stock?" Shea asked in quick fear.

"I don't think so. The only animal he got close to was my horse and he didn't get a chance to bite him."

"But you don't know what he might have been doing earlier." Shea glanced around the table. "We'd all better pay extra attention if we see an animal acting peculiar. Patrick and Miguel, you *do* remember that if a wild animal comes up to you, you should get away fast and call someone? Don't pet it. It may be terribly sick and make you that way."

The twins nodded solemnly, but had an uproarious time playing mad coyote after the meal. Hydrophobia was a fearsome plague that spread some years through the wild creatures who would occasionally be so afflicted by the deadly sickness that they'd attack anything they chanced upon.

A few days after Santiago shot the coyote, a sow went into running, frothing fits. She made for Chacho who was majestically stalking past the *ramada* where Talitha was slicing squash for drying.

Chacho had no fear of hogs, having taught several of them that he wasn't to be tempered with. When the sow lurched toward him, the cat arched his back and hissed. When she still came on, in spite of Talitha's scream, he lashed out, bloodying the sensitive snout, but the sow was past pain. Her teeth grazed the cat as he streaked away, understanding he was up against something outside normal experience.

A little foam dribbled from the sow's jaw. She stood stupidly a moment after Chacho's disappearance, then reared about and started in Talitha's direction.

Talitha was already halfway to the house. Socorro came out with a rifle, rested it on the rain barrel, and fired. The sow jerked. Blood flowed from her side, but, horribly, she ran on. Shea, running from the corrals, brought the animal down with his second shot.

She collapsed only a few yards away from the house. "Did—did she hurt you?" Shea asked Talitha, his face chalky beneath its tan.

Talitha shook her head, unable to speak for a moment. It had been so sudden, so totally unexpected! "But she tried to bite Chacho," she said through trembling lips. "I don't know if she scratched him or not."

James, behind Shea, screwed up his eyes and shouted furiously, "She couldn't bite him! She couldn't!"

"We'd better find him and have a look," Shea said.

When James coaxed his pet out of the mill where he'd refuged after fleeing the sow, Shea carefully went over every inch of the soft black fur. It began to seem that Chacho had indeed escaped when the probing fingers paused, searched, then drew back the hair to expose a small scratch.

Talitha sucked in her breath. Shea got wearily to his feet, holding the cat. But James cried ringingly, "That was already there! It was, Shea! Chusma got mad at Chacho this morning and she did it!"

"You're sure?"

James nodded his head, claiming the cat, cuddling

him protectively. Shea hesitated, searching those dark blue eyes that were at once so defiant and pleading.

"James, we can't take chances."

"Chusma scratched him!"

Shea shrugged and turned to Santiago who had come up during the examination. "We'd better have a look at the pigs. Kill any that look like she may have nipped them."

Two young hogs had bloody marks that might have come from a grazing fang or from rubbing into a projecting dead branch. Both were killed and butchered since at this point the meat would be unaffected. The sow was burned to make sure that nothing, wild or tame, dug her up and caught the disease.

"I don't know if it can be caught that way," Shea said grimly. "But no use risking it."

Talitha was jumpy for several days and kept a rifle with her when she was working in the field. She tried to question James more closely about Chacho's scratch, but he only grabbed up his pet and made off with him. No more mad animals turned up and the day the sow went wild was fading in memory when, about two weeks later, Chacho came into the house while they were having supper.

He was unsteady, weaving, stood on the threshold blinking as if the last rays of sun hurt his eyes. "Chacho!" James ran toward him, arms reaching down.

The cat hissed, arching its back, but James kept on. Talitha shouted at him, slipping from the bench. Shea caught James backward just as Chacho bit. The teeth spiked into Shea's wrist. Santiago stripped off his leather vest, dropped it over the cat, swaddling his claws and head, while Shea held James who gave one wild cry and began to sob.

"What—what's he going to do?"

"See if Chacho's sick." Shea spoke quietly though blood dripped from the punctures on his wrist.

Belen said, "Perhaps if we cauterize those bites right away . . ." He built up the cookfire and put a dulled knife to heat. Talitha snatched James away from Shea and gave him a hard shake.

"Did you lie? About Chusma scratching your cat? Did you lie?"

"I didn't lie, Tally! Chusma did scratch him!" James struggled to wrest free. "Let me go! Let me go to Chacho!"

Santiago came back, his limp heavier than usual, addressed James as *ahijado,* godson. "Your pet had the sickness. I put him down in the quarters, watched till I was sure."

"How—could you be sure?" James panted.

"He went into fits. I put him out of his suffering."

James gave a shriek that echoed through Talitha's nerves. Then he went very still, slipped from Talitha's hand, and started for the quarters.

"You must be careful how you handle him, godson," Santiago said, going with him. "I'll help you burn him."

In spite of her anger at James, Talitha's heart ached for her brother. As soon as Shea's wrist was cauterized, she left him assuring Socorro that rabies didn't always follow from a bite, and picked up Chacho's "toys": a round of bone that could be jerked by a piece of rawhide, a leather ball stuffed with cattail down, a battered eagle feather.

She took these out to where Santiago and James had made a pyre on the slope close to the burial of the scalps of Tjúni's village and Santiago's rancho. Thank heaven Santiago hadn't shot Chacho or split his skull. He must have smothered him. She placed the feather between his paws, the ball and bone by his head, helped James heap smaller branches on top as Santiago started the fire.

She held James in her arms and they both wept.

Life went on. The men began to brand yearlings and cull out cattle that would be driven to market. James rode with them for the first time, helped chase down recalcitrants, kept the branding fire going, and learned to use the iron himself. Though it was grueling for a six-year-old, Talitha was glad he was kept busy and tired. At that, she often heard him sobbing in the night, either in grief for Chacho or guilt for what might come to Shea.

Strange how they waited for that, as in a controlled nightmare. Everyone worked, ate and slept, not speaking of the horror that might come, though Socorro, heavy in the last weeks of pregnancy, knelt daily, a long time, before the madonna.

Then, when they were beginning to meet each other's eyes and smile, when surely the time of contagion must be past, or nearly so, Shea rode in one night and didn't want supper.

By morning he was delirious between spells of rationality. Socorro bathed him and Talitha brought joint fir tea which he drank thirstily, mumbling something that made Socorro's eyes glisten.

"He thinks he's lost in the desert again, as he was when I found him."

Sometimes he thought his dead twin, Michael, was with him, for he encouraged him, offered what was left in the canteen. Then he was in Ireland, pleading with his mother to eat, assuring her that he and Michael had more than enough. And then he cried out something about a scythe, how Michael mustn't know, but their father was finally avenged.

After a long period of such ramblings, he knew Socorro, smiled, and managed weakly to touch her face. "My miracle," he whispered. *"Querida,* you are more to me than all the ill that ever happened. I have been a happy, blessed man."

He slept quietly a short while. Then convulsions wracked him. Belen, Chuey and Santiago, coming for breakfast, heard the chilling news and came to stand in the door, shocked grief and dread in their eyes.

"You must not nurse him, Doña Socorro," Santiago said at last. "In one of the fits he might attack you, give you the disease. I'll stay with him."

Socorro shook her head. "He is my husband."

"The child you carry . . ."

"Santiago!" The beautiful eyes in the thin delicate face met and commanded the vaquero's golden ones. "I will stay."

He bowed his head. "I will be with you, then. I've seen this before, my lady. Before long we will have to tie him to keep him from hurling himself about."

Unnoticed, Talitha gripped the bedpost, forced down the primitive rebellious wailing that threatened to tear from her throat. Shea, bound like a frenzied beast? Shea, a danger to his worshiped Socorro?

The same disbelief must have overwhelmed Socorro, for, earlier composure breaking, she cried out pleadingly, "Must he die? Don't men ever recover?"

Santiago was helplessly silent but Belen stirred. "*Madama,* sometimes the Tarahumares can cure this."

"Tarahumares?" Santiago gave a bitter laugh. "Those heathen deep in their *barrancas* in the Sierra Madre? As well say the man in the moon has a cure!"

"We do not have to go to the *barrancas,* the great cañons," said Belen. "On the Rio Cocóspera not far from where it leaves the Rio de los Alisos, there lives a Tarahumare who has, I swear it, healed two vaqueros even after they were in fits. When one of Don Narciso's men was bitten by a skunk, an old Papago told us of the healer. We tied our friend to his saddle and took him to the Tarahumare. In three days he was well. A few years later, this Nōnó cured another of our men."

"Will you go bring him here?" Socorro asked, face brightening with hope.

"*Madama,* one must go to him."

Santiago's eyes had narrowed as he thought. "I believe I've heard something of this Nōnó. Isn't he a sorcerer?"

"His people thought so," admitted Belen. "He was a great shaman, known for his power in cures, but when several of his rivals died, it was thought he had turned his gifts toward evil. People avoided him and at last he decided to move far away."

"I don't care if he's a sorcerer or not if he can make Shea well!" cried Socorro. "Let's start at once!"

Belen looked astonished. Santiago's breath caught sharply. "My lady, you cannot go! If it will please you, if there's a chance, Belen and I will take Don Patrick."

"And if he died on the way, and me not with him?" Socorro got to her feet. "I will come."

Santiago flushed but said doggedly, "You are near your time. It is too dangerous."

The usually sweet mouth curled in abrupt savagery. "You speak of danger with Shea like this?"

"I'll come, too," said Talitha. "If—if the baby is born—I helped before."

Socorro hesitated a moment. "The children—Anita will look after them, and we can stop by El Charco to see if Juana and Cheno will help out here while we're gone. Yes, Tally, I'd be glad to have you."

Within half an hour they were ready to go. Socorro kissed the bewildered twins and told them to be good for Anita till she came back. James edged forward and touched her skirt.

"Doña Socorro!" That summer he had adopted the vaqueros' style of addressing her. "I—I—" He gulped. Though her gaze rested almost feverishly on Shea, whom the men were helping to his horse, she turned to the boy and caressed his black hair.

"What is it, *mi buen vaquero?*"

His desperate gaze flickered at Talitha, then came back to the tender face bending over him. "Chusma did scratch Chacho, Doña Socorro. But—I didn't look. I—" His throat worked convulsively. "I didn't know the mark on him was from her, I just wanted it to be so I believed it—"

Talitha's own throat felt filled with thick, choking blood. He hadn't been sure! He—he'd *hoped!* So Shea was dying. She caught her brother's shoulders and shook him, violently. He didn't resist, his head snapped back and forth, and this meekness of his now, now when it was too late, enraged her even more. She was drawing back her hand to strike him when Socorro put her firmly aside.

Cradling the boy's head against her heaviness, she brushed away his tears and kissed him. "My brave one, I know how one can hope when one loves. We are all in the hands of God. Instead of hating yourself, help the men while we're gone, and take good care of Patrick and Miguel. Will you do that?"

She smiled at him in a way that coaxed the shadow of a smile to his lips. He nodded. "I promise. I'll take very good care of them, Doña Socorro!"

"Good! They'll mind you a lot better than they will Anita."

Talitha's mind had cleared. She no longer felt like physically punishing her brother, but neither could she bring herself to embrace him, though there was a terrible yearning sadness for him in her as she gave a short small nod and said, "Goodbye, James."

She didn't look back as they started off.

Shea was lucid when they began the journey but after a few hours he grew restless and began to talk excitedly, trying to climb out of the saddle. Belen and Santiago tied him in the saddle, his hands to the horn, legs to the stirrups, and took turns leading Azul.

It was a terrible day. Sometimes he seemed to be in a stupor, head drooping forward. Other times he swore viciously, sometimes at soldiers trying to run up a white flag of surrender, sometimes at guards who were taking him to be branded or flogged.

He would cry out, "Socorro! Socorro!" but would not know her when she rode near and touched him, told him she was there.

At El Charco, they took him down for a while, drifting in and out of lucidity while they chafed his wrists and legs and hips where the bindings had left marks and fed him gruel. Socorro told him they were going to a healer who should make him well and he managed to smile painfully at her, lift his hand toward her cheek, before he sank into his illness.

Santiago left Pedro in charge. Cheno and Juana promised to go at once to the main ranch. The Sanchezes knew of the Tarahumare, and though Carmencita crossed herself, she agreed that he had cured men of hydrophobia.

"And of an ill they caught more often!" said Pedro with a grin before, sobering, he helped get Shea back into the saddle.

San Manuel was out of the way so they wouldn't be seeing Tjúni. Talitha was glad of that. South and west they traveled, stopping in midafternoon to rest Shea and massage his wrists and legs. His eyes were clouded, and when they gave him water he thought it was sand.

That night they stopped near the ruins of Guevavi, which had been the mission headquarters for the area, Calabazas being one of its *visitas,* until it was overwhelmed by Apaches over seventy-five years ago.

The ruins, dissolving back into the earth they had been made from, increased Talitha's sense of desolation and her uneasiness as night came on. No one had mentioned Apaches or bandits, but they made no fire and shortly after they had tended Shea and fed him a gruel of pinole, they ate their own meal of tortillas and jerky.

Santiago lay on one side of Shea, Socorro on the other. Belen settled at a short distance and Talitha huddled in her blanket near Socorro. The days were still hot, but the nights were chill. Shea had been loosely tied but he fought his bonds and babbled between stretches of quiet. In one of these, though she'd thought she couldn't, Talitha fell asleep.

They left the Santa Cruz next morning and struck south for the Rio de los Alisos. Fortunately, Belen knew the region which was at the northern edge of Don Narciso's holdings. He reckoned it was another sixty miles to the Tarahumare, two days' journey.

Talitha didn't dare ask the questions that drummed

in her head. What if Nōnó was dead or moved away? What if his medicine didn't work? Or supposing Shea died before they even got there?

Striking the river about noon, they followed it between rugged mountains, passing a few deserted ranches. They spent the night at one of these. Crumbling as its walls were, they'd offer some protection in case of attack.

Late next afternoon they came to the settlement of Ímuris where the kindly wife of one of the soldier-colonists gave them delicious small peaches, a cooling drink made from limes, which Talitha had never seen before or tasted, and a meal of stewed wild turkey and fresh tortillas.

"Pobrecito!" she murmured as it took both Santiago and Belen to hold Shea while Socorro got him to drink of the cooling lime mixture. "So handsome, so young!"

Her eyes widened and she crossed herself at mention of Nōnó. Yes, so far as she knew the old witch was still living. In a case like the Señor's, clearly any risk must be run. "But, *madama,*" she besought Socorro. "You should not go! Only think if he cast a magic on your babe!"

The three days' hard travel and fear for her husband had told heavily on Socorro. In spite of increased exposure to the burning sun, there was a transparency to her skin stretched over the fine bones of her face. Her eyes looked bruised.

"Why don't you stay, my lady?" urged Santiago.

"If—if you are needed, Belen or I would come for you at once," Talitha added.

She shook her head, clearly too weary for argument, but summoned a grateful smile and warm thanks for their buxom hostess. Santiago tried to pay her but she refused almost indignantly.

"No, rather may my good husband be succored if someday he's sick far from home! Go with God." Catching Talitha by the shoulder, she whispered harshly, "Have a care for the lady! Her time is near."

Talitha nodded. The woman's thought was kind but futile. Socorro wouldn't rest till they had brought Shea to the healer. Cutting directly east from Imuris, they soon picked up the Rio Cocóspera and shortly after that they saw a scatter of structures up ahead, gilded by the late sun.

A gaunt brown man rose from a cookfire by the *ramada* and watched as they approached. A coarse white woolen cloth was kilted about him with a broad, exquisitely designed, extremely soiled girdle. A matching band went around his head, somewhat taming a stiff mass of white hair. Shell earrings weighted down his ears and around his neck hung a mummified hummingbird. As the little group halted, he squinted at Shea with charcoal-colored eyes.

"The falling-down sickness?"

Belen explained while Shea muttered and fought his bonds. Nōnó asked a few questions, then made a heaving motion with his skinny shoulders. "I will try. But it is difficult, this hydrophobia."

"You have cured others," said Santiago harshly.

"Each man has a different fate," the Indian returned equably. "I do not know what this one's is."

"For your health, it had better be to live!" rasped Shea's partner. Socorro laid a restraining hand on his arm.

"You will do your best, señor?" she pleaded. "That is all we can ask, I know it!"

Nōnó gave Santiago a scornful glance, but his tone gentled as he spoke to Socorro. "I will do my best and that is all I can do. Bring him to this space before the crosses."

There were three tall slender crosses with small arms in a row between the *ramada* and the house built of stone and poles. Shea lay before the crosses on his blanket, quiet now, unmoving, after the shaman's treatment.

Nōnó had made a brew which, with the men's help,

he'd forced Shea to drink. Then he'd passed his hands over the sick man, blowing vigorously, and with a small wood cross, touched Shea's head, neck, back and shoulders. When Shea struggled and cried out, the shaman gave him another potion, accompanied with signs and mutterings.

Next Nōnó took several large stones from the edge of the fire and placed them in a hole in the ground. He covered them with aromatic branches, poured water in so that the stones hissed and steam rose thick and pungent, and commanded the vaqueros to place Shea in the hole where he could breathe the vapor.

Now that was done, the shaman had danced and chanted with his gourd rattle, and he concerned himself with his guests, bringing them a drink made of ground toasted corn, water and green herbs. He called this *iskiate*. He glanced somewhat longingly at two small bits of meat cooking on wooden spits.

"I have plenty of tortillas," he said, "but only two mice."

Santiago hurriedly assured him that they had plenty of jerky, though some tortillas would be welcome. They shared their peaches with him and he was especially pleased with the tobacco Belen gave him. After the meal, he gave Shea another gourd of some concoction.

Socorro watched the old man pleadingly. "Señor, do you think—"

"I do not think yet, señora, I only pray. But the medicine has not killed him, so it may cure."

Santiago sprang up, was checked by his limp, but loomed menacingly beside the emaciated Indian. "You gave him something that can kill?"

"What would you?" shrugged the old man. "It is a deadly illness. Small wonder that the cure, also, can bring death."

In the flickering light from the small fire, he looked very much a sorcerer. As if he somehow divined the chill shooting through Talitha, he studied her a moment and said, "I will make a gourd of medicine which

312

you must give him anytime he is restless. If he drinks it all, call me and I will make more."

"I will watch my husband," said Socorro.

Nōnó shook his head. "I am a shaman, not a midwife. You will sleep. The girl is young and can rest tomorrow." Ignoring Socorro's protests, he brought her a potion and stood over her till she drank it. "The storehouse beyond the steambath is empty if you want to sleep there," he said. Then he prepared Shea's draught, gave Talitha an admonishing nod, and retired to his house with no further words.

Socorro insisted on sleeping near Shea. The men spread their blankets on the other side of the crosses. "If you grow sleepy, *doncellita,* rouse me," instructed Belen.

Talitha pulled her knees up beneath her chin, wrapping her blanket close against the night wind. "Thank you, Belen." But she didn't intend to get sleepy.

She would watch this night, and pray to the Temple God of Nauvoo and the Mormon camps, to Socorro's madonna, to the elemental forces she felt in the dark night around her. A world without Shea? Unbearable!

XXI

In spite of her resolve, Talitha did drowse a time or two. When her head dropped forward enough to wake her, she dragged herself up, without the blanket, and stood there till the cold revived her. Only a few coals winked in the fire pit, freshened by the breeze, but in the boundless sky she found the Big Dipper and the small one, which Shea had told her about so that she could find the North Star in case she was ever lost at night—and very lost she felt this night, but the stars were high and grand and far away.

For Belen, the Big Dipper was *El Reloj de los Yaquis,* the clock, for it swung around each twenty-four hours though the last two stars in its bowl opposite the handle continued to point at the North Star. And to Belen and Santiago the Morning Star was the Star of the Shepherd.

She didn't want to think about James. She was too angry at him and, also, too full of pity. But she prayed that Socorro would be all right.

Shea woke early in the night. At his first stirrings she coaxed him to drink. He obeyed, though he seemed to believe she was Socorro and they were back at that *tinaja* in the dead volcanoes. His restlessness soon faded into drugged slumber. When he next began to toss and mutter, the horizon was graying. He finished the gourd that time, leaning against Talitha. He felt cooler to her touch and as she eased him down, his hand lifted weakly to her hair.

She didn't know who he thought she was, but it didn't matter. He must be better! Tears of relief ran down her face, but she scrubbed them away as Santiago rolled over, stretched, came instantly awake.

"Take your blanket to the storehouse where the light won't bother you," he said. "I'll watch now."

During the day, Shea was placed twice among the steaming leaves and Nōnó continued to ply him with potions. Socorro looked better after the sound sleep induced by the shaman's concoction, and Shea's improvement brought some color to her face.

Talitha slept till noon in the storehouse that was just long enough for her to stretch out, and then emerged to help make tortillas and a stew of jerky and parched corn.

"Good!" Nōnó beamed, as deftly and greedily he scooped stew into his tortilla. "I am too old to miss a woman except for cooking, but when it is time to prepare food, I sometimes wish I had taken another wife after my fifth one died."

"It's never too late," encouraged Belen.

Nōnó grinned, exposing excellent white teeth. "Ay, amigo, when the tortillas are made and the meal is over, I am glad to have my peace."

"Do Apaches never bother you?" Santiago asked.

Nōnó grinned even more widely. "Five Apaches were killed by lancers where my *ranchería* now stands. Their scalps were taken so their spirits are bound to the earth. No Apache wants to come here."

Belen's hand shook slightly as he poured tobacco into a shuck. "No one else, either, I should think!"

"It does make for a quiet life." Nōnó filled another tortilla.

"Aren't you afraid?" Talitha burst out.

He smiled quizzically. "Child, a shaman has his power from the light of his heart. Tata Dios Himself gives this. A shaman moves through air with the brightness of the sun, talks with Tata Dios and even sees him. Why should I fear Apache ghosts?"

When no one answered and the vaqueros fidgeted uneasily, Nōnó's eyes slitted. His tone grew sibilant. "And if I am a sorcerer as my enemies claim? Then who would dare to trouble me? For even after I am dead, I can take the shape of a bear or mountain lion and kill that one who offended me. Or I can be a shooting star and kill that man and take his heart."

"God pardon you, that is wicked talk," said Socorro. Her lips were pallid but she looked at the Indian with unwavering eyes.

"I don't believe it anyway," said Talitha. "Except that you might have a light in your heart that lets you talk to God and heal people."

Nōnó's jaw dropped. He stared at her a long moment. "You believe that?"

She glanced at Shea, under the ramada now to shield him from the sun. "Yes. I believe that."

The shaman chuckled. "You believe it because you want to." He filled another tortilla. "But that has power, too."

During the afternoon, he got out a knucklebone, and first with Belen, then with Santiago, played *la taba*. As with dice, the sides had different values, and the players kept score with grains of corn. When they tired of that, all three played quinze with four marked sticks.

Toward evening, Shea was able to sip some gruel. Socorro held the gourd, speaking softly, and when it was clear he'd do her no violence, the others withdrew to leave them alone for a while.

Santiago and Belen decided to go hunting but Talitha declined their invitation. She didn't like to see wild things killed, nor did she want to be very far from Shea. She took refuge from the sun under a big mesquite, was startled and a bit uneasy when the shaman followed her. He crouched down, as was his habit instead of sitting.

"You are not their child," he said after a time.

"No. But they have been very good to me." Her voice trembled. "He's going to get well?"

"I think yes."

A long sigh escaped Talitha. Having her hopes confirmed swept away her vague fear of the Indian and she beamed at him joyously. "I know Doña Socorro will pay you. But if I can ever do anything for you—"

"Will you give me a piece of your hair?"

Talitha gaped, instinctively raised her hand to touch the single long braid she had plaited to save trouble during the journey. She didn't like the idea of a reputed witch having a lock of her hair but could scarcely go back on her offer.

"Why—why, yes, but I don't have any scissors."

"I have a knife. Fine, sharp one."

That didn't cheer Talitha, but she waited resignedly while he ducked into his house and returned with a keenly honed blade. "Will you take it where it won't show too much?" she asked.

His fingers, dry as a snake's skin, brushed the back of her neck. Her flesh prickled in spite of the heat of the afternoon. There was a slight tug and then he was holding a long strand of bright hair, smiling at it in great satisfaction before he twisted some fiber around one end and tucked it carefully into a leather pouch.

"What will you do with it?" she asked, unable to keep a nervous tremor from her voice.

"Nothing to harm you." He touched the hummingbird hanging from his neck. "I do not carry this for magic but because the feathers are beautiful and the bird's heart so swift. It is good to be reminded of such things."

"What will my hair remind you of?"

"Why, who but Yerúgami, Mother Moon?" Nōnó pointed to one of the smaller crosses in front of his house. "That is she. The big one is Father Sun who guards through the day. But Mother Moon watches at night."

"Who's the third cross?"

"Morning Star, son of Yerúgami. He helps her protect Tarahumare in the darkness." He smiled shrewdly at her questioning look. "I know of the three Gods of you Christians and Christian Tarahumares, like the ones I worked with in the mines where I learned Spanish, would say the crosses are Father, Son and Holy Spirit. But it is not so. My people used the cross long

318

before *padres* came among us." In the dirt, he scratched two intersecting equal lines. "These are the four directions, the ends of the earth. It is older than any other cross, even the one of Tata Dios."

All this sounded heathenish but intriguing. Rather than try to correct Nōnó's errors about the Trinity, which she herself understood none too well, let alone where Mary and the saints fitted in, Talitha decided to learn more about Nōnó's faith.

"You have Tata Dios. Do you also have a devil?"

"Why would we want him? He's for Christians. But the Tarahumares who have become Christians have a devil and are more scared of him than of sorcerers." Nōnó chuckled contemptuously. "This devil has a long beard like a Mexican and only one eye. Since the strings and bow of the violin make a cross, he cannot play it but he is a great one with the guitar. The first Mexicans were born of him and his ugly wife, but the Tarahumares, of course, are children of Tata Dios and brothers of the stars."

His tone was ironic. Talitha doubted that he truly believed the Tarahumare traditions any more than the Christianized ones, but she probed further. "Is there a heaven?"

Again that slight smile. "Everyone needs a heaven. In ours are many large ranches stocked with the sacrifices made to Tata Dios. There are foot races every day, and games, and Tata Dios himself runs and plays with us."

Heaven, to Talitha, seemed tolerable only in comparison to a hell of eternal agony. She could only dimly remember the Mormon Terrestrial Paradise. But a heaven of ranches! That sounded highly desirable.

Between ministrations to Shea, Nōnó told Talitha many other things that day as they sat under the big mesquite. How the gray fox and owl foretell death; how some bears are not bears at all but dead shamans who cannot be killed; and about healing plants, which he showed her, taking her to one of the storehouses.

Palo amarillo for sore eyes and colds, *chilicote* for stomachache and toothache though Nōnó cautioned that the red beans must be used with care for they were poisonous. A number of plants reduced fever, *yerba de la víbora, copal* and *mató*. Verbena roots could be crushed into a poultice and the flowers steeped for washing wounds or boils. *Yerba buena* or wild mint was good for intestinal upsets, toothache and sore gums.

"Is there anything that would ease Doña Socorro when she has the baby?" Talitha asked.

He hunted around till he located the roots he wanted and put some into a small fiber bag. *"Lantana* helps at childbirth. Pound up the roots, boil them and have her drink the tea. Tea of cottonwood bark is good, too."

She thanked him gratefully and then asked what he'd used to cure Shea. "That is a secret, Shining Girl. But I can tell you that one part of his cure was *jículi.*" He led her to another smaller storehouse, opened the door enough to let her see a basket filled with small dried roundish things. Nōnó inclined his head, spoke respectfully to the basket and closed the door again.

"This is the cactus Mexicans call *peyote.* It brings visions and keeps one from hunger and thirst. Only shamans can handle it and it is kept by itself so it won't see or hear anything offensive. If I want to use some of it, I must offer *teswino* and meat. It is the younger brother of Tata Dios and he left it to comfort his people when he went to heaven."

Talitha blinked at all this. Nōnó had sounded skeptical, almost teasing, about many other things, but he seemed completely serious about this. He told her that *jículi* eased menstrual pain and, dampened or chewed, and placed directly on the afflicted part, had wonderful effects on fractures, swellings, wounds, burns and even rattlesnake bites.

It sounded useful if rather frightening. "Could we buy some?" asked Talitha.

Nōnó gave her a shocked look. "It would be very angry and might eat both of us!"

320

As if to make up for refusing, he gave her packets of roots and herbs, reminding her again of their properties, and then showed her his sucking stick. Examining her arm with sudden interest, he said, "You have some worms! Let me suck them out before they make you sick."

Before she could protest he put the tube, a piece of hollow reed about three inches long, on her arm, and sucked mightily. After a few minutes he unpuckered his cheeks, spat into his hand, and showed her some little whitish-yellow things that might indeed have been worms or parts of them.

Fascinated, Talitha rubbed her reddened arm and stared. "How did you do that?"

He grinned, tossed away the horrid little bits and produced something from a fold of his loincloth held in place by the broad girdle. Gingerly, Talitha examined them, rolled them in her fingers. "Why, they're little pieces of hide!"

"Buckskin," Nōnó nodded, delighted with his joke. "I put them in my mouth and while I'm sucking, they swell with saliva and look like maggots!"

"Ugh!"

"Don't make rude sounds. It is a very useful treatment."

"I don't see how!"

Patiently, he said, "Many people who come to me *think* they're sick, that the wind or sorcery has put some bad thing in them. If I suck out a stone, or much blood, or little worms like this, they go away happy. And cured."

She gazed at him between accusation, amusement and wonder. "I don't understand you, Don Nōnó. You believe some things and others you laugh at."

"Only a fool believes everything," he shrugged. "Only a worse fool believes nothing. Now you will excuse me while I make offering to the *jículi*. It is time the señor had more of it."

Next day, Shea was rational and could sit up, move around shakily, and the next day they left.

"Tata Dios protect you," the shaman said to Talitha.

"May He be with you," she answered, genuinely sorry to part with the old man. What a mixture he was, of knowledge and rascality, wisdom and superstition! She would have liked to adopt him for a grandfatherly teacher, visit him often. And she wondered what he would do with that strand of yellow hair.

They rested often for Shea tired and Socorro drooped in the saddle though her eyes, when she watched her husband, were full of joy. The kind woman at Ímuris fed them again, exclaimed at Socorro's extreme heaviness and tried to persuade her to stay there till her baby came.

"It will not be long, señora! And this jolting on horseback can't be good for you."

Santiago nodded slow agreement. "It wouldn't hurt you to rest a week or so, Don Patrick. Belen and I could go on to the ranch. Perhaps you can get an escort from here, but if you're not back in two weeks, we could come for you."

"Sounds sensible," Shea said reluctantly, eyes on his wife's thin face.

But Socorro shook her head. "It may be several more weeks before the baby. Patrick and Miguel have been without me too long as it is! I want them to see the baby when it's new." She turned to the soldier's wife. "You are very kind, señora, and I thank you a thousand times. But you will understand that I long to see my children and have the baby in my own house?"

"I understand. But oh, *madama*, I have fear for you!"

Socorro smiled and lightly kissed the woman's brown cheek. "Do not. If my husband can be cured of hydrophobia, shall I not be delivered of a child?"

The woman waved them out of sight. They rested twice that afternoon and camped well before sundown. Shea dropped off to sleep at once and Talitha coaxed

Socorro into resting beside him while the rest of them took care of the horses and got out food. Talitha also decided she'd better pound up those *lantana* roots Nōnó had given her. If they could just get home first! Apart from Socorro's comfort, James would be in torment till he saw that Shea was getting well, and in spite of her terrible first anger with him, Talitha did pity her brother.

Next day Shea was stronger but Socorro rode with a set face. During the night, she went into labor. In spite of the danger, there had to be a fire for light and Talitha put the roots to boil in a kettle of water.

Socorro drank meekly of the brew but though she gripped Shea's hands tight and moved with the pains, by dawn she seemed no closer to relief and she was much weaker.

"Sweetheart," Shea whispered, face strained and gray in the first light. "Try hard! Push!"

She obeyed but soon lay gasping. Helpless tears slid from her eyes. "Shea, I—I cannot!"

He glanced desperately at Talitha. "Your hands are still small. Can you see if the baby's placed wrong?"

Talitha washed her hands in hot water boiled after the root brew had been poured into a gourd. Last time, when she helped with the twins, she'd been too young to realize all the dangers. Now, with her own body that of a woman, she was cold with fear.

Carefully, she felt around the taut flesh as the tiny skull forced down and Socorro screamed. "I'm sure the head's in place," Talitha told Shea. "I can feel the fine hair on it."

"There's just not enough strength in the contractions," Shea groaned. "And she's getting weaker!"

"Perhaps if she sat up and we sort of held her—that's how the Apaches do. Let her hang on to that paloverde branch?"

"Let's try it."

Between them, they supported her in a squatting position. It seemed to help. She gripped the branch till her fingernails were white, made animal sounds and sweated. Then her hands loosened, fell limp, and she collapsed.

"Socorro!" Shea cried. "Socorro!"

She didn't answer. The pulse fluttered in her throat. Her breath came in quick shallow gasps. "We've got to get that baby out!" Shea rasped. "Even if we kill it, it's got to come!"

"Let me give her another drink." Talitha brought the root tea and coaxed some down Socorro's throat, washed her hands again as she turned to the task she dreaded. "Talk to her," she told Shea. "Hold her hands and get her to push."

He did this, talking of Patrick and Miguel, how excited they'd be with a new brother or sister. Socorro responded bravely, bearing down with the weakened contractions, trying to make them do their work. Talitha inserted her fingers on either side of the head, tugged as gently and firmly as she could with the next spasm. The head moved forward slightly, seemed to stick, and then with Socorro's next desperate effort, Talitha pulled and the head came through.

"One more big push!" she called. "One more!"

It came, and with it the slippery little body. As Talitha cut the thick, pulsing cord that still connected baby and mother, dark blood and mucus came out. Putting the baby in Socorro's arms, Talitha cleaned the afterbirth out of Socorro, leaned back to catch her breath.

"A girl!" Shea was telling Socorro. "She'll be beautiful, just like you!"

Socorro touched the damp fuzz on the little head and smiled.

But the bleeding wouldn't stop. Santiago, summoned hastily from the slope where he and Belen had withdrawn, worked with Talitha to staunch the flow, propping up Socorro's hips and legs, packing the cleanest garments they had between her thighs.

Nothing worked. Her life drained away before their eyes as Shea held her. She knew she was dying, asked him to take good care of the baby and call it after her own mother, Caterina. This done, she was quiet a moment before she opened her eyes to caress Shea.

"*Querido,*" she said to him in a tone so soft it was nearly inaudible. "We saved each other in the desert. We rode through the mountains. Now we have slept again beneath the stars—"

Her voice trailed off. She was smiling when the great gush of blood poured from her.

She was smiling when she died.

His big body wrenched with sobs, Shea held her close, pleading with her to come back, begging her to live. But her dark eyes couldn't see him though a tender smile lingered on her mouth.

Talitha took the baby. This red scrap to cost Socorro's life? It wasn't fair! If Socorro had been at home instead of jolting horseback through the heat in an agony over her husband, this would probably not have happened.

And Shea wouldn't have been bitten if . . . In a flash, she saw James as he'd been when they left, saw Socorro bending to kiss and absolve him. But it was his fault! It was!

Or was it hers, for insisting Juh's son come with her instead of staying with the Apaches? *I wish he had!* she thought miserably, immediately knew that wasn't so. She still loved James. And he was so little, only six, and how was he going to feel now, with Socorro dead?

Staring down at the feebly squirming infant, Talitha wondered what to do with it. She had cared for James almost from birth, but at least for a while he had been grudgingly nursed by one of Juh's wives. It was with vast relief that she remembered Anita whose Paulita was two months old.

Plenty of milk there, and it would be lovingly given. The baby could exist on water till they got home, which they could do tonight if they started soon. Shea still held his wife but Santiago was standing a little way off, staring at nothing. His hands clenched and unclenched.

Talitha washed the baby quickly and carried it to him. "Please hold her while I fix her a rag to suck on and make our *pinole*," she said.

To her astonishment, Santiago's tawny eyes were filmed with tears and his face seemed as young as James's. Talitha suddenly knew what her maturing senses had been detecting for a good while. Santiago had loved Socorro, too; as a man, not as a companion only.

"Who can eat?" he said dully, though he took the baby obediently enough.

"We all must," Talitha replied shortly though her heart was wrung with pity for him, swelling with her own grief and loss. "Shea's still far from strong and we need to get the baby home where Anita can feed her."

"Socorro, she's—dead," whispered Santiago.

"Yes, she is!" Talitha almost snarled at him. "But her baby's alive. We have to take care of it!"

Fighting tears that came anyway, she hurried to find a piece of cloth that could be used to get a little water down the child and pacify its instinctive need to suck.

It wasn't only Shea's miracle that was gone, but a grace and kindness that had blessed them all. How would they manage now? What would they do?

In an hour they were on their way. Shea carried Socorro in front of him, held by a sort of sling rigged to shift much of her weight to the cantle. He had swallowed the *pinole* Talitha urged on him but he seemed a long way off.

Talitha and the vaqueros took turns carrying the baby and dipping the twisted rag into the gourd of water Talitha had boiled. She had thought about mixing in a little brown sugar, but decided it might bring on a colic. Better wait for Anita's milk.

Wrapped in its mother's shawl, the baby sucked

eagerly on the cloth and slept most of the time, which was fortunate. Talitha felt sorry for it, thrust out of its warm, safe home, having to become accustomed to air and light. Instead of having a warm nourishing breast to soothe the abrupt change, small Caterina had only a watered bit of cotton torn from one of Socorro's blouses.

As the day wore on, Belen assumed the practical judgments such as when to stop and where to ford the river. Santiago seemed almost as dazed and remote as Shea. Talitha had made several diapers from what softer clothing remained after the attempt to staunch Socorro's blood, and when it was necessary, she stopped and changed the baby, rinsing the soiled cloth in water from the river and fastening it behind the cantle to dry.

By sundown they reached El Charco. The Sanchezes' amazed delight at seeing Shea alive was quickly smothered when they saw Socorro, but Carmencita got control of herself, hurried to feed them though tears ran down her plump face and she lamented continuously.

"*Ay, Dios! Pobrecita!* So lovely, so young! Poor Don Patricio! The small Miguel and Patrick! This tiny *niña!*"

Poor all of us, thought Talitha, exhausted. *And poor, poor James! He'll blame himself even if Shea doesn't.* But it was temporary surcease to rest under the *ramada* and eat the mashed beans, steaming tamales and fresh tortillas that Carmencita brought out to them.

It was also Carmencita who enfolded Socorro, lying near Shea on some blankets, in a thin woven coverlet, also Carmencita who took the baby and added a little goat milk to the water she sucked with increasing frustration from the rag.

"My Anita will take care of you," she promised the tiny creature. "I could send for her, Don Patricio, if you wish to stay here tonight."

Shea roused from some bleak ranging of the spirit. "Thanks, Carmencita, but we'll ride on. Tally, you can stay over if you want. You must be worn out."

She shook her head though she felt so weary that

she didn't think she could get into the saddle. As she almost hung by Ladorada, gripping the horn and willing her body to respond, Belen gave her a swift hand up.

"Courage, *doncellita!*"

He gave her hand a rough pressure, stepped aside as Carmencita handed up the baby. Santiago helped Shea lift Socorro in front of him, and they rode off in the twilight.

No light showed from the ranch but as they approached the corrals, their horses began to snort and sidle. A voice called softly, "Hair of Flame?"

"Mangus!"

The giant shadow rose before them. "You are healed," said the Apache. "It is good."

"It is not good, great chief. My wife is dead."

Mangus was still for a long moment. "She had a flower face, but she was very brave. My heart is on the ground." His tone sharpened. "Did she die by the hand of men?"

"No. In birthing."

A deep sigh came from the Apache. "The child lives?"

"Yes. A girl." Shea's tone was bitter and Talitha held the baby closer. Poor little thing indeed if everyone was going to blame her for Socorro's death!

"Perhaps she will be like her mother and brighten your days as she grows," said Mangus. He added slowly, to Talitha, "I came to tell you that the one who was your brother's father is dead, killed in a fight with Mexican soldiers. He will not be claiming his son. But the boy says he would like to go back with me."

Talitha gasped. "James said that?"

"Yes."

"It—it's because he feels to blame for Shea!" she cried. "And I was mean to him, I was so scared and angry! Don't take him! Please don't!"

"We'll talk of it later," the Indian said. "It's late. You must all be tired."

He waited, not offering to help, for the horses were nervous of his scent as it was. A horse got used to a certain kind of human odor, and a radically different smell upset it. But the ranch had come awake at the voices. A candle glowed from inside and Chuey and Cheno came out, tagged by a small boy who no longer swaggered, who no longer was shadowed by a large black cat.

"James!" Talitha called softly.

She wanted him close to her when he heard what had happened and she ached as she saw, even in the near-dark, that he approached her cautiously. Belen had helped her down and led away her horse.

Kneeling by James, she put her free arm around him and guided his hand to the baby's head. "This is Caterina, James. The new baby."

"Shea—he's alive! I heard him!"

"Yes." The lump in her throat swelled. She couldn't go on. But at that moment Chuey's shocked voice exclaimed, "Dead, Don Patricio? Doña Socorro?"

James twisted in Talitha's arm, but she held him. "Is she?" he choked. "Is she dead?"

Talitha could only nod as her tears fell hot and fast. Swallowing, with tremendous effort she managed to speak. "Remember what she told you, James. She didn't blame you. She—she bled so much! I couldn't stop it. She might have died anyway, right in her own bed."

"No, she wouldn't!" James wrested loose. She couldn't prevent him because she was holding Caterina. "I heard Juana and Anita! They said it was crazy for her to ride, that the baby would come dead or hurt some way!"

"Well, it didn't. The baby looks fine."

And everyone will wish she had died if it would have saved her mother. Though she'd had that feeling at first and traces remained, Talitha protectively gathered the little thing closer. All she could do for Socorro now was try to look after her family, especially this most helpless, friendless one.

"It's my fault," James said miserably.

"It's over. You didn't mean harm to anyone."

They were walking toward the house. As the women came out, Talitha gratefully handed over the fretting infant to Anita, briefly explained and asked her to feed and tend it. Then she looked around for James, found him by the corral with Mangus.

"Come in and sleep," she coaxed her brother.

"No. I don't belong there anymore."

"Of course you do! Now don't be silly, James! Come along——"

She tried to hold him but his body was rigid and tight. He pushed away. "Mangus says I can go with him."

"What?" Talitha's whisper echoed in her ears like a scream.

"I'm going with Mangus."

"You can't! Juh's dead!"

"He will be my son," said Mangus. "I will teach him our ways."

Maddened past restraint, Talitha blazed, "Yes, you'll show him how to kidnap women and burn men over slow fires! He can't go! He's my brother!"

"Half your brother," Mangus corrected, but he didn't sound angry. "You know well that Din-eh are not the only ones to steal women and torture men. Your brother will learn to stalk and hunt, find his way through every mountain range in this part of the country, whether claimed by Americans or Mexicans."

"Shea won't let you have him."

Mangus said patiently, "Hair of Flame has said the boy will always have a home at the ranch, but that if he wishes to go with me, he will not prevent him."

Feeling betrayed, Talitha stood helplessly in the darkness, glancing from the towering shadow to the small one. "James!" she cried. "Oh, James!" And he was not the boy precociously expert with *reata* and horses who squirmed from her embraces and followed the men, but the child she'd carried in a cradleboard almost as long as she was, that she'd fed with crushed piñons and water and kept alive in spite of Juh's women.

Mangus's hand on her was so kind that, to her own surprise, she didn't shrink from it. "Your brother can visit you. And if the white part of him is strongest, if he does not live well among the Din-eh, he can come back as he wills."

She grasped at that. A small hope, at least. Hadn't James been reared as white ever since he could remember? One part of her mind was even forced to admit that it might be best for James to leave for a while, get away from the people and place that would confront him daily with guilt. And Shea . . . He was too generous and fair to be unkind or vengeful, but who could blame him if he felt differently toward the boy he'd ransomed with his own pain?

Into the silence, Talitha said, "James? You won't forget us? You will come back?"

"I won't forget you!" he cried with an indrawn breath, and then, with a gasping sob, he ran away.

"I will watch him," Mangus said. "Go and sleep. I will watch Hair of Flame, also."

"How can you? Isn't he inside?"

"No. He has carried his wife to the bottom of the hill. He said he would sleep with her this last night before she goes into the earth." Mangus's tone held an edge of awe. "He does not fear her spirit!"

"No, how should he?" Talitha said.

Stupid with weariness and grief, feeling as if her bones were dissolving, she gazed toward the slope. So Shea, for one more night, would hold his love beneath the stars.

But the day would come, and the burial, trying to explain to Miguel and Patrick. James would go with Mangus and . . . *I can't bear it!* Talitha wept inwardly, stumbling as she walked to the house. *I can't bear any of it at all!* But she would have to.

XXII

Socorro was buried on the hill where the cross above her would be touched by the earliest sun and the latest. The vaqueros made a coffin of oak that had been curing for use in furniture and the women had dressed her in her best clothes and arranged the mantilla over her face. Shea added the jewels he had bought her, fetched up from Chihuahua by the *conducta,* an emerald ring and necklace, a rosary of gold and precious stones, a medal of Guadalupana.

On the hill, Shea tried to speak and could not. Nor could Santiago who stood with his face averted. At last Mangus loomed forward. "She who has gone away was beautiful in her face and in her ways. Her deeds were kind and she was valiant. Since it is not your way to kill a mount for one gone away, I will do that when I return to my own place."

"That would pain her," Shea roused enough to say. "Do not, great chief."

Mangus didn't answer, but turned and strode away. James went with him. They mounted their horses at the bottom of the hill and by the time Socorro was lowered into the earth, her grave heaped with stones and the cross raised, the travelers were out of sight.

In the days that Mangus had waited for the return of Shea's party, he had talked a little with Chuey and Cheno and made no pretense of liking them. He was troubled about the Americans pushing through his country, especially when they spoke of boundaries, though John Bartlett, the first Boundary Commissioner, had given him an officer's tunics, some blue pants with red stripes, epaulets, shoes and even a cravat. Unfortunately, these had been lost in gambling.

Even more unfortunately, Mangus had hoped to get some encroaching American miners to move their operations to Mexico and had gone alone into their camp, offering to take them to a valuable site. Not believing him or understanding who this huge man was, they wrestled him down and lashed him with a bull whip. That was two years ago. Mangus now believed the Americans to be as much his enemies as the Mexicans.

Startled out of his apathy, Shea said, "He didn't tell me about this!"

"Probably, Don Patricio, he felt it was not the time," said Chuey, pockmarked face very serious. "He said that as much as he could, he would protect this rancho, but if the whites crowd in and constantly enflame the Apache, he's not sure how long his friendship will keep the other groups away."

"We'll just have to take our chances," growled Shea.

"Which may rapidly improve," put in Santiago. "If the United States is buying this region for its railroad, it'll have to send soldiers."

Shea grimaced. Santiago gave him a slight smile. "I don't love the Americans, either. But at least they should be more numerous and better-armed than the presidio garrisons!"

"Captain Zenteno's doing his best," defended Shea, for on their fall drive to market in Tubac, they'd learned that Zenteno had been named commander of the whole sector from Santa Cruz to Tucson.

"The other garrison commanders will have to do what he says," agreed Santiago. "But look at what he's supposed to do! Keep in touch with the Gila Pimas and San Javier Papagos and convince them to muster in case of trouble; send six men to Calabazas to help guard the stock; stay constantly alert, defend the whole stretch of territory and still keep enough men at Tubac to repel attacks! Poor Zenteno! I bet he hopes the United States will take the whole mess off his hands!"

Shea didn't answer. He'd lapsed into the brooding silence that still claimed him much of the time though he had at least gone on living. And from that, Talitha argued to herself as weeks passed and he barely ate, was bound to gradually come a renewed zest, a return of energy. At first he wouldn't pick up Caterina, even look at her if it could be avoided, but lately he'd started watching her as she kicked on a blanket or slept in the big willow basket Belen had made for her.

That eased a pressing weight on Talitha's heart. She'd been afraid he might abhor the baby, or have nothing to do with it, which didn't matter so much now while there was Anita's warm breast, the fascinated twins to rock and cluck and coo, the vaqueros' rough adoration, and Talitha's own great love.

No, for a long while Caterina wouldn't miss one more worshiper. But as she got old enough to wonder, especially when she understood it was her father who ignored her . . . Well, Talitha had been terrified of that! Not now, though, for once Shea began to *see* his daughter, how could he not be utterly conquered?

The fair baby hair had been replaced with fine black curls that clustered softly around the tiny triangular face. Darkly imperious eyebrows slanted above eyes that were a deep blue-gray fringed with long black lashes.

"She'll break many hearts," laughed Santiago as she closed her perfect little fingers around one of his big brown ones. "And what a grip she has! The man she wants will never get away!"

"Don't start in on that already!" said Talitha rather crossly.

The baby had had colic in the night and she and Anita had taken turns walking her about. Now, while they yawned and struggled to get through the day, Caterina, the small devil, slept blissfully between gurgling happy bouts of squirming and reaching for the trinkets Talitha had tied to her basket.

"Why, Talitha!" grinned Santiago. "Do you fear you'll grow into this one's skinny old *dueña? Caray!* In a few years more you'll be famed from Hermosillo to Tucson! The visiting *caballeros'* horses will eat so much grass that we'll have to marry you off before we lose all the pasture!"

"Cojones!" She threw the corral expression "What balls!" at him, took wicked pleasure in the shock that widened his golden eyes, then made them narrow.

"Talitha! Only bad women, very bad women, talk like that!"

"You do. And Belen and Chuey and—all of you!"

He flushed. "Not in front of women," he said sternly. At the protest in her face, he added sheepishly, "If you're always around the branding and rough work, of course you'll hear things! Which reminds me that I must tell Don Patrick you're too old to go on as you have been."

"Too old?" She glared in outrage. "Why, I'm just getting strong enough to be really any help! You know that, Santiago! Don't be a burro!"

Something changed in his eyes, in his face. Suddenly he wasn't the big-brotherly person she'd taken for granted, but a man, one with a strangeness on him that somehow reminded her of Judah Frost, made her retreat though Santiago didn't move.

"How old are you?" he asked abruptly.

She blinked. "Fourteen next April."

His breath escaped in a sigh. He turned away. "Well, you're too old to talk like a vaquero or hang out with us, and so I shall tell Don Patrick this very day."

Talitha felt blind with fury. She could do housework, and did, without complaint, but she only felt alive when she was outside, and the baby's care took so much of her own and Anita's time that she rarely had a chance, now, to ride Ladorada, even seize a few hours to gather nuts or wild foods. And Santiago, for the sake of ideas thought up a long way off and a long time ago, wanted to condemn her to a life of cooking and household chores?

"Sangrón!" she shouted at him. *"Bembo! Zonzo!"*

Having called him hateful one, simpleton and stupid, she didn't dare, even in her outrage, to spit out the really bad names, so she ended rather weakly, "Shea won't listen to you! And—if he does, I'll hate him, too!"

At the hurled names, he had checked as if astounded, turned swiftly toward her, but the anger that flared in his eyes softened, as he watched her, into amusement. "Ay, Talitha, you are growing up! The kitten's getting claws. But it's not, you know, altogether unpleasant to be a woman."

The memory of Socorro bleeding flashed through her mind. It did through his, too, or he read her thoughts, for his face twisted as he whirled and went out, his limp heavier.

Ashamed, for she loved Santiago next to Shea, James, the twins and Caterina and knew that however obtuse he was, he truly wanted what was best for her, Talitha started to go after him and say she was sorry. Then she heard him laughing with the twins who had apparently ambushed him outside the door and decided that after all, he'd smiled, he'd known she hadn't meant it.

The twins' fifth birthday only a few weeks after their mother's death had been a hushed affair, but Shea had given them their first personal horses, Thunder, a steel-gray son of Azul, and Lightning, sired by Azul out of Ladorada, as creamily golden as the mare.

Talitha had helped work the young geldings and as Shea and Santiago gave the boys a boost into the fine new saddles brought up from Chihuahua, her heart swelled with the beauty of flame-haired Patrick on his dark horse, black-haired Miguel on his golden one. The boys had good hands and even in their jubilation they used the reins lightly.

As they went off for their first canter, followed by Belen, Shea's smile faded. His bleak gaze sought the cross on top of the hill. Hesitantly, Talitha put her hand on his.

"I think she can see them—and how proud it must make her!"

Shea patted Talitha's hand. At the evening meal for which she and Anita had fixed all the twins' favorite foods, he teased them gently and said they'd have to be top vaqueros to live up to their horses. He put them to bed that night and sang them a couple of lively Irish songs. But then he'd gone outside and though Talitha lay awake long after Anita, who was sleeping in the *sala* in order to suckle Caterina when she woke up hungry, had soothed both babies to sleep, she never heard him come in.

At last, unable to stand her worry anymore, Talitha put on her sandals and made her way in the light of a half moon to where she'd been certain he was. Only he wasn't kneeling or sitting by the grave. He lay upon it.

A terrible fear that he was dead froze Talitha, but she must have made some sound for he slowly raised his head. "Oh, Shea!" she cried. "Shea, please—"

"Go in, lass," he said. When she didn't move, he added dully, "I won't murder myself. There are the lads and now that—that new one. They're her own sweet flesh and I'll see to them, I swear it. But leave me be, Tally. Leave me as close as I can get to her now."

So she had gone back weeping, and finally slept, and morning had come. . . . Anita said it was a mercy and a marvel he didn't turn to mescal, but Talitha almost wished he would if it would help him rest, take the puzzled grief from his eyes. Still, life went on. Gradually, his appetite improved and he seemed to sleep better.

The twins had cried for their mother, but almost as desolately for James. Luckily, they had happy dispositions and responded to the vaqueros' increased male tenderness. On their new horses, they were improving the skills they'd played at since they were able to walk, and they slept among an array of Chusma's grandchildren with their small sister—when they had time.

Yes, thought Talitha, watching them now as they

338

flanked Santiago, that's how it is; if you're alive, you go on living. And after a while, you could laugh again. But why had Santiago's look, just for a second, reminded her of Judah Frost's?

She didn't like to think of that man. Nor, though she didn't want Shea and Santiago to lose the money they'd invested, did she want Frost to come back.

He did, on the day of the Feast of the Roof, celebrated that year only because of the twins. At the sound of approaching horses, Shea rose quickly and went to the door while the vaqueros got in reach of the rifles.

"It's Judah Frost," Shea said, sounding pleased and more excited than he had for a long time. "And there's someone with him."

With an almost doomed feeling, Talitha got out two more plates. Of course, he'd return. Like death, danger and evil. Why couldn't Shea sense that about him, why had he had to jump in and become his partner? Now Frost had an excuse to come back; and the man he'd brought along was probably as bad as he was.

She wasn't prepared for Marc Revier. Introduced by Frost as his partner and "the best mining engineer in the country, educated at the Royal School of Mines in Freiburg," Revier had steady blue eyes with good-humored crinkles at the edges, brown hair and a rather broad face with strong bones.

A scar slashed his left cheek and brow, so he must have been in a fight once, but it was hard to imagine. There was something sure and immovable about him as if he were part of the mountain whose secrets he searched out and though he wasn't as tall as either Frost or Shea, he seemed to be except when they were standing close enough for it to be obvious.

When he took Talitha's hand, bowing slightly, something warm and strengthening seemed to flow from his touch. Disconcerted, she mumbled a greeting and avoided his eyes.

She didn't want him to look into her; see how she

missed James and Socorro, how tired she got of the unending demands of the household, how much she worried for Shea. She could endure all these things by not thinking of them more than she had to and by simply doing whatever most needed it, but something about this man made her think he understood, and that she *couldn't* bear. It tore away her defenses, made her want to weep.

So, in a way she hadn't dreamed, he was dangerous.

But her armor hardened when Judah Frost smiled at her, a flame beneath the winter of his eyes. "Only four months and you're changing into a young lady. How proud your father will be of you!"

A knife turned in her heart. "My—father?"

"Jared Scott, no other."

"He—he— Where is he?"

"In San Francisco. Eagerly awaiting your arrival. He would have come for you himself, but he has a rich 'diggins' he can scarcely afford to leave. I told him I had to make the trip here and back anyway, on my own affairs, and would be most happy to escort you to him."

Talitha thought of her father. All she could remember was his dancing in the firelight and riding away with his battalion. Long ago. Before the Apaches. Before Rancho del Socorro and all that had happened since. It seemed more than just one lifetime ago.

"I can't go," she said.

Shea said quickly, "Now, lass, we can manage." To Frost he explained, "My wife is dead. There's a baby left and Tally's been wonderful with her. But if her father's found, of course she should go to him."

"I don't see why!" flashed Talitha. "He's gotten along without us seven years. My mother's dead, James with the Apaches! I don't know my father and he doesn't know me."

"But, Tally—"

She caught Shea's hand. "You're my family! You, the twins, Caterina! Don't make me go away."

He gathered her to him for a moment. She hadn't

been in his arms for a long time, since she was little, and she thought what a waste that had been for only now did she know how wonderful it was. But when her arms crept around him, he made a soft, smothered sound and stepped away.

"You've been our daughter, Talitha. You always will be. This is your home so long as you want it. But it's a hard life for you here. You'd have more chances in a town. Parties, pretty clothes, church, a chance to meet some young men."

"I don't want to meet them!"

"Not now, maybe, but you will in a few years. At least think about it. Mr. Frost is mighty kind to go to all this trouble."

Why had he? Frowning, she said rudely, "Well, I wish he hadn't! I won't leave unless you make me, Shea, and then I won't go to San Francisco!"

Judah Frost bowed with a hint of mockery. "Forgive me, Talitha. I truly thought I was serving your best interests. Perhaps you'll give me a letter to carry to him."

Admit that she couldn't write? Talitha's cheeks burned. "I'll send some message," she said in a strangled tone, and set about putting more hot food on the table, as Frost expressed his shock and regrets over Socorro. He was so perfect in his sympathy, so tactful in words and manner, that Talitha ground her teeth.

How she'd love to expose him! But she couldn't, not ever. He might kill Shea.

The Pajarito Mining and Exploring Company had been legally established and Shea and Santiago each held twenty-four percent of the stock.

"We've already found a vein of silver copper glance," said Revier with that slow, friendly smile at Talitha as she brought him fresh tortillas. "We've smelted it down and sent it to Guaymas where it ought to fetch a good price for the Asiatic market, perhaps as much as a dollar thirty per ounce."

"And it was carried on the Santa Cruz Freighting company's first trip," laughed Frost. "I raised the capital for the company while I was gone and Louis Jaeger up at Yuma Crossing's come in on it and is supplying teams and wagons. The next thing is to find a good port in northern Mexico so we won't have to go to Guaymas to sell or buy."

"I might be able to find such a place." Santiago's abrupt proposal brought everyone's gaze to him. "One of our vaqueros was part Seri. He told me of several natural harbors along the coast where his people use fishing boats."

"What'll do for flimsy small craft may not accommodate cargo ships," said Frost. "But I'd be most grateful for your efforts. When can you go and what sort of expedition will you need fitted out?"

"Why, señor," smiled Santiago, and there was something in his eyes that made Talitha uneasy, "I would need you to judge the value of the harbor for I have never seen the sea. We need no one else, just a pack mule for supplies. Thus we shall travel much faster."

"But Apaches—"

"The farther south we go, the less danger." Santiago lifted one shoulder in a shrug. "Besides, if we meet Apaches it'll make little difference as to our numbers unless we mean to recruit an army." His tone held the slightest hint of surprise; could the señor be afraid?

The pupils of Frost's eyes seemed to dilate. His jaw hardened. "When can you leave?"

Santiago looked at Shea. "It's a slack time from now till spring," he said. "I should be back by then."

"It's up to you," Shea acceded, but Talitha's body tightened in protest even as Frost suggested they leave next morning. She waited for a chance to catch Santiago by himself and after the meal when he said he was going to pack his *aparejos,* she followed him.

The vaqueros' quarters held only beds made of rawhide woven between posts driven in the earth, pegs for clothing, a bench and a chest. Saddles, bridles and ropes were hung up much more neatly than vests and extra shirts.

"Santiago." She paused in the door, but her hands reached out to him. "Don't go! Please don't!"

His head lifted with the swift grace she loved in him. He studied her intently. Then he turned and busied himself with his clothes. *Doncellita,* it is necessary."

"Why? Let him find his own port!"

This time when he looked at her, it was she who dropped her eyes. "Am I wrong? I had somehow believed Señor Frost's company unwelcome to you."

"It is. I don't like him—or trust him—one bit."

"Why is that?"

Should she tell? If Santiago went in the house right now, took a rifle, accused Frost of threatening Talitha with her friends' deaths, what would happen? Frost was wearing his gun. She didn't want to find out if he was as deadly as he claimed. The way he'd carelessly blasted that squirrel had convinced her. The only safe way would be for Santiago to shoot him without warning. She shuddered at that idea, knit her hands together and tried to speak calmly.

"I don't know. I just don't like him and I don't want you to go off together."

"Would it be better, Talitha, if I went somewhere else?"

She stared at him, puzzled. "Somewhere else? I don't want you to go anywhere!"

At her cry, his hands tensed on the shirt he was folding. "Don't make such uproar, *chiquita!* This Sangrón Bembo Zonzo will be back before you know it!"

She flushed. "You can't be mad over that still? Oh, Santiago, Socorro's gone, and James! Don't you go, too! Nothing will be the same!"

He looked at her for a long time, in a way that stilled the pleading that welled to her lips. "Nothing's the same anyway," he said at last. "It never can be. Believe me when I say I have to go for a while."

It was no use to argue. Tears forced from her eyes,

ran down her face, persisted though she brushed them angrily away. "You'll come back? You'll at least promise that?"

He came around the bed. To her bemusement, he took her hands. "I'll come back. Don't worry about that, my sweet little, fierce little Talitha. I could never stay away."

And then he pushed her out. As she walked defeatedly toward the house, she glanced up to see Judah Frost watching her.

All that day she was careful to stay where he couldn't find her alone, but that evening while she was tending Caterina, he came over and bent close, pretending to admire the baby. "So you don't fancy going to California?" he asked softly. The others, listening to some story of Marc Revier's, couldn't hear.

"No," she returned shortly.

"Then where, Talitha? Where shall I take you?"

"Nowhere!"

"Ah, but it must be somewhere. Some place, some time. I'm patient, Talitha, but be sure it will happen."

"I don't know what you're talking about, but I wish you hadn't come back and I hope I never see you again!"

"Careful, love. That big Irisher may hear. You'd hate for him to get hurt, wouldn't you?"

Talitha turned her back, tucking the covers in loosely at the sides so that perhaps Caterina would fall asleep before she managed to kick them off. The tall man behind her laughed under his breath.

"I have my ranch, Talitha, a freighting company and a mine. Try to get it into your head that what I want, I get. You are young and I can wait but in the end, I'll have you."

She was grateful for the approach of footsteps on the hard-packed earthen floor. Marc Revier smiled down at Caterina who made a bubbling laugh and reached for him.

"May I hold her?" he asked Talitha. His English was perfect, with only a hint of accent. "It's long and long since I had such a one in my arms."

Caterina looked not the least bit sleepy. Talitha picked her up in the blanket, handed her to the engineer who put her against his shoulder, steadying the back of her head with one big hand.

"You have children?" Talitha asked, relieved that Frost had moved away.

"No." Revier smiled at her over Caterina's fluffy hair. The dim light from fire and candle made his blue eyes seem dark, but she was glad she could still see the good-humored lines at his mouth and eyes. "But my sister had two small ones when I left Berlin, one this age. I was amazed, when she first compelled me to pick them up, how sweet the flesh of a child is. Healing, a balm."

He stared at something beyond them, then said, with a wry down-turning of his lips, "You don't need that healing yet, Miss Talitha. You must think me babbling."

She shook her head, liking this stranger in spite of his association with Judah Frost. "Sometimes, when I'm sad, playing with Caterina helps more than anything."

Which was a marvel. It was only of late that Talitha had been able to look at the baby without remembering her birth, Socorro's life draining, James going away. It must be even worse for Shea. She sighed and forced her thoughts down another channel.

"Will you go hunting for this port, Mr. Revier?"

"I've nothing to do with the freighting, except to smelt down bullion to be hauled. My work's at the mine and in looking for new locations."

The pleasantly different sound of his voice charmed her. She would have wanted him to go on talking even if Frost hadn't been holding forth over by the fire. "How did you chance to come to Sonora, Mr. Revier?"

"Well, like many people from all over the world, I first went to California. I was lucky to find enough gold to invest in this company of Mr. Frost's, and I was glad to leave California." He searched for words. "Everyone there seems to be running a fever and it gets more crowded every day. The easy gold is gone and the fighting's on for what remains."

"I hope it never gets to be like that here."

"So do I," he agreed soberly, then twinkled at her. "Let us hope for just a comfortable amount of silver that pays expenses and yields a reasonable profit."

"I think your partner wants more than that."

"Frost? Yes, he's ambitious, but mining's only one of his ways of getting rich."

Rich? It was a word she'd not heard much, but when she stopped to think, she supposed that Shea and Santiago, from selling horses and cattle and the half-profit from Don Narciso's mine, might be considered a *little bit* rich. If their investment with Frost didn't turn into a loss.

Tilting her head at Revier, she asked flatly, "Don't you want to be rich?"

He chuckled. "I want enough to do what I want when I want and how I want. That's riches, Talitha. The man so bound up in money-making that it owns him has no freedom, is as much a slave as one he might buy and set to work in his fields."

She approved of the sound of that though she didn't completely understand. "Don't you miss your own country?"

"Yes." He stroked Caterina's shoulders. "But I miss my niece and nephew more. I was schooled in England till it was time to study my profession, because my father admired the English to the point of marrying one, so it's been nothing new to be away. But I shall always love Berlin."

"Will you go back?"

"To visit, yes. I couldn't live there unless things changed much more than they're likely to in my lifetime. I need a freer air." Again his gaze reached far away. "On the March days of 1848, when King Frederick saluted the bodies of those who'd died on the barricades, and a few days later when he paraded through the streets in the red, gold and black tricolor of the new Germany, I hoped—we all did! I was a member of the Prussian constituent assembly that started in May to plan a new order where all men would vote, where the power of the nobility would be sharply curbed."

"But weren't you—" Talitha paused, embarrassed. "Your family must have been pretty well off for you to go to school in England."

"My father's a wealthy merchant—and a slave." Revier shrugged but a trace of pain roughened his words. "He disowned me for charging the barricades. Just as well. I have no bent for commerce but my brother-in-law does."

Talitha tried to picture a place called Berlin, a king saluting corpses and marching in red, gold and black, and some kind of big meeting with Marc Revier there. It was difficult. She'd never even been to Tubac and her memories of Santa Fe were of mud buildings straggling around a *plaza*.

Only Nauvoo, to her, had any echo of the far place he spoke of. She pictured him with his assembly in the shining white temple and suddenly his words took on reality.

"What did the—the whatever-it-was assembly do, Mr. Revier?"

"Oh, all summer, while the Danes and Prussians battled over who was to have the provinces of Schleswig and Holstein, the assembly debated points of a new constitution." He grimaced. "For our 'radical' acts such as striking 'by the grace of God' from the king's title, the assembly was exiled to Brandenburg in November and dissolved in early December."

Caterina had fallen asleep. Carefully, he placed her in the basket. "It's not as forlorn as I make it sound, Miss Talitha. Much of the assembly's work served as a basis for the constitution and though the king's ultimate authority was maintained, the lower house of the parliament is elected by universal suffrage."

"What's that?" asked Talitha with a furrowed brow.

"A vote by all men. The catch is that voting's based on taxpaying ability so that the wealthier seventeen percent of the voters control two-thirds of the seats." A fatalistic lift of the shoulder. "Perhaps a realistic improvement but scarcely what most of us in the assembly had hoped for. With my leanings known, it was impossible to find work. So that's why, Miss Talitha, I left the old world for the new."

"Shea left because of the famine."

"Did he?" Revier glanced at the men by the fire. "Of course, when you think upon it, the family of everyone who's not Indian did come from somewhere else."

Judah Frost was watching. It made Talitha uneasy though she'd have liked to talk with Marc Revier a long, long time. He gave her glimpses of a world beyond and though she didn't understand parliaments and constitutions, she'd like to have heard more about kings and barricades, that city called Berlin, his schooling in England. But they couldn't keep standing here, not with Frost's pale eyes on them.

"I'd better get the twins to bed," she said reluctantly. They were perched on either side of Frost.

Revier said, "Miss Talitha, that message to your father—would you like some help with it?"

"I can't write at all," she admitted.

Somehow, she didn't mind his knowing, though he must be the best educated person she'd ever met. Shea could sign his name but apart from that, he and everyone at the ranch was unable to read or write.

"Would you like to learn?"

There had been books at Nauvoo. Talitha remembered looking at the pages and wondering how her mother could read such wonderful stories from the little black marks. Mother had promised to teach her to read when they got to California.

Careless of whether Judah Frost noticed, Talitha threw back her head and smiled at Marc Revier. "I'd love to! But how can you teach me when you live so far away?"

"We've got a reliable superintendent now. I can get away every week for a day or so and leave you lessons to do in between. Shall we try it?"

"Oh, yes! The twins can learn, too!"

"Fine. If Mr. O'Shea agrees, I'll come next Saturday, so have your thinking cap on, young lady!"

Full of happy anticipation, Talitha nodded and advanced on the twins, shooing them off with the promise of a story. She was going to learn to read! She'd know how to write letters and keep accounts for Shea. But best of all, every week she was going to see Marc Revier! She'd still miss Santiago, but not anything like the way she would have without that deep gentle voice that seemed to caress away her fears and loneliness.

XXIII

After Marc's first "teaching" visit, the twins incessantly pestered Talitha as to which day was Saturday. Late in the morning they'd go to meet him, riding if Belen or Chuey could accompany them, otherwise going on foot. When this happened, he'd ride in on his durable buckskin with the boys up behind him, hanging tight so as not to jounce off. Arriving in time for the noon meal, he'd talk with Shea and the men till Talitha could leave Anita in charge and join him and the twins at the table.

Though Chuey and Belen both understood considerable English, they had no desire to read or write it so they went out to do some of the winter work, fixing corrals and building new ones, improving water tanks, mending saddles and bridles, all the things that couldn't be done from spring to fall when the cattle demanded their time.

Shea usually stayed. He swore at the pencil, grumbled that it was harder to control than a locoed horse, but he painfully copied the letters Marc wrote on a piece of the paper he'd brought from California.

Paper was expensive and they didn't waste it, but wrote on their pages over and over, crisscrossing till the letters were solid.

Because of his profession, Marc had a good supply of pencils and he left four at the ranch, along with a ledger, for his pupils to practice with. He also left books, and for these the twins endured the tedious alphabet.

"I thought the miners would have children," Marc explained, smiling as Patrick and Miguel gazed wide-

351

eyed at the elephants and tigers in one brightly colored book. "I hoped to have a small school for them. But our miners have no families and if they did, English wouldn't be that useful for them."

He had a geography, with maps. This fascinated Shea. He could never get over how small England was in comparison to the countries she governed. "Look at Canada! And Australia down there, and India! God's whiskers! No wonder she's been able to run it all over poor Ireland!" Absently, his fingers went to the old brand on his cheek. "One good thing I'll say for the Americans, they got properly shed of England!"

Talitha loved the engravings in the history book. Pyramids, sphinxes, temples nothing like the one at Nauvoo, Roman soldiers, Attila and Vikings—what a treasure of stories Marc seemed to know. She longed to read for herself and would sit up by the fire at night, spelling and sounding out words. It was slow, tantalizingly difficult, but by the end of January she could read most of a book of fables to the twins.

"I wonder if you hadn't already begun to recognize words when your mother read to you," Marc speculated. "However it comes, you're a joy to teach. You'll soon be ready for the books I brought for myself."

Shea was quick with ciphers. Buying and selling had given him a practical command of arithmetic, but to be able to make calculations in advance, subtract, multiply and divide—well, that intrigued Shea.

Marc's company was good for him, too. After an initial stiffening when he learned of Marc's English mother and education, he shrugged and said, "We're all here now, whyever, and the Americans soon will be!"

"I hope so," said Marc amiably. "With enough troops to keep off Apaches and bandits. We have a man on watch from dawn to dark, and at night, too, if we've seen anything suspicious during the day."

In December of 1853, Gadsden and Santa Anna finally struck their bargain. Negotiations had been temporarily sabotaged by William Walker's November try to take over Baja California. Though the filibusterer was swiftly defeated and chased into California, Santa Anna and most Mexicans believed the United States government was behind the attempt and considered it the first step in annexing all Mexico.

However, when Santa Anna's efforts to make alliances with European powers convinced him that France, Britain or Spain wouldn't aid him in case of war, he returned to bargaining with the exhausted Gadsden who certainly must have wanted his railroad to put up with all the disappointments and delays.

The treaty would allow the United States to purchase the land it needed for its nation-spanning route, a stretch between El Paso and Yuma, for $15,000,000. In return for assuming claims of Americans against Mexico, the United States would not be responsible for raids of Indians into Mexico as provided for in Article XI of the Treaty of Guadalupe Hidalgo.

The never-strong grip of Mexico on its northern frontier almost completely crumbled. Captain Zenteno at Tubac had a hard time keeping the people of his garrisons fed. In January, responding to pleas from starving Santa Cruz, he'd borrowed mules from Tumacácori and pack sacks from Calabazas, got together supplies, and started the slow trek south.

Apaches rode into them in sudden attack, killing two soldiers, driving off all the mules including the ones the men had been riding. Zenteno implored his government to provide some oxen and wagons for hauling supplies, but the harassed officials, with troubles closer at hand, left him to cope as best he could with the defense and provisioning of his sector.

That winter and spring of 1854 were filled with a sense of waiting, of inevitable change, while the United States Congress wrangled over land that the famous mountain man, Kit Carson, called "so desolate, desert and God-forsaken that a wolf could not make a living on it."

There was waiting in human terms as well, hoping that James would return, at least for a visit, and waiting for Santiago. He had said he'd be back in time for the spring cattle work. Surely he must come soon— if he were alive.

Marc hadn't heard from his partner, either, but he refused to worry and wouldn't permit Talitha to fret when he was around. "Judah's not about to get killed when there's a smart profit to be made," he said with breezy confidence. "Depend on it, they'll be back soon with the port located and a promise from the authorities to set up a customs office and develop the harbor."

It was impossible to be despondent when Marc was there. He fitted in as if they'd known him always and yet he was like nobody else they had ever met. He'd walk a cranky, toothing Caterina while discussing politics with Shea or telling the twins about Robin Hood, Dr. Faustus, King Arthur, El Cid, Rustum, Ogier the Dane and, to Shea's pride, of Cuchulain and Brian Boru.

He could sing, too, everything from German drinking songs to Gold Rush tunes, but best of all Talitha loved the old songs he'd learned from his mother, "Greensleeves" and "Western Wind," "The Gypsy Laddie" and many others, especially one he said had been made up by the poet Thomas Wyatt for Anne Boleyn, the woman he loved before and after she was Henry VIII's doomed queen.

> "Forget not yet the tried intent
> Of such a love as I have meant,
> My great travail so gladly spent,
> Forget not, oh forget not yet."

Hearing the male voice deepen richly, thrillingly as he sang, Talitha ached with the beauty and sadness of the song. Would she ever have a love like that? She didn't think she wanted to, watching Shea trying to live without Socorro.

He came in one evening while Anita was feeding the two baby girls and Talitha was trying to get supper while arbitrating a quarrel between the twins who were irascible from having bad colds and being kept inside out of the chill rainy spell that had settled in to drive Talitha completely to her wit's end.

After one quick glance, Shea commanded the boys to pick up the things they'd scattered all over the house, get themselves washed and set the table. He then took over the tortilla-making so Talitha could concentrate on the stew.

"I ought to be kicked!" he said angrily. "No wonder you look peaked! Anita's got her hands full with Paulita and Caterina, the twins are into everything, and you've got to cook and wash for all of us! Why haven't you said something?"

Astonished, Talitha said quickly, "It's all right, Shea! The twins wouldn't be like this if they didn't have those wretched colds and—"

"And nothing!" he cut in. "When we get started on the calves, I won't even be able to fetch the water and wood the way I can now. Tomorrow I'm going to get you some help!"

Foreboding shot through Talitha. "Where?" she demanded. "Who?"

"Maybe Juanita and Cheno can move up here."

"Juanita's going to have a baby," Talitha countered. "She'll want to be with her mother and even if she didn't, she wouldn't be any help while the baby's little."

Shea scowled, puckering the double brand. On an impulse, Talitha did what she'd always longed to, put up her hand and caressed the mark he'd taken for her brother's sake.

She felt him tense, wondered at the strange pinpoints of light in his eyes. Abruptly, he swung away, jarring her hand from him. "Then I'll get Tjúni."

"Tjúni?" There'd been no love between Talitha and the Papago woman but that didn't explain the denial, the heavy sense of warning that sprang from Talitha's

355

depths. "She won't come. She's got her own people at San Manuel."

"She was here to begin with." Shea was remembering back, to a time before Talitha had known him. She hated and feared that; it took him far away. "I never understood why she went off that way, but I think she'll come back when she knows we need her."

"We don't! Oh, Shea, please—I can do anything she can!"

He had moved a distance off. "No," he said. "You can't."

Talitha's body, which had been waiting, too, that winter, waiting to be charged with a woman's feelings, understood before her mind did.

Even then she fought against recognizing what Shea needed from Tjúni that he couldn't have from her, tried to calm herself by arguing that the Papago woman had been part of his life with Socorro, a partner in the founding of the ranch. It was natural for him to think of her. From his manner, Talitha knew it was useless to protest. But she had to turn her head to keep tears from falling into the stew and she wouldn't look directly at Shea for the rest of that evening. It hurt too much.

Tjúni came. Her body was fuller now, more richly curved, but her face had its old haughty cat-like beauty. Belen moved in with Chuey and Anita while a house was built for her and Talitha was glad to be spared sleeping in the same room with her till she woke one night and saw Shea moving quietly through the house.

A fiery blade seemed to turn in Talitha. When Shea didn't return in a moment, she got up and peered out the window, detected his shadowy form against the paler darkness. As Talitha watched, fingernails driving into her palms, she hoped desperately he was going to do what she'd so often prayed he wouldn't, go up the hill and mourn by Socorro's grave.

This night he went straight to the vaqueros' quarters.

As he vanished inside, Tjúni's exultant laughter echoed and reechoed in Talitha's head. Huddling down in her blankets, she pulled a startled Chusma close and sobbed against the warm soft body of the cat.

She was to do so often, though without Chusma, for the cat disapproved of such demonstrations and freed herself quickly or eluded capture. After Caterina started sleeping through the night, Anita had moved back with Chuey, so there wasn't even the soothing gentle rumble of her snoring.

Not that Shea went to Tjúni every night. Often five or six would pass before he moved quietly past Talitha. He never stayed long, either. Once he came back while Talitha was crying, unaware of his presence till he dropped to one knee.

"Why, Tally! What's the matter, child?"

"I—I'm not a child!"

From his voice, she knew he suppressed a grin and in the misery of that moment, she hated him for it. "Very well, Señorita Scott. What ails you?"

"Nothing!"

He was very close in the darkness. "Tally, you don't cry for nothing. Now tell me what it is. Maybe I can fix it."

Her breath felt shallow and tight as if invisible weights crushed on her. "Will—will you send Tjúni away?"

He was still for a heartbeat. "Why?"

In the main Tjúni ignored them regally. She had taken over the cooking and general management of the household, leaving Talitha to see to the twins and Caterina. "I—I just liked it better before she came."

Shea laughed, sounding relieved. "Nose a little out of joint, Tally? Young as you are, I guess you really were running the house. But you're able to get outside now, ride Ladorada and help with the outdoor work. I thought you liked that."

"I do, but not . . . Oh, Shea, tell her to leave and

357

I promise I'll do everything she has!" The words wrenched from her violently with no conscious decision on her part.

Silence deepened between them. Shea's voice was strained and husky. "Everything, Tally?"

Unable to speak, she moved toward him in the blackness, awkwardly tried to find his mouth with her own. Roughly, he caught her wrist, forcing her away.

"No, Tally! My God, you're the same as my daughter!"

"But I'm not your daughter, Shea! I—I love you. I always have, I always will!"

As if her cry had steadied him, given him a foundation from which he wouldn't move, he took her in his arms then, tenderly as a father would, and stroked her hair. "I'm glad you love me, darlin'. God forbid you should ever be sorry and strike me dead if you are. I love you, too. But you have your loves mixed up, little Tally. Because I am about the most father you've known, I won't take what should go to a very lucky man someday, the man you'll love for your mate."

She shook her head. "I love *you*."

"It's not the same."

Flaring at the weary patience in his tone, she demanded bitterly, "Do you love Tjúni?"

"No. And she knows that. But we were companions in the desert. She's wanted this a long time." He sighed. "Tally, we shouldn't be talking like this but since we are, try to understand. I don't know what you know about men, but I'm only thirty-five though that must seem a vast age to you. I need a woman sometimes. I've no wish to visit the overworked whores of Tubac, nor will I tamper with the wives of my vaqueros. Tjúni eases me and I pleasure her. We're hurting no one."

You hurt me.

Humiliated and desolate, Talitha tried to free herself, but Shea, kissing her cheek and rising, seemed not to notice.

*   *   *
358

Often that spring Marc carried the baby in the cradleboard that had been James's and went with Talitha to gather cattail roots, cholla buds and the stems of *yucca palmillo*. He helped shake the cholla buds in a basket of gravel till the spines rubbed off, and helped plant the first corn crop.

"You're teaching me more than I'm teaching you," he said one night after the twins had vied in showing him how to cast a *peal* and *mangana*.

"But you don't need to know what we can show you," Talitha laughed. "An engineer doesn't rope cows or plant corn or roast cholla buds!"

"This engineer plans to," he retorted. "As soon as the new boundaries are fixed, I'm buying some land of my own adjoining the company's."

"You plan on staying in the valley permanently then?" asked Shea.

Marc nodded. "It's got a grip on me. Marching mountains—everywhere you look, there's a range and behind it another, and another till they fade into the sky. Green gentle country can never hold me again." He smiled at Talitha. Weeks ago they had fallen into using first names. "So you see, Talitha, I'll be very grateful if you teach me all you can."

He was especially interested in medicinal plants. Talitha taught him what she knew and showed him the roots and herbs Nōnó had given her. "The *lantana* he told me to give Socorro didn't help, though," she said and was gripped with a wave of grief.

Socorro was dead six months now, and the sharpest loss was dulled, but when Talitha really thought of her, she felt a deep wrench of sorrow and rebellion.

To die at twenty-four, leaving a beloved husband and three small ones! It wasn't fair, it shouldn't happen! And James shouldn't be up in the mountains with Apaches, he should be here!

Revier said quietly, "Perhaps it helped enough to get the child born. If Nōnó cured Shea of hydrophobia, he must have powerful skills."

"Yes, and he told me a cure for snakebite that sounds awful enough to work." Resolutely, Talitha directed her thoughts away from the ache of remembering Socorro. There had been so many happy times. She'd try to think of them, not those last hours.

"And what is this awful remedy?" Marc teased.

"Catch the snake and kill it, then take out its liver and gall and smear the gall on the bite. Eat as much of the liver as you can." She made a shuddering face. "Ugh!"

Marc chuckled. "It might work, Talitha. I had a biology professor who thought very strong antitoxins are present in the bile of some animals. And in the Talmud it says hydrophobia can be cured by eating the liver of the dog that bit you! Nōnó's in good company."

That led to his explaining what the Talmud was and comparing it with the Koran, the Bible and the Zend-Avesta. Talitha darted him an incredulous look. "You didn't have to learn all these things to be an engineer, did you?"

His blue eyes danced. "No, indeed. But let me tell you an important fact: all things being equal, streams tend to meander. And so do I. Most engineers don't like that. They have their T-squares and angles and want to go in straight lines. But that's ridiculous!"

Talitha eyed him dubiously. "It is?"

"Of course it is! It's against nature which has precious few straight lines." He blew out his cheeks and she guessed he was voicing an ingrained aggravation. "Men are crazy and scientific ones are the worst! What do they use for boundaries? Rivers! Rivers that shift drastically with any big flood! Now why, instead, not use a mountain range or a ridge that's not going to alter?"

"From what you just said about streams meandering, I should think you'd like rivers for boundaries," said Talitha.

His scowl changed to a surprised grin. "So I should! It's one place where the engineers haven't triumphed."

She shook her head in laughing puzzlement. "I don't understand you, Marc. You're an engineer yet you grumble about their methods!"

"Mining engineers are different," he said smugly. "Just remember this, my dear; there's a rock at the bottom of everything!"

Casually, he taught her and the twins a little about minerals. How volcanic magma turned to igneous rock which might then become sedimentary or metamorphic; how conglomerate rocks were formed of many small rocks or pebbles cemented together by clay in some alluvial dump; and how the study of rocks led to a grand and staggering view of the world, a time before man existed, when plants and creatures both immense and miniscule left their traces in mud now hardened to stone.

It fascinated Talitha to hear Marc apply his scientific knowledge to everyday things. He pointed out that the white rocks at the bottom of a pool attracted enough light to permit algae to form. On a cold day, when they saw a prairie pheasant or paisano lying on a rock with its wings spread, he surmised that the dark patches in its plumage were soaking up sun to raise its body temperature. Once when they rode far enough west to find saguaros, he pointed out that the nesting cavities made in them by woodpeckers and flickers, and later used by sparrow hawks, elf owls and other birds not only provided a great measure of safety from predators but maintained a fairly steady temperature.

"Which is good in winter," he said, "but how wonderful in summer when, I'm told, temperatures can go well over a hundred!"

Talitha laughed. "Oh, well over a hundred. For days and days and days!" She studied a saguaro cavity with fresh respect. "It's too bad we can't live in something like that!"

"Well, your thick adobe is a good insulator. Or people could get many of the same benefits by building in the side of a hill or partially underground."

"But that would be so dark!"

"Not as glass gets more plentiful. One whole open side would give a lot of light and sun heat."

"Which we certainly don't need in the summer!"

"Heavy curtains could shut it out then, Talitha." He rubbed his chin thoughtfully, reined his buckskin around for it was time they got back to the ranch. "It's all a matter of properly using man's brain on what God has provided."

Without Marc's wise and cheerful company most weekends and the challenge of studying in between, Talitha wouldn't have been able to bear Tjúni's presence even though Shea didn't, at least openly, treat her any differently than he had before.

Talitha wished desperately that Santiago would come back and supply a balance. Since the night Shea had refused her, there'd been constraint between them. They seldom looked directly at each other or spoke more than was necessary. Talitha was sure that Tjúni had noticed and was glad of the estrangement.

It would have been a relief to pour all this out to Marc, but Talitha couldn't babble about Shea's private arrangements. Santiago would see and understand, though, without any words. With him there, she wouldn't feel so alone. Apart from wishing he'd come for the comfort of his being at the ranch, she was increasingly worried as March advanced.

There were always Apaches and bandits but William Walker's filibustering had made it even more hazardous for strangers to go wandering about Mexico, especially if they were looking for ports convenient to the region Mexicans felt had been all but stolen from them. So, while she hoped Judah Frost would never return, she prayed that Santiago would.

It was strange to start working the cattle that spring without Santiago urging Noche to turn some escaping steer, expertly roping the most elusive yearling, filling the air with good-natured obscenities flavored with Spanish color and elegance.

There was quite a mix of brands and earmarks. Santiago, a partner, shared those branded with Rancho del Socorro's S; the Vasquez brothers used a V, Chuey Sanchez had an S lying on one side, and his father and brother at El Charco branded with a circle. Belen still insisted on contributing his share to Talitha. Her pile of *señales* had grown till she'd long ago had to start keeping them in a box Shea had made for her. It had used to give her a glow of ownership to see her Cross T on an animal but that had been when she vaguely dreamed that one day she and James would have their own small place near the ranch.

James. That ache, unlike the one for Socorro, seemed to get worse as time passed with no word of him. He'd gone off, blaming himself, thinking all of them blamed him; a terrible load for a little boy who wouldn't have his seventh birthday till this July.

So Talitha got no particular thrill out of burning the Cross T on this twentieth unbranded cow that she and Belen had caught. As he let it up and she stepped out of its way, Belen straightened and peered up the arroyo.

"That horse—it looks like Señor Frost's!"

Whirling, she gazed beyond the mist-gray mount, straining to glimpse the gleaming black of Noche, but there was only the big gray and the pack mule. Talitha dropped the iron, untied Ladorada and urged her into a gallop.

Judah Frost's handsome thin lips curved in a smile as she drew up beside him. "So eager, Talitha? You rejoice my heart!"

"Where's Santiago?"

"Here comes your worthy guardian. Allow me to explain once and for all, my dear. I'm quite fatigued—"

"Is Santiago alive?"

Frost sighed plaintively. "Of course he's alive. Very much so. Now please wait till the others gather 'round."

Shea and Chuey were waiting with Belen when Frost

reined in Selim and slid from the saddle to shake hands with Shea and nod a greeting to the vaqueros.

"We found a port," he said, "but you want to know about Santiago so I'll tell you about him first. By now he must be married to a very pretty woman of mature years, the widow of a prosperous ranchero. We stopped at her home for shelter—she lives about halfway between Hermosillo and the proposed port, and she and Santiago made friends so quickly that I assure you I felt very much out of it. By the time we had rested enough to go on our way, she had persuaded Santiago not to."

Shea looked dumbfounded. "Just like that? I'd have thought he'd come for his cattle and share of the mine proceeds."

"His fair widow has more cattle than she can keep track of," Frost grinned. "And she didn't favor letting her potential husband risk himself in Apache country since it was on a trip to Tucson that her first one was killed. Santiago said to tell you his cattle are for his godson, young James. Talitha and the twins are to share the mining profits, with you in charge, Shea."

Standing as if an invisible current dashed against him, Shea didn't speak or move for a time. Then, with a heavy shake of the head, he said slowly, "Hard to believe! After all this time, he's gone just like that. I sure wish he'd have come back himself to talk it over."

Talitha's feelings echoed Shea's words. Santiago had promised to come back. It was hard to believe that he'd just stop someplace and forget all about them.

"My dear Shea," chuckled Frost. "It wasn't with talking the lady got her way! And Santiago did want to break the news to you but she pleaded so tearfully it would have melted anyone's heart, let alone a prospective bridegroom's."

"There'll be a priest to marry *them*," Shea said under his breath. He seemed to contract his loosened body, drew himself up straight. "Well, after he's been wed awhile, perhaps he can journey this way now and then. And you must tell me how to find him."

Frost gave directions from Hermosillo, in such detail that Talitha was reluctantly almost convinced. Then, since it was growing late in the day, Shea called a halt to the branding and they all rode for the ranch.

At the sight of Tjúni, Frost shot his host a quick glance, then smiled at Talitha. "So this is why you're out playing vaquero! You've got someone else to make the tortillas and watch the baby."

Talitha flushed. She had washed her hands and gone straight to pick up Caterina who had stopped nursing at Anita's breast when Talitha appeared. Gurgling with delight, Caterina seized fistfuls of Talitha's hair.

Shifting her to a shoulder and patting to bring up any air bubbles, Talitha stared at this man whom she feared as she had never feared Apaches. He threatened not only her body but the very core of her being, what her mother and Socorro would have called a soul.

Talitha wanted to shout that she didn't fully believe him about Santiago, but that could bring on trouble for Shea who now saved her from answering Frost's belittling remark.

"Tally doesn't play at vaquero. For weight and size, she's as good as they come."

"Really?" murmured Frost. His polite tone, at least to Talitha, held an edge of amused derision. "I suppose I'm judging her by eastern girls. At her age, they've scarce put away their dolls."

"I still have my doll!" Talitha flashed at him.

"Indeed?" he murmured. "I'm glad to hear it."

"Why?"

He said blandly, "It's refreshing to hear that such an independent young lady clings to her toys."

The wonderful doll brought up by *conducta,* named for Talitha's mother and once besought to keep Juh from claiming James, was little more of a toy than the madonna in the *sala* but Talitha wouldn't have told

Frost so. She felt instinctively that the more mistaken he was about her the better.

Caterina burped milkily on her shoulder. With a final hug, Talitha gave her to Anita who was fending off nine-month Paulita, promising to feed her as soon as they went to their own house to cook for Chuey. As Talitha helped Tjúni finish preparing supper, Frost leaned back in one of the rawhide chairs and described the two harbors he and Santiago had located on the Sonoran coast.

"The northern one would be less than two hundred miles from Tucson and the southern slightly more." He placed his chin on slim, pyramided fingers. "I'd reckon on getting goods from San Francisco in about forty days compared to four months coming through Yuma, and the cost should be about six cents a pound as compared to fifteen to eighteen."

"Sounds good if the Mexican and Sonoran governments will open the port." Shea was interested in spite of his shock over Santiago.

"I've talked to the governor and think he will. He's even hinted at letting goods pass duty free through Mexico into the United States since a thriving new port would help the Sonoran economy."

Shea whistled. "Maybe I should have bought into your freighting business!"

"There's still time," Frost grinned expansively. "Anyway, nothing's going to happen till the Gadsden treaty's been settled. By the way, Congress is quibbling over it; that may be a while."

At Shea's urging, he stayed the night, sleeping in the vaqueros' quarters while Tjúni grudgingly spread her pallet in the kitchen as she had before she went away that fall the twins were born. Passing through the *sala* as Talitha readied Caterina for the night, Shea paused and gazed down at his daughter.

Her tiny fingers reached for him. With a kind of sigh, he offered a brown finger, laughed in surprise as

366

she closed her chubby honey-colored fist around it, holding so tight that he could raise her.

"God's whiskers! She hangs on!"

"Yes." Talitha could scarcely speak. This was the first time he'd laughed at his baby, looked at her with anything but pain and guilty resentment. Talitha's heart swelled. *Oh, let him love her!* she pleaded silently to mother, madonna and Socorro; God, if He listened. *Please, let him love her.*

At least, after all these months, he was *looking*. If he looked, he had to love. Caterina was such a beautiful, funny baby with eyebrows that puckered fiercely when her wants weren't promptly attended to. She spent hours each day now rocking on her knees and could already hitch herself along a little way before she collapsed.

"Well, my lass, come here then," Shea told her as she squealed and refused to let him go. Awkwardly, he held her at arm's length. "She doesn't weigh much," he said anxiously to Talitha. "Do you think she gets enough to eat?"

If she didn't, this would be a fine time for you to notice it, thought Talitha but she was too overjoyed at his interest to chide him. "Of course she does! Anita still feeds her and I give her ground piñon nuts in honey and water, the way I fed James."

He frowned, obviously not satisfied. "She feels too light to me."

"She wouldn't, if you'd been holding her since she was tiny."

Talitha bit her lip, but he seemed not to notice the indirect reproof.

"Reckon I'd better start getting milk out of one of those old range cows. The babies can get used to it gradually and when Anita's milk gives out, they can change over entirely."

"I don't know what's gotten into you." Talitha frowned. "Socorro fed both twins till they were almost two and you never worried about them."

"That was different! *She* saw to things then. Now it's up to me. And this one is going to have what she needs!" He squinted at Talitha across the baby's shoulder. "A glass of milk a day wouldn't hurt the twins. Or you, either! You're skinny as a post!"

"Milk?" Talitha echoed. Milk belonged to Nauvoo, before they'd had to cross the icy river in the night. It belonged to a long time ago. "Me, drink milk? Why, Belen would laugh his head off!"

"Never you mind that." Shea uncurled his daughter's hand from his hair and put her back in her basket. "Starting tomorrow, there's going to be milk! And it's time you had your own room, you and little Katie."

"I don't mind, Shea." She couldn't say how comforting it was to have him just a wall away, except for the occasional hours he spent with Tjúni.

"You're almost a young lady! Time you had a proper bed and place instead of a pallet in what'll be the living room if we ever get that civilized! As soon as we get back from selling the cows, we'll get that room of yours started."

She didn't argue. It was good to have him wanting to do something more than the necessary things. In spite of her misgivings about Santiago, Talitha went to bed that night in a glow of happiness. Shea had held the baby, really looked at her, and for the first time had given her a name!

Katie. A wee Irish name, with none of the haughty stateliness of Caterina which Talitha had already begun shortening to Cat. It was going to be all right. Shea had started to love his child.

XXIV

Talitha had avoided being by herself where Judah Frost might find her but next morning after breakfast when he was preparing to leave, he asked her if she had the letter for her father.

"I have business in San Francisco and I can see Mr. Scott with no trouble," he offered smoothly. "I'll tell him about you, of course, but I'm sure he'd welcome something in your own hand."

It was a reasonable, even thoughtful, suggestion, but Talitha wanted nothing to do with this handsome cold-eyed man and though she wished her father well, she shrank from an entanglement that might jeopardize her place in Shea's household.

"Perhaps you could just tell him—" she began, but Shea, ready to go out the door with Belen and the twins, faced about sternly.

"You write your father, Tally. If you can't spell all the words, Judah will probably help you. We'll be working the mesquite thickets over behind the second ridge today. You can join us there." He nodded at Frost. "Have a safe journey and come see us when you're back."

Frost rose to shake hands. "Be sure I'll do that. I feel quite at home here."

Yielding to the inevitable, Talitha located a clean page in the ledger and sat down at the table, sucking in her cheeks as she concentrated on the letter. Fortunately, Marc had taught her how to spell most of the words she'd need for such a message, but Frost's presence, now that the men were gone, seemed to scramble her brains.

"Dear Father," she began, stopped to bite into the pencil. She had already decided to say nothing about James. "I am glad you have done well in California. I am fine and live with a nice family. Mother died after the Apaches caught us."

What else?

Her attention shattered completely as Tjúni took the water bucket and went out. Hastily scribbling her name at the bottom of the page, Talitha jumped up, folded the letter and thrust it at the tall man who seemed to loom over her though he hadn't moved.

"Thank you, Mr. Frost. I've got to hurry now and catch up with the others."

"Talitha!" he exclaimed in pretended hurt. "So long since we had a word in private and the moment we have an opportunity, you want to run off!"

"I don't want any private words with you!"

His eyebrows raised. "None at all? Come now, Talitha, there must be something you'd like to say without your estimable foster father overhearing."

Goaded, she narrowed her eyes, challenged him. "That story about Santiago—I think you're lying!"

"Why would I do that?"

"I don't know. I—I just can't believe he'd decide to stay down there like that and never even come to tell us."

Frost considered her. "Especially since he was in love with you?"

Talitha stared in blank dismay. Frost took a long step toward her, crystalline eyes probing. "Surely you knew that, my dear?"

"No!" She tried to refuse to think of those times Santiago's gaze had changed, when the lazy gold of his eyes turned to flame; or of the puzzling things he'd said before he went away.

"He never told his love?" It sounded like a mocking quote. "Perhaps not since you're so young. But he told me. That was why he went with me in the first place, to get away from the temptation of constantly being near someone he felt honor bound not to approach for several years yet, if ever."

Talitha's head whirled. She wanted to hurl denial at this man who watched her, ostensible sympathy failing to cloak the cruel pleasure he took in her confusion. But she believed him. It made sense of Santiago's bewildering behavior, trifling little things she'd never confronted squarely.

"Ah, you begin to understand." Frost's white even teeth were startling in his deeply tanned face. "Is it a wonder he turned with relief to a ripe, handsome woman who adored him? If you care for your friend, Talitha, you should rejoice that he's so happily delivered from the torment of daily beholding what he couldn't possess." He paused a moment. "Especially since he'd been through all this before."

"What do you mean?"

Frost tilted his head. "Did you never guess that he loved Doña Socorro?"

That, too, made certain things fall into place. Once again, against her will, Talitha had to believe.

"So you should see that Rancho del Socorro had become impossible," continued Frost in that soft commiserating tone. "There he was, between grief for the woman he'd never had, and desire for the one he felt forbidden." Pausing, Frost added the remark that completely convinced Talitha. "Santiago got gloriously drunk the night he decided to accept his importunate widow. He told me if he had any real hope that you'd turn to him in a few years, that he could ever have you, then he'd have returned. But he's sure your heart is so full of Shea there can never be anyone else."

Did everyone guess? Think her bad or forgetful of Socorro, or pity her because of Tjúni? A hot tide of blood washed through Talitha, she felt it staining her face, scalding her body.

Blindly shoving the letter toward Frost, she made for the door but he caught her arm. "Another moment, love!"

"I'm not your love! And Tjúni will be back any second!"

"Tjúni won't start back till she sees me step outside."

"You—you asked her to leave?"

"Heavens, no!" he laughed. "Good God, you may have to be told about people's feelings, but most women don't. She'd be delighted if you rode off to California with me, let me escort you to your father."

"Well, I won't!"

He sighed. "I thought not. So I think I should tell you what's in my mind. But first—" He drew her to him, bent his silvery head.

Talitha didn't struggle; in her dread, a part of her knew it would be useless, might further enflame him.

His lips were so cold on hers that they seemed to sear, then warmed as if he drew life from her. A tremor ran through him. He tightened his hold till she felt she was suffocating and still she feared to resist, ignite the passion she could sense beneath his control.

When at last he raised his head, she almost fell. He steadied her with a smile that was possessively intimate. "I don't ordinarily kiss little girls, Talitha. But you're at a dreamy age. Now you have a starting point for your reveries."

"If I dreamed of you, it would be a nightmare!" Backing toward the door, she rubbed her mouth vigorously with her hand.

"You'll dream. And after a while you'll start to try to imagine what comes after the kiss."

"I won't!"

"You will." His long fingers touched her cheek, caressed the side of her throat. "You'll be ripening for me, Talitha, and I can be patient, for I've many worlds to conquer. But in four years, when you're eighteen, then you'll marry me. If I still want you. I think I will."

She stared at him disbelievingly. "You must be out of your mind! I'd sooner marry a rattlesnake!"

"An interesting alternative and most symbolic." His eyes were like starshine reflected from a deep, frozen well. "Bear this in mind, sweet Talitha. I'll wait. But only so long as you encourage no one else. As Shea's partner, I'll stop by often enough to know if I have a rival. I have no intention of leaving your maidenhead for someone else to garner."

"I—I wish Shea knew what you're really like!"

He cocked an eyebrow. "Do you, love? What a shame it would be if I had to kill a man of whom I've become quite fond."

"He might kill you instead."

"Not unless he shot from ambush and you know he'd never do that."

"If you ever hurt him, I'll kill you any way I can!"

Scanning her, he nodded approval. "I dare say. That's what attracted me to you from the start, Talitha, your spirit. But you can't shoot me till I do something, can you?"

He offered his revolver.

If only she could! Take it and blow that smile through his face! But she couldn't, not like this, and he knew it, though it made her furious that he could go around bullying and threatening simply because he had no conscience and other people did.

As she spun away, his laughter followed her, and for a long time after she'd joined the men at the branding, that soulless crystal sound echoed in her ears.

That evening the men choused two cows with fairly full udders into the smallest corral, keeping their calves outside. Belen held one cow's head by the horns while Chuey kept a rope on her hind legs and Shea endeavored to milk.

She bawled wildly, her offspring answering from the other side of the corral, while Shea squatted, a gourd between his knees, and managed to coax out alternating streams of milk before they dribbled to nothing.

Shea swore at her but his labors produced only a few drops. "The old beast won't let down her milk," he grunted. "Chuey, Belen, could you do better? I haven't milked since I was a lad."

"I've *never* milked." Chuey sounded insulted. "And neither has any vaquero I ever heard of."

Belen shook his head. "I am not capable, Don Patricio."

Shea stood up, disgustedly eyeing the scant results. "Let her loose and turn her calf in. We'll keep them in the corral a few days and see if they don't tame down."

As soon as the first cow was placated by reunion with her big splotch-faced calf, the men advanced on the second cow. "Wait a minute!" called Talitha.

Early spring grass grew thick and green on the outside of the corral. Climbing over, she gathered an armful, and, clutching it to her, clambered back into the corral.

"A good idea, *doncellita*," said Belen. "Let's see if it works."

This cow was either more placid or more used to men. Chuey got her hind legs in a loose cuffing that he could yank tight if necessary and Belen stood where he could grab her horns if she started to turn on Shea, but during the time that Shea milked, she luxuriated in the grass Talitha held while talking gently to her.

The gourd soon filled. Shea rose with a heartfelt sigh. "Hell, turn the other old fury out and let's use this one!" He gave her a grateful slap on her bony rump. "Being as how you're a civil creature, I'll call you Mollie after a most obliging wench I knew once. Let her have her calf now."

So Caterina got her first cow's milk that night, watered down and sweetened with a bit of honey. Patrick and Shea drank the rest for Anita said frankly, "I don't think, Don Patricio, that cow milk is intended for human children. However, if it proves to agree with Caterina, I will let Paulita have some."

It agreed with Caterina very well. The twins loved it. After a few weeks Paulita had her share, too. Talitha took on the chore of supplying enough grass or succulent plants to keep Mollie complacent at milking time, and learned to milk, though the vaqueros continued to scorn that occupation.

Talitha refused to drink milk herself. She wanted no links with her far-off childhood other than memories of her mother, but it was possible there would be other babies to feed sometime and no human milk for them.

The act of insuring that his daughter had plenty of nourishment was a turning point for Shea. His appetite returned, he laughed more, and instead of staring moodily at the twins in the evening, he told them stories of his boyhood in Ireland, carefully selected, Talitha was sure, and of his adventures since. Their favorite story was of how he had died and Socorro had saved him. Next to that, they thrilled to how Socorro and Tjúni had earned Mangus's gratitude by rescuing his women from the scalp hunters.

Talitha wanted the boys to know their father could also be heroic. One day she told them of how Shea had endured a second branding for her brother's sake, a child who was nothing to him. She wept at the end of it. The twins, abashed, tugged at her and patted her consolingly.

"Don't cry, Tally!" Patrick begged. "James'll come back!"

"If he doesn't, we'll go find him when we're old enough," Miguel promised.

Alarmed, Talitha swept them close and gave them an admonishing shake. "You mustn't do that! Just because Mangus is our friend, don't think most Apaches are!"

Patrick squirmed out of her grasp and looked proudly up at the twin cradleboard hanging on the wall of the *sala,* still ornamented with feathers, turquoise and little bags of pollen. "Mangus brought that for us! Almost like we were Apaches!"

"Well, you're not! And don't you dare go wandering off unless you want me to really cry!"

Miguel kissed her, hazel eyes solemn. "We won't

worry you, Tally! Daddy says we mustn't ever do that 'cause you—you've—" He struggled to remember, finished triumphantly. " 'Cause you've already got too much on your shoulders!"

She did, though Shea's renewed interest in life and his children was a tremendous relief. She was resigned to his visiting Tjúni but it left a bitterness. When she thought of Santiago, guilt warred with a sense of abandonment.

What good was it for someone to love you if it made them go away? Frost's avowed intentions hung over her like a boulder balanced on a high cliff, potentially deadly but not an immediate threat. A lot could happen in four years. As freakishly as his desire had fixed on her, it could swing away.

All these things weighed on her much more than work. Except for Marc Revier, she had no one to confide in. There was much she couldn't say, of course, but with him she felt some of the same ease and comfort there had been with Shea before that awful night she'd tried to keep him from going to Tjúni.

She didn't dream of Judah Frost, but now and then a memory of his icy, searing kiss constricted her heart. With all the travelers who got killed on the way to California, she couldn't see why he shouldn't be one of them, but had an unhappy certainty that he'd always manage to survive. There was something uncanny about him, something not quite human.

A cousin of Chuey's, Rodolfo Sanchez, had left Don Narciso's employ and turned up in time to help drive the cattle to Tubac in early summer. Rodolfo was of indeterminate youth with a huge mustache that almost hid his lower face. Tjúni's little house was finished now, built with a common wall joining it to Anita and Chuey's, and Shea launched the building of a large room for Talitha and Caterina.

It would join the bedroom of the main house with the vaqueros' quarters, now shared by Rodolfo and Belen. Except for a gap between Tjúni's place and the *ramada* Belen had taken over for blacksmithing, the courtyard was now enclosed. With its peach and pomegranate trees around the well, it was a pleasant spot.

James's seventh birthday came and went that July and Talitha grieved silently. Even though she knew he'd have no way of telling the date, she'd hoped he might somehow come back by then.

Frost came instead, with considerable news. In June, after making so many changes in it that Gadsden himself lobbied against its passage, Congress approved the Gadsden Treaty. For ten million dollars the United States purchased what would now be the southern part of New Mexico and the Sonoran lands south of the Gila to the agreed boundary.

"The United States has the land for its southern railroad now," said Frost. "When it finally decides to build it, or even before, if settlers start coming, the Apaches had better stick to their mountains."

Talitha thought of Mangus. Then she remembered her uncle's and grandfather's slaughtered bodies, the misery of her own mother. Could there ever be peace between whites and Apaches?

Belen said doubtfully, "For two hundred years Spaniards and Mexicans have tried to tame the Apaches. Why should the Americans succeed?"

"Because they're rolling west like a great wave and what doesn't bend before them will be swept away." Frost smiled at Belen. "Do you realize that you have a choice now? You can remain a citizen of Mexico or become a citizen of the United States."

Chuey spluttered. "Me, a Yanqui?"

Belen's seamed face showed disdain. "I never was Mexican, but Yaqui, born on the Rio Yaqui in Potam, one of the Eight Sacred Pueblos located by angels who marched with Yaqui prophets to sing the boundaries. That is my true home and what I am. As to what government claims *this* region, I care not at all except I hope it will control the Apaches."

The scars stood out on Shea's cheek. "So I didn't

get away from them after all!" he said with a bitter laugh.

"What?" Frost's eyebrow tilted in polite interest.

"An old story." Shea reached for the bottle of mescal though he'd had the one drink he usually took with company. "Well, I suppose I can stand it if the bastards don't come poking around giving a lot of orders. And maybe they will bring peace to the——" He glanced at Frost. "What *are* we now?"

Frost raised his glass in a toast. "The western part of Doña Ana County, Territory of New Mexico, United States of America. Of course it won't be official till the boundary's run."

"New Mexico!" Shea echoed. "You mean we'll be governed out of Santa Fe? Hell, man, that's five hundred miles away!"

"If you don't want to be interfered with, that should suit you fine," grinned Frost. "However, as soon as enough Americans move into the region, they'll start agitating for a separate territory that they can run, and then they'll push for statehood." His grin broadened at Shea's dazed look. "Things are going to change fast and furious so we might as well enjoy the proceedings and profit by them. Unless, of course, the North and South separate."

"There's talk of that?" Shea asked eagerly.

"There's certainly a race on for keeping at least a balance of power in Congress. The Kansas-Nebraska Act that was passed the end of May repealed the Missouri Compromise, which was passed back in 1820 when Maine was admitted free and Missouri slave. Till then the balance between North and South was kept by alternately admitting a free state, then a slave one. The compromise excluded slavery in the Louisiana Purchase north of the line 36°30'."

Talitha remembered something Marc had said, for he was appalled at slavery's existence in a country founded on the ideals of freedom and equality. Talitha had never seen a slave, except those in Apache camps where her mother had been one, but she hated the thought of one man *owning* another.

"When California was admitted as a free state," she asked, furrowing her brow, "wasn't there another compromise? About what to do with the lands taken from Mexico in the war?"

With a groan, Frost spread his hands. "Don't expect me to give you all the details of *that* mess! It was poor Henry Clay's dying attempt to settle differences between the North and South and the Senate debate ran from the end of January till past mid-September, months after Clay died."

"What did happen?" Talitha prompted. If she was going to be an American again, the doings of the government concerned her a lot more than they had when they'd seemed as distant as Santa Anna's machinations in Mexico City.

Frost pursed his handsome, if thin, lips. She tried not to think of how they'd felt on hers but a memory of that icy fire ran through her. A wail from Caterina gave her an excuse to leave the table, but the amused glint in his eyes told her that he knew what she'd remembered.

"California was admitted as a free state," he enumerated. "New Mexico was organized as a territory and Texas was given ten million dollars to abandon its claims to any New Mexican lands. The Territory of Utah was established with the provision of 'popular sovereignty' which was also applied to New Mexico. That means when the territories apply for statehood, they'll be admitted as free or slave, depending on what their constitutions say. The Southerners got the Fugitive Slave Act. Northerners got the slave trade abolished in the District of Columbia. Something for everybody. But the Kansas-Nebraska debate opened the whole fuss again. With the Missouri Compromise repealed, there *can* be slave states north of 36°30', provided that a territory's constitution allows it."

"What a wrangle!" muttered Shea. "You think there could be war?"

"It's possible. Hot-headed Southerners have been wanting to secede for years. Because the House is elected in proportion to population, the North has an ever-increasing advantage there. If the South loses a balance in the Senate, too, it's almost sure to leave the Union."

"And the North would fight that?"

Frost smiled. "What do you think? If they'll fight a war to gain land from Mexico, will they wink at losing a great part of the original nation?"

Giving his head a hopeful scratch, Shea said, "Sounds like the Americans may be too busy to worry about us for a while."

"The officials, maybe, but you can bet fortune hunters will be pouring in. As I passed through Fort Yuma, Major Heintzelman was entertaining a young Kentuckian, Charles Poston, whose party had been exploring in Sonora and up along the Santa Cruz. They found some rich copper ore at the Ajo mine some distance west of here and he's on his way back to California to organize a mining company."

After a moment, sighing, Shea made a resigned grimace. "It's a big country. Guess we can't have it to ourselves forever."

"Poston's going to make it one way or the other," Frost chuckled. "Damned if *he* hadn't been hunting for a port. Why, while he was resting up at Yuma, he and his German friend Ehrenberg laid out a town on the land opposite the fort and called it Colorado City! In fact, my freighting partner, Jaeger, took some shares in the townsite. And, Shea, speaking of freighting, are you still interested in being my partner?"

"It sounds like a good proposition. Don't think I'd ever buy into a railroad, though. Hate those great thundering, smoke-belching monsters!"

"They could take your cattle cheap and fast to better markets."

"I'd rather sell for less and be spared the racket and ugliness."

"The railroad's going to come, Shea. But let's talk about freight."

Shea became a partner in the Santa Cruz Valley Freight Company, another link with Frost which Talitha regretted but felt powerless to prevent. She was somewhat relieved by his treatment of her. He made no effort to see her alone and when he left next morning, he said he had a lot of business to attend to in widely scattered places and didn't know when he'd be back.

The letter he brought from Jared Scott was also a relief. In large, clear writing, the father Talitha scarcely remembered said that he rejoiced to hear she was alive since he had sadly given up all his family as dead. "A mining camp is no place for the young lady you must be," he wrote. "But when I can, I'll come to see you. Mr. Frost assures me the family caring for you has no financial problems and regards you as a daughter so I shall let my great debt to them stand for now and repay them at a later time." He ended with love and prayers that she remained steadfast in the Mormon faith.

Talitha snorted at that. He expected a six-year-old to remember what she'd never understood? She'd been far too busy trying to keep James alive. James, who hadn't come back for his birthday.

The ache of that faded slowly as summer wore on. Marc was busy with his ranch, as well as the mine, and came less often, but Caterina was walking now and investigating everything she could climb through, upon or under, so she took most of Talitha's time and energy.

Small and wiry, she was still light enough to be carried in the cradleboard and, oddly enough in view of her general restlessness, she was perfectly content to stay laced to the board, hung from a tree or wedged securely in some rocks, while Talitha gathered the late summer bounty: acorns, mesquite beans, berries, wild grapes and currants.

Caterina's first birthday passed without celebration. She didn't know the difference and the anniversary of her mother's death renewed the pain of that loss. For several days Shea stayed drunk on mescal.

Talitha was glad when he sobered up and went again to Tjúni; glad, too, when she ceased being so aware of those night visits because she had moved with Caterina into their fine new room.

For the first time since Nauvoo, Talitha had a real bed, woven rawhide fastened to posts. For Caterina, there was a high-sided box bed made of bent willow branches covered with rawhide. The Judith doll occupied a deep niche by Talitha's bed and a chest and bench completed the furnishings. Talitha's heart swelled with pride as she put Caterina down on a Saltillo serape spread in front of their very own fireplace.

"Shea, it's beautiful!" she whispered. "Ever so lovely!"

Forgetting the strangeness that had come between them, she threw her arms around him in a tempestuous hug. He kissed her on the forehead and stepped quickly away.

Patrick and Miguel were six in October, and though no presents they could get would ever be as cherished as Thunder and Lightning, they were delighted with new sombreros trimmed with silver conchos and beautiful knives of the sort called Bowies but on a smaller scale, the blades designed with a pattern of gold tracery.

These, Shea told them sternly, were for work, not playing, though when they were a few years older, Belen would show them how to handle the blades in a fight should it come to that.

Enchanted, Caterina laughed and reached for the bright steel her brothers let flicker before her, blinked in astonishment when the knives disappeared into leather scabbards.

This year it didn't matter, Talitha thought. *But next*

year, she's having her birthday! A nice one. The day
Caterina was born shouldn't remain one of gloom be-
cause it was also the anniversary of Socorro's death.
Socorro would have hated that.

Marc Revier came for the Feast of the Roof, bringing Christmas gifts since he didn't think he could come
back till well into the new year. For the twins he
brought Dickens's *Christmas Carol* and Lear's *Book
of Nonsense*. There was a bright animal alphabet book
for Caterina and to Talitha he gave books by two
English sisters, *Jane Eyre* by Charlotte Brontë and
Wuthering Heights by Emily.

"And so you'll understand more what's going on in
what's now your country," he said, "here's *Uncle Tom's
Cabin* by Harriet Beecher Stowe. It's one of the most
important books ever written because, though few
Southerners are like Simon Legree, it shows the iniquities of owning humans as if they were cattle."

He spoke so fervently that Shea looked at him hard.
"You're with the North, then, in this business?"

Marc's blue eyes met his host's steadily. "I am, sir,
so much that if war comes, I intend to serve on the
Union side."

"Still rushing the barricades?" Shea bantered.

Grinning at that so the scar across his left cheek
and brow seamed whitely, Marc's tone was serious.
"Many of my homeland's ills come from being so frag-
mented, so class-ridden. I left because I was stifling beneath an old, decaying order, and became a citizen of
this country. I would fight here with a sense of hope.
That things could change, that the dream of freedom
can be reality."

"If I fought," said Shea, with equal deliberation, "it
would be against the Union."

"Oh, Shea! Why?" cried Talitha. "You can't believe
in slavery!"

"No more do I! But I don't think the United States
had any business pushing into Mexico, I don't think it's
got any right to hold on to States that want to un-unite

and . . ." He paused, smiling sheepishly as he met Talitha's gaze. "All right, lass! To hell with that, what's it to me? I'd fight the government that put this brand on me and my brother."

Marc nodded. "I can sympathize with that. I hope, Shea, we never have to fight each other."

Shea looked somber. "Aye, that's the hell of it, to know the man you kill! Much of that and there wouldn't be any wars."

If you had to fight men you liked; but what of men you hated? Looking at these two, one loved with her whole being, the other very dear, Talitha prayed that distant threatening war would never come.

XXV

As spring ripened, so did Tjúni. She continued her work to the last and had her baby alone, down by the creek, washing both herself and the boy child before bringing him to the house.

Pain twisted slowly through Talitha as she looked at the infant. What wouldn't she give for him to be hers? Thank goodness, there was nothing of Shea in the dark eyes and black hair.

"He's a fine baby," Talitha forced herself to say to Tjúni. "Would you like the cradleboard for him?"

Tjúni clasped the child jealously to her full breast, smiled proudly as he pushed with strong little hands, found the nipple and sucked. "My son no need Apache cradleboard!" she scorned. "I have one ready. For him, all ready."

Her joy in the child was so blazing that Talitha couldn't cling to her resentful envy. After all, the Papago woman had worshiped Shea for years, held herself aloof from other men though she could have had no hope that Shea would ever turn to her. And the boy was Shea's. So Talitha vowed to care for him and help as much as Tjúni would permit.

She wasn't to have the chance.

That evening when Shea came in and saw the baby, he stopped dead in his tracks for a moment. Something flashed in his eyes. Self-hatred? Grief? Then his face masked as he knelt beside Tjúni and smiled at his son.

"Born the fifth day of the fifth month in 1855! Guess we'll have to call him Cinco!"

Tjúni's face glowed. "You like?"

"He's a fine boy." Shea touched the fine black hair,

385

then the woman's cheek. "You're all right? No troubles?"

She laughed. "No trouble, having baby! I want. Want much!"

Shea's jaw hardened for an instant. "Well, you have him," he said abruptly, rising. "Take it easy till your strength comes back."

Talitha and Anita tried to do her chores, but Tjúni refused. Though Cinco thrived, as the days passed a sort of shadow seemed to veil the young woman's first delight. Early in June, when the child was a month old, Talitha heard voices one night, coming from the window of Shea's bedroom, audible through the open door and windows of her own room.

"You no come to me," Tjúni said.

"It's too soon since the child."

"Indian might think that. Indian want wife feed baby long time so it grow strong. But you not Indian."

Shea said nothing. After a time, the woman spoke again. "I give you fine boy. You make me wife?"

There was a strangled breath. "No, Tjúni."

"No priest. Just before madonna the way you—"

He cut in harshly. "I told you how it was. That I didn't, couldn't love you but I needed a woman. You said that was all right. You said you knew herbs—that there'd be no baby."

"You no want him?"

"I didn't say that! He's mine and I'll take care of him, give him a share of what I have. But you cannot be my wife, Tjúni, now or ever."

"Papago not good enough?"

"That's not it and you damn well know it!" After a time he added more gently though with great weariness, "My wife, my one wife, is dead. I can't put someone in her place."

Tjúni's voice thrust like a dagger. "Sleep with dead wife, then! I go to own place! My son all mine! San Manuel his, he need nothing of you!"

"Tjúni, listen!"

"I listen enough! My boy not have your name, then he be Papago! I find him Papago father!"

In a moment Talitha heard angry footsteps padding across the courtyard. Next morning, Tjúni and the child were gone, and though Talitha had never been able to like her and had, through this past year, been smolderingly jealous, she still felt sorry for her, sorry that a love cleaved to for so long had produced at the end only bitterness. But Tjúni had her son now, and, for his sake, had found the strength to break away from Shea. Talitha sighed and hoped it would go well with them.

The boundary survey was run across the Santa Cruz Valley that June about a dozen miles south of Calabazas and skimming the edge of the *sitios* making up Rancho del Socorro. Though the garrison lingered at Tucson, the little force at Tubac left what was now foreign soil and journeyed southward.

Once again, the region was left without protection, though the Germans struggled to hold on at the Calabazas sheep and goat ranch, a few Mexicans remained at Tubac, farming beside the Apaches *de paz,* and a hardy Kentucky settler called Pete Kitchen had located in the valley, making his house a citadel.

The Pajarito Mine continued to operate but as Apaches raided and menaced up and down the broad valley, Marc Revier was never out of reach of his rifle and it was September before he came again to Rancho del Socorro, having asked a well-armed group of Americans who were scouting for mine sites if they'd guard the Pajarito while he was gone for a few days.

He looked fatigued and his face was thinner. "Judah's in Washington lobbying for that railroad," he said, taking Caterina on his knee and letting her play with his watch. "While he's at it, he'd better get the bigwigs to send some troops down to this part of the country they were so anxious to take over. It must be just about as bad as it was when you first came."

"Few more settlers," Shea observed. "And Tubac always has been an on-again, off-again kind of garrison. Anyhow, from the way it sounds, the mountains are going to be chock-a-block with miners." He grinned. "Maybe you could form your own army if the Americans don't send one pretty quick."

Talitha tried to coax Marc into staying for Caterina's birthday which was only a few days off but he said it wouldn't be fair to the exploring miners to delay them that much longer.

"Anyhow, if I'm too slow in coming, they may decide I'm dead and just take over," he said whimsically. "If I turned up after that, they might be tempted to make their conclusion a true one."

He rode off next morning, looking refreshed, promising to come oftener as soon as the Apache danger lessened. Shea had listened assentingly to Talitha's purposefully excited plans for Caterina's second birthday. With Anita's help, the table was loaded with special food, and after the feasting, Chuey played his guitar while the vaqueros sang *"Las Mananitas":*

"On the morning you were born
Were born the flowers . . ."

Caterina, on Shea's lap, listened gravely, her blue-gray eyes dreaming. "More sing?" she asked when Chuey ended with a final strum and a courtly bow.

"Later, darling," said Talitha. "Now it's time for your presents."

The twins, with Belen's help, had made her a *reata* of horsehair. Very special horsehair, black and cream, garnered from the manes and tails of Thunder and Lightning.

"Just as soon as you're big enough, Katie-Cat, we'll teach you how to use it!" promised Miguel, rubbing her back as if she were one of the kittens that continued to be born of Chusma's descendants and all too rapidly grew from cuddly palmfuls to stalking, independent miniature panthers.

Grasping Miguel, Caterina gave him a tremendous hug and planted a noisy kiss on his cheek as Patrick neatly looped the rope beneath his twin's leg and gave a tug that sent him scrambling.

"That's how it works, Katie-Cat!" Patrick shouted gleefully as he braced for Miguel's lunge. They wrestled on the floor a minute.

"Bad boys!" Caterina shrieked. She never liked to see them fight. At a word from Shea, they rolled over, panting, and watched as the vaqueros brought their gift.

It was a hobbyhorse made from walnut rubbed by hand to a sheen, but instead of straight pieces of wood, the legs and body were shaped and the head was a truly beautiful piece of carving. A small rawhide saddle with *tapaderos* strapped around the middle and a horse-hair hackamore fitted over the muzzle, reins looping about the saddle horn. Mane and tail were golden, contributed from Ladorada's groomings.

"*Con permiso,* Don Patricio," said Belen, and at a nod from Shea, the bandy-legged, broad-chested vaquero lifted Caterina from her father's lap and put her in the saddle, showing her how to thrust her small feet in the covered stirrups. "Ride this steed joyously, *chiquita,* until you get a real one!"

He got a kiss on his weathered cheek, and thanks in Spanish, before Caterina climbed down to go and similarly thank Chuey and Rodolfo.

"Come on, Paulita!" she commanded her playmate who, though four months older, was content to follow cautiously in Caterina's usually violent wake. "We can both ride!"

They did, Caterina rocking with such vigor it was lucky Belen had tested the rockers to make sure they wouldn't go past a certain angle and somersault the riders.

When Paulita had had enough and Caterina could be coaxed off, Shea produced a small rocking chair and a doll that would most certainly have to be put up till Caterina could play with it and not crack the china head, hands and feet. Fortunately, she could play with the soft, floppy rag doll Talitha had made her.

Cuddling both dolls, she rocked for a while in the chair. Then, carefully, she made Paulita sit down with them, grasped her *reata* and hauled herself into the saddle.

Everybody exchanged glances. Patrick put it into words. "What you going to be, Katie-Cat? A mama or a vaquero?"

"Mama *and* vaquero!" she assured him, not missing a lusty pitch forward or back. As they all laughed, she rocked harder and sang in a kind of rhythmic croon: "I be everything! I be everything!"

Later, after everyone had gone to bed, Talitha noticed a soft glow of light cast through the door on the wall. With a sinking heart, she realized a candle had been lit in the kitchen. Through the evening, more than once, she'd seen Shea's eyes flick toward the niche where the mescal was kept. Was he going to do as he had last year, get drunk to drown the loss of his wife and stay that way for days?

I won't have it! Talitha thought. *If he has to get drunk sometimes, all right, but he's not going to do it on Caterina's birthday!*

Jumping out of bed, she pulled on her dress, ran barefoot across the hard earth of the patio. Bursting into the kitchen, she found him sitting by the dead fire, the bottle in his hand. His head turned toward her, eyes unfocused in a dulled stupidity that made her ache, want to comfort him at the same time it sent her furious.

After a morose stare, he looked back at the ashes. "Go to bed, Tally." The words blurred as if a clumsy tongue couldn't shape them.

"Not till you do!"

He seemed to forget her. Unsure of what to do,

Talitha stood with hands clenched, body rigid, while she inwardly prayed. *Socorro! Socorro!* How strange that her foster mother's name should be the word for aid or help, for succor.

No flash of enlightenment or inspiration came, but when Shea lifted the bottle again, outrage sent Talitha diving forward. Snatching the mescal, she deliberately poured it into the ashes in the fireplace.

"Patrick O'Shea!" she shouted into his angry, astounded face. "Sober up and listen to me! This can either be the day your wife died or the day your daughter was born! Which way do you want it?"

"Oh God, Tally! I——"

She cut in mercilessly, willing her words to cut like a whip through his drunkenness. "Socorro's gone, Shea, but would she want this? Caterina's got her whole life ahead. How's she going to feel in a few years when she notices that her father goes into a drunken binge of mourning on her birthday?"

Shaking his head, he buried it in his hands. Resisting the overwhelming sympathy that made her want to cosset him, Talitha ended with harsh challenge.

"Which are you going to turn your mind to? Your wife's dying or your daughter's life?"

He looked up at her. Tears streaked his cheeks and she longed to caress the branded one, take all his hurts into herself to suffer in his place. But that couldn't be, each person had to bear his own grief. He stood up, a trifle uncertainly. His jaw hardened and for a moment she wondered if he were going to hit her, at the least give her a shaking and tell her to mind her own business.

Instead he laughed. "God's whiskers! That's just what Socorro would've said. Only she might have kicked my shins and called me 'redhead burro'!"

His gaze went to the hobbyhorse, the *reata* over the saddle, the dolls embraced in the rocker, for Caterina had fallen asleep in his arms and been carried to bed without them. "It was a good birthday, wasn't it?

Don't you suppose the madonna—well, she was a mother, too—"

Talitha nodded. This time she could let her tears fall. "I'm sure that somehow Socorro was with us tonight, and that she was happy." *That she helped me with you.*

Shea grinned. "Wouldn't do for her to be with me all the time, especially when I go in to Tubac the way I'll have to once in a while now that Tjúni's packed herself off!" He yawned and stretched. "Get to bed with you, Tally! I'm about to fall asleep on my feet."

Back in her own room, Talitha stood beside Caterina's high bed. "Happy birthday, Katie-Cat Caterina," she whispered. And then to her mother, Socorro, God or Tata Dios, she added as she climbed into bed, *Thank you. Thank you.*

It was March of 1856 when Judah returned from Washington with the news that he'd taken a wife, the daughter of a powerful senator. "Leonore won't come out, of course, till I can have a suitable home built for her in Tucson," he explained. At Shea's congratulations, he smiled broadly.

"She's a beautiful creature. If I run for political office, as I may do, she'll be a most elegant asset."

Shea gave him a questioning look but Frost was saying that the last Mexican troops had left Tucson early that month under command of Captain Hilarión García, the same soldier who'd come to the aid of Calabazas during the big Apache raid almost three years ago. "Didn't see anyone at Calabazas when I rode through," added Frost. "Know what happened?"

"Hulsemann came over sometime before Christmas. Said the Apaches were too much. He'd decided to drive the stock to Ímuris and asked if a couple of my vaqueros would help since he wanted to leave his partners to hold down the hacienda. The Vasquez brothers and Rodolfo went." Shea shook his head regretfully. "Looks like Gándara double-crossed Hulsemann, who was, as you'll recall, his partner. One of Gándara's men, the prefect of San Ignacio, confiscated all the stock, so for all his work and danger, Hulsemann got nothing."

"He's still alive," Frost said carelessly. "And speaking of partnerships, partner, it's about time I got back and tended to our freighting enterprise! Solomon Warner's opened a store in Tucson and a fourteen-mule pack train brought in his supplies from Fort Yuma the last of February. The Santa Cruz Freighting Company should have had that job!"

"Have you been to the mine yet?" Talitha asked, for though she hated speaking to Frost, she hadn't seen Marc since Christmas and with nothing left to plunder at Calabazas the Apaches might give more attention to the miners.

Frost held her eyes a moment before he yielded an answer. "Everything at the Pajarito's fine. Marc besought me to take over so he could junket about a bit, but I put it to him that I had to get a home for my wife and line up some freighting contracts. He saw the reason in that though he was mightily disappointed."

"How's your lady going to take to Tucson?" Shea wondered. "Don't suppose she's ever seen anything like it."

"You can bet our last cow she hasn't!" Frost laughed. "I'd guess the town has a couple of hundred people, not more than a dozen being Anglo-Saxon. But that'll change." He turned his glass in his hand, took a slow sip. "She vows she'd live with me in a cave or tent, and though I think she'd quickly change her mind about that, she's romantical enough to think things are picturesque instead of heathenish and dirty." He added in a tone of near-contempt, "She'll adore fiestas and *bailes*."

Talitha pitied his bride. But she also drew a deep breath of relief as if an invisible weight had been lifted. He was *married*. He couldn't bother her anymore. Not now. Not when she was eighteen. Not ever!

*　　*　　*

That September of 1856, Tubac came alive as it had never been before. Charles Poston, the young Kentuckian Frost had met in Fort Yuma the previous year, hadn't raised his mining money in San Francisco but in Cincinnati. With the patronage of the Texas Pacific Railroad Company, he'd organized the Sonora Exploring and Mining Company with Major Samuel Heintzelman, the former Fort Yuma commander, as president. In San Antonio he outfitted his party of frontiersmen and miners with Sharps rifles and Colt revolvers and started his long trek.

At Mesilla, the governmental center for what was now Southern New Mexico all the way to the California border, the enterprising Poston had been appointed deputy clerk for the western part of the Gadsden Purchase by the clerk of Doña Ana County which made him the closest thing to a government official for hundreds of miles.

He also met with Dr. Steck, the Indian agent, who was still trying desperately to wangle land, seed and farming implements for the Indians in his charge, as well as enough rations to carry them till crop time. Steck helped Poston make a treaty with Apaches living near the Santa Rita mines east of Tubac wherein they agreed not to molest any operations he might open in the region so long as the miners didn't bother them.

Poston was busy, also, in Tucson, now occupied by United States troops, for though he gave his men two weeks to enjoy the fiesta of St. Augustine and rest from their journey, he helped organize a convention that met late in August. Mark Aldrich, a merchant, the mayor or alcalde, chaired the meetings which passed resolutions urging Congress to make a separate territory of "Arizona." Nathan Cook, a mining official, was selected as delegate and sent to the House of Representatives with a certificate duly signed by deputy clerk Poston.

This accomplished, Poston proceeded to Tubac and set up headquarters. A sentinel was posted in the tower to keep constant watch for Apaches and bandits. Animals were loosed in the corrals and company property stored in the guardhouse. The doors and windows that had been hauled away were replaced by pine whipsawed from the Santa Rita mountains, and Shea, who reported all this after driving cattle over for sale that fall, added that a big dining hall and lounge had been furnished very comfortably with homemade bunks, tables and benches.

"It's an interesting lot there and no mistake," Shea chuckled to Talitha. "Herman Ehrenberg, a German engineer, fought against Mexico twice, once for Texas and once for the United States. The geologists and such graduated from American and European universities; they sound just like Marc! Now that there's some protection, peaceful Indians and Mexicans are starting to come back and Poston's hired miners at fifteen to twenty-five dollars a month and rations. The whole valley's booming!"

"You like them, then, the Americans?" Talitha quizzed.

"Hell, Tally, they're not Yanquis, they're good people and damned fine to have as neighbors! Next time I go, I'll take you." He grinned, cocking his head. "Those good-looking, educated bachelors will swarm like bees to honey!"

And he wouldn't care. He'd be relieved if she married one of them, probably, except then he wouldn't have an English-speaking person to look after three-year-old Caterina. Would she herself always be a child to him? Hurt, Talitha gave her patched skirt a yank and said scornfully, "No fancy gentleman's going to pay court to me in these clothes!"

Shea looked at the dress and frowned. "God's whiskers! That *is* a rag, Tally! Why haven't you said you need some new things?"

"I don't, around here."

Only last summer had she and the other women of the place succeeded in using the last of the garments salvaged from the Cantú ranch. Carmencita was expert at altering and sewing and Anita had some of her skill so Talitha used a needle only to mend.

"Any woman ought to have a few pretty dresses," Shea decreed, assuming what Socorro had called his "burro" look. "If you want different cloth from what the mining *conducta* brings up, we'll have the Santa Cruz Freighting Company get you something from San Francisco or even St. Louis. Just make out a list of what you want."

Talitha stared at him. "I don't know," she said helplessly. "I don't know what ladies are wearing or what kinds of material there are."

Grunting, Shea's brow furrowed deeper before it cleared and he laughed triumphantly. "Judah'll know, or if he doesn't that high-falutin' wife of his sure will!"

"I don't want Mr. Frost doing any favors for me!" Talitha protested, but Shea ignored her.

"Rodolfo's been wanting to go to Tucson and see some cousins, though I suspicion a girl's the big attraction. I'll tell him to go in the morning. You want to write Judah?"

"No!"

"Then I'll just send a message," said Shea, unperturbed. He had long ago decided not to heed her obvious dislike of his business partner.

Now that Tubac was occupied by well-armed men, abandoned ranchos along the Santa Cruz came back to life and mines seemed to be everywhere.

"There must be a hundred and fifty mines within sixteen miles of Tubac," Marc Revier said on a visit to Rancho del Socorro. "Most of them are primitive affairs, but some are taking out a good amount of ore. The Ajo's copper ore's packed to Yuma on Jaeger's mules, then sent by the Gulf of California to San Francisco for shipment to Wales. We're still freighting our bullion to Guaymas."

With danger from Apaches considerably lessened,

Marc came perhaps once a month, sometimes bringing newspapers and periodicals given him by friends he'd made in Tubac. He remained a favorite with the twins, who were eight years old, though they didn't study much now that they could tag the vaqueros from dawn to dusk. Caterina happily added him to her subjects and scarcely let him out of her sight during his visits.

Whether it was this or something else, there was, Talitha thought, a change between them. The old ease was gone and he no longer teased her or lured her into arguments. When he called her "Miss Scott," that was too much.

"Marc!" she cried reproachfully. "Do you want me to call you Mr. Revier?"

"No, of course not!" Flustered, he looked directly at her, his blue eyes distressed. "But you're growing up, Miss Talitha. You must be treated with respect."

She made a rude noise. "Friends can respect each other without being stuffy!"

He bowed. "Whatever you prefer, Miss Talitha."

Repressing an urge to pinch him and see what he'd do, she sniffed disgustedly. "For heaven's sake, Marc, I turned sixteen in April but I haven't changed! I'm the same person you taught to read and write, the same one who showed you what plants were good for food and medicine. Those things are real!"

"Those things are very real."

"Then can't you act the way you used to?"

His gaze swept her face before he seemed to physically wrench it away so that he looked toward the mountains, hands crossed behind him. "No, Miss Talitha, I can't act the way I did when you were a child. Nor can I, in conscience, behave as I would were you a few years older." With a wry laugh, he swung about, rumpling his brown hair. "You're in between, my dear, but that'll change. Meanwhile, could I escort you to the Christmas festivities at Tubac? A number of respectable ladies are coming from as far as Magdalena, Tucson and Sopori for the holidays and you could, I'm sure, share a room with one of them."

As she stared at him in surprise, he laughed and was almost the old Marc. "Shea thinks it's a wonderful idea, in fact, he's coming, too. And he's assured me you're going to have a party dress!"

A *real* party? And Shea coming! People from all around! Talitha thrilled, so breathtaking was the prospect, though it was also fearsome.

Except for that trip to Nōnó, she hadn't been off the ranch since Shea and Socorro brought her and James home from the Apaches. If she watched the ladies, though, she could copy them, keep from making any horrible mistakes. And Marc was as traveled and educated as any of the mine officers. It would be good for Shea to have some fun, too, though Talitha hoped, if any of the women were single, Shea wouldn't have an eye for them.

"Oh," she said in a small voice, remembering. "The children! Shea and I can't both go off and leave them at Christmas."

"No more will you," Marc said cheerfully. "I'll come the day before Christmas and we'll all be with the children Christmas Eve. Sometime the next afternoon, I'll take you to Tubac."

"But Shea—"

"Will ride over after I take you home. They'll be making merry till the New Year so he won't miss anything."

It sounded too grand and strange for belief. Giving in to delight, Talitha scooped Caterina up and spun in a circle, all thoughts of what Marc could mean by his cryptic statements completely scattered. There was going to be a party and she was going to go!

As the first week in December passed and her dress material hadn't come, Talitha worried that it wouldn't appear in time to be made up.

"Don't fret," Shea admonished. "Rodolfo said Judah

promised to have it delivered special if it missed a regular run, and I've left word with Mr. Poston to have someone bring it straight over from Tubac when the wagons drop it off there."

She scolded herself for getting so wrought up, but there was simply *nothing* she could wear. If the material didn't come quickly, she couldn't go and that made her heart sink.

Then Judah Frost rode in one evening with a large bundle tied behind his saddle. "Personal delivery for Miss Talitha Scott!" he called as he worked at the knots. "Santa Cruz Freight—farther, faster! That's our motto, Shea. Aren't you proud to see your partner living up to it!"

"Mighty proud," grinned Shea, shaking hands. "Chuey'll see to your horse. Come in and warm up!"

Torn between relief at getting the material and annoyance that Frost had brought it, Talitha thanked him politely and put the package to one side while she went back to preparing supper, though she was longing to peek at the contents. There'd been a most enticing rustle in the moment she held the parcel.

"God's whiskers!" Shea exploded, taking over the stew. "Here you've been fidgeting for weeks over whether that stuff would get here in time! Open it!"

"Yes, Tally! Open!" urged Caterina, dancing around her. Even the twins pressed close though they'd been teasing her about the new dress, saying she ought to wear the trousers she used for working cattle.

Her fingers shook as she unfolded the coarse wrappings, the layers of paper, to reveal a rich shining blue, the color of the sky. When she started to pick it up, she saw that it was already fashioned into a marvelous gown, the three full flounces of the skirt patterned in flowers of deeper blue which were repeated at the deep heart-shaped neckline.

"Oohhh!" breathed Caterina, touching it with awe.

"Brocade," said Frost. "Leonore had her own seamstress make it from *Godey's Lady's Book*. She bade me tell you those pagoda sleeves are the height of fashion. A mercy, isn't it, that they finally do narrow at the top?"

Talitha slowly examined the series of false sleeves, each one requiring so many stitches that it made her dizzy to think of it. Let alone those extravagant flounces! "Oh, that poor seamstress!" she said. "So much work for one dress!"

"Leonore brought with her one of those new-fangled sewing machines," Frost said airily. "Josefina, the seamstress, loves it." He turned to Shea. "I was sure you'd want Talitha to have all the necessary things, so I took the freedom of asking Leonore to select them."

"We're much obliged," said Shea heartily. "Tally, you'll be the grandest lady at the party!"

"I fancy Leonore will be quite impressive," chuckled Frost. "Let me hold the dress, Talitha, while you look at the others. That cloak of blue cashmere trimmed with swan's-down is to go with the brocade but you can wear it with other gowns, of course."

A miniature cape, similarly lined with brocade, fell out of the larger one and Caterina snuggled and pranced about in it when Frost said it was a gift for her from Leonore who, he added with a curving lip, very much wanted a little girl of her own.

"The gray-blue gaberdine is a riding habit," Frost explained. "You are especially to note the stylish *Mousquetaire* cuffs, slashes faced with steel-gray velvet like the trim on the basque."

Shaking her head at the handsome costume with its fine cambric underblouse, Talitha carefully placed it on a bench. "I don't know when I could ever wear that riding! The thickets would tear it to pieces."

"The cows would sure laugh if you came after them in that rig!" chortled Patrick and hugged Miguel in the ecstasy of that thought.

"Times are changing," said Frost, unruffled. "I wouldn't be at all surprised, Talitha, if you didn't go riding with some of the officers who've moved in at Calabazas."

"What officers?" demanded Shea, smile fading.

"Major Enoch Steen with four companies of the First Regiment of Dragoons. Toward the end of November, he established Camp Moore at the old stock ranch and you should just see the place! Overrun with carpenters, blacksmiths, laundresses, ambulances, cook wagons, freight wagons, teamsters and all sorts of hangers-on! Steen's trying to rent the land from Gándara, but if the price is too high, he says he'll sit tight anyway. Gándara, as off-and-on governor of Sonora and a big landowner all the time, should be damned glad to have someone checking the Apaches."

"So they've finally come," Shea muttered.

"Oh, they'll not be concerned about your differences with them almost ten years ago," Frost shrugged. "With the territory full of Apaches and real outlaws that've been run out of California, Sonora and Texas, they won't have time to pester settled, respectable folk but will be very glad you're here. The next dress is simple, Talitha, for home occasions when you want to look nice but not elegant."

It looked elegant to Talitha, poplin the silvery green color of the underside of a cottonwood leaf, with a pointed bodice and flared half sleeves over long fitted ones. This dress had only one flounce and a plain oval neck. Frost grinned as she laid it aside and bent toward the remaining parcel.

"Perhaps you should open that in privacy; Leonore thought you would need—other things."

Shea cautiously eased an arm beneath the cloak and dresses. "Come, lass, let's get this plunder to your room where it won't be getting dirty!"

"I can't hang them on pegs!" Talitha wailed.

"No need," soothed Frost, following with the brocade. "I brought some wicker hangers. They're in that package."

"It's mighty kind of you to do all this, and of your lady wife," said Shea. "Of course I'll pay for the seamstress and material and all, but there's no way to pay for all the pains you and Mrs. Frost took."

"Please do thank her for me," said Talitha, unable to bring herself to be grateful to him.

"You'll have a chance to thank her yourself at Poston's gala," smiled Frost. "She hopes perhaps you'll share a room with her."

There was nothing to do but murmur that she'd be glad to. What was Leonore like? To go to all this effort for someone she'd never seen, she must be kind and generous. And to send the small elaborate cloak for Caterina—yes, she must be sweet!

Resolutely Talitha determined to form her opinion of Leonore completely apart from her loathing of Frost. She couldn't imagine why he'd gone to so much trouble when, married, he must have given up those ridiculous plans he'd had earlier. Perhaps he simply wished to ingratiate himself with Shea.

However it was, Talitha thought, as the men dropped the clothes on her bed and withdrew, she now had a most wonderful party dress, and she was going to enjoy it!

XXVI

For several days before Christmas Anita and Talitha prepared tamales, nut and seed cakes, *pipián,* turkey with *mole* sauce, a ham Shea had obtained from Pete Kitchen who was raising pigs on Potrero Creek, acorn stew, pumpkin, beans simmered with chilis, and *pozole.*

The O'Shea children would get their presents Christmas morning since Shea felt this was the proper time, but January fifth would be when Talitha would steal over after dark and leave gifts for Paulita and her small baby brother, Ramon. Little Juan Vasquez, son of Juana and Cheno, would be given his cuddly toy during his visit, for the Sanchezes would come feast Christmas at the home ranch. Though at two-and-a-half Juan was as big as Caterina, he was almost a year younger, and obeyed her in all things. Paulita, when she'd had enough of Caterina's imperious leadership, had learned to simply vanish.

And Cinco? Talitha wondered, a shadow creeping over some of her eager anticipation. Did he get presents? Was he a happy little boy? He must be starting to walk now at a year-and-a-half. Last Christmas Shea had given Pedro Sanchez a large bundle and asked him to get it to Tjúni, but she'd refused to even open it. There was a man in her dwelling, Pedro had said when he returned the parcel. A Papago.

Shea had told Pedro to give the things to little Juan and as far as Talitha knew, he hadn't tried further to stay in touch with his son. Tjúni had clearly decided to break her ties with him. Maybe it was best but Talitha felt a sad little pang when she thought of small

Cinco, and always this reopened the hurt of remembering another little black-haired boy, her brother, James.

Not a word had come from him and it was more than three years. Was he all right? Had he forgotten them at the ranch? He'd be ten in July, he must be growing tall. Talitha clung to the belief that he was well, somehow assured that Mangus would let her know if anything happened. Though Mangus, at Socorro's death, had seemed to forget Rancho del Socorro.

There was so much sadness, when she let it come. Usually Talitha kept very busy, refused to linger on griefs that had no remedy, but this day her longing for James swept over her with such force that she knelt by Caterina and hugged her close, drawing comfort from the warm sweet little body and its innocence of what could happen in the world.

Marc brought Scott's *Ivanhoe* and Irving's *Sketch Book* with droll Rip van Winkle for the twins. Caterina giggled over Lear's *Book of Nonsense,* and for Talitha there was a slim *Sonnets from the Portuguese* by Elizabeth Barrett Browning. There was also a beautiful fan, black lacquer and parchment, ornamented by a dragon of flame and gold.

"I don't think you'll need it for the party," he smiled, "but it should look pretty on your wall."

"Dragons," mused Talitha, spreading the fan so Caterina could admire it. "I wonder where people got the idea."

"Lightning, perhaps. But they were, till Christian times, signs of good fortune and happiness. I like to think the ancients imagined a beast that could, by its wings, lift itself off the earth, soar high above, as they hoped man might one day."

Talitha shook her head. *"I* like the earth. But the dragon's glorious. You shouldn't bring me presents anymore, though, Marc. I'm not a child."

"But you're my hostess," he countered. He patted the

fringed leather pouch beside his plate. "Besides, didn't you make this for me?"

"But it didn't cost anything!" she protested.

He ran a finger along the lacings. "You made it which is much better. Alas, I can't write poetry or paint fans!"

"He's got you, lass." Shea laughed from the head of the table. "Now you'd better make sure you have all your things together so you can leave right after services. It gets dark early."

To wear three new dresses in one day! The very thought was dizzyingly extravagant. But, looked at another way, she'd never had a really new dress before, and these were going to last a long time.

She wore the silver-green poplin for the feast with the Sanchezes and then changed into the dashing riding habit for the little ceremony in the *sala*.

Shea led in prayers while the madonna smiled down at them, and then Talitha read the story of Jesus's birth from Luke.

Caterina kept stroking the facings of her cuff slashes. "I like velvet," she said afterward. "It's soft as a kitty! When I'm big like you, Tally, I'm going to have a whole dress of it!"

"I'll bet you do!" Talitha gave her a hug and returned several ardent kisses, also kissed Miguel's smooth cheeks though Patrick evaded her.

"I'm too old for that stuff, Tally! Save it for the dragoons and miners."

She made a face at him. Since she didn't have a side-saddle, Shea helped her mount. "All these skirts!" he whistled, helping her arrange them as modestly as possible though the soft gray leather boots showed. "May you never have to ride for your life rigged like that!"

"I'd shed the skirts and maybe whoever was chasing me would pick them up and let me go!" she laughed. "Now, Shea, you *will* come?"

"Soon as you're back, lass. Now don't you worry about us, just have a grand time!" He swung Caterina to his shoulder, and with the twins, Sanchezes and Vasquezes, waved them on their way down the valley.

Talitha kept turning to wave back. When Caterina's vigorous farewells were hidden by a slope, she felt a wild impulse to whirl and ride back. Since Caterina's birth, she'd never been away from her for more than a few hours. A lump swelled in Talitha's throat. She blinked fiercely, but her eyes kept misting.

"Tears?" Marc reined close to her, brushed at the dampness on her cheek. There were people with hard blue eyes and bright blue eyes, but Marc's were receptives and deep and very warm. "What can be wrong for one so pretty as you on her way to a fine party?"

She bit her lip but Marc had never made fun of her and so she blurted, "I—I've never left them before!"

"And you fear they can't manage a few days without you?" he teased. "Or are you afraid they can?"

"Marc!"

Hurt and surprised by his unexpected query, she urged Ladorada ahead, but he soon caught up, and for the first time, he didn't preface her name with "Miss."

"Talitha, I never knew your little James, but starting with him, you've been looking after babies since you were only a child yourself. You act as a mother to Caterina and the twins. But you're not! You have to start thinking of your own life."

She stared at him in shock. Taking a deep breath, seeming as vexed at himself as he was with her, he added more temperately, "For all your sakes, Caterina needs to understand that you're not her mother, that in a few years you'll marry and have your own home."

"But I—don't want that," she faltered.

He frowned. Suddenly, his eyes *were* hard. "You don't want what?"

"To marry." She couldn't meet his probing gaze and looked backward as if for reassurance but the ranch

406

was out of view. "I—I don't ever want any home but the Socorro!"

She saw his knuckles go white on the reins. He didn't speak for a while and when he did, it was in a carefully controlled voice. "It's natural for you to feel that now. The O'Sheas have been your family."

"They always will be."

He said with forced patience. "You're growing up, Talitha. You'll love a man. When that happens, you'll want to go with him."

Maddened at his reasonable tone, the way he seemed to think his age gave him the right to predict what she'd do, Talitha flung at him, "I *do* love a man. I always will. I never want to leave him!"

Marc flinched as if receiving a blow he hadn't seen coming. He drew himself up rigidly, speaking under his breath. "Shea!"

"Yes, Shea! He's not my father! And—and he's not old, either!"

"No," agreed Marc in a dazed way. "I suppose he's not. But he's much older than you, Talitha."

"He's only thirty-eight."

With a wry chuckle, Marc said softly, "And I've feared my thirty was too much difference!"

"Your thirty?" Talitha stared. Slowly, reluctantly, she had to understand. "Marc! Please! You—you can't!"

His eyes again were deep soft blue, watching her steadily. "But I do." His pleasant mouth quirked. "I have—I don't know for how long. I don't know when the love I felt for a beautiful brave girl-child changed into love for girl-almost-woman. It changed as a body changes." He added gently, sadly, "As you have changed yourself."

She looked away, devastated.

"I—I'm sorry."

"Don't be. I tell you only to rouse you to the fact that there are other men in the world than Shea, only

407

so that if you ever wish to leave Socorro, you'll know I'm more than a family friend."

Glancing at his profile, the strong but good-natured jaw, she wondered why she'd thought of him as so much older when he was younger than Shea. Not that age had anything to do with it. She had loved Shea, worshiped him, from the hour he took Juh's brand. She would love him till they both were dead and maybe afterward. He was her eternity.

But she loved Marc, too, as a friend and teacher. Wretched at wounding him, she said in a rush, "You don't have to take me to the party, Marc. Let's go back and Shea can ride with you instead. I—I'll say I don't feel good."

Which was certainly true.

"No. I want to take you to this party." He smiled at her, challenging gaily. "For this little time, I'll pretend you're my lady. I'm going away soon, to look for locations out south of Yuma Crossing. So I won't be a trouble to you."

She didn't know what to say. Infrequent as his visits had become, she would still miss him. He'd filled some of the void left by Santiago; Santiago, who, according to Frost, had also chosen to stay away because he loved her.

Why can't they love me the way I love them? she thought desperately. But that was as futile as asking why Shea didn't love her as she did him.

Tents were spread along the fork at Calabazas, housing the soldiers till the log barracks could be finished, and what seemed to Talitha like swarms of people came and went among makeshift hovels of brush and canvas.

Fording the river, Talitha was glad to get away from her first glimpse of American civilization since her capture by Apaches. It had been like a vast noisy anthill.

Settlers who'd fled the Apaches, both Mexican and Indian, had taken up farms again. There were a number of families, at Tumacácori and along the three miles between the old mission and Tubac.

As they approached the walls, the lookout in the three-storied tower flourished a greeting and Marc waved back. Their horses were taken in hand by a boy who flashed a grin and said *"Mil gracias!"* for the coin Marc gave him.

Adobe houses, most with garden plots, spread around the towered headquarters, and the flag of the mining company, a pick and hammer, now flew above it. Laughter and a roar of voices floated from the main hall. Talitha involuntarily moved close to Marc.

"They won't eat you," he teased, "though I'm sure they'd like to! Come, let's find out where you're to stay so you can change before the party."

Stowing her bundle and his own saddlebags by the door, he brought her into a long room jammed with people. Army officers, resplendent in dress uniform and swords, proud *hidalgos* and *hidalgas* with the look of Spain, men who bowed over Talitha's hand in courtly fashion as Marc introduced them as officers of various mining companies.

There were merchants from Tucson and ranchers from the whole length and breadth of the Santa Cruz Valley. There were several ladies, too, from Camp Moore; one German metallurgist's wife spoke a delightful hesitating English, and two Frenchwomen were accompanying their husbands who had colonization schemes in Sonora.

Talitha's head was spinning. She smiled distractedly at a captain and lieutenant who were both trying to supply her with a cup of punch. "Mescal, ma'am, but it's really quite good!" while Marc, with perfect good humor, told them they'd have to wait till after she was rested to press their acquaintance.

"Here you are!" Judah Frost's head was inches higher than those of most of the men as he made his way through the crowd. "Where's Shea?"

"He's coming day after tomorrow," Talitha explained. "Marc brought me."

The pupils of Frost's winter twilight eyes contracted to tiny points. "Oh, did he? Well, come meet your host and my wife. She'll show you where you'll be staying." Over his shoulder, he said perfunctorily, "Thanks for bringing her, Revier."

"The pleasure was mine." Marc stayed beside them. "I must greet Poston, too. Then I'll take your things to your quarters, Miss Talitha."

"No need," said Frost tersely. "A boy can do that."

"Of course. Nevertheless, Judah, as Miss Talitha's escort, I'll see that she's comfortably settled."

By then they had reached a group before the fireplace where a dark-bearded, wavy-haired young man was bantering with a black-haired young woman, who, though small, held herself with sweet regality. She turned at Judah's touch on her arm.

"Talitha! You must be!" Catching Talitha's hands, the woman kissed her while Talitha could only stare. With a slight frown, Judah Frost's wife said, "Something's wrong? The ride has made you ill?"

Frost said briskly, "Talitha can outride most men, Leonore, but perhaps you'll show her your room so she can change. Talitha, as you'll have gathered, this is my wife. I seldom get to introduce her formally. Now let me acquaint you with our host, Colonel Charles Poston. Charles, this is Miss Talitha Scott. Her guardian is my partner in several enterprises and owns Rancho del Socorro of which you must have heard."

"Indeed I have." Poston bowed low, regarded her with a shrewd twinkle. "The only ranch not to be abandoned between Tucson and Magdalena! I look forward to meeting your guardian, Miss Scott."

They talked a few minutes till he was called to superintend the making of eggnog and Talitha found herself relaxing. Poston, like most of the men here, was young, perhaps thirty, boyishly full of enthusiasm for the prospects of Arizona.

These were *her* people, Talitha realized. *Americans.*
And though her family had been forced west for safety
to live according to their religion, she couldn't repress
a glow of pride and liking for these spirited, rollicking,
daring ones.

Slipping her arm through Talitha's, Leonore said,
"Come, dear, and change! The habit becomes you wonderfully with that sort of cavalier dash. I can hardly
wait to see the evening dress." She said to Marc who
had waited purposefully, "It's the first house across the
plaza."

"I'll meet you there," he nodded, and slipped through
the throng.

Frost separated the women, a hand on the elbow of
each, steering them through the crush. Talitha ignored
the amused way he watched her, schooled herself to
look more closely at Leonore, something which, after
the first startled glance, she hadn't trusted herself to do.

There were differences. Leonore's face was softer, her
mouth wider, eyes not so deeply set. She must be about
the age Socorro had been when she died, but she looked
much younger, as if she'd never worried, been hungry
or thirsty or faced death.

Probably she hadn't.

Frost's voice sliced through her happy chatter.
"You're thinking, Talitha, that my wife resembles some
hidalga you've known. No mystery in that. She's from
one of New Orleans' creole families, and more Spanish
than French."

"Deplorable to look like so many other women!"
Leonore bubbled. "But in Washington, where I acted
as Papa's hostess after *maman* died, I was considered
exotic. That, after years of being confused with my
innumerable cousins, was absolutely delicious!"

Dropping a kiss on the tip of her ear, Frost admonished her not to be late to table and left with Marc
who'd placed Talitha's bundle on a bunk in the small
room, lit by the fragrant piñon logs in the fireplace.

Leonore wasn't as addle-pated as she let on, but efficiently undid the pack and shook out the gleaming brocade. "I didn't procure a crinoline for you, dear, because even though they may look *très chic* on Empress Eugénie who started the new rage for them, they're unbelievably cumbersome! When Papa roared about my coming to live where I might be massacred by Indians, I soothed him with the reminder that in a place where *I* could set the fashion, I would at least not catch fire from sweeping too near a hearth!" She shook her head decidedly. "Let me hang up the habit while you put on this other starched petticoat. No corsets, either! Oh, my dear, what heaven it is to be free of such tortures!"

Talitha had to laugh. Leonore, temperamentally, was so different from Socorro that she looked less like her with every impudent wrinkling of the nose, each lilting sweep of the hands.

Even what Leonore would consider necessities were an unwelcome hindrance on Talitha's free movement.

Garters, holding up the black silk stockings that felt so sleek and elegant, cut into her flesh, and the drawers, fastened at the waist with a drawstring, chafed her legs. But for this occasion, Talitha was prepared to suffer.

"Ravishing!" Leonore cried, when the last tiny button was fastened, the last seam smoothed, and shimmering brocade molded Talitha from slim waist to the tender lift of her breasts. "It was fitted on me, you know. Judah thought we were of a size except that— you won't be angry—you still ran to boniness!" Her laughter tinkled. "Bony! My usually observant husband hasn't looked at you closely of late! You're slim as a willow but all the curves are there! There's a candle, let me light it so you can do your hair."

Talitha tried to do something with her thick unruly mane, gave up in exasperation and started to braid it. It would just have to coil around her head the way she wore it in summer for coolness.

"Ah, no!" Giving the mirror to Talitha, Leonore took the comb. "Let it shine! See, it sweeps back and up, so, then some pins to hold it at the crown and from there, it falls free!"

Talitha stared in wonder at the face watching her from the mirror. Smooth honey-tanned skin made eyes, beneath strong-arched ash-colored eyebrows, as luminously blue as the brocade, and the hair style narrowed her face till the squareness of jaw was drawn into the shadow of high cheekbones. If Shea could see her, he'd *have* to know she was no child!

That he wouldn't dampened her glow a bit, but she put down the mirror and gave Leonore an impulsive hug. "You've made me look beautiful! And all the bother with the dresses—how can I thank you?"

"It was fun for me," Leonore assured her. She frowned at the black kid slippers Talitha was putting on. "I'm sorry I could find nothing to go better with the dress, but bootmakers out here aren't prepared yet to cater to ladies." She carefully smoothed the ruching at the square neck of her dark rose silk, perfected one of the long soft curls escaping artfully from a carved ivory comb. "Isn't it nice our colors don't clash?"

When Talitha stared in confusion, Leonore laughed and kissed her cheek. "Talitha, how funny-sweet and solemn you are! I believe I'd like you even if you were dark like me! But as it is, you'll be queen of the fair and I'll hold court for gentlemen who prefer brunettes! Put on your cloak! It's just a short way but the wind's chill."

Besides several big tables that looked permanent, planks had been laid across sawhorses and set with what looked like every eating utensil and dish in Tubac. A dozen dressed turkeys hung from the ceiling beams as if to assure the guests there was plenty to eat. Marc had been waiting by the door. As they came inside and he took Talitha's cloak, hanging it on a peg, he drew in his breath audibly.

"You could break my heart before," he said in her ear. "What you'll do now—oh, Talitha!"

Eluding several officers who jumped up to proffer stools or parts of benches, Marc escorted her to where Frost and Leonore were finding seats.

Frost inclined his silvery head and his eyes, too, showed silver. "My wife's taste is equaled only by your loveliness, Talitha." He tilted his head, smiling. "What a difference four years make! By the time two more pass, you'll doubtless have succumbed to prayers and entreaties and become somebody's wife."

Did he want her to remember that was when he'd vowed to have her? Talitha felt cold. "I doubt I shall marry, Mr. Frost," she said, accepting the stool Marc pulled out for her.

"Don't plague the child, Judah," chided Leonore. "My heavens, look at the kinds of meat! What are they?"

Poston chuckled at her from the head of the table. "We already had beef and mutton, but we've been hunting, too. Behold, madam, you may choose quail, turkey, duck, antelope, deer or bear! We haven't much variety in vegetables, but we have plenty in meat!"

While pretty girls and women moved about serving food, Poston introduced the others at his table. Besides his German partner, Hans Ehrenberg, there was Fred Hulsemann who now kept the company store while he looked for a way to recoup the $50,000 he'd lost in the Calabazas venture; Charles Schuchard, in charge of mining operations down at Aribac who frowned in puzzlement at Talitha till she reminded him of the spring when, accompanying Gray's railroad survey, he'd sketched the ranch house for Socorro.

"Of course I remember! How is Señora O'Shea? A very gracious lady!"

Talitha froze, blessed Marc when he said quickly, "She must have been. Unfortunately, I never met her. She died some three years ago."

Schuchard murmured condolences while Poston presented Colonel Douglas from Sopori, a flamboyant older man got up in Spanish holiday garb. Beside him were

414

a soft-eyed lady, Doña Rosa, and her husband, Pete Kitchen.

Pete Kitchen? Whose house was a fortress, who had started a graveyard below it, peopled with raiders for whom his gentle wife burned candles and prayed? Meeting his quizzical blue-gray eyes, Talitha realized she'd been staring.

"Oh, Mr. Kitchen," she babbled. "We've really been enjoying one of your hams."

He grinned, his florid face losing some of its grim lines. "Well, I hope you don't find any arrowheads in it! Them pesky Apaches have shot some of my pigs so full of arrows that they looked like walking pin-cushions!" He turned to the two officers seated across from Talitha. "Thought your dragoons would put an end to that, but oh, no! Every full moon here the varmints come again!"

"I'm just a surgeon," grinned the red-headed hand-some young man who reminded Talitha of Shea. There was even the slightest hint of Irish in his accent.

He proved to be Dr. Bernard J. D. Irwin and the balding fortyish officer beside him was Captain Richard Ewell. His beaked nose and eyes that seemed to pop from their sockets gave Ewell a birdlike look as he set his gleaming head to one side and began to reminisce about his experiences with the Mescaleros in New Mexico.

"It'll either have to be reservations or complete extermination," he said in a shrill, rather squeaky voice. "Until they learn to farm and raise livestock instead of stealing it, they'll have to raid to live, and they sure won't farm till they have to!"

Talitha thought of James. It would be a few years yet before Mangus took him on any raids but he could be killed in camp by soldiers like Ewell at almost any time. The thought took away her appetite.

"It would help if the Mexican government would do anything," growled Kitchen. "But here's Pesqueira and Gándara wrangling over Sonora, and the Liberals and

Conservatives at each other's throats down in Mexico City. Nobody seems strong enough to take hold and give the country any leadership."

The talk turned to filibusters. "It would be an act of mercy to Sonora to annex it and give it decent government and protection," Frost said. "We need a port as much as we need a railroad. We're as close to Lobos, the harbor I found, as we are to Fort Yuma, and at Lobos goods wouldn't have to be shifted from ocean-going vessels to river craft."

"Gentlemen," said Irwin pleasantly, "don't you realize that our government is almost in as desperate a case as that of Mexico? All this gobbling up of western land on top of the quarrels between North and South has brought on a monstrous fit of indigestion. It's going to be a while before the older part of the nation can give even a feeble chew at what it's bitten off."

Poston frowned. "It's true the House of Representatives wouldn't seat our delegate when it met this month, but a bill was passed to build a wagon road from El Paso to Fort Yuma. Congress is doing something."

"And Arizona's not without influential friends," pointed out Frost. "Railroad men and financiers and speculators from both coasts and Ohio have a stake in what happens here."

"To hell with financiers!" rumbled Kitchen. "I just want them Indians to stop shooting my pigs!"

Fiddlers were tuning up and, while eggnog was served around in cups, gourds and glasses, the music started. It reminded Talitha of those nights by the Mormon campfires, of her parents dancing, and a great wave of longing swept through her, to be loved and protected as she had been then, not to have to decide what to do and worry about whether or not it was right.

Marc's touch roused her. "Shall we dance?"

"There's not room," she demurred, but he nodded to where one makeshift table had been cleared away and people were forming two lines facing each other.

"The Virginia reel," he smiled. "It's more game than dance. You can't go wrong if you watch the others."

Leonore was already on her feet, urging up her husband. In a moment, they were in the lines as the dancers at each end came forward to meet and circle in the center.

Then the fiddlers moved into a sort of gliding music that swooped and then paused. "A waltz!" Marc laughed down at Talitha, drawing her into the open space. "What an excuse to have my arm around you! Don't stiffen, my sweetheart. Just follow what my hands say."

She liked the waltz after the first difficulty of being so close to a man, his lips only inches from her ear, his arm hard and warm and strong against her back, dipping her low, whirling her expertly in the little area they shared with Ewell and Doña Rosa, Frost and Leonore.

As the dance ended, Dr. Erwin bowed and asked for the next.

"I really can't dance." Talitha blushed. "Mr. Revier's been teaching me."

"Then you've been a most apt pupil." His voice had a lilt so like Shea's that she had a stab of loneliness for him. "My feet are much bigger than yours, Miss Scott, so you're risking more than I am!"

She smiled. Taking that for assent, he swept her into another waltz. He *was* from Ireland, had left in boyhood and had graduated from New York Medical College.

Testing him, she told him of Nōnó's curing Shea. Irwin's glance was thoughtful, not incredulous. "For sure, the natives must know things we don't. That *jículi* sounds as if it could be a very useful anesthetic or pain-killer."

He was so interested in what she could tell him about medicinal plants that they went on talking after the waltz, standing near the fireplace.

"Here comes your escort," Irwin said resignedly as

Marc came toward them. "Forgive my boldness but I'm on duty tomorrow and can't waste time. Are you engaged?"

"No," said Talitha.

Her heart misgave her as his face lit up but there was no time to say more before Marc claimed her.

To her relief, Judah Frost didn't attempt to dance with her that evening, though necessarily, in the reels and country dances, he partnered her fleetingly, his hands cool on her, steel in his lightest touch. Her mind churned with questions which chased each other around and around, finding no answers.

Why had he married someone who looked so much like Socorro? What would Shea feel when he saw her? In baffled anger, Talitha felt as if Frost were crouched above them all like a giant cat, watching amusedly till time to spring.

So she danced her turns with Colonel Poston, Captain Ewell who paid extravagant compliments when he wasn't teasing in a half-paternal manner, several other officers and Charles Schuchard who said he'd love to sketch her some day.

When at last the fiddlers stopped and the guests who lived nearby went home, Talitha was so sleepy she could barely struggle out of her lovely, lovely dress, though as she hung it up, she caressed it with a smile. In it she had first felt the heady power of being a woman.

Leonore smiled, smoothing creams into her skin. "Yes, my dear, you were a great success! Isn't it fun?"

Talitha nodded and snuggled under the covers. She wouldn't want to do this very often, but the admiration of vital, energetic men was just as intoxicating as the mescal in Colonel Poston's punch and eggnog! Sighing blissfully, she was asleep before Leonore blew out the candle.

XXVII

Talitha and Leonore, still in bed, sipped the chocolate brought them by the Indian girl who built up the fire so the chill would be off the air before they were ready to dress.

Talitha felt lazy to the point of wickedness, but her head throbbed slightly from unaccustomed potations and she wiggled her toes luxuriously and determined to enjoy this opportunity for decadence since she might never have another.

Leonore was exclaiming on the problems of American ambassadors abroad where a plain citizen's garb, recently ordained by the Secretary of State, might be considered an insult at court functions, and an inflammatory reminder of the United States' origins.

"Poor Mr. Buchanan—he'll be our new president, you know—Pierce lost the renomination because Northern Democrats couldn't stomach his proslavery stand on Kansas—well, Mr. Buchanan didn't know what to wear to the Court of St. James, so he missed the opening of Parliament and the way the newspapers, court and even the House of Commons carried on, one would never have guessed England on the brink of war with Russia!" Her laughter chimed like small bells. "Papa says the minister thought of arraying himself like George Washington! Fortunately, he had the wit to know he'd look ridiculous and appeared at Queen Victoria's levee in plain garb. She received him graciously, which settled the matter, at least in England, but after all, Victoria's so *dowdy* she can scarcely cavil at anyone! Empress Eugénie sets style for all civilized society."

"But you don't like her hoops," Talitha objected.

"No, and I pray they are out of fashion before ever I return east! But," sighed Leonore, "how I'd love to see her dressing room at the Tuileries! Revolving mirrors! Separate rooms for hats and bonnets, footwear, parasols and cloaks. Each morning a doll of the Empress's size is dressed to the last detail and sent down in the lift for her approval. It's very seldom that she accepts the costume without much altering and trying of various accessories."

If that was what sipping chocolate in bed could lead to, Talitha wanted none of it! Jumping up, she turned her back to Leonore and dressed quickly in the gaberdine.

"The French have rulers like that again, after the Revolution?"

Leonore shrugged her slim shoulders. "After the Terror and a strong dose of Bonaparte, I think they welcomed the Bourbons." She patted back a yawn. "Would I rather sleep or have breakfast? Breakfast, I think!"

Since it was decided, after a leisurely breakfast, to ride over to Tumacácori and see the ruins, Talitha suggested to Marc that they might as well continue from there on to the ranch.

"Oh, I'll miss you!" Leonore cried, but nodded understandingly when Talitha explained that she didn't want to be away longer from Caterina. "My dear, you must come visit us in Tucson! Promise you will, and bring the little girl with you! She sounds adorable!"

"Sometimes she is," laughed Talitha. "But I can't imagine Shea letting her go on a visit for many years to come!"

"Ah, I'll see to him!" said Leonore confidently.

Looking at the gay sparkling young woman, so like yet so different from Socorro, Talitha felt a sense of warning. She was going to tell Shea how remarkably Leonore resembled Socorro but would that make him more or less eager to meet her? The similarity was a chance of common Spanish heritage, but it was no accident that Judah Frost had married this particular Washington belle.

As they walked about the ruins of Tumacácori—the church roof fallen in though the dome was in reasonable repair—and gazed up at the crumbling bell tower, Talitha told the story Tjúni had given her about the mission. Early in the century the Indians, Pima and Papago, living about the mission received title to four *sitios* of land nearby for grazing and farming, though if they abandoned the region for three years, they lost claim. This was a common provision for grants along the frontier.

During the sale of secular lands, Gándara had acquired the mission property though the Indians were rightfully owners of it and the surrounding lands. Officials had asked to see their title and had kept it. Then, in that Apache-beleaguered winter of 1848, the inhabitants took their *santos* and church furnishings to San Xavier where they were inventoried and kept separate.

"Gándara treats the land as his," Talitha finished. "And since the Indians had to abandon the place, he probably has some legal standing, but it's still a cheat!"

Shortly afterward, she thanked Colonel Poston for his hospitality and said her farewells to Leonore who kissed her and again insisted that she visit Tucson. Frost only bowed, eyes unreadable, and Talitha turned Ladorada sharply away, glad to escape his constant surveillance, which, in a way, made her jumpier than a direct onslaught since she didn't know what he intended.

As they passed Calabazas Marc said, "Did you find Dr. Irwin as interesting as he obviously found you?"

"He's very nice." Her cool tone was betrayed by a blush.

Marc gave a short hard laugh. "And he's very near the Socorro, damn him!"

"I've already told you—"

421

"I know what you've told me!" His tone was savage. "The more I think about it, Talitha, the less I know whom to feel sorrier for, you or me! Shea will never see you as anything but a daughter."

"Then I'll be his daughter."

Marc reined in his horse and stared at her. His eyes smoldered. Springing down from his horse, he tossed the reins around a jutting broken limb, took Talitha's from her astonished hands and did the same. He brought her out of the saddle, holding her as she slid to the earth so that his whole body pressed hard against her.

She had no strength, nor did she truly wish to stop him. It was as if this was something that had to pass between them. He held the back of her head in his hand, kissed her forehead and eyes and throat, taking her mouth last.

Embraced by his whole being, swept with fire, she felt her lips soften under his. He groaned and gathered her closer till her breasts ached and her legs melted. She was dizzier, much dizzier, than she had been from the punch and eggnogs.

"I could take you!" he breathed. "Maybe I should. It might put all this eternal daughter nonsense out of your head, or more to my purpose, out of your body!"

Sweat stood out on his face in spite of the chill breeze. Roused for the first time, she pulsed with hunger for his kiss, for more, more of that rough sweetness, whatever would be its end. She thought, too, that if he had her, it would tame his longing, quench his impossible wish for marriage.

"Marc, if you want me—"

"Want you?" His voice was strained, husky, before, gazing at her, he moved his head back and forth as if he were deeply, secretly wounded. "My God, Talitha, you think that would make me stop loving you? Can you really believe that I could have you and then go away?"

Shamed, she couldn't answer. Face set, he helped her mount, gave her the reins, and was swiftly back in the saddle. Talitha was mortified at the way she'd responded to him, but as they neared the ranch and she began to think of how it would be never to see him, her misery deepened. Marc was her dear friend who had taught her to read, opened a different world. He was special, not like anyone else.

"Marc," she said, just above the sound of the horses. "Won't you ever come back?"

He regarded her somberly for a moment. Then the lines about his eyes crinkled and he smiled. "I'll be back. Unless you marry or die, Talitha, you may depend on it that every year or two or three, I'll come back to see if you've changed your mind."

"You will be careful?"

"Absolutely! Life with you would be rapturous—some of the time, at least—but I find it sweet, anyway." As they stopped by the corral, he helped her down, hands tightening before he let her go. "If you need me, Talitha, send word. If I'm alive, I'll come."

Shea was with them then, and the twins, pouncing on the chewy nut candy she'd saved for them. Caterina, in her own cashmere cape, hugged her about the legs till Shea swung his daughter to his shoulders.

"Have a good time, lass?" he inquired, eyes searching.

Talitha forced herself to meet his gaze. Could he guess what had almost happened on the way home? Blessing Marc for his restraint, she hugged the boys and started for the house since Chuey was taking care of Ladorada.

"It was wonderful, Shea! There was a nice Irish doctor from Camp Moore and Pete Kitchen and Mr. Schuchard and—oh, well, you'll have to go yourself!"

"And that I will!" Shea said. "Even if I do have to rub elbows with some blue-belly Yankees! Will you be riding back with me, Marc?"

"Yes, if I can have some coffee first."

"And some of whatever there is to eat," Talitha insisted.

She fixed him a plate of turkey and ham left over

from the Christmas feast, mashed beans and tamales, trying to think how to warn Shea. At last, unable to think of any subtle method and with time short, she said, "Mrs. Frost, Shea—she's beautiful! And I couldn't believe my eyes! She could be Socorro's twin."

He paled. She went on rather wildly, "It's the Spanish blood. Of course, when you talk with her, the likeness fades, they're so different. But it's startling at first glance."

"Then she's a very lovely lady," Shea said, recovered. His eyes thanked her. He ran a hand over his clean-shaven jaw, lingered a moment at the blotted brand. "Even if there's anyone from my old outfit at Camp Moore, I doubt we'd know each other after ten years. An Irish doctor, is it? Now him I'd like to meet!"

When Marc was ready, the two set off. Marc's good-bye to Talitha was curt but as he turned to mount, he said softly, "I will be back."

Talitha had been gone only one day, yet it seemed years. Caterina looked much bigger and the twins seemed to have grown by inches. Then, gradually, the excitement wore off, and Tubac became unreal, the officers with their sabers and epaulets, Leonore's chatter of empress and queen, Poston's eggnog, the dancing.

It was like a brightly colored dream. That Shea moved in it kept it in Talitha's mind. It was as if their life, real life, was suspended till he came back. She'd miss Marc, but life at the ranch would settle into its accustomed rhythm and things would be as they were before.

She was wrong. Just as Socorro's passing had marked the end of one time, and Santiago's departure another, those holidays that opened into the year of 1857 were the start of Shea's drinking.

Not as before, after Socorro's death, when he'd drunk himself into insensibility. He was controlled about it now, drinking only after the children were in bed, working the same as usual, though he had been drunk that day Judah Frost brought him home from Tubac, so drunk that Frost half-carried him into the house.

"I'll put him to bed, let him sleep it off," Frost said as Shea weaved and smiled foolishly. "He was all right when we left Tubac but started nipping at Calabazas."

Caterina was frowning up at her father and the twins looked puzzled. Belen scooped up Caterina, wrapping her small serape around her. "Come, *niña,* let's see what horse you're going to ride this summer! Patrick, Miguel, advise us, *por favor!*"

He hustled the children out. Frost's mouth twisted. "The good servant, protecting his master from ignominy."

Talitha said nothing. Sick at heart, she turned back the covers and pulled off Shea's boots, leaving Frost to help him undress. She had no mind to let Frost catch her alone. Slipping into her serape, she hurried outside, intending to join Belen and the children at the big corral. Frost caught up with her before she was out of the courtyard.

"I'm sorry, Talitha. Truly, this isn't the effect I'd planned for my charming wife to have on Shea."

"Effect?" Talitha stopped, looking up at him. She drew the serape closer against the biting cold, but there was no protection from the ice-gray chill of this man's eyes. "Planned?"

"You don't think I married Leonore solely because her father is a power in banking and can push legislation favorable to my interests, do you?"

"You—you might love her!"

His sculptured lips curved down. "She's ornamental. A pleasant enough bedmate. She'll serve till I have you; in fact, she may help considerably in that acquisition."

"You—you're crazy!"

He shook his head, smiling. "Saner than your beloved Irisher! Ah, you didn't think I'd seen that?"

She turned toward the mountains. His words struck

425

sharp and cruel as the wind. "I thought my senses, so finely tuned where you're concerned, my dear, were playing tricks. When observation convinced me they weren't, I pondered for some way to make this unfortunate predisposition less of an obstacle." His chuckle grated on Talitha's nerves. "So when I went to Washington, what should I see there? A girl who looked like Socorro would have if she'd enjoyed a life of ease and time and money to preen."

It was so cold-blooded and calculating that for a moment all Talitha could think of was what this knowledge would do to sweet, generous, bubbling Leonore. Perhaps she'd never have to know, but Talitha's feelings rebelled at her friend's being used like a puppet by this ruthless man. She'd better learn all she could of what twisted scheme he had in mind.

"But you've married her. How does Shea come in?"

"I can't foresee exactly. Leonore's a romantic little goose and full of sympathy. Should they fall in love, I'd expect Shea to struggle nobly for a time. Then, discovering the truth, I could magnanimously arrange a divorce."

"And they could marry."

Talitha didn't think the pain that streamed through her sounded in her voice, but Frost seemed to sense it as an animal scents blood. His nostrils quivered.

"Yes." He smiled. "And I don't think, Talitha, that you could bear living with a new Mrs. O'Shea!"

Her heart turned to ice at the thought. Tjúni had been bad enough, but a real wife—a woman Shea would love at least in part as he'd loved Socorro?

"I wouldn't live with them," she said slowly. "But I wouldn't marry you either."

He lifted a dark eyebrow. "Time changes many things, my dear. I'm in no hurry. As long as her father's in the Senate, Leonore's valuable to me, so I rather hope Shea's struggle against coveting his partner's wife will be a long one." He laughed softly. "What, not urging me to stay the night? Never mind, I've business in Camp Moore."

Talitha went back to the house. Staring down at Shea, she ached with love and pity. She shouldn't want him for herself. If he found someone to love again, she'd make herself glad though it would be beyond her power to share their roof. And she mustn't get frantic notions just because he'd had too much to drink at a celebration. So had most of the men. By tomorrow, he'd be fine again, except for a ringing head.

The next day he was sober and worked with the men on mending a corral but after the children were asleep, he'd gone to his room. Next day, hanging up clothes, Talitha saw the half-empty bottle of mescal behind his bed. The morning after that, it was nearly gone, and the next day, there was a new bottle, drunk a third of the way down.

This was no binge. It was steady, methodical night drinking. After a week, Talitha confronted Shea one night when, bottle in hand, he was going to his room.

"Shea." Her tongue stuck to the roof of her mouth. "Was it bad for you, meeting Leonore?"

"Bad?" His brows knit and she wanted to smooth away the baffled pain. "Yes, it was that, Tally."

"Do—do you love her?"

If he did, Talitha resolved to tell him Frost would make no barrier. Far rather see him with another woman, though she herself would have to go away, than watch him grapple with this dull silent misery.

Shea laughed out in surprise. "Love that pretty little butterfly? For all she's sweet and winsome, she's like the foam swirling on water. Socorro was the water."

Talitha's heart beat again; she realized she'd been holding her breath. Along with sorrow for Shea came a flood of relief. He didn't love her, not as she wished him to, but at least he didn't want anyone else, either.

He continued slowly, "Seeing Leonore brought it all back, though, seeing someone so like Socorro in looks, it roused up the yearning for my own dear lass. It made me know that even if I found a face and form like hers, what I really loved is gone, the shining spirit of her."

"But, Shea—drinking like this—"

He smiled wearily. "Tally, it is how I sleep."

She would have given anything in the world to comfort that bright head, hold him in her arms against the yearnings and torments of the night. But he didn't want her. He wanted the woman buried on the hill.

For the first time, Talitha almost hated her foster mother. In the dim *sala,* facing the dark madonna, she cried wordlessly, *Can't you make him lift his heart out of your grave? Can't you let him go?*

It was still January when Captain Ewell with several dragoons and Dr. Irwin stopped at the ranch. Major Steen had been ordered to find a new location and had sent Ewell, out of earshot referred to as "old Baldy," to scout for one.

While they ate and rested, the captain and doctor debated the merits of a small plateau abut five miles to the west. "It's surrounded on three sides by a marsh," argued Irwin. "Bound to breed malaria and fever. Damned poor place if you ask me."

"I didn't ask!" snapped Ewell. "Didn't even want you along, but you would come, you hot-tempered, red-headed, mule-stubborn Irishman!"

Irwin bowed. "The same to you, Captain, excepting the Irish and red hair which I'm bound you wish you had!" He winked drolly at Shea. "The captain's about to burst a blood vessel since he can't cut loose in front of Miss Talitha. He can swear the hide off a mule and his curses can be parsed!"

The captain's eyes seemed ready to pop out but he choked, coughed and managed a chuckle in the depths of his beard before he said flatly, "That elevation gives a good view of the country and has plenty of wood and good water. I'm going to recommend it to the major."

"And I'll disrecommend it!" Irwin growled. "But who ever listens to doctors till they need one?"

A short time later, they mounted up and were on their way. "Come anytime, gentlemen," invited Shea, with a particular grin for Irwin. "We've enjoyed your company."

Irwin's blue gaze strayed to Talitha. "I can think of one advantage to the captain's marsh," he laughed. "It would be much closer to the hospitality of this ranch. Miss Talitha, I hope you could spare the time one day to show me that *canaigre* plant for coughs and sore throats. Half of the men are barking their heads off."

"Wait, I'll send some with you now," she said.

Running to the storeroom, free of mice thanks to Chusma's horde, she put all the dried roots she had in a piece of cloth and took them to the doctor. "A piece can be chewed and swallowed," she said. "Or it can be powdered and mixed with something sweet."

As he took the packet, his big hand closed over hers longer than necessary. He thanked her and said he'd be back.

"A good man," Shea approved as the party rode off. "And born in Roscommon! Have you a taste for being an officer's wife, Tally?"

Speechless with hurt, she stared at him. How could he say such a thing? As if he were the only one who might hold to one love! His smile faded as he looked at her.

"Tally," he said. "Oh, Tally, girl, you must be giving the young men a chance!"

Fighting back tears, she cried in fierce pleading, "Shea, even if you can't love me, you need a woman, you need someone. Let me be with you for that!"

"You don't know what you're saying." His face was taut. The brand stood out white and bloodless. "A man'll come who can give you all his heart and youth and soul. I won't ruin you for him, Talitha." His voice was hoarse and he clenched his hands behind him. "Don't ask me to damn myself, lass, for that's what it would be if I abused your sweet child's love in such a fashion!"

"Socorro wasn't much older than I when you met!"

There was a flash of his old smile. "But I was ten years younger! Give over, Tally. Teach the doctor plants and let him have a chance to teach you other things."

She held his gaze steadily, willing him to accept her as an equal, a woman to his man. "It's you I love, Shea." Then she turned and walked to the house.

She found herself enjoying Irwin's visits, though, and it would have been presumptuous to discourage them since he talked with Shea more than he did with her, and became a favorite of the twins and Caterina. Many plants were dormant, but she showed him the ones she could. Caterina and the twins went with them on these expeditions and Talitha was glad that, lured by the doctor's interest, they were bound to learn a little.

He soon had generous amounts of elderberry bark, its tea good to cause vomiting or cure constipation; joint fir for fever and kidney pain; walnut hulls for cleaning maggots out of wounds; green oak bark to make a cure for diarrhea; root of ocotillo for painful swellings; cholla root for a laxative; agave pulp for wounds. John, as he asked them to call him, was a keen observer and jotted down notes on wildlife, birds, plants and terrain. He didn't come every Sunday but as spring approached, Talitha began to feel disappointed when noon came without him.

One morning he came so early that he must have left camp before sunup. "Why don't we ride to Tubac and enjoy Colonel Poston's entertainment?" he suggested as soon as he had admired Caterina's new kitten and extracted a splinter from Patrick's hand that no one else had been allowed to touch. "The superintendents from other mines come for dinner and neighbors are always welcome."

Shea laughed. "My head can take Colonel Poston's hospitality only once a year! But, Tally, you could go with the doctor."

"Oh, I couldn't!" she exclaimed, blushed at her rudeness, and tried to cover it by saying that she was in the middle of making panocha.

The sprouted wheat meal and brown sugar pudding, after mixing, had to set an hour before it baked very slowly for several hours, and did indeed take time and care, but she hadn't even thought of the waiting batter when she first refused.

A glint in John's eyes told her he guessed this but he smiled charmingly. "I'd rather have your panocha any day, Miss Talitha, than the colonel's venison, even though he's now getting champagne and Scotch to go with it."

Settling by the fire with Shea who was mending a bridle, Irwin gave them the latest news. Just as the Santa Cruz Valley in Arizona was being repopulated, in northern Sonora ranches that had been abandoned for twenty and thirty years were coming back to life. For good prices, Sonorans supplied staples like wheat and sugar to the miners, soldiers and settlers of southern Arizona, and also profited in the trade of luxury goods brought in through Guaymas.

"But the honeymoon's over," regretted Irwin. "A certain Henry Crabb started recruiting colonists in San Francisco for the Gadsden Purchase this January, only when he got to Yuma, he let them know he planned to join Pesqueira in putting down Gándara's forces, and colonize in Sonora. Probably, back before Pesqueira got fairly well established, he had made some kind of deal with Crabb—Crabb's brother-in-law is an influential Sonoran named Ainsa. But Pesqueira doesn't need Crabb now and he's whipping up the populace against this latest filibuster."

"Surely when Crabb gets word of that, he'll drop the idea," scoffed Shea.

The doctor shook his head. "He left Yuma heading for Caborca early in March, a few weeks ago. He's sent two men to see if there aren't some fight-hungry adventurers in Tucson, Tubac and Calabazas who'll join him."

Shea gave a long, low whistle. "Poston would never fall for such a shenanigan?"

"Not he. He told them he depended on Sonora for supplies and labor and tried to make them see the expedition was bound to fail and could only destroy the present good feeling along the border. But some of his miners went. I would reckon about thirty-three men, most from around Calabazas, have taken off toward Caborca."

"Then God help them. Pesqueira won't. The fools! Don't they know how Mexicans feel about Americans, first the war taking the spread from New Mexico to California and the Gadsden Purchase whacking off Sonora's northern half? Greedy damn Yanquis!"

"Just like England?" Irwin grinned.

"More than a little, man!" Shea tossed the bridle to the floor, getting up. "Here's the North saying the South can't go its own way. Here they are, dilly-dallying about making Arizona a territory when Santa Fe ignores even Mesilla, which is where our nearest court is!" He let out an exasperated breath, shrugged aside governmental iniquities. "I know you're not a horse doctor, John, but would you have a look at a canker in my old Azul horse's ear?"

"The men say I should stick to horses," Irwin laughed, and, with Caterina and the twins, followed his host outside.

"The panocha was very good," Irwin said that evening. He and Talitha were briefly alone in the storeroom where she was getting him dried elderflowers to

432

treat colds and stomachaches. "But I think there was another reason why you didn't want to go to Tubac."

She said nothing. "Well, Miss Talitha? Will you go with me next Sunday if I can escape emergencies? People seem to wait till Sunday to come to me with ails they've had all week."

How could she explain that she didn't want to lose him as she'd lost Marc? Slowly, miserably, she said, "That would look as if we were—keeping company, John."

His eyebrows climbed. "My dear, why shouldn't we?"

She swallowed, involuntarily stepping back. "I—I thought you came here to see all of us!"

"So I do. I like the O'Sheas tremendously, and love wee Cat." In the dim room, his eyes seemed to catch and hold the light there was. Silence mounted between them, a growing tension. "You told me you weren't engaged."

"I'm not." What could she tell him, that he'd accept? "But I—I do love someone."

The red head, painfully like Shea's, went back sharply. "I can't believe any man you cared for wouldn't have carried you off by now, even if Shea didn't approve," Irwin said at last. "Nor can I believe there's a man who, given the chance, could fail to love you."

"This one doesn't." Talitha couldn't keep the bitterness from her tone.

Irwin sighed. "But you hope he'll change?"

"Even if he doesn't, I won't."

A smile crept into his tone. "Let's see now, next month you'll be all of seventeen, isn't it?"

She didn't answer that. After a moment, he took her hands, raised them to his face. "Very well, my stubborn lass! But now all's clear between us and you won't be leading me on——" His voice twinkled. "Why not ride out with me sometimes?"

"You still want to?"

"Of course! The señoritas are pretty little things and dozens have poured in from the despoiled parts of

Sonora where they've lost their men from Apaches or
civil war, but their interests run to romance and *monte*.
I'd much rather talk with you. At least sometimes."

"Well," she said doubtfully. "If you're sure—"

He kissed her lightly on the forehead. "I'm sure.
I can be a good friend to you, Talitha, though I'd
hoped to be more." He chuckled irrepressibly. "And
there's the chance you may realize in time what a rare
catch I'd be!"

They were both laughing when they went inside.
Irwin told Shea he'd like to call for Talitha next Sunday.
After a startled glance at her, Shea said heartily that
would be fine. Talitha's heart made an odd little somersault.

Maybe, if she kept company with the doctor, Shea
would be jolted into seeing her as a woman, admitting
she was grown up. That might make a difference. Anyway, John Irwin was handsome, brilliant and fun, and
now that he understood matters, she was going to enjoy
his companionship. Once he was transferred from this
remote wilderness post, he'd forget all about her, but
they could, for now, ease each other's loneliness.

XXVIII

It was in April that John Irwin brought news of what had happened to Crabb's expedition. On April 11th, with sixty-nine of his men, Crabb had fought his way into Caborca. In some low adobes across the street from the church, the Americans held out for six days against ten to one odds. Crabb persuaded them that surrender might bring them safe passage across the border.

Instead, after giving up their weapons, they were shot at the next sunrise. Crabb's head was severed and preserved in mescal. The bodies were left for hogs, and a few days later Crabb's rearguard of sixteen was overwhelmed, marched into Caborca and shot.

Four sick members of the expedition had been left at a trading post on the American side. Mexican troops crossed the border and shot the remaining would-be filibusterers.

"Now Major Steen's supposed to find out for sure which side of the border that trading post is on," the doctor said. "The Mexican commander insists he didn't come on American soil. What's more, he's written to the major, putting it to him that he should punish the filibusterers who were recruited from around here but didn't go very far into Mexico."

"Should sort of check people's enthusiasm for stealing territory," Shea remarked dryly.

"It's stirred up a lot of old hatreds. Pesqueira's closed the border again and all our supplies have to come from Yuma or the east."

The interests of Sonora and Arizona were so interlaced that by the time Camp Moore was completely abandoned in June for Fort Buchanan, Captain Ewell's marshbound slope, trade with Mexico was in full swing again and the region prospered as never before with soldiers to check the Apaches and the mines paying good wages.

Tubac thrived in particular, with Poston holding open house with a lavish hand. Visitors were welcome as long as they wished to stay and when they journeyed on, their mounts were shod gratis and they were given free provisions.

As a territorial official, Poston felt empowered to perform marriages, which he did, and threw in a wedding feast to boot. Because priestly visits had been rare for years, and because it cost $25.00 to be married in Sonora, many couples were married by the commandant of the Sonora Exploring and Mining Company and he was godfather to numerous children.

To solve the problem of scarce currency, the company paid workers with *boletas*, printed slips of pasteboard with the picture of an animal. A pig was 12½¢; a calf, 25¢; 50¢ for a rooster; a dollar for a horse, five dollars for a bull, and ten for a lion. When a merchant collected enough of these, the company redeemed them with bullion.

Well-armed Tubac itself wasn't molested by Indians, but the dragoons weren't a month gone from Camp Moore when Apaches raided Calabazas and stole thirty-one mules and a dozen horses.

Under pressure to control the Indians, the high command of the Department of New Mexico mounted a campaign that summer to crush and disperse the Mogollon, Coyotero and Gila Apaches.

Weeks of combing the Gila region and scouting the rugged Chiracahuas accomplished nothing beyond the taking of a few prisoners and burning some cornfields.

It was June 27th before any real battle was fought. Twenty Apache warriors were killed, at least one shot after being made a prisoner at order of Colonel Bonneville, the commander of the joined forces. Twenty-six women and children were captured.

"Bonneville's being cheered as the 'Hero of the Gila Expedition,'" growled John Irwin in disgust. "Didn't succeed in doing anything but making the Apaches madder!"

But it showed that the Army was serious about checking the Apaches. Talitha feared greatly for James. "John," she said, "will you tell Major Steen, Captain Ewell, pass the word to all the men, that if they find among the Mimbreños a blue-eyed boy of about ten, he's my brother?"

Irwin's eyes widened. "Your brother?"

It hurt so much to think of James that she never spoke of him except when, occasionally, the twins would still wonder if he wasn't coming back and she could only say she hoped so. She prayed for him every night, though, to whatever Powers might listen, and implored her mother and Socorro to help him if they could.

Now she told the young doctor about James, that he was the son of Juh, and why he'd gone away with Mangus.

"Poor little lad," Irwin muttered. "Near four years, and no word of him?"

She shook her head. Her throat ached too much for speaking.

"I'll pass the word," he assured her. "And Steen can notify the other posts."

She thanked him and added, "I think Mangus would get word to me if James were dead. Even if he didn't, I think I'd know, I'd feel it." Her grief welled over. "Oh, John, I was so angry when his cat bit Shea! Socorro forgave him but I didn't! I was supposed to take care of him! Instead I drove him away!"

Irwin held her tenderly and let her cry. Producing a big handkerchief, when the storm was spent, he made her blow her nose. "Sniffing produces catarrh," he admonished. "And now, young lady, put this nonsense of failing your brother out of your head for good and all! You saved his life to start with, you got him away from the Apaches, and you were yourself a child when this hydrophobia business happened."

Talitha shook her head, refusing to be excused.

Unbelievably, he laughed. At her stare, he said, "Haven't you ever thought that your brother's probably having a dandy time?"

"What?"

"Why, sure! He's hunting, learning weapons, skylarking with friends, wandering the mountains! Lord, he's doing everything boys enjoy when they can get out of work! Don't feel too sorry for him, Talitha."

Now why hadn't she thought of it like that? Remembering her time with the Apaches, Talitha had to admit that the boys had seemed to always be having fun; in fact, the children were treated well and never punished after the manner of whites. A weak, deformed baby might be exposed, or a twin, if it couldn't be cared for, but children who lived were indulged and loved. Talitha had allied herself closely with her mother and then been so fiercely engaged in keeping James alive that her own existence had not been normal.

Beguiled at this thought, Talitha brightened, only to sink again into worry. "That may be true, but if the Army's going after the Apaches, really trying to conquer them, it won't be much fun to be one!"

"No," agreed Irwin. "It won't."

Talitha and Caterina were picking currants along the creek in September when Talitha saw a pale gray horse coming. Judah Frost? Not wishing him to catch her alone, Talitha picked up the basket. "Let's go to the house, Cat. I think we have company."

"Dr. John?" cried the child eagerly. She still had a pointed chin and the dark peak of her hair increased the heart-shape of her face. She raced ahead, tanned legs flashing in the tall grass. "No!" she cried in mingled disappointment and fascination. "It's the silver man!"

That was her name for Frost. Though the twins continued to admire him, Cat refused to sit on his lap and watched him from the safety of Shea's proximity, or Talitha's, peering at him with the curiosity of one of the kittens she usually cuddled.

Shea had been working young horses in the corral. Leaving it to the vaqueros, he came, twins at his heels, to greet Frost. All of them came inside after the horse was cared for. Talitha let Caterina pass around the currants while she made coffee and started supper.

"This is for you, Talitha." Frost put a letter on the table. "Courtesy of the Jackass Mail, or if you prefer formality, the San Antonio and San Diego Mail Line! Started with pack mules this summer, but now they use coaches except for a hundred miles of sand west of Fort Yuma where the coaches have to be unloaded. Mules pack passengers and mail over that stretch, but from there on, it's coach all the way!"

"From your father?" Shea asked Talitha.

She nodded, glancing up. "He says he's selling his mining interests and taking up land north of the Gadsden Purchase. He's heard of a rich valley watered by the Verde River beneath the Mogollons."

"But that's really Indian country!" Shea protested.

"He knows that. But just as the Mormons in Utah generally have stayed friends with the Indians, he thinks he can live among them here."

"They don't have Apaches in Utah," Frost drawled. "Best send a letter back by me, Talitha, and try to dissuade him."

"And ask him to come and visit us," Shea urged. "He's welcome to stay here if he wants, or take up land close by."

"He seems set on this Verde River country," Talitha said. "But I'll write him. He does say he'll stop by here."

The thought panicked more than pleased her. Remembering Jared Scott made her uncomfortable. She knew she should love her father but she didn't know him, and even though she was old enough now to understand why, as a soldier, he'd had to leave his family, she would always in the deepest part of her, not reachable by fact, feel he'd abandoned them. At least he didn't talk about her living with him, apparently realizing it was too late for that. Talitha wished he'd just forget her.

Through supper, Frost gave news. The people at Tucson were angry that Fort Buchanan wasn't located nearer to them. A Collector of Revenue had moved into the big house at Calabazas and ran a little store as well as levying the twenty percent duty on goods from Mexico. Poston was elated at the arrival of more heavy mining equipment from the Missouri Valley, fetched in by twelve six-mule wagons by Santiago Hubbell. At a charge of $233 per ton, the wagons were freighting back very rich silver ore to Kansas City for assay. Poston wanted to spread Arizona's fame as a mining area.

"And we've sent another delegate to Washington to push for territorial status," Frost said. "Sylvester Mowry. He's soldiered around Yuma, believes in the region's future, and just resigned his lieutenancy, though he's a West Pointer, to be able to work for what we need."

"Will Congress seat him?" frowned Shea.

Frost shrugged airily. "Even if it doesn't, he's got powerful friends. He's from a wealthy Rhode Island family and has the backing of financiers from that state and a lot of Southern congressmen. Seated or not, he can get bills introduced, maybe even passed."

"Still trying for that railroad, Judah?" grinned Shea.

"We'll get it!" Frost reached inside his coat and produced some papers. "By the way, friend and partner, here are figures on your investments in the freighting and mining companies. Do you want a draft for your share of the profits or shall I get you some of Colonel Poston's bullion?"

"Why don't you just reinvest it?" Shea said carelessly.

"Fine. Revier's located a good prospect south of Yuma not too far from the *Camino del Diablo,* and the sooner we can start there, the better. Guess I'll go see him before I leave for Washington."

"You're going back there?"

The handsome silver head nodded incisively. "I'm going to lobby with all I've got for that railroad and a territory!" His almost colorless eyes flicked Talitha. "My wife is homesick, anyway. So we'll stay till spring."

Homesick? Had she begun to know what kind of husband she had? What *were* Frost's plans for Leonore now that his hope to lure Shea with her had failed? Talitha was suddenly afraid for the young woman who'd been so kind to her.

She didn't hear Shea's question till he put it twice. "Talitha, wouldn't you like to go to Washington? See the sights, do some shopping? Mrs. Frost suggested it, didn't she, Judah?"

"Indeed, she did," said Frost smoothly. "Why don't you, Talitha? You'd be the toast of Washington, with Leonore's sponsoring, and I assure you we won't be crowded in her father's mansion."

In front of Shea, Talitha could scarcely tell him she'd rather go to hell than spend months in his company. "I can't leave Caterina," she said.

"Sure, you can," urged Shea. "God's whiskers, Talitha, if Anita's too busy now she's got three little ones, we'll hire someone from Tubac. And there's plenty of money for you to pay your own way and get all the clothes you could want."

Talitha gave him a searching look. "Do *you* want me to go?"

"No, lass, but—"

"Then I'm staying here." She cleared the dishes, banging them more than necessary. "I wouldn't know what to do in a big city and wouldn't like it if I did!" Avoiding Frost's amused gaze, she added, "Please thank Mrs. Frost for me, though. And tell her I hope she'll enjoy the trip and come back well and happy."

After the slightest hesitation, Frost said, "I'll tell her."

Apart from the Army, most Americans coming to Arizona were merchants or miners, but at least one family settled there in 1857. Irwin told Talitha that a widower named Pennington with his twelve children and three wagons had been forced to drop out of a California-bound wagon train because one of the girls was sick. Elias Pennington must have had westering in his blood because he and his wife had left the Carolinas for Tennessee and that state for Texas, where Mrs. Pennington had died.

At the doctor's suggestion, the O'Sheas and Talitha rode over with him one Sunday to visit the new settlers, the twins on Thunder and Lightning, Caterina perched regally on Mancha, the black and white spotted mare she'd fallen in love with and insisted on having though Chuey and Rodolfo grumbled that such were fed to the hogs on Don Narciso's ranches. Azul was retired from working cattle though Shea still rode him for other purposes, as Talitha used Ladorada. For hard riding she was training a filly out of her beloved mare, named Ceniza because of her curious ash color.

It was the first time Talitha had seen Fort Buchanan. In spite of Irwin's grumblings, she was shocked. They had to splash through a *cienega* or marsh to reach the slope at the bottom of the foothills, and then crude huts were scattered over perhaps a half-mile without any apparent plan. Log barracks were being raised, some of peeled pine which Irwin expected to serve well, but he swore about the ones made of oak with the bark left on.

"Already decaying," he gritted. "And there's nothing I can say to convince the commander that heaps of manure and filthy pigpens breed more disease on top of the fevers from the marsh!"

The Penningtons were close to the fort. Their cabin looked sturdier than most of the fort buildings and comfortable with household things from the east gracing the rough homemade furnishings. The house seemed full of daughters. Eight of them, from pretty Larcena, who was about Talitha's age, on down. The younger girls swooped on Caterina at once. The four sons shook hands with Shea, bobbed their heads shyly at Talitha, and faded to the back of the room while Shea and Mr. Pennington got acquainted.

Larcena made coffee and the sisters passed around great pans of what they called cinnamon rolls. One, two, then three of them melted in Talitha's mouth. The ranch grew wheat, but the coarse flour produced by the little mill was nothing like this! The twins didn't stop at three rolls. Before they could gobble all of them, Talitha sent them to fetch the things she'd brought.

One of Pete Kitchen's famous hams, bacon from their own hogs, candied pumpkin, nut cakes, strings of chilies, bags of beans, parched corn, sunflower seeds, piñon nuts and dried peaches. Talitha answered eager questions about what some of the foods were and how to use them, adding that she'd be glad to show them where and when to gather wild foods.

"Nice folks," remarked Shea, as they left late that afternoon. "Pennington and his sons are supplying hay to the fort, and teaming. The girls do some sewing for Mrs. Steen and one or two other ladies."

"As if they didn't have enough sewing for themselves!" Talitha hooted, still overwhelmed by the enormous family.

"Pennington may be hard put to it to hold on to a housekeeper. The dragoons must be drawn to that house like bears to a honey tree. But it's good for you to have some females to visit with."

"We're all too busy for much of that," said Talitha. "But it's good to know they're close."

She saw Larcena again at Colonel Poston's Christmas party to which John Irwin escorted her. Larcena was with a young man named John Page, and from the way they looked at each other, it wouldn't be long till Elias Pennington lost a daughter.

Marc Revier was there. Talitha's heart skipped as she saw him. He made his way to her as she turned from Colonel Poston's gallantries, bowed and said to Irwin, "Well, doctor, I suppose I must thank you for bringing Miss Scott though I'd rather planned on having that pleasure myself as soon as I'd rested."

Irwin laughed. "It's lucky for you, Revier, that you were generous in letting me dance with her! Tonight you'll have your reward."

It felt good to see Marc, like a completeness, the easing of an ache so deep and masked she'd hardly known it was there till it stopped hurting. Taking one of his hands between hers, she cried, "Oh, Marc! It's been a whole year!"

"How well I know it." He was thinner, browner, and there were deeper lines in his face, but the blue of his eyes seemed even brighter. "And how has the year passed with you and all of the O'Sheas?"

"We've missed you sadly! Won't you come tomorrow and stay a few days?"

"I'll come, gladly, but will have to be off next morning. I'm checking on the Pajarito Mine while I'm here and can't leave the Tecolote very long. My assistant's honest but fresh from the East and I'd rather he learned his lessons while I'm around to keep them from being disastrous."

Pete Kitchen was there, and Doña Rosa; Charles Schuchard, Ehrenberg, Colonel Douglas, William Mercer, the Collector of Customs, and guests from Tucson and Mexico. The dress uniforms of the Fort Buchanan officers gave added swagger and this year there were imported wines and Scotch.

Through dinner and the dancing, the two men goodnaturedly vied for Talitha's attention. She had a marvelous time, though it wasn't the same as it had been the year before when Marc held her. The strength of his arm made her want to melt against him, close her eyes and follow his lead.

Once when she had been doing just that, she opened her eyes to find him watching her in a way that sent a deep, almost painful thrill through her. The pressure of his hand increased and her body brushed his.

"Marc," she breathed. "Marc, don't—"

"Don't what, Talitha? Love you?" His laughter was harsh. "I've tried all year to stop and what happens? One look at you and I'm deeper in than ever!"

She shook her head. "Please, Marc, don't make me feel guilty. I—I'm so glad to see you again. It doesn't seem right for you to be so far away."

"Yet you still won't come with me?"

She said desperately, "I like you so much! In a way, I must love you! But it's not what you want, not the way it should be."

He drew her out of the dancing, shielded her with his body. "Marry me and I'll take a chance on that!"

Frightened of the treacherous softness in her body, dismayed at the hunger in his eyes and hands, a hunger which by its very strength seemed to compel her to yield to it, she thought of Shea, invoked his branded face.

"Marc, I can't."

"You loved me tonight," he said beneath his breath. "I felt it in you."

"No!"

Anger stiffened him. His eyes veiled. "I'll take you to your escort. I'm going to be riding on to the Pajarito tonight."

"You—won't come tomorrow?"

"I won't. Much as I'd like to see the family, I can't be around you, Talitha. Especially now that you're lying to me and to yourself!"

"That's not fair! It's not true!"

"Maybe not fair, but it's true!" He paused by the door, his hand beneath her arm cruel in its grip. "If I took you to one of the rooms, Talitha, if I held you and loved you, you wouldn't stop me. Your body answers mine." He moved her grimly along toward John Irwin who was drinking with Poston. "But I don't want you that way. So I'll have none of you!"

He made his farewells to the two men, thanking Poston for the entertainment. "Give your family my greetings," he said to Talitha and started to go.

Did he mean he was dropping out of their lives for good? "Won't you come some other time?" she asked.

He shrugged. "It's a long way to the Tecolote."

Then he was gone, stiff-backed, and though Talitha danced with officers, engineers and ranchers, sipped the wine John Irwin brought her, and forced herself to laugh, for her the party was over.

Long after Irwin saw her to the room where she was staying, long after she was in bed, she thought of Marc riding through the cold night, and then, after his chores at the Pajarito, striking west for that deadly country where so many Gold Rushers had lost their lives, to thirst or the *Areneños*. She wouldn't even know if he'd reached the mine safely until some roundabout word came from Frost.

She didn't think she loved Marc. How could she, when she felt as she did about Shea? But she missed Marc terribly, not just his smile and voice, but the strength of his arms, the strange, exciting fire that had coursed between them. Most of all, he had been her trusted friend. She wept for that, far into the night.

"Red eyes, my dear," John Irwin said next morning as they were riding home. "Did that miner say something that I should be shooting him for?"

His tone bantered but there was an underlying steel in it. "He didn't say anything he didn't have a right to," Talitha admitted ruefully.

Irwin's eyebrows raised. "A right to make you cry?"

"I did that, John." She managed a shaky laugh. "If I won't marry him, I can scarcely expect him to be my friend if he finds it impossible. He says he does."

The doctor sighed and the storminess left his face. "So that's the way of it. Can't blame Revier, Talitha. You'll have to cry." His mood changed and he grinned at her, very handsome with his fringed gold epaulets

446

and plumed hat. "But why do that when you can smile at me?"

"You won't—" She broke off, flushing.

"Give you the either-or like Revier?" Irwin shook his head. "If you encouraged me, Talitha, who knows what would happen? But you won't and my instincts of self-preservation are pretty strong. I can be your friend and enjoy it. You may even," he offered outrageously, "cry on my shoulder about Revier while I tell you about the girl who jilted me!"

"John!" she giggled in spite of the tears pricking at her eyes. A rush of affection for the kind, gruff young redhead went through her. How lucky she was that he was of no mind to issue ultimatums! But even as they teased and talked, cantering in the bright frosty morning, deep within her, she longed for Marc.

Sylvester Mowry hadn't been seated by the House, and in spite of strong support from financiers and railroad interests, the bill for the organizing of Arizona Territory was voted down.

"But at least the El Paso–Yuma road's coming along," Irwin told Shea. "Leach, the superintendent, thinks it'll be done by summer. Nothing fancy, mind you, but wagons can get over it. Eighteen feet wide on the straightaway and twenty-five feet on curves."

Shea chuckled. "Reckon it'll be a long time before anyone'll have to worry about passing! But that's sure a long dry stretch."

"Leach is drilling wells and making cisterns to catch rainwater."

"God's whiskers!" complained Shea, but with a twinkle. "Soon won't take any kind of fiber to cross this country!"

"Just wait till Butterfield gets his Overland mail and passenger service running this fall!" The doctor added wryly, "There are still Indians to keep things lively. The news we get from Fort Fillmore near Mesilla is that a gang of toughs named the 'Mesilla Guards' are waylaying peaceful Mescaleros. Seems they agree with our ex-lieutenant Lowry who's all for extermination."

"It'll likely get worse before it gets better." Shea stared at the fire and Talitha knew he, too, was thinking of James and Mangus.

It was a strange year for Talitha, 1858. It was as if there were so many things she had to endure silently that her energy spent itself in that: in worrying over James, wondering why Santiago had never come to see them, grieving helplessly at Shea's use of mescal as his night companion, her aching for Marc.

Not that she acted sad or very often felt truly miserable. She did the work of the days and seasons, heard the children's lessons, and warmed herself by cuddling Caterina, and making up stories when she ran out of them. Warmed herself, too, by riding with John Irwin or showing him plants.

The Butterfield Overland Mail went into service that September between St. Louis and San Francisco. On its first return trip, Jared Scott stepped down at Tucson, slept in the plaza since there was no hotel, bought a horse next morning, spent that night at Tubac, and reached Rancho del Socorro at nooning.

Talitha didn't know him, the broad-shouldered man with an outthrusting red beard and hair that gray was starting to tame. Then, as he came toward her, she saw his eyes, warm russet, and he smiled, holding out his arms.

"Tally! Tow-headed as ever!"

It was like being hugged by a bear, but Talitha decided that she liked him. Shea welcomed him heartily, the vaqueros bowed, Patrick and Miguel stared at this father of the girl they considered their big sister, and Caterina was much intrigued with his watch and chain.

"For sure I'll never go back to California now!" he groaned laughingly as they all sat back to eat. "That stage! It has to cover twenty-eight hundred miles in twenty-five days or less which means jolting along at an average five miles per hour. The horses get changed at each relay, but the passengers don't."

He took a long drink of milk, having refused coffee, settled back and beamed. "But it's fast, and I'm finally here, and I do thank God for keeping you safe, Talitha!" He nodded to Shea. "I surely am thanking you also, sir, from the bottom of my heart." He glanced around, puzzled. "And where's your good wife?"

Shea's face paled. Stricken, Talitha said quickly, "She—she's dead, father."

His burly jaw dropped. He apologized hastily to Shea but Talitha braced herself for some questions. Scott went out with the men that afternoon to see the cattle, but he came in alone while Talitha was getting supper and watched her for a while with his big head at a worried tilt.

"When did Mrs. O'Shea die?"

"It's five years now. When little Cat was born." Talitha said it deliberately, reminding him that there were children dependent on her. "We had an Indian woman living here awhile, but since she left, I've managed with Anita's help."

"Don't take offense," this stranger-father rumbled, rubbing his neck. "But Mr. O'Shea's a young enough man that it don't seem fittin' for you to keep house for him."

Talitha gave him such a surprised look that he colored and fidgeted. "Don't be put out with me, honey. I know well enough these folks saved you from the heathen and when it comes right down to it, you know Mr. O'Shea a sight better'n you do me. But—"

Caterina chose that moment to come burrow her dark head against Talitha and peer out flirtatiously at this new man-creature. She still had that heart-shaped face clustered about with slightly curling black hair, and there was a translucent quality to the sun-kissed skin.

Giving her a hug and telling her to set the table, Talitha said gently to her father, "Shea does his best, but all three children need me, especially Cat. It's my chance to pay back what was done for me." She almost added: *and James,* though she checked in time. No use in inflicting that knowledge on Jared since James had apparently chosen to stay for good with the Apaches.

Jared nodded slowly. "You're right, Tally." He sighed, watching her as if trying to find in her face something he'd longed for. "I must give thanks to God for sparing you, at least." His shoulders slumped heavily and he stared out the door at the sunset. "Somehow, seeing you the age Judith was when we started keeping company brings it home. She's really gone. Not waiting somewhere."

Rising, he stumbled out the door.

He had supper with them, answered Shea's questions about California, and held Caterina on his knee, letting her listen to his watch tick. Though Shea urged him to stay as long as he wished, Scott, who'd slept in Tjúni's house which was now the twins' bedroom, left next morning after breakfast.

"I'll try to let you know where I'm situated," he said at parting. "But cut off like that Verde country is, I'd reckon we can't exchange news very often. Mr. O'Shea wouldn't take anything for your keep, Tally—said he was the one in debt. But keep these nuggets, and here's a little bag for each of the youngsters."

He gave her a small, heavy leather pouch and three smaller ones. Kissing his rough cheek, Talitha felt deep-buried grief stir. For several days after he rode away, she mourned silently for her mother who was dead, for James, gone away, and for this father she didn't know and for whom she'd had no comfort.

XXIX

A comet blazed that autumn and winter for several months. The vaqueros said it portended a disaster. One of sorts did befall the Santa Cruz Valley that December in the coming of the Vicar General of the Diocese of New Mexico, Father Joseph Machebeuf. Sent by Bishop Lamy to minister to the long-neglected people of Arizona, the vicar frightened all the couples Colonel Poston had married by declaring the marriages null and void.

In spite of this scorning of his authority, Poston cheerfully surrendered all the sheets and tablecloths that could be scrounged to make a confessional. Machebeuf held services, and after some discussion with Poston, consented to regularize the colonel's ceremonies for seven hundred dollars paid to the Church by the Sonora Exploring and Mining Company.

Poston was having trouble with his eyes as well as with Machebeuf. He went back east that Christmas and Arizona was left with no territorial official at all, though the Customs Collector and a notary public did perform marriages, as well as a Reverend Tuthill, a Methodist who preached at various ranches, at Tubac and at Fort Buchanan.

Eighteen fifty-nine was a strange period for the region. Mules, horses, cattle and oxen were driven off by Apaches and seldom recovered, though dragoons pursued when possible. Twenty head of cattle were stolen right out of the corral at Fort Buchanan. Fifteen were recovered, but a few days later three horses were successfully run off, and the next day, twelve more cattle.

The Pinal and Coyotero were after plunder but if

they happened on a small party, it was wiped out like that of two sergeants, recently honorably discharged after long service, who were killed only twenty-two miles from Fort Buchanan, barely started on their way back to the States.

Captain Ewell, now in command at the fort, was planning a campaign against the Apaches but couldn't get the necessary horseshoes, ammunition and equipment from the Santa Fe quartermaster. "Swear?" said John Irwin dryly. "What he says would take the scalp off an Indian! I look for him to burst an artery any day! What's worse, we're losing a company of dragoons and getting one of infantry! Infantry after Apaches!"

In spite of this constant danger and thievery, there were now seven farms along the Sonoita, and even a hotel a few miles from the fort, as well as one in Tubac.

Dr. C. B. Hughes had set up practice in Tubac though John Irwin, very skillful at amputations, still had numerous civilians come to him for help. There was a sutler's store at Fort Buchanan, and Fred Hulsemann, once of the ill-fated Calabazas ranching venture, now ran the Sonora Exploring and Mining Company's store in the old barracks.

The company flag flew above, and inside Hulsemann sold everything from calico to Colt's Navy pistols and carbines. He was also the postmaster and until a regular government route was put in service, the company sent mail to Tucson each Friday and returned with whatever the Overland Mail, East and West, had brought for the Tubac region.

A mescal distillery was located on the Sonoita, and the Findlay ranch near Calabazas was installing a grist mill with French burr stones which would certainly produce wheat flour fine enough for cakes and bread.

And there was a newspaper! On the third of March a young man named Edward Cross brought out the first *Weekly Arizonian* at Tubac. The four columns on each of the four pages were tightly packed with news of Indian depredations, mining, developments in Mexico and the States, advertisements for a hotel in El Paso, merchandise that could be ordered from Cincinnati, a druggist in San Francisco and the San Antonio–San Diego Mail line's schedule. The first issue also carried a notice of the death of James Gadsden, whose efforts had made the region part of the United States.

John Irwin brought the O'Sheas a copy and Talitha read it to Shea. He found it so interesting that he subscribed, and weeks when no one passed by to drop off his copy, he rode to Tubac after it.

Early in May, some Mexican workers murdered their employer, a young man named Byrd who had treated them well. They escaped to Mexico but gave an excuse for half a dozen Anglo toughs to terrorize the Mexicans in the region. They went along the Sonoita, driving away the workers, and at the mescal distillery, they killed four Mexicans and one Yaqui.

When the gang rode up to Rancho del Socorro, Shea and the vaqueros stood them off till they went on for easier pickings. Shea rode to the fort and Colonel Reeves, the new commander, sent fifteen troopers out to find the murderers, and soon captured three.

Shea attended a meeting in Tubac on May 14th when the leading citizens met to condemn the "Sonoita Massacre" and assure local Mexicans that such outrages would be punished and were not approved of by the citizenry. Copies of the proceedings were sent to officials in Sonoran towns, but in spite of this, many miners and laborers left Arizona.

The prisoners were sent to Mesilla for trial. That sort of distant justice brought on renewed demands for local courts and peace officers, which would increase through the summer, for it was a troubled one.

Apaches thieved on both sides of the border and Mexicans thieved in Arizona. The Overland Mail was harassed by Apaches who claimed they weren't getting enough rations and Mangus Coloradas closed up Apache Pass with stones.

Late that June some Mexicans were passing a farm near Tumacácori when some dogs barked at them. The men went at the dogs with knives, and when the owner of the house, John Ware, went out to see what was wrong, the men stabbed him. His partner, James Caruthers, came out, shot one Mexican and knocked down the one who began the attack, a Rafael Polanco.

The others ran. In spite of Dr. Hughes's efforts, Ware died the next night. Polanco was brought before a meeting of Santa Cruz Valley citizens, questioned and sent to Fort Buchanan with the request he be taken to Mesilla for trial.

The citizens' meeting went on to resolve that until regular courts were established, they'd organize temporary courts and deal justice to murderers, horse thieves and other criminals. They also elected a constable and a Justice of the Peace who proceeded immediately to try a case of theft.

The Justice, James Caruthers, who'd just seen his friend and partner die, sentenced a horse thief to receive fifteen lashes. These were meted out by the new constable and everyone, including Shea, rode home feeling that they had taken an important step in bringing order to a region rapidly filling up with every kind of thief and killer run out of California and Mexico.

In reading Shea the paper having the account of the meeting, Talitha skipped the story of how a dragoon deserter from Fort Buchanan had been court-martialed and sentenced to fifty lashes, branding with the letter D, confinement, heavily ironed, at hard labor, and to be drummed out of the service.

It was interesting, in July, to read a brief notice of the duel fought between Cross, the *Arizonian*'s editor, who opposed Arizona's being a separate territory, and Sylvester Mowry, who advocated it. Burnside rifles at forty paces. The first shots were harmless; on the second round, Mowry's rifle failed to discharge. He was given another shot which Cross waited for, without arms. Mowry fired into the air, and all concerned retired to the company store for a drink, the two principals inserting a notice in the paper retracting their earlier insults.

A few weeks later, Mowry bought the paper and moved it to Tucson. He was again elected delegate for Arizona, but for the third time, he wasn't seated, though he did succeed in getting ten bills introduced for the admission of Arizona as a territory. All of these were defeated and by spring of 1860, Arizonans decided to set up a provisional government.

In March, Mesilla deposed New Mexican appointees and elected their own. Further west, it was planned to hold a convention in Tucson April 2nd through 5th, but for a time people were more concerned with the fate of Larcena Page, Elias Pennington's daughter.

She was living with her lumberman husband in a cabin at the mouth of a cañon leading to the pines of the Santa Ritas. One morning after Page went to his work, Larcena and a ten-year-old Mexican girl who lived with them were getting ready to do the washing when Apaches carried them off.

As soon as the alarm was spread, dragoons and volunteers combed the area, and though they followed the trail, they never caught up with the abductors.

Two weeks later, Pinals brought the child to Captain Ewing, saying they'd taken her away from some Tontos and that Larcena had been killed.

For a wonder, she wasn't. Sixteen days after her capture, Larcena dragged herself across the trail the lumbermen must follow and they carried her home more dead than alive, though she recovered to tell what had happened after the Apaches took her.

She'd been weak from recent fever and ague, not able to keep up, and by sunset, her captors decided to kill her. Stripping off all but one garment, they thrust their lances into her, wounding her eleven times, threw her over a rock ledge and hurled big stones after her to finish the murder.

Landing in a bank of snow, she lay there unconscious

for several days, but when she roused, she cleaned her wounds with snow, thought about the direction the Apaches had driven her, and where the sunset was in connection with the cabin.

Almost naked, barefoot, she had to crawl when her feet gave out and scratch holes in the sand to sleep in at night. On the fourteenth day, she found a lumberman's camp and a little flour. She ate this and though she was too weak to go the few more miles to her home or the lumbermen, she did drag herself out to the road.

When they heard that Larcena was back, Talitha and Shea rode over to see her, taking gifts of food. Having eaten nothing but grass for over two weeks, Larcena was emaciated and she would carry the scars of her fearful wounds to her grave. One of her sisters had come to nurse her, but she was glad to see Talitha. Talitha held her hand and they stayed like that till Shea said it was time to go.

"Poor lass!" he muttered, as they started home. "Won't there ever be any safety here? Why was the United States so set on having this country if it didn't intend to protect the people? Now that they've replaced one company of dragoons with one of infantry, Fort Buchanan's even worse off than it was."

"Do you think the provisional government will do any good?"

With a shrug he answered, "It can't make things any worse than they are, that's certain!" He stiffened at the sound of hoofbeats, pulled his carbine out of the sling, then stared in gleeful surprise at the approaching horseman.

The mist-gray horse cantered lightly along the creek bottom, rutted now by the stage that traveled from Tucson to Fort Buchanan. The horseman swept off his fawn-colored hat, but even before that Talitha recognized him.

"Judah!" Shea called. He rode alongside and clasped hands, slapping the other man's shoulder. "What brings you, man? Or more like, what's kept you away so long?"

"Oh, I've been busy in Washington during the legislative sessions. And last summer Leonore had a passion to see Paris and London again." He shook his silver head. "Poor Leonore! So happy, expecting our first child. I hope she never knew she lost it when she fell down a wicked flight of stairs. She died an hour later."

"Judah!" breathed Shea, paling. "That sweet young lady! Sorry I am, man!"

Frost looked down like one controlling grief. "I try to remember that she had no pain. The fall paralyzed her. And I believe, with the child coming, she was happier than she'd ever been in what was a remarkably happy, though short, life." He paused. "It's been some months now. I'm more—philosophical."

Shea nodded gratefully. "It's good to see it like that. And it's good to have you back. Did you get to Tucson in time for the convention?"

"Be sure I did!" Judah smiled. "Thirty-one delegates from thirteen towns voted to establish a provisional territorial government to function until the federal government gives us one."

"How are they going to finance it? Tax on top of the customs we already have to pay for what we're forced to import from Mexico?"

"That's one of the big questions," grinned Frost. "I'm heading back to Mesilla to look things over and see what should be done. Maybe this will convince Congress that Arizona can't be governed out of Santa Fe and they'll give us our rights during the next session."

He went on to tell how "Baldy" Ewell and his dragoons had brought in the little Mexican girl, Mercedes Quiroz, who'd been captured with Larcena Page and given to Ewell by the Pinals.

Church bells had been rung and everyone gathered in the plaza to welcome the child and her escort. As many as could crowded into the church, a small house enlarged with a porch by Father Machebeuf when he found the old church too ruined for use. Young Mercedes knelt at the altar and the whole populace joined in thanks for her rescue.

"Ewell was quite the hero," Frost said. "They gave him a place of honor at the convention and proposed to name one of the new counties after him; in fact they laid it on so thick that the good captain retired in confusion. But he enjoyed the big dance got up that night in his honor." His cold eyes rested on Talitha. "So you've been to visit the other captive?"

"Yes." Talitha spoke shortly. She was stunned by the news of Leonore's death, and didn't believe Frost's account of it though she couldn't think that even he would murder lovely, warm-hearted Leonore.

"A wonder Mrs. Page lived," he mused. "She's lucky the Apaches don't scalp the way Comanches do or she'd have to comb her hair over a bald spot for the rest of her life."

He went on to say the freight line was doing well and that Marc Revier had three mines operating in the mountains south of Yuma. "I need to see him, too, before I go to Mesilla," Frost said. He glanced quizzically at Talitha. "I can scarce credit that he hasn't been to see you since I left these parts!"

"He came to Colonel Poston's Christmas party that year," shrugged Talitha. "I haven't seen him since."

Not to anyone, much less to Frost, would she try to explain how forlorn and desolate Marc's anger had left her. But sometimes even now, after all these months, she dreamed of his hard arms holding her, his mouth turning her blood to sweet fire. She never thought that way about Shea; it would have been a kind of sacrilege to imagine him loving her with his body until he wanted that himself.

It was sundown when they rode up to the corrals. Rodolfo took Ceniza whom Talitha had taken for the long trip instead of Ladorada, and Talitha hurried in to start supper with no real hope that Cat would have left off tagging the twins in time to put the *pozole* on to cook.

She had, though, and was engaged in trying to make tortillas with dough that was too watery. Meal was stuck at the edges of her silky hair where she'd pushed it back impatiently and when Talitha came in, she sighed between relief and exasperation.

"Help me, Tally! This old stuff sticks and sticks! Patrick said I couldn't do it but Miguel thought I could!"

"You can," promised Talitha. "You can do the hard part, pat out the tortillas. We just need more meal, like this."

Correcting the *masa,* she joined in the tortilla making. Cat rubbed her hands till they were free of dough, took a piece and started over. Talitha nodded approval as the thin round cake took shape. "Your mother never really learned to make tortillas, Cat. She'd be proud of you."

Patrick burst in the front door, followed by Miguel. When they weren't tumbling in a Patrick-instigated jumble, that was their usual order of progression. At eleven-and-a-half, Patrick came to Talitha's shoulder and was thin and wiry. Miguel was a fraction shorter and his bones were covered in a supple way that reminded her of Santiago.

Santiago, gone so long with never a word! Marc also. Talitha pushed that lingering sadness away and thought, as she watched the boys, that Socorro would have been proud of them, too, handsome, eager, spirited as young colts.

"I knew you'd need Tally!" Patrick whooped.

"She didn't!" defended Miguel. "Look at that tortilla!"

"Look at the *masa* all over her face!" jeered Patrick. At the sound of voices, he ran to the door to the courtyard. "Why, it's Mr. Frost!"

He pelted out but Miguel, frowning, scraped his sister's face clean of the scrappy meal and started setting the table.

"The silver man?" asked Caterina, jumping up, running to peer out.

In a moment Patrick brought Frost in and Shea poured him a drink while he told Caterina how she'd grown and answered Patrick's breathless questions, behaving like an old, trusted friend. But his eyes, when Talitha met them once, were chill as winter ice.

Had Leonore fallen? Or been pushed? And now that she was out of the way, did he remember his one-time plans for Talitha? She was twenty that month. There was no longer any reason for him not to begin his wooing. When she refused him, what would he do?

Cold to the heart, Talitha put leftover venison on the table, the kettle of *pozole,* and tortillas. She sat as far as she could from Judah Frost but even with Patrick, Cat and Belen between them, she still felt his eyes.

Shea and Frost sat talking long after the twins and Cat had gone to bed. Though she hated being around the man who had menaced her since the day he caught her in the hot spring below the Place of Skulls, Talitha preferred to know what he was saying and doing while at the Socorro, but his talk of railroads and politics, after the long ride to visit Larcena, made her sleepy, and, stifling a yawn, she put down the dress she was letting out for Cat, said good night and went out through the courtyard. A figure rose out of the shadows.

Before she could cry out, hard fingers pressed on her mouth, but lightly. "Talitha!" the man whispered. "Don't say anything! I must settle with him in there, that Judah Frost! But I had to see you first. Just a moment. My God, you've grown up beautiful!"

"Santiago!" She kept her voice down, though she was light-headed with joy. "So Frost *did* lie! What happened?"

"You'll hear about that when I call him." Hands she

460

remembered from childhood smoothed her face. "Will you kiss me, Talitha?"

She went into his arms. He gave her a lover's kiss, sighed and turned toward the door. As he stepped inside, his face was a rigid mask darkened by shadows, but the candlelight doubled the blaze of his golden eyes.

"So you're here, Señor Frost, Señor Scalp Hunter." Santiago's voice rasped like a snake in dead leaves. "I do not have to hunt you, then." He came forward, a Bowie in his hand. "Don Patrick, you must learn how our partner bribed officials into accepting that I was a bandit and condemning me to slave labor in the mines. Six years of it!"

Shea stood as thunderstruck as Talitha, who had followed Santiago inside. Frost had risen. A little smile played about his lips though his revolver was hung by the door.

"I would have died long ago, my partner," went on Santiago, yellow eyes fixed on him, "if I hadn't endured in order to kill you. You didn't need to taunt me by saying you were with the scalp hunters who destroyed the ranch of the Cantús!"

"One of *those* scalp hunters?" Shea choked.

Santiago's lips parted tightly over his teeth. "And one of those who killed Tjúni's people! The only one who escaped her arrows and those of Doña Socorro."

"I heard the Yaquis in your region were rebelling," said Frost conversationally. "I wondered if you might be among the convicts they freed. But then I was sure the overseers would have finished you years ago."

"The Yaquis freed and fed me till I was strong again." Santiago shifted the knife. The light streamed off it in a point of trembling fire. "Go outside, Talitha," he said. "You must not see this. Don Patrick, give him a knife."

Frost held out his hand as if to receive a weapon, but in a twinkling, there was a puff of smoke. He held a small gun that must have been up his sleeve.

A hole appeared between Santiago's eyes. He took a staggering leap forward, crashed to the floor. Both Shea and Frost made for the guns by the door, but Frost was closer. Grabbing his revolver, he clicked the hammer on the empty, and fired the second cartridge as Shea snatched down a rifle.

Spun halfway around by the shot's impact, Shea fell, bleeding from the shoulder. Talitha reached for his rifle but Frost caught her arm, wrenched her forward.

"Listen, partner," he told Shea. "Don't follow me, you or your men, and I'll leave the girl safe at some ranch. She dies if you come after us."

Sweat stood out on Shea's face. "You hurt her and I'll find you even if you're in hell!"

"You'll try that anyway, won't you, for the sake of your friend?" Frost nudged Santiago's body with the toe of his elegant boot. "No, all I need's a few days' start. If you wish to track me, then, on the Devil's Road, the best of luck to you!"

As Belen ran in, Chuey and Rodolfo behind him, Frost held the revolver to Talitha's ear. Under this threat, he made Chuey securely tie the other vaqueros and then marched him down to saddle horses. When this was done, Frost's bedroll and canteens secured, Chuey was compelled to tie Talitha in the saddle. Then Frost crashed the revolver down on the vaquero's head.

"Let's ride," he said to Talitha.

Mounting, he took Ceniza's reins. They moved swiftly into the dark night.

She must be dreaming. Santiago dead? Shea bleeding? The man in front of her a scalp hunter? But it was no nightmare. Rawhide bit into her wrists though Chuey had tried to tie her loosely. Tied to either stirrup, her ankles chafed.

Shea was wounded in the shoulder, but unless it gangrened he wouldn't die from that. Santiago's wound looked fatal. And all these years of his slavery, everyone had believed him happily married and forgetful of his old friends. Rage at that and his cruel, sudden death warmed Talitha.

"The dragoons will be after you," she cried above the sound of the horses. "And we've a Justice to hang you here; you won't have a chance to get away on the road to Mesilla!"

"That red-headed Irish surgeon can look after Shea, but no one's coming after me till they know you're safe."

"So long as you're taken, I don't care what happens to me."

"Don't you, my dear? We'll see about that!" He laughed softly. "I'll leave you at some ranch as I said I would, but I'll be back for you when circumstances are less pressing."

"Shea will trail and kill you if the dragoons don't."

"Good luck to him, if he can," said Frost airily. "Whatever happens, before I leave you this time, I'm going to have you, Talitha." He laughed at her involuntary sharp intake of breath. "You may decide you'd like to come with me."

For a moment she thought of feigning, pretending willingness till he relaxed and gave her a try at a weapon, but her horror of him was so great that she knew she couldn't deceive him. She nerved herself to seize any glimmer of opportunity, though.

If he got his head start into the fierce country of the *Camino del Diablo,* he might never be found.

Marc Revier, unsuspecting, would give him provisions, and from Fort Yuma he could go overland to California or take a boat down the Colorado to the Gulf. Or he could go south on the Devil's Road and lose himself in Mexico. There was every good chance that he'd get away unless she could stop him.

How?

Assessing matters, she decided she'd just have to act quickly if any chance came.

Her thoughts kept going back to Shea. Thank goodness, John Irwin was good at probing and he'd do his best for Shea. But she wished she could have helped.

And Santiago . . . If only he could have been back with them awhile, if the bitterness of his captivity could have been a little forgotten among his friends, if he could have known Cat and enjoyed the twins! There'd be none of that now. But at least she had kissed him.

"The gun you used on Santiago," she said slowly. "It's very small."

"But, as you've seen, it kills. Mr. Henry Deringer of Philadelphia made this one. No good for distance, but effective across a card table or a bed."

"Do you still have your scalping knife?"

"What a lurid mind you have! I never scalped anyone. Left it to the others." He chuckled. "Fair money while it lasted."

"I hope they remember to tell Tjúni about you! If word about you gets around the Papagos, there won't be anything left for Shea or the dragoons!"

He said, strangely, "You hate me so much that taking you should be exquisite pleasure."

They rode in silence after that, past the hotel, Findlay's ranch, Calabazas, barked at by dogs, but unchallenged. He let her drink once and relieve herself but stayed beside her.

Going west from the river, Frost led Ceniza onward, into the mountains. Night changed to gray light, the east began to flush, fingers of dark cloud kindled and the sun hurled itself above the mountains.

"This is far enough," Frost said.

He turned to her with a smile.

XXX

He took her, grinding her body between his and the blanket tossed on the sand of a dry wash. Talitha was glad of the pain which kept her from thinking. She fought him savagely but he only laughed, pinioned her arms more cruelly and kept himself locked inside her wildly threshing body.

Then as something gripped him, as he swore, moaning, holding her as he drove sledgingly for his release, she knew beneath her shock and dread that there must be for him, after this, a moment of rest, a time of recovery.

How could she use it?

She didn't know where the little gun was, but the revolver should have several more cartridges in it, perhaps even four. It lay on his trousers a few yards away.

Talitha endured the hurtful thrusts, waiting. His rhythm faltered. "Fight me, damn you!" he gritted. "Fight me!"

The brutal hardness inside her was softening. This man had not had his fulfillment—*could* not, she realized with bitter triumph, unless she gave him her struggles.

She laughed softly, tauntingly, but couldn't afford to enjoy his humiliation if she wanted to seize that moment he would be disarmed by gratified lust.

It wasn't hard to battle him. She tried to bite his wrists that clamped her arms, writhed and twisted, and as she did her best to unseat him, yielding to her hatred, she restored his weapon and he pierced her with it, thrusting with mounting need till he cried out, shuddered and collapsed on her.

His weight pinned her. He lay like one dead. She felt smothered by his breath, drenched by his slime. To give him his pleasure and then not be able to take advantage of his slackening! She could have wept.

She searched the area she could see with her uncovered eye, but there was nothing with which to attack him. Then his exhaustion was over. He raised on an elbow to caress her body, smiling as she set her teeth and managed not to flinch from his cold deft hands.

"You suit me well," he said. His fingers touched her throat, gently, absentmindedly pressured. "Lucky for you to have kept virgin. Otherwise, I'd cut your throat. I claimed you for myself when you were a child. I'll be back for you."

"Yes, come!" she spat at him. "Come so they can kill you!"

He laughed and took her again. This time her battling wasn't calculated. It was a despairing frantic attempt to be free of him. The end came quickly. Again his weight made it impossible to move with stealth.

"I wish I could keep you with me another day but you might not be able then to get back to safety—and I want you safe, Talitha, until I come after you."

Hurt, battered, she opened her eyes and wished her hate could blast him dead. "I can get over this. It was something you did, not my fault. But I'll never live with you. I'd rather die."

"I think I can change your mind when the time comes." He handed her his canteen again. "Sorry I can't feed you but I'm short on rations. Follow this wash, my dear. It'll bring you to the Kitchen ranch and Doña Rosa will fuss and feed you while old Pete swears and gets up a crowd to chase me! Put on your clothes and start walking."

"You're keeping my horse?"

"Just long enough to trade it for food and whatever loot I can get. Don't want you reaching Kitchen's too fast."

She threw the canteen at him, ducked and reached

for the gun. Her fingers almost closed on it before he kicked it away, numbing her hand where his boot grazed it. Scooping up the heavy revolver, he held it while he pulled on his trousers.

"No more tricks, my sweet, or I'll tie you up and you can just lie here hoping your friends find you before some bandit or Apache does!"

There was nothing she could do but put on her clothes. A little way down the wash, she turned to look at him. "I hope you do come back," she said. "I want to kill you!"

"You won't do that, love. You'd hate for Shea to join Santiago." His soft mocking laughter echoed in her ears as she made her aching despoiled body move along the dry watercourse.

He's hurt me, she thought. *Forced himself inside me where only the man I love should have gone. But I can wash away the blood. The pain will go. It wasn't my fault, I didn't cause it. It was like being struck by lightning or dropped on by a wildcat. It is a wound like any other. I won't let it fester and turn me sick. No. What matters is that Santiago is dead. I must hurry so the men can go after Frost!*

Kilting up her skirts, she ran. When she was gasping, she walked, and when she had her breath, she ran again.

Grain and other crops greened the rich bottom land overlooked by Kitchen's fortified house on a hill, with a small graveyard beneath it. As Talitha approached, the watchman on the parapet shouted and in what seemed a twinkling, Indians materialized from fields and the direction of the buildings, enclosing her as Kitchen himself came out, squinting till he recognized her.

"Miss Scott! The Apaches get you?"

Shaking her head, she gasped out what had happened except for what Frost had done to her. Doña Rosa hurried to her, made her come inside and gave her strong coffee.

"I'll send a couple of my Opatas to tell Mr. O'Shea you're safe," said Kitchen. "But I'll get after that scoundrel with my best trackers. He won't have more than a six-hour start. A couple of my men know that Devil's Road pretty well. We should take him."

"Shouldn't you send to Fort Buchanan?" Talitha asked.

"Can't hurt though by the time they get in action, Frost will be caught or gone for good. Might as well alert our constable, too." Kitchen eyed her keenly. "Want a drink of mescal, girl? You look all done in."

"If I could just rest a little . . . And would you have your men watch out for my horse? She's sort of a creamy gray."

"Don't you worry, you won't have to walk home!" he assured her, giving her hand a rough pat.

He strode off to see to the expedition. At once, a wooden tub appeared and half a dozen girls of all ages trooped to it with buckets and gourds of water, hot and cold, while others went on with their carding, sewing and spinning.

"My nieces," smiled Doña Rosa. "They make our home happy and help me with the work." She sprinkled a handful of mint in the water, put out a bar of soap, and arranged a screen so Talitha could bathe in privacy. "We'll wash your clothes," she said, draping a clean cotton skirt and blouse over the screen. "Wear these till your things dry."

If she noticed there were no bleeding cuts on Talitha while there was blood on her clothing, she was too wise and kind a woman to force confidences.

The hot herb bath took away all of Frost's smell and much of Talitha's soreness. Dressed in her borrowed clothes, she wasn't hungry when she first sat down to the meal Doña Rosa urged on her, but the tantalizing smell of bacon lured her to begin and she was soon relishing it along with fried potatoes, a delicacy she'd never tasted except at Poston's last Christmas party, since Shea flatly refused to have potatoes grown at So-corro.

"I'll have their taste in my mouth when I die," he'd said when John Irwin mentioned they did well in the region. "Treacherous they are, too. I still smell them rotting in the ground while my mother starved to death."

There was peach conserve, crusty bread and a spicy, refreshing herb tea. When Talitha could eat no more, one of the nieces took her to a room with several beds. Talitha lay down on one and slept so quickly and so soundly that she later was sure that Doña Rosa had given her a sleeping draught.

She didn't wake till twilight. For a moment, she didn't know where she was, or even who she was, but her senses were reclaimed abruptly by herself when she knew Shea's voice, recognized it before she could have given her own name.

He shouldn't be riding yet! Sitting up, she tensed against the bruised ache between her legs, put on her sandals and hurried through the hall to the *sala*.

Shea started to rise at sight of her, but she pushed him back. Beneath his shirt, his shoulder was bandaged and his arm hung in a sling. Scanning her, he saw a clean, rested young woman and visibly relaxed.

"I hoped Frost would leave you here, lass, but how glad I was to know you were safe!"

"You ought to be home in bed!" she scolded. "Is your arm hurt, too?"

"No, the sling's just to keep it from flapping around and aggravating the shoulder. John Irwin says I'm lucky the shot missed the socket." In spite of his grin, he was pallid. "Belen's with me. Can't track in the dark but we'll leave at first light tomorrow."

"Shea, Mr. Kitchen and six of his men have gone after Frost. They left about noon. If they don't find him, you can't! And you shouldn't be jostling that wound!"

"There'll be dragoons after him, too, but that doesn't

mean he's not my job." Shea's eyes smoldered with blue fire. "Frost killed my friend after making him a slave. All that might never have happened if I hadn't thought Frost was such a fine fellow. No, Tally, I'm going after Frost. I intend to kill him."

No use arguing. Talitha only hoped Kitchen's men had already caught up with Frost and that by the time Shea reached them, there'd be nothing left for him to do.

An Opata had brought in Talitha's horse. Escorted by two of Kitchen's most trusted men, Talitha left for home next morning shortly after Shea and Belen rode west.

Santiago was already buried, up on the hill beside Socorro. Trudging up there with Caterina and the twins, Talitha planted wild flowers on the grave and hoped that Socorro had met his spirit and taken him into that unknown world.

Two of the four who had started Rancho del Socorro lay under its earth and Tjúni was gone to her own portion. It must make Shea feel lonely. Talitha knelt, arms encircling Cat and the boys, and seemed to feel, in the sun and gentle breeze, the feel of Socorro's hand, the loving in her smile.

Be with Santiago. Please be with us.

Though no one had said so, Talitha had believed for some time that Socorro had been raped by those *Areneños* who killed her father. It hadn't blighted her, though. Rising, Talitha felt comforted by her foster mother.

I'll do my best for your children, she promised. *Just as you did for James and me. And please understand about Shea. I would never have loved him like this if you hadn't had to go away. You were his miracle, his only one.*

John Irwin was vastly relieved to find Talitha at home when he rode over from Fort Buchanan that night. "I wanted the worst way to go with Shea or the search party," he said, holding her hands as if afraid she'd vanish. "But I had several people who were close to dying and I couldn't leave them."

He swore when he learned that Shea had gone in pursuit of Frost, then tried belatedly to hide his concern. "He's a tough Irishman, Talitha. May take his shoulder longer to heal than if he'd been sensible, but he'll be all right." Still holding one of her hands, he let out a gusty breath. "When I heard that blackguard had carried you off, I thought I'd go crazy! Hope Kitchen's already caught up with him and hung him!"

He didn't stay long after that, saying he had to look in on some patients but would come over a week from Sunday if he could. She had to send for him earlier, for ten days after her abduction, Marc Revier and Belen brought Shea home, delirious and fevered.

Areneños had killed Frost, borrowing a trick from the Apaches to roast him head first over a small fire so that his face was charred past recognition. But the man wore Frost's clothes and the remains of his gray horse, evidently feasted on, lay close by. Kitchen found and buried the ruined body and pushed on to the Tecolote mine for water and food. They were on their way back to the Santa Cruz when they met Shea and Belen.

Shea was already running a fever and in pain from his shoulder. Kitchen guarded him the short way to the Tecolote and urged Marc to keep him quiet till his wound healed, but as soon as the fever went down, Shea had insisted on starting out.

"He was upset over not avenging Santiago himself," Marc explained. "And he seemed worried about you though he said Frost hadn't hurt you."

She couldn't meet Marc's deep blue eyes, busied herself with sponging Shea's hot face and chest. Chuey had already been sent for John Irwin.

"Thanks for bringing him home," she said, trying not to cry as she watched Shea's gaze fix on something beyond her. "He—he will get better, won't he?"

"Of course! I think the wound was healing when jolting along tore it open again. Now he's content to rest, he'll be good as new in no time."

But Shea wasn't resting. His hands worried the sheet, he tossed constantly, and when Talitha got him to drink some willow tea, he thought she was Socorro. Desperate, she gave him a brew of one of Nōnó's sedative herbs and that sent him into heavy slumber.

Anita had cooked supper and Marc made Talitha eat while Cat curled up on her father's bed and assured Talitha that *she'd* take care of him.

When Irwin came, he took off the old bandage, cleaned away pus and dead flesh while Talitha held the basin, and doused the wound with mescal which brought Shea up cursing him for some sergeant of over a dozen years ago.

Caterina refused to go but held her father's head, whispering to him soothingly through her tears.

"Keep him as quiet as you can," the young doctor said. "Make him drink a lot and feed him only broth till the fever's down." He frowned at Talitha. "Can you dress the shoulder? It'll be draining for a few days."

She nodded. Though the ugly wound sickened her, it had been worse, much worse, to watch Socorro bleed to death, or Shea branded. Over her shoulder, Irwin looked at Marc Revier.

"You can stay awhile?"

"I've got a good assistant."

"Marc," protested Talitha, "you mustn't—"

"Of course I must. Besides, now that you and the O'Sheas hold the main interest in the mine, we need to talk about that when Shea's able."

"I'll come Sunday unless everyone at the fort comes down sick," the doctor promised. "Send for me earlier if the wound looks tainted."

After coffee and a stout drink of mescal, he rode back to the post. The twins had gone sleepily to their little house, and Caterina, pale after Shea's ordeal, had collected an armload of kittens and gone off to bed.

Marc brought Talitha a glass of water and mescal.

"Drink it," he ordered when she made a face at the sting of it. "Your nerves need settling."

"It'll make me sleepy. I've got to sit up with Shea."

"No. I'll sleep in his room and I'm so used to keeping an ear cocked for bandits or *Areneños* that he won't stir much without rousing me."

"But you must be tired!"

"I'll catch up tomorrow. Makes no sense for both of us to be sleepy."

That was sensible and he was solid and sure and kind; his eyes were so deeply blue they hurt her, and she'd missed him terribly. Tears welled up in her eyes. "It's so awful, Marc. If Santiago could only have been home with us awhile, if we could have made him happy again—"

"Ifs are no use, darling." Kneeling by her so that she had to meet his gaze, this one of the men she loved said grimly, "Frost took you, didn't he? Is that your wound, Talitha, why you won't look at me?"

She wanted to tell someone. It had been a secret poison the healing air and light couldn't reach. Yet she was ashamed for him to know, and for Shea it could only be a grief, something to add to the guilt he felt for accepting Frost.

"Talitha?" Marc insisted. He took her face between his hands and kissed her. Gently, cherishingly. "Oh, my love, you don't have to bear it alone. You *are* strong and brave, but use my strength, too; let me help you."

So she told him. Everything, from the time Frost found her at the spring. "If I had warned Shea and Santiago then, maybe they could have killed him. Maybe none of this would have happened. Leonore might even be alive. But I was so afraid Frost would kill Shea!" A new dread plunged her into deeper self-accusation. "Marc! If Frost hadn't wanted me—"

"Stop that!" He closed her mouth with his and this time there was passion and longing and anger in his kiss, along with the tenderness that never left him. "I've suspected that Judah had strange tastes, but to lust for a thirteen-year-old! Don't blame yourself for his craziness."

"But—"

"If you'd told your menfolk, the only way they could have killed an expert like Judah would be to shoot first, ambush him. You know they wouldn't do that, just because he'd made threats that might have been exaggerated by the mind of a young girl."

"I should have done something! It—it was like letting everybody think we had a harmless snake in the house when I knew he was a rattler!"

Marc shrugged. "He was gone most of the time. You naturally hoped he just wouldn't come back. Don't brood over that, Talitha. Your men wouldn't have killed him without warning. With warning, he was sure to get at least one of them, possibly both." He drew her to her feet. "And now it's time for you to sleep."

In confessing to him, she felt as if a great load had dropped from her. She felt now an overwhelming need to be cleansed of Frost, to have his piercing of her obliterated. Looking straight up at Marc, touching the scar that crossed his cheek and brow, she said, "Please love me, Marc. Lie down with me and love me!"

He went rigid. His breath caught in. "Are you sure?"

In a way, she wasn't. Her body still ached from Frost's ravishing. She passionately wished to blot out that possession but knew she must be honest with Marc.

"This doesn't mean I love you," she said painfully, reaching for his hand. "But I need you! Oh, Marc, help me. Make me clean again."

For a moment, she thought he would refuse, but then he moved with sudden resolution, got his bedroll, spread it in the *sala*. At first it disturbed her that Shea was right behind the wall, and she tried to hurry Marc, but he kissed her into quiescence before he let his trembling hands smooth her, caress her with a reverential joy that made her glow, come alive with charged tension.

When at last he took her, there was only a second of fright, a moment's memory of pain, and then he was marking her with new feelings, laving her secret parts with his loving, dissolving the cruelty and contempt that Frost had marked her with.

In peace, they rested in each other's arms till Shea grew restless. Then Talitha dressed and brought him more of Nōnó's sleeping brew before Marc walked her to her room. She slept well that night for the first time since her drugged sleep at Doña Rosa's.

By the time John Irwin came on Sunday, Shea's fever was down and the shattered flesh was starting to knit. "In a few days, your worst problem will be keeping him quiet," the doctor grinned. "My opinion is that people heal faster if they do move around once they feel like it, but don't let him out to rope or ride till that hole closes!"

He turned a quizzing eye on the engineer. "How long can that mine manage without you?"

"We'll find out, won't we?" retorted Marc.

After Irwin had gone, he took Talitha's hand and kissed it slowly. They had made love every night, naturally, with no questions or discussion, though he must know now that what had begun as Talitha's desperate need to erase her body's violation had become as ecstatic for her as it was for him.

"Our handsome doctor fancies you himself," Marc said with a twinkle. "He'll be glad to see the last of me and I must go as soon as Shea can talk business."

He drew Talitha against him. His head rested against her breasts. She trembled at the warmth of his breath through the cloth. "Will you tell him, Talitha? Or shall I?"

Warning ran through her. She stiffened. "Tell him what?"

"Why, about us." Marc frowned up at her, puzzled. "That we want to marry."

She blinked. The thought hadn't entered her mind,

but she knew now that it should have. She'd been blindly selfish, healing her hurts with Marc's love, not thinking ahead. Carefully she said now, "Marc, I—I'm sorry. I can't marry you."

He put her from him, stood up and moved away. As if only then could he trust himself to look at her, he faced about. "Why not? You can't think because Frost—"

She shook her head. "I know you'd have me in spite of that. But I can't leave Shea and the children."

"Shea, you mean."

Helplessly, she spread her hands. "I told you that—what we've done—didn't mean I loved you."

He put clenched fists behind him. She knew he was making a tremendous fight for control, hated herself for his pain, yet there was nothing she could do.

"You love me," he said wonderingly. "I'm not wrong about that. I know you love me."

She nodded, swallowing. "But I love Shea, too. I loved him first, all these ways and all these years."

Marc gave an abrupt nod. "Finally I understand. Shea is god to you. I'm only a man."

She put out her hands in pleading, but Marc turned away. "I'm getting back to the mine. When Shea's well enough, you and he can decide if you want to make any changes in the mining company. Since Frost has no known survivors, I'd assume his shares would be split equally among the remaining partners, you, Shea, the children and me. So I'll carry on as usual unless he sends me word to the contrary."

"Marc, I'm sorry."

He gave her a crooked smile. "So am I, Talitha. Maybe I should do what Frost did, steal you away. But I don't want you if you don't want me."

He didn't kiss her goodbye. He was gone within the hour.

Talitha cried herself to sleep for several nights. What was wrong with her? She *did* love Marc; when she passed the place in the *sala* where he'd loved her so sweetly and so strongly, she was convulsed with longing and it wasn't only or chiefly for those delights that she missed him.

During the hours they'd watched by Shea, he'd talked with her as he used to about the world outside, books and people and ideas. He'd revived the twins' and Cat's sporadic interest in arithmetic and reading. Less abrasive than John Irwin, his convictions were at least as strong. There was about him a sureness, a steadfastness that made Talitha feel safe.

He might be partly right about her feelings for him and Shea. Certainly, Marc was to her a *man*. Shea had been her childhood god, but mingled with her worship was knowledge of the part of him that made her almost see him as a starved, half-orphaned child.

Socorro's death had orphaned him again as well as taking his beloved mate. It was the lonely child in him Talitha couldn't abandon, but this was nothing she could have explained to Marc Revier even had she found the words.

So she told Shea only that Marc had needed to get back to the Tecolote and added what he'd said about the business. Grimacing as he shifted on the pillows, Shea said, "I suppose I'll have to get the freighting and mining partnerships straightened out. You and James will have Santiago's share since I'm sure he'd have liked that. The railroad venture's probably a bust, though I'll have you help me write to the bank in San Francisco and see if they know anything about it. But I don't want to think about it yet."

"Then don't."

During those days of his mending, she was glad for Cat's spritely ways of entertaining her father with songs she'd made up, the kittens' latest tricks and demands for stories about Ireland and what she called "the first days" when Socorro had found him and they had found Santiago and all of them had been sought by Tjúni.

"I can remember Viejo," Cat said, furrowing her

brow. "And Cristiano's still alive. I'm sorry Azul and Castaña are dead but we have lots of their colts. Why did Tjúni move away from us, Daddy?"

"She wanted to live in her own way."

"Will I ever meet her?"

"It's likely you will sometime."

"I want to. I can't remember mother at all and only a little about Santiago." She hugged her father, careful of his shoulder, and kissed him resoundingly. "Oh, Daddy, I'm glad you're not dead!"

He buried his face in her hair, and Talitha thought how strange it was that this little girl who'd never had a mother had so much motherliness in her, even for her father.

The twins were of real help at that spring's roundup and were quite proud of themselves when they returned from helping drive the cattle to Fort Buchanan, now feeling they were full-fledged vaqueros.

Shea praised them but fretted to be out and at work so it was a good thing John Irwin got by often enough to examine the shoulder and say it was doing well but needed a bit more healing time.

Irwin was delighted that at last his advice was being heeded and the buildings were being moved to a healthier location farther from the marshes.

"We're to be made a six-company post," he said. "Captain Ewell grumbles about having to button our coats and go by military etiquette, but I think he rather looks forward to some ladies. We should get a lot of young lieutenants whose fresh-married brides will follow them anywhere."

"Don't you have a bunch of foreigners at the post?" asked Shea.

"Like you and me?" laughed Irwin. "There are thirty Irish, right behind fifty-eight born Americans. Then there's nine each from Germany and England, five from Scotland, two Swiss, three Canadians and one each from Mexico, France and Denmark."

"God's whiskers!" Talitha knew Shea was remembering that about half of the U.S. Army he'd served in had been foreign. "You wonder what brought them here, though it's easy to know as far as the Irish are concerned."

"Well, they've had a host of occupations. Harness-maker, tailor, farmer, carpenter, blacksmith, painter, white-smith, sailor, miner, baker, shoemaker, potter, dyer, machinist, hatter, paper-maker, nail-maker, cabinet-maker, tile-cutter, silver-plater, rope-maker, bookbinder, and editor."

"God's whiskers!" said Shea again.

XXXI

The events of that summer and fall of 1860 were, to Talitha, like shadows dimly moving behind a dark window. Gold was reported near the Santa Rita copper mines in New Mexico and the usual horde of gold-seekers hurried there, creating more problems with the Apaches. Ex-Governor Gándara's forces raised an army in Arizona and entered Sonora to renew their off-and-on battle with Pesqueira. Tubac postmaster Fred Hulsemann gave up that post in disgust since he was never paid and the government had failed to supply a mail route. Sylvester Mowry, who had bought the Patagonia Mine in April, was installing a steam engine, mill and reduction works. In October Colonel Pitcairn Morrison and the 7th Infantry came to Fort Buchanan and except for a second lieutenant of dragoons, John Irwin was the only one of the former officers left.

Talitha was glad of his visits. He was gallant and attentive without making her feel that he wanted more than her company, and he was good for Shea.

Santiago's death and Frost's duplicity had marked Shea. He wasn't even very enthusiastic about the dozen heifers and bull, Illinois stock, that he'd bought, after considerable wheedling, from William Oury of Tucson, heavy stock that should breed more beef into the scrawny Mexican cattle. Shea sat brooding most evenings and though he still didn't drink in front of the children, he emptied more mescal bottles and it began to show on him, in puffiness around his eyes, a slight thickening at the waist that had always been so hard and slender.

He was in a private misery Talitha couldn't lighten. Often, she saw him gazing at the crosses on the hill,

Santiago's by Socorro's. He said to Belen once, "Have the Sanchezes seen Tjúni's boy?"

"Pedro did during roundup. Cinco's five now, a fine sturdy lad." Belen squinted as if wondering whether his further news would be welcomed. "He has two brothers now."

Shea looked at the twins a little distance off, gentling a young gelding, spoke as if to himself. "And he has two half-brothers here. I wonder if they'll ever know each other." He added to Belen, "Remind Pedro that if Cinco ever needs a home, he has one with me."

In November, Irwin brought news that Lincoln had been elected president. "And that means Arizona won't be made a territory since both the Mesilla and Tucson conventions were red-hot Democrat and Southern," said Irwin. "McGovern, who became our delegate when Mowry resigned, has instructions to ask a Southern congress for territorial status if the Union splits." He shook his head. "It's crazy to see so many would-be territories clamoring for recognition just when the nation's falling apart. Colorado, Nevada and Dakota have set up provisional governments, too, which they want acknowledged. My guess is North–South problems have to be settled before much attention's paid to the west."

Shea said bitterly, "The United States had no business taking over this part of the country if it couldn't defend it and give it decent government!"

Irwin looked at him strangely and turned the talk to other things. After the doctor had gone, Shea turned to Talitha. "Sound young man. Irish. You mean to have him, lass?"

She colored. "No."

He watched her narrowly. "Marc Revier, then? I can't remember much from those days I was mostly out of my head, but a few things did make me think you were mighty fond of the lad."

"He's no lad! He's thirty-three, almost as old as you!"

Shea's mouth jerked down. "I've eight years on him, Tally, and a lifetime in them. I feel like an old man."

"You're not! Shea, if you'd just take care of yourself—"

He hushed her with a wave of his hand. "No temperance lectures, Tally." He eyed her levelly. "What I want to know is when you're going to marry. You're past twenty. I know Revier loves you and I reckon you care for him."

"I don't want to marry him. Or anyone." She swallowed till she could trust her voice to be steady. "I want to stay here, Shea. The twins don't need me, but Cat does."

He bowed his head at that, but in a moment renewed his attack. "If you'd marry Revier, a manager could be found for the Tecolote. You know I bought Don Narciso's mine after the Gadsden Purchase. Marc could take charge of that and live here."

Hope flared in her a moment at the suggestion, but she didn't like it. Knowing how she felt about Shea, Marc would never consent to a combined household. Besides, she sensed in Shea a sort of withdrawing, a planning to make himself unnecessary.

Talitha leaned forward, catching his hand. She wouldn't let him slip away, wouldn't let him ease out of his place as head of the ranch and the household.

"If you want to see me married so much, why don't you ask me?" she demanded angrily.

His jaw dropped. He put her fingers away from him, shaking his head. "My God, Tally, I can't do that! You're like my daughter!"

She moved swiftly, kissed him on the mouth. For a moment his arms tightened around her, his lips warmed under hers. Her breasts crushed against him and she moaned at the sweet pain. Then he put her roughly from him, stumbled to his feet.

"I won't, Tally! Ruin your life with my sour one? I'm not that wicked!"

He reached down a bottle and started for his room. Desperate, Talitha caught his arm. "Shea, I'm not a virgin. Frost had me. And I love you, I want you! I don't want another man!"

"Frost?" Turning slowly, he took her in his arms, held her as he had when she was a child. "How awful for you, lass, and you never told me!"

"I thought it would just upset you for no reason. But you mustn't think I'm some innocent young girl. Shea, please! If—if you can't marry me because of Socorro, that's all right. Just let me be with you."

He groaned. By the way his body changed, she knew that he desired her. She pressed closer, offering her lips, but he tore himself away. "I didn't protect you from that devil but damned if I'll do worse! You need a young man, Tally, one all your own! God damn me if I'll be spoiling your life."

He flung outside, into the darkness, and she knew where he was going. Up to the hill where his heart was buried.

After a time the constraint between them eased, but there was tension of a different sort. From the shocks that fanned through her when they accidentally touched, from the look she sometimes found in his eyes, Talitha knew that Shea at last saw her as a woman. His love for her might be that of a father, perhaps he couldn't *love* her any other way, but his body was aware of hers now.

With a sort of despairing triumph, she waited. The time must come. And then surely, surely, she could make him happy, make him want to live again. She couldn't be for him what Socorro was, but she could comfort his loneliness.

It was shortly before Christmas that Belen brought in a baby about six months old, holding it in his scarred rough hands as if fearful of breaking it.

"Don Patricio!" he cried. *"Doncellita!* This is Santiago's child!"

As the family gathered around, amazed, he gave the

baby to Talitha who stared at the petal-soft brown skin, large tawny eyes and tiny mouth. "How—?"

Belen breathlessly explained. Santiago, when released by rebel Yaquis from hard labor in the mines, had been sick. One of the girls who helped care for him loved him even though she knew he was determined to return to Rancho del Socorro. When she fell ill a month ago, she'd besought her brother to bring the baby to Santiago, not only wanting him to have her, but because she'd have a safer rearing than among the embattled Yaquis.

"Santiago told the girl of you," Belen said to Talitha. "She was jealous, for she suspected you were in his mind even more than vengeance on Frost. But when she told him she was pregnant, he married her and promised to come back when he'd settled with Frost."

Caterina had come close and pressed the baby's little fist to her cheek. "She can stay with us? I hope she's a girl!"

"You get your wish," smiled Belen. "She's named Tosalisewa, which means 'white flower.' "

"Too much for me!" said Shea. "I'll call her Sewa." Wonderingly, he touched the soft black hair, the dimpled cheek. "Santiago's child! Thank God, she's come to us, though it's a shame that poor lass, her mother, died. I hope she and Santiago were happy in the short time they had. Can we see the brother? I'd like to find out all he knows about Santiago."

Belen shook his head. "When I told him Santiago was dead, he was going to take the child away, but I persuaded him you'd all love her for Santiago's sake, so he took food and departed."

The baby's mouth began to tremble. Her eyes closed, so did her fists, and she gave a wail of protest so soft it was almost a question. "She's surely hungry," Belen said. "An aunt had been nursing her, but on the trip she's had only watered pinole."

"Fetch Anita," Talitha said, giving thanks that in

June Anita had produced a second son, Tomás, and had more than enough milk.

Anita's warm breast solved the most important of Tosalisewa's needs. In a few days, she'd recovered from slight diarrhea caused by the pinole and was sleeping as soundly in James's willow basket as if it had always been her haven. The basket was in between Talitha's and Caterina's beds. When the baby whimpered, Caterina was often there first.

Little Sewa, as they came to call her, was by way of being outrageously spoiled. Caterina lugged her about in James's cradleboard in a way that made Talitha marvel to remember that she'd been somewhat younger than the eight-year-old when she'd had to mother James.

Shea loved the child for his comrade's sake as well as for her beguiling self. "Her eyes will be gold like Santiago's," he said once. "*Tigre* eyes. Strange in a girl, but won't she be a beauty?"

Talitha nodded, grateful that there had been loving care for Santiago; and that something of him lived on to be cherished by all of them.

January of 1861 brought more snow than anyone could remember, covering valleys as well as the peaks. Early that month all the livestock of the Santa Rita Mining Company in the mountains east of Tubac were stolen by Indians, and there were smaller thefts from the San Pedro to the Santa Cruz. The hard winter brought hunger to the Apaches, but they were not much afraid of being caught by infantry.

John Irwin was to have his share in what proved a bloody lesson on both sides. On February 1st, Lieutenant George Bascom, fresh out of West Point, left Fort Buchanan with fifty-four enlisted men, mostly infantry mounted on mules. His orders were to find Cochise, friend and son-in-law of Mangus, and make

486

him return livestock and a twelve-year-old boy he was suspected of carrying off.

Cochise met Bascom at Apache Pass and denied that his band had stolen either the boy or the cattle. Bascom threatened to hold him prisoner. Cochise escaped but six of his people were held hostage. Expecting trouble, Bascom sent to Fort Buchanan for medical help. His messengers came across what was left of a wagon train. Eight men had been tortured and killed.

Sent to Apache Pass with supplies and a small relief column, Irwin picked up several Coyotero prisoners along the way and got to Apache Pass shortly before dragoons arrived from Fort Breckinridge in New Mexico, summoned by the Butterfield agent in Tucson after an express rider brought news of the slaughtered wagon teamsters.

Cochise held three men from the stage station captive and offered to exchange them for Bascom's six prisoners. Bascom refused unless the allegedly abducted boy was turned over. Cochise and his Chiricahuas killed their station men and vanished.

Bascom and Lieutenant Moore from Breckinridge hanged the three Chiricahua men, one Cochise's brother, and also Irwin's three Coyoteros close to the burned wagon train, but they couldn't track down Cochise and went back to their posts.

"I advised Bascom to hang the prisoners," Irwin said truculently when he came to Socorro late in February. "Men tied to wagon wheels and roasted—Wallace, the station attendant, who'd been the Apaches' friend and voluntarily went to talk with them, dragged to death behind a galloping horse! And you haven't forgotten Larcena Page, have you? Did you know her husband was killed about a week ago? Apaches shot him while he was escorting a provision wagon!"

Numbly, Talitha shook her head. Poor Larcena! But Irwin's bitter gaze brought her back to the fear that haunted her. "I—I was thinking in a few years you might hang my brother like that."

Irwin stared, then remembered. He passed his hand across his face wearily. "Talitha, I'm sorry. But if your brother *will* run with savages, he'll wind up killing as they do."

"And you?" she thrust.

"I'm sorry," he said again. "I did what I felt to be my duty." He rose, reaching for his hat, but Shea commanded him to sit down. After learning details of John Page's death, he sighed heavily.

"Cochise maybe didn't have the Martinez boy and Bascom probably shouldn't have tried to hold him, but once it was done and Cochise killed those wagon people and station attendants, I don't see what else could be done. What do you hear about the seceding states, John? Have they held a convention?" For after South Carolina's secession in December, seven of the southernmost states had followed, including Texas.

"They had a convention in Montgomery, Alabama, several weeks ago," the doctor said. "Framed a constitution and set up a provisional government with Jefferson Davis, the former U.S. Secretary of War, as president."

"Do you think the Confederacy will recognize Arizona as a territory?"

Irwin snorted. "Jeff Davis will recognize anything that gives him an outlet to the West Coast. The South could use the minerals and if it could take over the whole Southwest, including California, it wouldn't be a weaker neighbor of the North for long. But Lincoln won't allow the Union to dissolve. The South will have to fight. It can't do anything for Arizona."

"The United States hasn't done a hell of a lot!"

Irwin laughed, then sobered. "It was making a start. Now . . ." He shrugged. "The Union itself's at stake."

There had been a meeting February 4th in Tucson to debate secession, but the resolutions passed expressed faith in the Union. However, when the Overland Mail stopped in March, a sense of being abandoned by the national government grew swiftly. On March 12th Congress passed a bill routing the Overland Mail through South Pass instead of along the southern route through Arizona, but a week before this, the company had stopped the route because secessionists, as well as Apaches, were running off their stock and raiding stations and wagons.

At a meeting late in March delegates resolved to support the Confederacy and ask for territorial status.

And in April, a few days before Talitha's birthday, James came home.

She screamed when she first looked up to see a young Apache standing in the door. Boots came to his knee. He wore a deerskin loincloth and a red headcloth. His body was brown and muscled, lithe and wiry. But when she saw his eyes, blue in that dark face, she knew him, and her fear changed to joy.

"James!" she cried, running toward him.

He permitted her embrace, but stood so still that she reluctantly moved back. "James! You've come!"

He put down his bow and quiver. His English was hesitating, deeply accented, and his voice was changing, sometimes a boy's, sometimes a man's. "Mangus said I should. No one is left at the stage stations, the wagons do not come anymore. The soldiers may kill a few Apaches, but they cannot do much. This will be Apache country again. But because of his old promise, Mangus will not harm this ranch. I am here to warn Pinals and Coyoteros that Mangus still protects you."

It was clear that he considered himself Apache. Juh, dead, had his son back. Grief welled up in Talitha as she remembered Judith. But James could not, of course, nor could he remember how Juh's wives would have let him starve.

He was alive, he was well. And he was back! He would be fourteen in July. In late September he would have been gone seven years. But the earliest years he remembered had been here. Surely, surely there was a chance he'd come back in heart as well as body. She wished Santiago were alive, he'd had a special bond with his godson.

Cat ran into the kitchen, stopped at the sight of the boy-warrior. Amazingly, she didn't scream. After one glance at Talitha, she darted forward and caught his hands, hugging them to her cheek.

"You're James! You're *our* James! You'll stay with us now, won't you, forever and ever?"

He stared at her. It was like watching a wild proud animal that could be fierce beguiled by the antics of some smaller creature, suspicious, yet wanting to join in the frolic.

"What's your name, little girl?"

"I'm Cat or Katie or Caterina." She added disdainfully, "The twins call me Katie-Cat, but that's a baby name."

He smiled and touched her hair. "I shall call you Caterina."

At the sight of his brown fingers resting in the black glossiness, Talitha thought of scalps though she knew Apaches seldom took them. "The twins will be glad to see you," she told her brother. *Brother,* not Apache. "They still speak of you and wish you'd come home."

"My home is the mountains. I visit here."

Clinging possessively to his arm, Cat said, "Oh no, James, this is your place, too. You can have both! Come on, hurry! We have to find the twins! And you must see Santiago's little girl, Sewa."

Miguel fell at once under James's sway, not that he tried to lead. Patrick, jealous, taller than James, and as heavy though over a year younger, made one taunt about Apaches. The ensuing tangle resulted in a draw, both boys too exhausted to fight further, and after that, they were friends. James was enchanted with Sewa and often took the cradleboard from Caterina and carried her himself.

He'd kept up his roping skills—how, it was probably better not to ask—and made a good hand for the spring roundup. He was a fine horseman, too, though he said Tordillo had been slaughtered for food last winter when food was scarce.

It pleased him greatly to know Santiago's cattle were his. "I won't have to kill my horse again to eat," he said. "I wouldn't have done it, but the children starved."

He was soon on easy terms with Chuey and Belen, but Rodolfo was nervous of him even though James had matter-of-factly accepted white clothing. He wouldn't cut his long hair, though, and wore his headcloth.

He was respectful to Shea who welcomed him wholeheartedly, bringing home to Talitha the thought that however Shea mourned Socorro, he'd never blamed James for setting in motion the events that led to her death. James remembered, though. And he'd stiffened with shock when he heard what had happened to Santiago. Sometimes Talitha saw him and Cat outlined on the hill by the crosses.

"What are you doing up there?" she asked Cat one day.

"We take them flowers." Cat wriggled restlessly against Talitha's arm. "James says I look like mother. Do I, Tally? Will I be as pretty as she was?"

"Prettier, I think. You've got your father's eyes."

Cat shook her head. "I don't want to be prettier. Just *as*."

Talitha laughed and kissed her, but there was a small bewildered knot of hurt in her. She was blessedly happy to have her brother back, glad and relieved that he'd slipped into place without trouble, that he and the twins were companions and that instead of seeing Cat as a reproach and reminder of his childish transgression, he was protectively fond of her. But in that last closeness, Talitha felt excluded, shut out.

Where she'd once been the most important human in James's world, now she was the woman in charge of the house, respected and obeyed where once she'd been loved. He showed more affection to Anita, who, recovering from shock, soon petted James as much as he'd allow and brought him special dishes.

Cat had James's love now, and she returned it with adoration. When John Irwin came and James faded away, she faded with him. She, who wept over dead animals, went hunting with him. When he wasn't working cattle, they were inseparable.

The twins were usually along, too, so Talitha didn't think anyone but she noticed the special bond between them. Cat's motherliness found in James someone who needed it as much as tiny Sewa but who couldn't accept tenderness from an older person. In her, he had a lovely soft little being who thought him completely wonderful while sensing that in some deep part of his soul, he needed her.

They had each other. The twins had always shared everything. And Shea had his bottle.

Why? Talitha wanted to shout at him when that secret current flowed between them and he hastily left or busied himself with something that dissipated its force. *Why? You don't have to love me, just let me love you!*

There was a kind of waiting in the days, a mounting tension in the atmosphere, as the air grows heavy before a thunderstorm. When John Irwin brought word that war had broken out, Shea said nothing at all, but a few days later he rode into Tucson.

When he returned, he called in all the men and Anita, the twins and James as well. "I'm convinced the North won't give Arizona the government and peace we need," he said. "I'm equally sure the Confederacy will, so I'm going to fight for it." He handed Talitha a large envelope. "While I'm away, Talitha's in charge, with Belen foreman. I've seen a lawyer and made a will. Tomorrow I'll go see the Sanchezes, and then I'll leave as soon as I can."

He glanced from startled face to startled face, added heavily, "It comes hard to leave you, with dangers all about. But we know Mangus still holds his hand over the Socorro, and James should be more help, in case of a raid, than I could be. I've talked with John Irwin and the Fort Buchanan commander. Even though they know

I'll be fighting against their uniform, they've promised to be watchful for you. Irwin, especially, will assist in any way he can. Are there any questions?"

"Can't we go with you?" the twins cried.

Shea encircled each with an arm, roughly. "I hope my going now will keep you both from having to fight later. You're to help Tally and do what Belen says. I rely on you."

Cat flung her arms around his neck, clinging wildly. "I don't want you to go, Daddy! Please don't go! I don't want you to leave me!"

His face twisted and he held her close. "I don't want to leave you, sweetheart. But I must."

She sobbed heartbrokenly. James came and led her away. "Caterina," he said with a sternness that halted her weeping though tears continued to flow. "A man must fight when his time comes or he is no man. Your father is a man." She buried her face against his arm but made no more protests.

The vaqueros inclined their heads. Belen stepped forward. "Don Patricio, I will die before harm comes to your children or the *doncellita*. Go with God. Return to us."

Shea's visit to the Sanchezes took two days. While he was gone, Talitha searched frantically for some way to make him change his mind, but she thought of nothing. He was determined, she knew he would go, and she thought she would die without him; never to see his face, not to know if he was well or if he was even alive.

After everyone else had gone to bed the night of his return, Talitha was finally alone with him. "I went to the San Manuel and wished Tjúni luck in case I don't see her again," he said. "Cinco's a fine little lad. Looks pure Papago except for a reddish cast to his hair when the sun hits it. If it ever comes in your way, Talitha, will you be his friend?"

She nodded, too angry and sorrowful to trust herself to speak.

"There's one more trip I'd like to make," Shea continued, eyes holding hers. "Let me go to Marc Revier. Let me say you want him to come."

"No."

Shea's breath sounded dragged from him. "Tally, Tally! I want you to be happy, have your strong young man."

"Is that why you're going away?" She looked at him in sudden dread. How could she bear it if her trying to be with him had caused this? "Oh, Shea, if it is, then you stay here! I can go to my father."

"And take away the center of the house?" He sighed deeply. "I could wish you'd go with Revier, Tally, or he'd come to you. But till there's a man you love, your home is here."

"I love you. It's you I've always loved."

He didn't speak but watched her with tormented eyes. Coming around to him, she knelt beside him, carried his hand to her breast, held it above her heart. "Shea, love me before you go away."

"Tally, I mustn't."

"Why? What can it matter if you're leaving? It's not something you'd have to live with."

He put her fiercely from him, got to his feet, crossed to the other side of the table. A pulse hammered in his temple, beat in his throat. "God above, girl! Have you any notion how hard it's been these weeks to keep my hands off you, keep from warming myself with your sweet fire? I'm not going off to fight because of you, but if I didn't do that I'd sure have to do something else!"

"You could take me."

He stared at her.

"I want your baby," she said in a whisper. "I want you to come alive again and laugh and be happy, Shea, please—"

He took a long breath. His tall lean body relaxed. "I don't deserve such loving, but I would lie to say I don't

want it. But you must have your chance, Tally. I belong
to the first times, to Socorro and Santiago."

"You can belong to my time, too."

"Maybe. Maybe." He smiled at her and it ran over
her heart like sun, letting her hope. "Let me fight my
battle, Tally. That's how I started my life in this new
world. It may be how I can finish that life and begin
all over."

Her blood seemed to race after being frozen. "Shea,
you mean—"

He threw back his shoulders, looking younger than
he had in a long time. "If I come back, and you're still
of a mind, we'll marry."

And then he was around the table and she was in
his arms. She had never been so happy. She had never
been so sad.

She could scarcely believe it. But—*when he came
back?* That could be so long. And a quickly suppressed
voice whispered that he might not come back. She
looked up into his eyes, caressed the scar on his cheek.

"Shea. Oh my love, we can wait to be married. But
please don't make me wait for *you.*"

"But, Tally—"

"Let me have that. Let me have that to remember.
Shea, if you leave me without that, I don't think I can
bear it. Just this night, be my man."

He took her in his arms, swept her up and carried
her to his room. He loved her with sweetness and fire.
Sometimes, he slept. Talitha never did. This time was
too precious. She kept her hand lightly on him, loving
him so fiercely that she didn't know how she could endure life without him. But she had this, and so did he.
Something that might bring him home.

Next morning, Talitha, the twins, Cat and James
rode with him as far as Fort Buchanan. Talitha had
brought Sewa in her cradleboard fastened to the saddle
horn. Dismounting, Shea shook hands with his sons,

kissed Cat and Sewa. Last of all, he kissed Talitha and it was a man's kiss to his woman.

"I want to come back now," he said, laughing, though his eyes were moist. He glanced at the children. "Take care of them for me, Tally. Take care of yourself."

Unable to speak, she tried to smile and nodded her head.

They watched him out of sight in the bright new day, Cat weeping softly. Talitha could only bear the overwhelming loss and desolation by remembering. At last he loved her!

Nothing could take that away.

When they could no longer see him at all, Talitha reined her horse and led the way, back to the Socorro. She would hold it for him. And wait.